KNIGHT
AWAKENED

Text copyright © 2012 by Coreene Callahan
All rights reserved.
Printed in the United States of America.
No part of this book may be reproduced, or stored in a retrieval system, or transmitted in any form or by any means, electronic, mechanical, photocopying, recording, or otherwise, without express written permission of the publisher.

Published by Montlake Romance
P.O. Box 400818
Las Vegas, NV 89140

ISBN-13: 9781612183039
ISBN-10: 1612183034

KNIGHT
AWAKENED

COREENE CALLAHAN

For you.
I knew the moment we met you were worthy and would
find the one destined to love you.
I'm so glad I was right.

The Prophecy

And out of the ashes seven warriors shall rise.
Bringers of death, they shall wreak vengeance upon
the earth, until shadow is driven into darkness
and only the light remains.

—The Chronicles of Al Pacii:
written in the hand of Seer

CHAPTER ONE

It was twilight when he made his move, the moment day folded into dusk, the space between light and shadow. He'd watched her all day, marked her progress through the marketplace between stalls and calling vendors, watched her and the little one go about their business never knowing he trailed like a phantom in their wake. A hunter tracking his prey. Now, concealed by the twisted limbs of large beech trees, he watched from across the clearing as she ushered the girl-child over the threshold and closed the planked door behind them.

His gaze centered on the tiny stone cottage. Xavian Ramir absorbed every detail—the thinning thatched roof, the crumbling chimney, the missing mortar between the stones, and the aging wheelbarrow beside the small garden—then scanned the shadowed forest beyond as he'd been trained to do. *Study the angles. Flesh out the target. Define the variables.* Old habits died hard. An unfortunate truth for the woman preparing to eat her evening meal.

He smelled the stew. Rabbit, most likely. The decadent aroma mingled with the grey curl of wood smoke as it escaped, twisting up to meet a darkening sky. His stomach growled. Xavian ignored the discomfort and distracted himself by picturing her.

1

Raven hair spilling over the curve of her shoulder, she stirred the pot, hazel eyes intent on its thickening contents. Aye, he'd been close enough to see them, memorize their shape, the exotic up-tilted outer corners framed by dark brown lashes. He saw the supple curve of her cheek, the lushness of her lips, and imagined them wrapped around something other than the wooden spoon she no doubt used to taste the gravy.

The muscles roping his lower abdomen tightened. Aye, she was a tidy little bundle, but that didn't explain why Vladimir Barbu, new lord to Transylvania, wanted her. Hunted her, had gone to extremes to find her. Not entirely, at least. The recently ascended voivode might want the lass in his bed, but Xavian guessed the reasons the warlord had hired him struck closer to the coffers than his heart. What did she have that Vladimir wanted?

'Twas a question that bothered him more than he liked. Curiosity was a luxury, one he couldn't afford. For an assassin operating at the top of his game, the curse of conscience signaled trouble...the kind he wished he'd never met. But now that he'd been bitten, the bug—the need to know—burrowed beneath his skin, festering until he itched to solve the mystery. So now he must decide. What was more important? The coin he needed to see countless boys rescued and his fledging academy through the coming winter, or her life. He hated to choose. A mother. Jesu, he hadn't expected that. He flexed his hand and felt the gash on his forearm throb with the movement. The injury was courtesy of a brother-in-arms, the latest in a long line of those sent to kill him.

"Ram?" the soft voice, vibrant with the fullness of youth, came from behind.

Qabil. His new apprentice, borrowed without permission. Hell, *borrowed*. 'Twas a matter of opinion, one the old man would dispute with his dying breath. Mayhap *stolen* was a better word. Xavian's lips curved, finding satisfaction in the theft. But as much as he relished the blow to his former master, thankfulness took precedence. Qabil hadn't been with the bastard long enough and still possessed the wonder of innocence, and despite himself Xavian was grateful the lad had been spared.

Xavian glanced over his shoulder, dipping his chin to acknowledge the call. With a flick, he undid the buckle in the center of his chest, slid the double harness from his shoulders, down his arms, and handed the twin swords he favored to Qabil.

The lad blinked, alarm darkening his eyes. "But—"

"Hold them," he said, not wishing to explain he didn't want to frighten the woman or her child. His presence—his size and strength—would do that well enough without being armed to the teeth. The fact he was rarely without the weapons made him itch to strap them back on. He felt exposed without the curved blades on his back, though it meant naught in the scheme of things. He needed her occupied, unsuspecting while he made his decision.

Wide-eyed, Qabil's hands shook as he hugged the weapons to his chest. "What if the hunters track us here?"

"Quick in. Quick out," he said, understanding the lad's fears. Halál's hunter assassins were naught to scoff at when they came in packs. Less than a full day's ride wasn't enough distance. Xavian knew it—so did Qabil—but he couldn't leave the woman. Not now. "Keep the horses ready."

Xavian waited until his apprentice lowered his gaze and nodded before he turned his attention back to the cottage. Tension coiling in the pit of his stomach, he listened to the boy's footfalls fade, then said, "Cristobal, you're with me. The rest of you spread out. If she runs, I want all escape routes blocked."

Like the ghosts they'd learned to be, Cristobal and Razvan shifted out of shadow while Andrei and Kazim dropped from swaying tree limbs above. They landed on silent feet behind him, not a whisper of sound to indicate their presence. Faded beech leaves scattered across the turf as his men moved to flank him. Dressed in black from head to toe, their clothes were designed with precision in mind and mirrored his own. Each of them lived in the dark, thrived on silence and the spaces between, the ones devoid of emotion and lined with simplicity. None of them liked ambiguity and sure as hell didn't accept hesitation in the role they'd been forced into playing.

Cristobal raised a brow. "Uneasy?"

"Nay." Xavian shook his head. "Merely undecided."

"The plan?" Andrei asked, the richness of his French accent alight with purpose.

"Reconnaissance." Pushed by a gentle breeze, the dark leaves of the beech murmured as he admitted, "I wish to know more."

The least bloodthirsty of their group, Razvan nodded. "I don't like the bastard...He lied."

"Mayhap," Xavian said, unconcerned for the moment about Vladimir and his motives. His focus was on the lass and the mystery of her circumstances. He couldn't deny his curiosity, a novel prickling sensation he didn't often experience. "Liar or nay, his coin is still good."

Kazim snorted, amusement alive in his dark eyes.

Acknowledging the humor with a shrug, Xavian palmed the dagger he kept snug against the small of his back. The blade rasped against leather, the whisper sounding loud in the silence. A crease between his brows, he set the point to his forearm, to the wound left by the former comrade he'd sent to the devil but days ago. He fisted his hand, inhaled sharply, and with a flick, opened the gash. A red rivulet, heated by life's essence, tracked south across the back of his hand as he left his men to move into position. Eyes on the cottage door, he strode toward the inevitable, blood dripping from his fingertips.

CHAPTER TWO

Her heart ached. It always did when she thought of Bianca. Sitting at the rickety wooden table spoon-feeding her sister's daughter proved no exception. Sabine, with her golden hair and gentle soul, was like her mother in every way but one. The eyes. Bianca's had been dark, carrying wisdom beyond her nineteen years. Sabine's were mismatched, one green, the other blue. The fact her sister wasn't here to see their beauty, the subtle shifts in color, was all her fault.

Afina Lazar's throat tightened, the guilt so thick she found it difficult to swallow. She was failing…at everything. Motherhood, the healing, the promise she'd made to Bianca on her deathbed. A death Afina had failed to stop, been helpless to stall, to ease the pain as her sister slipped away. She stroked her little one's hair, murmuring encouragement as she took another spoonful rich with rabbit meat.

They were lucky to have it. The summer game had proved more crafty than usual, avoiding her traps and homemade arrows with little difficulty. Sabine's growling belly most nights spoke to the truth. She needed some luck to get them through. Was a little divine intervention too much to ask? Couldn't the goddess of all things afford them their fair share? Afina hoped so. Otherwise the coming winter might not only turn harsh, but deadly as well.

What would she do if she couldn't fill their winter stores in time? She couldn't go home. Nothing but certain death lay in that direction, no matter how plentiful the food supply. At least here, she held some small chance of survival, of fulfilling her role as protector to the Amulet of Orm. As she spooned another mouthful into Sabine, her attention drifted to her satchel—the one that carried her healing supplies. The stupid amulet, bane of her existence, a curse upon the women of her line. She wanted to rip it from its hiding place beneath the leather lining and toss it into the nearest ditch, but knew she never would. High priestess to the Order of Orm, her mother had died doing her duty, saving the wretched thing from Vladimir Barbu...the murdering swine.

Afina rubbed her aching temple, wanting to forget, wishing for another way. But none existed. Her mother had made a fatal mistake, and now Afina was left to pay the price. Vladimir needed her to complete the ancient rite—the ritual that would crown him Lord of Transylvania. She must stay hidden and out of his greedy grasp: to protect her people and her daughter and honor the goddess she served.

A promise made was a promise kept.

She needed her word to mean something, and her sister's death to mean more. If she abandoned the cause now, after two years of running, she was as gutless as her mother had accused her of being.

The memory of harsh words lashed her.

Tears pricking the corners of her eyes, Afina turned her mind away and scraped the bottom of the wooden bowl, scooping up the hearty gravy for her child.

Sabine's small fingers grasped hers, her tongue peeking out to touch her bottom lip. "I do it, Mama. I do it."

Her little cherub. Afina smiled. The tightness banding her chest eased as she relinquished the spoon. "All right. Would you like a little more, love?"

Even knowing she needed to ration the rabbit stew over the next few days didn't keep her from asking. She wanted to make sure Sabine was satisfied. It had been so long since they'd had any meat, and if that meant eating less so her babe got her fill Afina was happy to go without. Mayhap tomorrow, were they lucky, she would snare another.

Fortifying herself with hope, she left her stool and headed for the hearth. The heat from the fire wrapped her in a warm embrace as she reached for the ladle. A sharp rap sounded on wood. Afina flinched, her heart stalling as she spun toward the door, wooden spoon raised in defense. White knuckled, she stared at the wide grey planks, alarm fighting logic for supremacy.

It couldn't be Vladimir…it *couldn't* be. The swine wouldn't knock. Kicking down the door was more his style. The thought calmed her a little, but not enough. She didn't want to answer. It was late and intuition warned nothing but trouble waited outside. Silence hummed, the vibration loud, stretching her nerves tight.

"Go away," she whispered, unable to take the echoing hush. She hoped voicing her wish aloud would make it come true, would chase the unwanted visitor into the coming night. "Go away."

"Door, Mama. Door!" Sabine bounced on her stool, eyes bright while she tapped the spoon against the side of the bowl.

Afina leapt the distance between them to grab her daughter's hand. Placing her index finger against her lips, she mouthed, "Shh, love."

She held her breath and counted to ten. Nothing. Not a whisper of sound from the other side of the door. Eleven, twelve, thirteen…A second knock followed the first. Oh, goddess. Whoever was standing on the threshold didn't plan on going away. Afina swallowed and, ladle raised, moved toward the entrance, acutely aware it also served as the only exit.

"Mistress?" The voice, smooth and deep, rolled through the rough-hewn planks in a warm wave, sucking away her tension like sand in an undertow. Afina fought the pull and tightened her grip on the impromptu weapon.

"W-who…" Fingertips brushing the pitted wood of the door, she willed strength into her voice. "Who's there?"

"The priest in the village told me to come, mistress," he said, his tone full of gentle reassurance. "I'm in need of a healer…have come seeking your care."

She closed her eyes and lowered the ladle. Father Marion, the parish priest, had sent him. Thank goodness. She might not be part of his flock, but the priest had always been kind. Could even be relied upon to send her ailing parishioners from time to time.

Afina lifted the bar, cracked the door, and came nose to sternum with a wide, very male chest. She blinked, startled by his size, and stared at the pitch-black leather jerkin. A moment passed before she allowed her gaze to climb over well-set shoulders, a strong neck, only to collide with ice-blue eyes set in the most incredible face she'd ever seen.

Handsome didn't begin to describe him. Lethal appeal, strength tempered by charm. Cropped short, his hair was shot with gold threads, a bronzy color that matched the hammered coins she'd once taken for granted. A mistake she knew not to make with him. His intensity said it all. He was a warrior wrapped inside aristocratic features.

She tensed, guard up, instincts screaming for her to slam the door in his face. His unusual eyes holding hers, he slid his foot between the door and the jamb as though aware of her intention. "I will pay, mistress."

Catching a flash from her periphery, Afina's gaze strayed to the gold coin perched in his fingertips. By the goddess, it was more money than she'd seen in two years. Enough to secure their future, not only for the winter, but in the years to come. She bit her bottom lip, her mind compiling lists and tallying costs. She'd be able to buy a goat, warm clothing, the extra seeds for their garden, see to the repairs, and still have plenty left over. And the only thing standing in her way? Giving aid to a man who radiated aggression and gave new meaning to the word *frightening*.

Could she do it? What if she disappointed him? She wasn't the best healer. In truth she was a terrible one. Everything she knew she'd learned from Bianca. The healer in their family, her sister had made sure Afina understood the basic principles before her death. On the run, their survival had depended on presenting a united front, but she'd only ever been a helper. And were she honest, not a very willing one. She didn't possess the stomach for it, shying away from injuries she knew she couldn't handle. But she couldn't afford to do that any longer. Sabine needed her to be strong. Otherwise they would starve to death.

She met his gaze then shied, looking away. "Y-you're hurt?"

He nodded, raised his arm, and held it out for her inspection. Blood dripped in a steady stream, leaving droplets on the edge of a wooden floorboard. Without thinking, she reached for his hand, cupping it with her own. He stiffened. Unease forgotten in the face of his pain, she ignored his reaction to her touch and admonished, "Why didn't you tell me you were bleeding?"

Bumping the door aside, she tugged on his arm, wanting a better look at his injury. He hesitated, resisting the gentle pull as though uncertain he wanted to cross the threshold. She tugged again, her focus on the nasty gash bisecting the outside of his forearm. "Come into the light, sir. I cannot see the extent of the damage if you remain out there."

He inhaled. The slow, deep breath alerted her to his tension, signaled nervousness of some kind. Afina knew the emotion well, fought to contain it with every breath she took. Day in and day out, she struggled with worry, an edginess she wore like a scent. He wore it too, though it smelled different. Lean and hungry with a touch of rebellion. Aye, under all the lovely bone structure was a man in need of repair and the soothing touch that went with it.

Empathy stole into her heart, and all of a sudden, she wanted to make him feel safe. Absurd—completely laughable—considering she doubted anything made the hard-faced warrior afraid. Add that to the fact he scared her witless and the notion made her think she'd lost her mind. But if she was to tend his wound, she needed him to trust her.

Squeezing his hand, Afina deployed a technique that had served her well in the past. She put them on familiar terms. "What is your name?"

He gave her a strange look and let her pull him past the doorframe. "Xavian."

"I am Afina," she said, infusing her tone with warmth she didn't feel. "And that wee cherub is Sabine, my daughter."

Forever friendly, Sabine gave him a toothy grin, rapped the spoon against the edge of the bowl, and chirped, "Hello!"

Afina dropped his hand and gestured to a stool before turning to retrieve her healer's satchel. "Sit. I will gather my things and tend you at the table."

Again he hesitated, but in the end obeyed and took a seat, as far from Sabine as he could manage. Afina hid her smile. A grown man afraid of a wee lass. 'Twas inconceivable, but true. She'd seen it many times. Observed men hardened by battle and hurt by war fairly run in the other direction when faced with a child. When she encountered someone like that, she knew they'd forgotten joy, had no idea how to handle an energetic bundle filled with nothing but merriment.

Curbing the inappropriate burst of amusement, she grabbed her bag and the large bowl from the shelf above it. Hands full, she turned and nearly jumped out of her skin. Another man, dark to Xavian's light, stood in the open doorway. Her breath stalled as his black gaze swept her then the tiny confines of her cottage. The door swung closed behind him with a click, and her grip tightened on the satchel. Leather groaned in protest as alarm knocked around inside her head.

Xavian studied her expression then glanced over his shoulder. "Relax, mistress. 'Tis only Cristobal. He's with me."

"Oh," she said, resisting the urge to pound on her chest to restart her heart. She took a shallow breath. No matter how much she disliked having two large men in her home, she must stay calm. Xavian required her skill, such as it was, and she needed the coin he offered to secure their future. She pushed past fear and set the bowl along with her bag on the tabletop.

Sabine greeted the newcomer in her usual fashion. "Hello!"

"*Salutari*, little one," Cristobal said, a smile in his voice. Hooking a stool with his foot, he sat across the table from her daughter.

Sabine grinned.

He grinned back.

Afina blinked, amazed by the exchange. Fierce-looking men didn't generally engage her two-year-old in conversation. Neither did they reach into the pouches at their waists and offer her toys. But as Cristobal rolled the dice across the table to Sabine, she forced herself to reconsider, to remember a lesson long forgotten. Never judge another by appearance alone.

"Cristobal enjoys children."

Xavian's deep voice stroked along her spine, leaving pin-pricks of heat in its wake. Afina flinched and dragged her attention from the strange pair. She collided with his ice-blue gaze, wondering what that meant, exactly. *Enjoy* in the way a wolf does a lamb or a child his favorite playmate?

An image of razor-sharp teeth and lupine eyes flashed through her mind. She cleared her throat. "Towels. I will fetch them then begin."

She forced herself to move at a steady pace and, with quiet efficiency, gathered the rest of her supplies. Xavian tracked her movement. She felt his focus keenly, registered his gaze as prick-les exploded across the nape of her neck in a warm rush of sensa-tion. The tingle of awareness frightened her, made her tense with the need to rush him out the door. Something about him wasn't quite tame. She got the sense the only rules he followed were the ones he made for himself. And for a girl who needed the rules to feel safe, that wouldn't do.

Afina set the small kettle she carried on the table. Iron bumped against wood. The uneven thump sounded loud in the stillness, an unanticipated announcement of her ineptitude. She paused, waiting for the accusation, any sign he understood the cryptic message. He said nothing and waited, patient in her mo-ment of hesitation. In a flurry of movement, she placed the folded towels to one side then flapped one square open and spread it on the wooden planks. Without being told, Xavian placed his forearm on the linen and, with the flick of his fingertips, gestured for her to begin. She quelled the urge to run in the other direction, wanting to scoop Sabine up and head for the hills so badly the impulse made her mouth dry.

The rattle of dice and Sabine's giggle rippled, joining the crackle of fire in the hearth. Grateful her daughter was occupied, she flipped her bag open and extracted a small vial of liquid. Lightning quick, Xavian encircled her wrist, his grip just short of bruising. Air rushed from her chest in a puff, and her gaze shot to his. The instant she made contact, he raised a brow, a clear question in his eyes.

She swallowed. "Distilled witch hazel. I must clean the wound before I stitch it. Otherwise you will suffer an infection."

He held her captive a moment more then uncurled his fingers, releasing her from the calloused shackle. She drew a soft breath and, spreading the liquid on the linen, shifted closer. His heat reached out, wrapping her in warmth scented by male and something more. Rich and earthy, he smelled fresh and clean, like the forest after a summer storm. Afina inhaled and dabbed at the wound, sifting like a bloodhound through the complexities of his scent, wondering how he'd come by it. Did he use a special soap? What blend of herbs would create an aroma so full of woodsy delight? She leaned toward him, nose twitching, brain working to unravel the mystery ingredients.

He shifted, and she flinched as the backs of his fingers brushed the curve of her cheek. Unaccustomed to being touched, she stayed stone still, afraid to look at him while he pushed the hair that had fallen into her face over her shoulder. His hand hovered close, and hers stopped above his injury, a stunted breath tangled in her throat.

His tone soft and even, he murmured, "There, now you can see what you are doing."

Afina nodded her thanks and straightened on a shaky breath. Her gaze averted, she reached into the satchel and pulled out a fine bone needle. "I'll stitch it closed then apply salve and wrap it."

His chin dipped, and he angled his arm to give her better access. Fighting queasiness, she imagined Bianca, pictured her steady hands, replayed every instruction her sister had given her, and set needle to flesh. Her stomach clenched, rolling in protest. She inhaled through her nose, ignoring the slight tremor in her hand and, with steady precision, closed the gash with tight, narrow stitches.

"You've a gentle touch," Xavian said, his voice mild and full of approval. "You are very good at this."

Afina almost snorted. Good at it? Was he soft in the head? The man obviously hadn't been hurt very often. She wasn't stupid enough, however, to correct him as she tied off the threads. If he wanted to believe she was an accomplished healer, so much the better. His ignorance walked her one step closer to the gold coin. Hmm, she could almost taste the goat's milk.

"You'll need to keep it dry," she said. "No water or soap on the wound."

Slathering thick ointment over the injury, Afina peeked at him from beneath her lashes, wanting to be sure he paid attention. The goddess preserve her, he was well put together, much too appealing for his own good. Good thing he frightened her. Otherwise she might be tempted to talk with him awhile, to make him stay a little longer.

She gave herself a mental slap. What was the matter with her? She didn't have time for a man, never mind the inclination. No matter how compelling, Xavian needed to go...and go quickly.

Bandage in hand, she wrapped his forearm, tied a knot just below his elbow and, tone brusque, instructed, "Change the bandage every day. The stitches need to remain for ten days then you can cut them out one at time. Be very careful about it. You don't want to reopen the wound."

"Many thanks, Afina."

Her name rolled off his tongue as though he were tasting it, a predator savoring his next meal. A shiver chased dread down her spine, causing a visceral chain reaction. She'd done as he asked and tended his wound, but the idea he wasn't finished with her grabbed hold, clanged inside her head until instinct coiled, preparing her to flee. Muscles tense, she shifted, moving away from him and toward Sabine a fraction at a time.

"Ram?" Cristobal's voice cut through the haze of fright, momentarily interrupting her tension. Something about his tone caused her to pause and take stock of the question embedded in the summons. The chill of Xavian's eyes moved from her to his friend. Time slowed, altering perception as Afina watched Cristobal reach out and grasp Sabine's small chin. With a gentle touch, he turned her daughter's face toward Xavian and said, "The eyes."

A muscle jumped along Xavian's jaw as his hand curled into a fist on the planked tabletop. "Hell."

"Aye," Cristobal murmured, clearly understanding the meaning behind the expletive.

Her gaze swiveling between the two, Afina struggled to breathe. What did they want with Sabine? The question sank deep and panic rolled in. She exploded around the edge of the table. Something was wrong. Very, very wrong.

She needed to reach her child...now, this instant. "Sabine, come—"

Xavian struck, reaching out so fast she didn't see him move. The heat of his hand shackled her wrist. A moment later, he hauled her up and back, away from Sabine. Her throat clogged and instinct surged, unleashing the ferocious need to protect her child. Xavian was talking, but she didn't hear him, too focused on getting to Sabine as he continued to draw her toward the door. Using the momentum of his pull, she rounded on him, teeth bared, feet and fists flying. He cursed and yanked, spinning her until she landed, back to his front, shoulder blades pressed to his muscled chest.

Sabine whimpered.

Afina screamed and bucked his hold, heart breaking, tears pooling in her eyes. One hand wrapping both of her wrists, he cupped her throat, fingers searching.

"No," she said, her voice weakening as he applied pressure to a sensitive spot on the side of her neck. "Let go...let me go!"

"Easy, Afina."

"Please! P-please don't hurt her...d-don't hurt my baby."

Tears streaming from the corners of her eyes, the black void of unconsciousness beckoned. Afina fought the pull, fear for Sabine anchoring her in the light. Xavian murmured, mouth close to her ear, his low tone reassuring, but she knew better. He was the angel of death, right hand to the devil.

CHAPTER THREE

Xavian swung Afina into his arms, all the while berating himself. He'd frightened her, made her believe he would hurt her child. Not the best move, all things considered.

Had he stuck to the plan she might have agreed. Now she would fight him every step of the way. And he couldn't blame her. He didn't deserve anything less. In his defense, though, the girl-child's eyes had surprised him, making him move before he'd been ready.

Mismatched. One green, the other blue…Bodgan's eyes.

Xavian had stared into a pair of identical eyes just days ago, watching their life force drain away. Did it matter that Bodgan had attacked first? That his intent had been to slit Xavian's throat and carry his head like a trophy back to the old man? Nay. From the moment he recognized Sabine's coloring, an awful ache sliced him wide open.

He closed his eyes and relived the desperation in his comrade's voice. Watched his blood flow and listened to him beg, *You owe me, Ram…find her near Severin…blond…healer…provide. Remember…the code.* He'd rasped the last words, gasping on the certainty of death.

The code. Could he ever forget?

'Twas sacred among their kind, a gift given to the dying. One favor, a request made of the victor without the possibility of denial.

He never imagined, however, his present mission and the vow made to Bodgan would collide. That the woman he hunted for Vladimir would prove to be the healer and the blond child, his former comrade's daughter.

Jesu, a simple promise and now he stood neck deep, condemned with choice. The options slashed, opening old wounds until he bled, unable to stem the flow of regret. 'Twas new, the constant questioning, an affliction he'd not suffered before a year ago. He didn't like it, mourned the simplicity of his life before he split from the group, Al Pacii. Tired of the folly and Halál's indiscriminate killing, he'd left alone. He'd wanted a new start, a future far from his past and the innumerable sins for which God would never forgive him. Instead, the past followed along with the four, the men that now stood at his back.

He hadn't asked for leadership. Didn't want it. But somehow, responsibility found a home on his shoulders. Now his men looked to him. Had handed the power of their futures into his care, and Xavian refused to fail them. He must find a way through, give them all new purpose if they were to survive Halál's wrath.

His fingers curled, flexing around soft flesh and lax muscle. He looked down at the woman he cradled like a babe in his arms. More responsibility. Two wee bundles he could ill afford. What the hell was he going to do with them?

His immediate impulse was to keep Sabine—satisfy his promise to Bodgan—but hand Afina to Vladimir, take the coin and forget about her. 'Twas a reckless reaction, one fueled by emotion. He recognized it for what it was...anger. Hell, he didn't even know Afina, and he was angry with her for so many things: for welcoming Bodgan, for bearing his child, for giving his former friend the gift Xavian yearned for...acceptance. The notion stirred him, tossing up debris from the murky bottom of his soul.

No matter how hard he fought, the truth always came back to haunt him. Now was no different. The craving uncoiled like a wounded animal, howling for a woman to call his own—a special lass to love and be loved by in return. Xavian scowled. Love. 'Twas naught but a fool's dream, a false hope he couldn't encourage. He needed that kind of aggravation like a dagger between his shoulder blades.

Even so, the imagined loss stung as he crossed the clearing.

Andrei slid from the shadows and raised a brow.

Xavian unclenched his teeth long enough to snarl, "Cloak."

The Frenchman's chin dipped an instant before he unhooked his mantle and tossed it in Xavian's direction. The heavy wool arced, moving on the wind, a black stain on the muted grey of the coming night. Shifting Afina, he caught the cape with one hand and swept beneath the curved canopy of the large beech tree. Sabine whimpered behind him, the only sound to indicate Cristobal ghosted in his wake.

Sensing the audience at his back, Xavian inhaled to steady the volatility rolling around inside his chest and glanced over his shoulder. His men stood in a semicircle, a question in their eyes. Arms curled around Afina, he protected her from their probing gazes and said, "Clean it up. Take what is useful. Leave no trace."

His men nodded and moved toward the cottage, their feet silent, movements efficient as they obeyed his command. Cradling the girl-child, Cristobal headed in the opposite direction, toward Qabil and their horses. He heard his friend murmur, the cadence of his voice soothing as he stroked Sabine's hair, reassuring her with both tone and touch. Xavian shook his head, amazed a hardened assassin, a man with blood on his hands—as much as his own—could be so good with a child.

It defied logic, and Xavian struggled to wrap his mind around the blatant contradiction as he spread the cloak on the ground. Afina would stir soon if he didn't hurry. He wanted her senseless for a while…at least through the night. He wasn't ready to face her yet, or the fury she would no doubt deliver. The reaction smacked of cowardice, but he didn't care. He needed time: to adjust, to formulate a plan, to make a final decision.

Fallen leaves rustled as he came down on one knee and set Afina in the middle of the dark wool. The breeze stirred, pushing the branches above, and moonlight spilled, bathing her in light. He drew a deep breath and swept the hair from her face while he palmed the small vial he always carried. The thick strands clung, and unable to help himself, he wove the locks between his fingers, enjoying the softness even as he admonished himself for the pleasure.

Tight pressure moved behind his breastbone. With a scowl, he shook free of her tresses and brushed the corner of her mouth. She shifted, turning her head to follow his touch. He flicked the stopper from the glass and caressed the full curve of her lower lip. As she sighed, his heart clenched, but that didn't stop him from tipping the vial and dripping two droplets into her mouth.

Her eyelashes flickered. He cupped her cheek and murmured, using the soothing rhythm of his voice to keep her quiet until the drugging tonic took effect. She settled like a kitten, content with his tone and the heat of his body surrounding her. With an eye to her comfort, he shifted her a little then wrapped her in the warm mantle. He didn't question his need to be gentle, simply accepted and let it go as he scooped her up and headed for the horses. He needed to move fast. Of a sudden, a half-day's ride between him and the enemy didn't seem nearly far enough. Not with Afina and Sabine now in the fold.

❦✚❦

Unhappy birds argued somewhere overhead. The high-pitched chatter made Afina's head hurt, and she shifted sideways. Away from sharp-edged pain, toward heat and a spicy scent she couldn't place. Goddess, that was nice...rich with warmed leather and wood smoke. With a hum, Afina snuggled in, pressed her cheek to something solid, and swallowed the bitter taste in her mouth. The tang turned rancid, telling her stomach the smallest twitch would be treated like an enemy invasion.

Enemy.

The word echoed inside her head. Something was off. The "what," though, was proving to be a problem. Her brain wasn't working right. Everything was foggy. A fuzzy collection of barely there thoughts jumbled together with images that didn't make sense.

Afina shivered, tried to catch the memory. The birds above yammered and the vague impression thinned, leaving her mind blank but for one thought.

She didn't feel dead.

Something told her she ought to, except...heaven should feel more, well, heavenly, without the terrible sting buzzing between her temples. The other problem? Everyone was supposed to get along in heaven, and a flock of engaged fowl seemed a bit disorderly, disrespectful of the goddess's master plan.

Well, whatever the strategy, it wasn't working. The argument had become a screaming match, driving the ache into the back of her skull. Mother Mary, why couldn't they find another tree? Why couldn't…Wait a moment. Trees?

Afina cracked her eyes open. Filtered through something, sunlight drilled her and agony clawed, leaving spots in the center of her vision. She tried again and saw a collection of blurry green blobs. Leaves. Which meant trees. Not something she had anywhere near her cottage. The beeches stood all the way across the clearing and—

The ground shifted beneath her. A sauntering roll, more gentle than jostling.

Still her stomach rebelled, clenching in protest as Afina looked to her left. Her vision wavered, moving from dark to light and back again. Concentrating hard, she squinted at a fuzzy outline. The black mane came into focus first, followed by pointed ears and the shape of a head. A horse? She blinked to clear the fog and tried again.

Uh-huh…definitely. A horse.

Afina frowned at it. Much as she'd always wanted to, she didn't own a horse. So why was she on one? A dream come true or—

Oh, gods, her head hurt.

Letting her eyes slide closed, she settled against her warm cradle. Later. She'd figure it out later, when Sabine woke up to break her fast. For now, she would—

The stallion sidestepped. Her stomach went with it, pitching as the jarring movement sent her brain sloshing inside her skull. Afina gagged, fighting the burn while nausea fisted a hand around her windpipe.

A deep voice cursed. The warhorse settled, but it was too late. Bile churned, and she coughed, lost to the horrible spasm clogging the back of her throat.

"Breathe." Warm hands rubbed circles on her back.

Afina shook her head. Breathing sounded like a good idea, but she couldn't find any air. The pressure banding her chest squeezed, compressing her lungs until cramps took over, taking her along for the ride. Dry heaves hit and she doubled over, palms flat against her breastbone, eyes watering as she fought the convulsions.

"Jesu." With gentle insistence, someone tugged at her, pulling her upright. The position helped, allowing her to take a shallow breath. "Good. In through your nose, out through your mouth."

The tone drew her, held her up high, away from the pain. She drifted toward it, following the deep timbre without question, and took another breath, this one fuller than the last.

"That's it, *draga*."

Afina blinked away tears. *Draga?* Oh, that was nice. No one had ever called her "darling" before. And that voice. Incredibly deep, with a soothing cadence that reminded her of warm honey and sugary sweets. Her favorite, but…wait a moment. Something was wrong with that image. She shook her head, ignoring the pain as she tried to clear her mind.

"Take another." Strong fingers stroked through her hair, massaged her nape, attacking the tension under her scalp. "'Twill help the unease pass."

Her stomach twisted, trying to escape through her spine. "W-who?"

"Breathe first, love. Worry about me later."

Worry about him? Should she?

He made it seem like a worthwhile idea, being so gentle…calling her love. That wasn't right either. For all she yearned otherwise, there wasn't a person she knew who loved her but Sabine. The thought jolted through her. Where was her daughter? Sabine was never out of her sight—never. But she wasn't in her lap and that meant…

A chill nipped at her and Afina stilled, fighting a tremor and rising fear.

"*Rahat*, you're pale." A big hand ghosted over her, holding her steady as he pulled a thick blanket around her shoulders. Soft wool tucked beneath her chin, he cupped her face. "I'm sorry. I gave you too much."

"P-poison?"

"A tonic."

"S-Sabine." Planting her palm against his chest, she pushed herself upright and forced her eyes open. The world spun, flipped once before righting itself. "Where is s-she?"

"Safe with Cristobal…still asleep."

"Did you—"

He shook his head. "We didn't give her any. She is napping 'tis all."

His reply made sense. The sun hung high in the sky. 'Twas sometime after the noonday meal—prime naptime for Sabine. Still, how could she trust him? The answer? She couldn't. The mental fog hampering her cleared, allowing her mind to gain speed. Memory rushed back with acuity, unscrambling the picture, laying out the puzzle, damning the man who held her.

Xavian.

His name whispered through her mind, scraping her raw as she remembered: his injury, her cottage, the promise of the gold coin, and the sweetness of goat's milk. All lies. Nothing but a clever ruse designed to get him inside her home. The bastard.

Sitting sideways in his lap, she raised her gaze to meet his, hammering him with the silent accusation.

His hands went still on her nape as a wary light entered his eyes. "Careful, lass."

His voice rolled over her like warm milk: soothing, coaxing...hateful. She detested the fact she liked the sound of him. It was treason, a betrayal of the senses—one that made anger burn and her stomach settle. Beast. Cad. Kidnapping dolt.

Afina shrugged his hands away from her throat. "Stop the horse and give me my daughter."

Watching her like a predator does its prey, he said, "Not yet."

The quick denial killed self-preservation and unleashed rage. With a quick jab, Afina elbowed him in the ribs, felt him tense, and swung around with her fist. She'd never hit anyone before—had never wanted to—but the bastard thought to stand between her and Sabine. He'd done it in her cottage. Afina wouldn't allow him to do it again.

The white points of her knuckles came round, heading for his eye socket. Xavian countered and, with a quick hand, caught her fist midvolley. She launched the second, twisting against him, fighting for balance on the saddle front. He caught that one as easily as he had the first and held, imprisoning her knuckles against his palms.

Poised in front of him, both hands trapped, Afina's eyes went wide. Goodness, he was fast and...she swallowed...warm. The heat in his palms sucked the body chill out through her fists. But the warmth didn't reach his eyes. The pale blue was icy, direct in a way that made her shiver.

She clenched her teeth to stop them from chattering. Yes, he might be good at playing the wolf, but that didn't mean she must play the rabbit. Fear. No fear. It didn't matter. She refused to show it or give up and retreat.

Xavian raised a brow. "What now?"

"All I want is my daughter," she whispered, berating herself as she gave ground and looked away.

"Ready to stop fighting?"

She nearly snarled at him, wanted to yell "no" so badly her teeth ached. She nodded instead, her pride no match for the quiet throb of fear. Sabine was so little—so innocent—and if promising to behave would see her daughter returned Afina would give her word. Keeping it, however, was another matter. As soon as the cretin handed her Sabine, she would direct her boot to the softest part of his anatomy.

"Look over my left shoulder."

Her head swiveled so fast she wobbled in the saddle. Xavian steadied her and, with a gentle tug, pulled her off the saddle horn and back into his lap. Afina barely noticed. She was too busy searching for Sabine, scanning the riders behind them. Cristobal broke away, guiding his steed to the front of the pack. His dark gaze met hers a moment before he shifted the cloak-wrapped bundle in his arms.

Hardly able to breathe, she clutched Xavian's shoulder and waited. He lifted a corner of the mantle, smoothing it away to show the mop of blond curls surrounding her cherub's sleeping face.

Afina exhaled in a rush. "Blessed be the goddess."

"See?" Forgotten in the struggle, Xavian reached for the cloak pooled around her hips. Adjusting the wool, he drew it up until it lay snug against the nape of her neck. "Hale and whole."

"Can I have her?" Meeting his gaze briefly, she pleaded with her eyes before returning her attention to Sabine.

"In a while."

"But—"

"We cannot stop now, Afina," he said, keeping his tone soft enough to soothe her but strong enough to hold the line. "'Tisn't safe. At nightfall, when you are recovered and strong enough to carry her, I will give her back."

Her bottom lip quivered. "Promise me he won't hurt her."

"My word," he murmured, his throat tight. He swallowed past the knot, disliking her distress. It made him want to soothe her, to touch her until the pain left her eyes and she settled against him as she had during the night. Pain and pleasure—a sorry couple, but intertwined when it came to Afina. His reaction was telling...temptation and need wrapped into one.

Unable to resist either, he traced the edge of her eyebrow, using the caress to gain her attention. When her eyes met his, he brushed the bedraggled tresses away from her face. "I've no intention of hurting her...or you."

"Too late." Her brows drawn tight, she leaned away from his touch. "You took us against my will. Let us go if you wish to keep your word."

"Nay, you stay with me." Xavian winced but didn't show it. Christ, he hadn't meant to say that, to sound so possessive, as though he'd taken her for himself. Aye, he liked the look of her—had imagined bedding her a dozen different ways—but that meant naught in the scheme of things. He'd taken Afina for a purpose, one that didn't include making her his own.

"What...why?" Anger and bafflement winged across her small face. Xavian took a shallow breath, trying not to be enchanted as he watched her teeter between the two emotions. Fury won out and she glared at him, eyes narrowed, expression militant. "I don't have anything you want."

"Not true." He kept his expression neutral, unwilling to show his attraction. He'd not spent much time with women—most of the encounters had been brief, ending when he received his pleasure and gave some in return. But instinct warned if she guessed how much he desired her, it wouldn't take long for the manipulation to begin. "I'm in need of a healer for my new home. Your skill is sufficient for my purpose."

"And if I am unwilling?"

"Can you afford to be?"

She said naught, simply stared at him, the unspoken vulnerability in her silence difficult to bear. For some reason he disliked her uncertainty, the notion she preferred abject poverty to him. But this wasn't about him. 'Twas about the lads in his care and the importance of his academy to their success. Afina could contribute, give the boys something they'd never had: softness, caring, a woman's touch.

With the boys forefront in his mind, he pushed for an answer. "What did you have in that hovel...what are you leaving behind? Wealth? Stature? The—"

"Independence," she said, cutting him off with an undeniable growl.

"What good is that, *draga*, when you cannot feed your own child?"

Intense pain flashed across her features a moment before she looked away. Xavian killed the urge to take the harsh statement back. It might hurt her pride, but she needed to hear the truth. Both she and Sabine were too thin. 'Twas obvious to anyone who cared to look they'd not had enough to eat for a while. The baffling bit—the thing he couldn't understand—was the fact he cared enough to make her admit it.

"I was doing fine," she said, her tone thick with emotion and something else. Stubbornness. He knew the flaw well, possessed it himself, but now was no time for her to become mired in illusion.

He raised a brow, challenging her statement with silence.

Her knuckles turned white in the black folds of the mantle. "I was."

"Do not lie to me." He leaned forward, bringing them nose-to-nose. As much as he admired her spirit, he wanted her to understand. He never tolerated dishonesty. He'd endured years of deceit, been suffocated by subterfuge and manipulated without mercy. 'Twas best she learned he valued the truth now. Otherwise naught but trouble lay ahead. "Be honest with me, Afina. In the end, 'twill get you most of what you want and all of what you need."

"I don't want anything from you." Chin tilted in defiance, she planted her hand on his chest and shoved him away. "Honest enough?"

Her petulant tone drilled him. He clenched his teeth on a smile, enjoying her wit even as he wished it wasn't so quick. "Better."

She huffed, no doubt unsatisfied he refused to give ground. Amusement spread like a disease, infecting him with good humor. He shoved it away, rejecting the ease he shared with her. 'Twas too dangerous. It made him want to get closer, to ignore her purpose, his vow, and follow desire's urging. But he couldn't do it. Connection was something he'd never done well and didn't want.

Shuffling sideways, Afina helped him gain control, putting as much distance between them as she could without falling off his horse. "You won't let us go, will you? No matter that I wish it."

"Nay, you belong to my circle now." Shifting in the saddle, he gave Afina more room. He wanted her comfortable, well able to ride into the night. With the afternoon light waning, they had miles to go yet. The hunters wouldn't rest, and as much as Xavian yearned to turn and fight he didn't want his new healer anywhere near the battle. "Accept what you cannot change, Afina. 'Twill go easier…for everyone."

Lips pursed, she clung to the saddle horn, refusing to look at him. Xavian stared at her profile, debating whether to say more. Nay, he'd said all he needed to. She understood his message, knew he would not let her or Sabine go. 'Twas enough for now. She would test him before long and run.

Good. Let her try.

The sooner she realized escape was futile, the sooner she would accept her new life. No matter how much she taxed his patience, he would see his responsibility through to the end. He'd made a promise to Bodgan to protect her from all comers. The Transylvanian lord wanted her for a reason. An important one. His objective concerning Afina might have changed, but he knew Vladimir's wouldn't. Now he must cultivate her trust to find the truth. Odd, but as he urged Mayhem into a gallop, his gaze on the obstinate set of her chin, Xavian found himself looking forward to the challenge.

CHAPTER FOUR

Vladimir Barbu took the stairs two at a time. He launched himself off the second-to-last step, avoiding a rotted tread to touch down on the upper landing. With a curse, he swerved around a pile of debris deposited by the decaying roof and turned right toward his solar. Strides long and pace steady, he slammed through the door and, with a flick of his wrist, closed it behind him. The hinges screeched, raking icy fingers down his spine. He glared at the metal brackets over his shoulder.

Hell and damnation, he would string Anton up by his balls when he found him. Lazy good-for-naught. He was to have fixed the door days ago. Vladimir scowled. His jack-of-all-trades needed another thrashing, but he would throw him in the stocks first. He wanted the incompetent arse sober when he delivered the reprimand. Otherwise the drunkard wouldn't remember the beating, never mind the reason for it.

He rolled his shoulders and turned his attention to the chamber. The luxury reached out to stroke him. With a sigh, he allowed the collection of plush pillows, daybeds, and thick tapestries to draw the tension from his muscles. A veritable oasis, the round tower room was the only one finished in the rat hole he now called home, the only one he'd possessed enough coin to refurbish.

Now he had precious little left. Certainly not enough to replace the castle roof, any stair treads, or shore up the crumbling walls of the great hall. But he didn't care. The large turret, with its square windows and generous proportions, was his favorite place...the opulent sanctuary he deserved. 'Twas a right he claimed as acting ruler of Transylvania, the people's protests be damned. He'd worked for years to take the title; brutalized, maimed, and killed to be next in line. And Afina wasn't going to ruin it for him.

Damn the lass to hell.

Two years of searching. No matter who he sent after her, the result remained the same. She evaded him at every turn. And he was running out of time.

He needed the Amulet of Orm to wear the crown of Transylvania, for King Charles of Hungary to deliver a decree and make his title official. Until then, he was naught more than the interim lord, a circumstance subject to change.

If only Ylenia, former high priestess, had done as instructed. Had she lied and told the people the amulet had accepted him—glowed as it always did when handed to the true ruler of Transylvania—then she would still be alive...and he would already be king.

He curled his hands into fists. Stupid wench. She'd ruined everything.

Without the sacred talisman, he lacked the leverage to force King Charles's hand. Superstitious to the point of obsession, the royal jackass refused to ignore ancient lore—the tradition of the amulet—and anoint him voivode. He must find the trinket and fake its glow. If he didn't, he would never sit his arse on the throne and do what Wallachia had done a year ago: sever all ties with the Hungarian monarch and create a country and kingdom of his own.

Damnation, where in the hell was Afina?

He needed her...for more than just the power she would provide him. He wanted her under him, over him, in whatever position he could get her as long as it involved his bed. He would settle for Bianca, but 'twas Afina he craved. She wore the mark, the crown of the goddess stamped on her skin, the symbol marking the next High Priestess of Orm. Without her support, the king would never accept him. And without his blessing, the coffers, the treasures of Transylvania, remained out of reach.

His nostrils flared as he imagined what he would do to her—with her—when he found her. An eye for an eye. He suffered, and when he finally got his hands on her, she would too.

He growled. Where the devil was Henrik?

He'd ridden all the way from the marketplace to meet the bastard. If he wasn't—

A soft sound caught his attention.

Scanning the chamber again, Vladimir caught a flash of movement in his periphery. Bare-chested, a man came through from the alcove, silhouette haloed by the sun flooding through the high windows. Another outline followed, shapely, much smaller than the first. The pair paused, heads aligned and close together.

Vladimir sighed and pivoted. His back to them, he crossed to the other side of the room, his progress muted by the thick Turkish rug underfoot. Grabbing a bejeweled cup from the exquisitely carved sideboard, he tipped the matching pitcher, pouring a tumbler full of red wine. Goblet in hand, he turned to lean on the lip of the cabinet.

Legs crossed at the ankles, he sipped the wine and watched them. A cloud passed overhead and the sunlight faded, giving him a clear view of the man's face.

Hazel-gold eyes trained on Vladimir, Henrik fastened the ties on his trews then bent to kiss the curve of the wench's bare shoulder. "My thanks, sweet."

Vladimir raised the goblet in silent salute. Christ, the warrior had no shame, didn't care that he'd been caught tupping a servant by the lord who employed him.

A rosy hue in her cheeks, she peeked at Henrik from beneath her lashes. "Tonight?"

Vladimir's hand tightened around the tankard, jealousy rolling like wildfire through his veins. If only Afina had looked at him that way. If only she'd wanted him with the same intensity, the crown would be his, and so would she.

His mind on how best to punish her, he observed Henrik with the wench and almost snorted. The warrior's patience was laughable. He'd already tupped her, for Christ's sake. Why be so gentle? But then, he guessed the man wasn't renowned for his skill with the lasses for naught. Vladimir shook his head. Gentleness. Such an abysmal waste of time.

With a nudge, Henrik pushed her toward the exit. "Off you go, lass."

Eyes bright, the maid scurried toward the exit, her fingers busy lacing the front of her gown. She paused on the threshold, gave the warrior one last lingering look, and disappeared over the threshold.

The latch fell with a click, and Vladimir asked, "What have you learned?"

"Not much." His gaze fixed on him, Henrik palmed a tankard from the marble mantelpiece. Something cold moved in the warrior's eyes as he swirled the wine then raised the cup to take a sip.

Vladimir clenched his teeth, disliking the blatant show of disrespect. The urge to draw his sword—and Henrik's blood—almost overwhelmed him. Self-preservation prevailed, however, stilling his hand. The man standing before him was no lightweight. A full-blooded assassin trained by the old man, Henrik could no doubt kill him with naught more than his little finger.

"Then why the hell are you here? Couldn't find someone else's servants to screw?"

"You're selection is good, Vladimir," he said, his bored tone somehow laced with enmity. "But not so fine I'd travel cross-country to bed one."

The crass bastard. How dare he come here empty-handed then disregard his authority as though his position held no importance? His hand tightened on his cup. "Then I'll ask again...why are you here?"

"Rumor has it you've hired Xavian Ramir."

"What of it?"

"I like to know when I have competition." Interest interwoven with menace sparked in Henrik's strange golden eyes. "Hedging your bets?"

The hostility embedded in the assassin's voice swirled in the space between them, and the muscle roping Vladimir's abdomen twisted, tying his stomach into knots. He forced himself to relax and, affecting a manner of unconcern, swirled the wine in his goblet. "I want her found...two working on the problem is better than one."

Henrik prowled toward him, his movements predatory, his feet soundless as he skirted a plush daybed. Trailing a finger along the top of a silk pillow, he stopped a few feet away and flicked the gold fringe on the tasseled cushion. "Is it?"

Vladimir shifted against the sideboard, aware he clung to his perch by a fingertip. He must tread carefully. Henrik was unpredictable at best, violent at worst. If he showed weakness, the animal in the assassin would sense his disquiet and go for his throat. Icy fingers brushing the nape of his neck, he waved the comment aside, feigning a confidence he didn't feel. "What do you care?"

"He is a comrade, of sorts."

Of sorts? What the hell did that mean? Had Ramir been trained by the Halál as well? Vladimir knew so little about the man, had heard about him through a string of associates. 'Twas said the warrior-assassin single-handedly won the Battle of Posada for Basarab, the new ruler of Wallachia. If rumor held true, Ramir massacred half of the Hungarian army and sent the other half fleeing for their lives.

Vladimir raised a brow. "Is he as good as I've heard?"

"Better."

With a soundlessness that unnerved him, Henrik ghosted around an armchair, drifting within striking distance. Alert to the possibility of attack, Vladimir held his breath then let it out when the assassin moved away, toward the blaze roaring in the fireplace.

"Better than you?"

Henrik's mouth quirked at the corners, but he said naught.

The subtle evasion bothered Vladimir. Why was Henrik so interested in Ramir? What did he know that he wasn't telling? Whatever the cause, it signaled trouble, the kind he didn't like. Who he hired was no one's business, least of all Henrik's. But assassins were a strange bunch. He'd learned that truth the hard way, had yet to recover from his folly...from forcing the encounter and Ramir's subsequent attack. Hell and damnation, his knee still ached and the meeting had taken place well over a month ago.

He breathed deep, trying to calm himself. Ramir was the rarest sort of savage. Skilled precision coupled with a cunning Vladimir admired but seldom saw. He clenched his teeth. If only Ramir had taken the coin. He'd wanted to give him half to start and half when he delivered Afina, but the bastard hadn't bitten. His distrust had been palpable. He'd neither refused nor accepted, merely evaded, too intelligent to commit to the mission either way. The hesitation made Vladimir think Ramir was no longer an asset but a liability, one that needed to be dropped off the nearest cliff.

Curious about Henrik's association with the famed assassin, he tested the waters. "Can you find him?"

"Who?" Grabbing a sleeveless tunic from the chair in front of the fire, Henrik pulled the black leather over his head and attacked the side laces. "Ram?"

"Aye." Vladimir took another sip and lounged against the sideboard, trying to appear as though the assassin's reply didn't matter. The truth? He hung on tether hooks, itched to know whether Henrik could track the bastard.

Henrik shrugged, as noncommittal as his blasted comrade.

Tension pulled at the muscles bracketing his spine. Should he? Shouldn't he? 'Twas a toss-up considering Henrik's violent streak, but…aye. It was worth the risk.

"There's additional coin in it…if you can track him," he said, tempting Henrik with the one thing he knew no one could resist. Ready coin.

A black brow raised, the assassin slid a knife into a sheath high on his chest. "How much?"

"Thirty pieces of silver." Vladimir paused, sitting on the fence, not sure which way to hop. After a tense moment, he made the leap. "To take him out."

"Eliminate the competition?" Henrik's mouth curled at the corners. The smile never quite reaching his eyes, he strapped twin swords on his back and headed for the door. "I thought you'd never ask."

She needed to make her move…soon. The Carpathians loomed, a silent predator waiting for them to come within easy reach. She'd never been so close before, had never wanted to be anywhere near them. People said the inhospitable mountains ate people whole, that strange things—unholy things—happened on the great peaks, and below, in the deep valleys. A godless place filled with naught but inky darkness and bad intentions.

And Xavian was leading them straight into the belly of the beast.

Afina shivered, catching a glimpse of the jagged teeth through a break in the trees. The sharp angles and soaring cliffs snarled at the sky, piercing greyish-white clouds to taunt the heavens with a curled lip. She clung to the saddle horn and cuddled Sabine closer, her unease so strong the heat leached from her body. The chill sank bone-deep, turning muscle to ice, freezing her ability to form an adequate plan.

At least her brain was working well enough now to know she required one. Fast. Faster than fast…before the little-used trail they followed carried them into the mountains. Once they left the forest, her chances of escape went from slight to nil. She needed the thick shadow and dense foliage to shield her when she bolted. Finding cover on barren rock faces, sheer cliffs, and the narrow paths of the Carpathians would prove too difficult, especially with a chatty two-year-old in tow.

Time was running out.

Judging by their pace, she had two, mayhap three days at most. Nervous tension swirled in the pit of her stomach, wreaking havoc with her resolve. She drew a long breath and stroked Sabine's hair, trying to steady herself. One slip, a moment of inattentiveness was all she needed. By the time her captors registered her absence, she'd be gone, so deep in the woods they'd find it difficult to track her.

The mossy turf would conceal her footprints, wouldn't it? She could hide in the shadows, use the trees for cover, the streams to disguise their scent and trail, couldn't she? Afina swallowed, praying she was right. So many factors to consider, too many chances to make a mistake. And yet she only had one to win her way free. Xavian wasn't stupid. He no doubt expected her to run. It wouldn't take a genius to figure out. She'd signaled her intent the instant she failed to fall in with his plans.

She shifted in the saddle, wanting to kick herself. Why hadn't she played along? It would be much easier now if he believed she was a happy captive. Now he watched her like an alluring angel— a fallen one. Stupid. Idiotic. Completely witless. Why did she always think of these things too late?

Afina adjusted the sling around her shoulder. Lulled by the steady beat of horses' hooves, Sabine swung in the well-worn fabric, struggling to keep her eyes open. Afina watched her silver eyelashes flicker and prayed for good fortune. She didn't hold much hope. Luck had never been a friend of hers, unless, of course, the bad kind counted.

Afina stifled a snort. Abysmal luck, indeed. Poor decision making had landed her here, not fortune, but she refused to dwell on her failures. No matter how inept her skill, she needed to move forward. She held no sway over the past. It was over and done, but the future lay ahead, and feeling sorry for herself was never a good strategy.

She huffed. Forget *good*. She would settle for mediocre if it got her far enough away from her captors. It was like being in the middle of a male wolf pack. Silent, muscular ones who wore aggression like a scent.

Armed to the teeth, their sun-bronzed skin and serious eyes screamed of experience, a depth of skill she didn't need to see to believe. World-weariness reflected in their faces, sad and startling in its intensity. Could that be why they wore nothing but black? The style of clothing differed, yes, but each wore ebony in one form or another. A strange preference, but one she guessed held importance for them. Instinct warned this group did nothing without reason. She wasn't sure how she knew, but something told her when Xavian acted, the logic supporting his decision was well thought out in advance.

There was something unseemly about that. A methodical precision that made her feel safe even as it scared her to death. She felt the push-pull, the fear and attraction each time she looked at him. How could he heat her blood and frighten her at the same time? Was that what Bianca had felt for Bodgan? Had the emotional opposites pulled her sister into a passionate entanglement? Prompted her to meet with him in secret, risk all to have him in her life and rejoice when she found herself with child?

Afina chewed on her lower lip, weighing the probability. No matter the contradiction, it seemed a distinct possibility. One she disliked...immensely.

With a frown, she drilled the back of Xavian's head with a look. She refused to let that happen to her. She wouldn't permit him to lure her the way Bodgan had lured her sister. Bianca's death stood as an excellent example. Nothing but pain came from becoming entangled with a man, and Afina intended to remember the important lesson.

"Look, Mama! Birdie."

Yanked from her thoughts by Sabine's excited chirp, Afina jumped. "Yes, love, I see it."

"Pretty." Pointing to a low-lying branch, her daughter bounced in the sling, swaying against Afina's side before popping her thumb back in her mouth.

"It is, but hush," she said, registering the ripple of masculine power around them. The disturbance, a slight ruffling of muscle, reminded her of how a wolf might react when startled—lip curled, fur standing on end until it found the source of disruption, declared it a non-threat, and smoothed its fine pelt back into order. "We must be quiet, cherub."

Xavian glanced over his shoulder, sharp eyes settling on her. Afina bit her bottom lip, quelling a shiver. His gaze swept over her, pushing brittleness into her bones until she felt fragile, as though she might break into tiny pieces. Stiff in the saddle, she feigned confidence, unwilling to show weakness to a man who possessed none.

Without taking his attention from her, he spoke to Cristobal. The dark man nodded and urged his mount forward as Xavian drew his warhorse to the edge of the path. The huge beast tossed his head but stayed true, obeying his master's command to wait. The moment she came alongside them, he nudged his steed into a walk.

He bumped her leg and her horse sidestepped, making room for him beside them on the trail. Muscled thigh a hair's breadth from hers, his scent engulfed her, a subtle invasion of male spice and forest musk that soothed even as it unbalanced. Hmm, he smelled so good. She wanted to lean in and immerse herself in the pleasant complexities of his fragrance.

She swayed in the saddle and, without thought, let her senses lead. Drifting toward instead of away from him, she watched his eyes flame as he raised his hand. His heat reached her before his fingertips, moving across her skin in a warm ripple of sensation. She sighed as he traced the ridge of her cheekbone then moved lower to brush the corner of her mouth. He paused, his gaze roaming her features before he cupped her cheek and made another pass, stroking her bottom lip with the pad of his thumb.

Afina sank into the caress, parting her lips when he applied more pressure. His taste, salty-sweet, invaded her mouth and pleasure hummed, flooding her with delight. The unfamiliar sensation rocked her and awareness struck like a thunderbolt. She flinched. What on earth was she doing? Why was she welcoming his touch...encouraging his kiss? His kiss. She almost moaned, the idea of his mouth on hers sending her sideways into delight.

Oh, no. She was in trouble. The serious kind that made girls act like fools and men like lechers. She needed to get a hold of herself and away from him before she did something stupid. Like offered him her trust—along with her body—on a silver platter.

Heat pricking across her cheekbones, she turned her face from his hand. He made a sound of regret and leather creaked as he shifted in the saddle, putting distance between them.

Scrambling for a distraction, she blurted, "I'm sorry, she doesn't mean—"

"Hi!" Mismatched eyes trained on Xavian, Sabine smiled at him around her thumb.

The twin swords strapped on his back bobbed as he dragged his gaze from her to Sabine. A crease between his bronzy-gold brows, she saw uncertainty flicker in his eyes an instant before he said, "Hello, Sabine."

"Look, Mama." Her voice a flutter of excitement, Sabine pointed to the man beside them. "X."

"Yes, it is," she said, stomping on the butterflies wreaking havoc in her belly.

Needing a distraction, she took inventory of the warrior while his attention remained on her child. Stealth wasn't exactly her forte, but she picked out small details, cataloguing the weapons he carried...well, at least the ones she could see.

Aside from the twin blades he wore on his back, two knives were strapped to each thigh, a pair made their home on his chest, one low, the other high, while yet another rested at the base of his spine. She spotted a few more buried in leather sheaths in his saddle. Good goddess, the man was a walking arsenal. How in Hades was she going to escape from that?

"How old is she?"

His deep voice stroked her, a warm caress that drew her gaze back to his. "Almost two. Her birthday falls in a month or so."

He tilted his head, expression thoughtful. "Do all children suck their thumbs?"

Afina blinked, thrown by the simple question. Such a strange thing for a battle-honed warrior to wonder. What was he playing at? "I'm not sure. She's the first one I've ever had."

He nodded.

She stiffened as his focus left Sabine to settle on her. The horde of butterflies flapped their wings a little harder and sensation spiraled below her belly button. Afina glanced away and, not knowing what else to do, reissued her apology. "I'll do my best to keep her quiet from now on."

"'Tis all right." He nudged her with his knee.

She shied away from the gentle bump, but got the message. He wanted her to look at him, and goddess help her, she needed to avoid that at all costs. He unsettled her, stirred her soul-deep with his quiet ways and inherent strength. Qualities she'd always thought she might like in a man.

She remembered the times she and Bianca had lain awake at night, whispering like pea-gooses. Cocooned, safe from the outside world, they'd shared secrets and dreamed of the men they would someday marry. She never imagined a few years later Bianca would be dead along with her dreams. The pain of that made it hard to breathe. Afina forced herself to anyway, but...

Goddess help her, she missed her sister. Every evening at sunset. Each morning at daybreak. Bianca was never far from her thoughts.

Her vision went blurry. Afina held the sorrow at bay, tucking the tears along with the precious memories away. She wanted to keep the good times for herself, not share them with the man who had taken her freedom—the autonomy Bianca had tried so hard to teach her. Anger burned the back of her throat. Who did he think he was? What gave him the right to decide her future?

Setting her teeth on the question, she took strength from her sister's memory and, raising her head, met his gaze head-on. Approval sparked in his eyes an instant before he reached out and flicked the underside of her chin.

She jerked away from the playful tap and frowned at him.

The corners of his mouth tipped up. "The lass can talk. We are in no danger here."

In other words? They were alone in a place where no one would hear them scream. Afina swallowed, righteous indignation dimmed by a healthy dose of wariness. Self-preservation took precedence over pride. She could be angry with him another time, after she knew for certain he wouldn't lose his temper and hurt her.

"Oh, good. That's…ah, good."

"You're spooked." Head tilted, he considered her. "Why?"

"Oh, I don't know," she said, her tone testy. "Being kidnapped has a way of unsettling a girl."

He snorted. "'Twas more a liberation than a kidnapping."

"In your opinion, not mine." She pursed her lips, irritated by his attitude. "You cannot go about dragging people from their homes…no matter your opinion of their situation."

"Why not?"

Why not? Surprise overriding mental agility, she grasped the first reason that came to mind. "It's impolite."

He tossed her a look of disbelief. "Politesse. A waste of time. Why would you imagine I possess social graces…that I've been taught any?"

"It is a universal truth, not something that needs learning." Her hand tightened on the reins. She resisted the urge to wrap the dark straps around his neck and strangle him. "Everyone—even those without manners—knows supplanting another's will is wrong."

"Even when the greater good is served?" Something sparked in his eyes: a gleam, one that told her he liked sparring with her. Warmed by the discovery, she almost smiled at him. She killed the urge, needing distance between them, not friendship. "Let us say, when a person is starving to death?"

"We weren't starving."

"Close to it, *draga*."

She bristled and, tired of the argument, changed the subject. "Where are you taking us?"

"Have you a faulty memory, lass?" She glared at him. His lip twitched. When she didn't respond to his teasing, he shrugged. "I told you...home."

"Forgive me for not knowing where that is."

"The Carpathians." Lifting his large hand, he pointed to a break in the large trees flanking the path. Tree limbs swayed in the gentle breeze, rustling the leaves as she spotted the unholy beasts standing in the distance. Deep-seated pride laced his voice when he said, "My keep, Drachaven, is located there. Not far from the Jiu River."

"In the mountains?"

"Aye."

She stifled a shiver. "I've no wish to go there."

"You've a day or two to become accustomed to the idea," he said, tone soft with what she thought might be understanding. He raised a hand as though he wished to soothe her with his touch. She leaned away, a protective arm curled around her daughter. A muscle jumped along his jaw as he looked from her to the path ahead. "My home is now yours."

"Your interest in us makes no sense."

She shook her head, intuition igniting suspicion. Xavian wasn't telling her the whole truth. He could have chosen from any number of healers in Severin, ones with good reputations. So the question, the one bothering her: What had made him come after her? From what she knew of him there must be a reason, above and beyond his injury. No random event had brought him to her door, Father Marion notwithstanding. The more she thought about it, the more she realized he'd used the priest's name as a way into her cottage; a nonviolent tactic to achieve his goal.

Narrow-eyed, she stared at him, sorting through the possibilities. "Tell me why you wish us to make our place with you. Do you even need a healer?"

"I do." He glanced at her sideways, assessing her from his periphery.

What he was looking for, she didn't know, but his silence unnerved her. He used it to effect, she realized, crushing his opponents with a well-placed pause. She refused to take the bait and be the first to break the hush. If he wanted a standoff, she was more than ready to give him one.

After an intense moment, he sighed. "You are a thinker, Afina. That may prove to be a problem."

That nailed it. Sir Tell-the-Truth was withholding information. "For a man who demands honesty, you seem to have difficulty using it yourself."

He chuckled, the sound rusty with disuse. Surprise creased his face before he smoothed his expression. "Touché, but choosing not to inform you of something does not mean I am lying."

"A lie of omission, then."

He shook his head, the gleam of enjoyment returning to his eyes. "Patience, Afina."

Patience, her foot. "What if I don't have any?"

He bumped her with his knee again, the movement playful. One corner of his mouth tilted up, he put his heels to his steed's flank and said over his shoulder, "Learn some."

Her lips pursed, she watched him ride away, wishing she held a sharper weapon than her tongue. How dare he lecture her about untruths then refuse to adhere to the same rules he demanded she follow? Irritating, domineering dolt. Her gaze centered on the back of his head, she racked her brain, trying to assess all the angles. What was he hiding?

Whatever it was, she knew it must be important. Big. Huge in a way that scared her. Did it have something to do with Vladimir? Her heart stalled, refusing to beat as panic closed her airway. A little light-headed, she clung to the saddle horn and tightened her hold on Sabine.

Her daughter squirmed, an irritated, sleepy wiggle. "Mama?"

"It's all right, cherub," she whispered around the lump in her throat. Loosening her grip, she rubbed the center of Sabine's back, soothing her with rhythmic circles. "Shh, go to sleep now. Everything is all right."

And it would be. She wasn't lying. She would find a way out of the mess she'd made. Pry them out of Xavian's talons to keep Sabine safe. She'd made a promise to her sister, and now her actions must support that vow.

Escape was the only option. No matter how afraid, she must break free.

Dread burning a hole in her stomach, Afina closed her eyes and prayed that luck, just this once, chose to befriend her.

CHAPTER FIVE

Xavian clenched his teeth as the blade nicked his thumb. Turning the chunk of wood in his hand, he shifted on the moss-covered log and glanced down at his hand. Blood welled on his skin. The third cut in less than an hour. He frowned, disgusted by his lack of concentration. 'Twas a problem, one that rarely plagued him while he engaged in his favorite pastime.

Normally carving kept him calm. Sane. Better able to sink inside himself and withdraw from the brutality life handed him, day in and day out. All without leaving his perch.

The perfect escape for an imperfect man.

And he was thankful. Thankful for the old assassin who'd taught him to whittle as a child. Thankful for the ability to disappear inside a world of his own making, far from Halál and the harshness of his former life with Al Pacii. But the real boon? Working with his hands helped him relax, providing an endless source of satisfaction. He loved taking a rough piece of wood and transforming it into something useful…something beautiful.

But not today.

The half-finished figurine did little to ease the tension. The well-worn handle of his carving knife felt awkward in his palm and distraction gave way to clumsiness.

With a sigh, Xavian sucked the droplet from his thumb then leaned forward to prop both forearms on his bent knees.

Afina was driving him daft. Concentration seemed an impossible mission with her flitting about the campsite, nimble fingers stealing what she needed.

He should stop her, but he wouldn't. Not when he knew her aim. He'd been waiting for her to make her move for days. An hour ago, she had, slipping a pouch of dried meat into her healing satchel.

Xavian stared at the wooden block, unable to keep his lips from twitching. His little troublemaker had been busy, gathering supplies in preparation for escape. Plucky lass. If naught else, he admired her tenacity. 'Twas mayhap what he liked best about her, aside from her beauty. The innate toughness allowed her to adjust under less than optimal circumstances. A rare trait in a woman and one that made him wish to give her what she wanted.

But he refused to let her go.

His newfound conscience squawked, calling him selfish. He conceded the point, but the fact he enjoyed having Afina and the little one around changed naught. His logic was sound. He'd taken them for a purpose. He required a healer, and she, his protection.

Vladimir was power hungry, a warlord with serious ambition. Promise to Bodgan aside, instinct told him the bastard would hurt Afina if he managed to capture her. Xavian's hand tightened around the wooden block. Nay, he wouldn't allow it. Drachaven was her home now, and he, her overlord. 'Twas his duty to ensure she thrived, and hers to serve him well.

The trick would be in breaking her willfulness without damaging her spirit. He didn't want her broken, just tamed a wee bit. Eyes narrowed, he flipped the knife into the air, watching it rotate end over end while he went over his plan. The old oak he sat beneath swayed above his head and a whisper of sound ghosted from his left.

Without looking away from the arc of the blade, he asked, "Where is she?"

"At the stream, bathing the little one." The voice came from the opposite side of the tree.

Catching the knife hilt midturn, Xavian fingered the grip's worn leather. "Who's trailing them?"

"Razvan."

"Out of sight?"

"Aye," Cristobal said, rounding the enormous trunk. Standing between the oak's gnarled feet, he propped a shoulder against the rough bark. "Afina has no idea we are tracking her movements. Razvan will let us know if she makes a break for it."

"Good." Xavian tossed the weapon again, fighting an unpleasant sensation as it banded around his chest.

Light from the setting sun flashed on the blade while he banished regret. She required a lesson. One he hated to deliver but knew was necessary. When she found the courage to run, he would follow…close enough to protect, far enough to make her believe she'd succeeded before he showed himself. He wanted her to understand she held no chance of escape. The only way to accomplish that was to hand her hope then take it away.

He scowled, dreading the moment she realized she'd failed. He imagined her hazel eyes filled with anger, then hurt. 'Twas the hurt that almost changed his mind. Almost, but in the end logic tamed emotion, and he said, "Make sure she is watched at all times. I mean to give her some room to run, but not so much that I lose her."

Cristobal nodded, his expression pensive as he flicked an acorn with the toe of his boot. Xavian recognized the look.

'Twas one that always appeared before his friend called him on his behavior. Preparing for Cristobal's rebuke, he wiped his carving blade on his trews and searched the tree line at the lip of the clearing. Afina had been gone too long. Had she given his man the slip? Was she already on the run?

The thought barely registered when he heard Sabine giggle. Awareness flickered, and his body tightened, knowing wherever the little one went Afina followed. His focus fixed on a break in the shrubbery, he heard Afina's voice, tone soft with coaxing. A moment later Sabine came charging out of the underbrush, a stick clutched in her wee fist. With a bellow to rival a knight on a battlefield, she raised the small branch and roared toward the other side of the clearing.

Preparing their evening meal at fireside, Qabil ducked, avoiding decapitation as the little one sped past, her gaze fixed on Kazim. The warrior hit his knees, grabbed his own stick from beneath the fallen leaves, and met Sabine's downswing. She shrieked with laughter when Kazim growled and parried another thrust, seemingly thrilled by his reaction.

Xavian shook his head. Jesu, mock battle with a two-year-old. His lips curved, enjoying the melee and Sabine's enthusiasm as she struck again. Amazed by his men and their willingness to not only protect but play with the girl-child, he flinched when she swung left and thumped Kazim on the shoulder.

He glanced at Cristobal. "Bloodthirsty little thing."

Dark eyes agleam with good humor, his friend shrugged. "The healthy ones usually are."

Xavian snorted. How the hell did Cristobal know so much about children? 'Twas a mystery that intrigued him more than it should, but he refused to pry. His men deserved their privacy, had earned the right to their secrets. And so had he.

"Sabine!" Afina's voice rang across the clearing.

Xavian watched emotion tumble across her face, bafflement combined with dismay. Hopping over a fallen tree trunk, she hustled toward the impromptu battlefield, all lithe curves and swaying hips. He swallowed, unable to keep himself from absorbing every detail—from the rippling length of her dark hair and flushed cheeks to the enticing curve of her breasts. His blood heated, nudging the traitor below his belt.

He clenched his hand around the figurine, trying to douse the lust as Andrei intercepted her halfway across the clearing. Xavian stilled, aggression swimming in his veins, and waited. If his man touched her, a little too long or a little too much, he would enter the fray; something the Frenchman would regret afterward. Lucky for him, Andrei did naught but stand in her path and talk. The smooth sound of his French accent drifted, the soft cadence designed to soothe Afina's fear for her child.

After a moment, she backed away and glanced at him, a clear question in her eyes. His heart turned over. Hell, she looked to him for reassurance. The realization made him feel unaccountably good—proud that she trusted him to keep her daughter safe. Fighting the tightness in his throat, he nodded, letting her know 'twas naught but a game. No cause for alarm.

The tension holding her shoulders square softened. She nodded in return then cringed when Sabine whooped and struck. And struck again, the crack of wood echoing as she brained Kazim with her makeshift sword.

The warrior chuckled.

The girl-child grinned, and Afina shook her head as she turned to join Qabil by the fire.

Cristobal shifted, placing his back flat against the oak. Arms crossed over his chest, his gaze settled on their new healer. "How long will you let her run?"

"A day, no more."

"She'll exhaust herself," his friend said, concern in his tone.

Xavian glowered at the knife hilt, guilt infecting him like a disease. Why did he react to her this way? Jesu, 'twas baffling. He was a hard man, an intelligent one not given to flights of fancy. How was she able to tie him in knots when naught else did? The answer escaped him, but self-preservation warned he needed to get whatever ailed him under control...now, before he lost himself in hazel eyes flecked with green and gold.

"Aye," he said, shaking vulnerability off like a wet dog did water, "but the lesson will be learned and not easily forgotten."

"Tonight then...when all is quiet." Cristobal rubbed against the rough bark, chasing an itch.

"More likely on the morrow, at the bazaar."

"She knows we are stopping there before heading into the mountains?"

"Aye."

Xavian had made sure of it. Had told Qabil to let their destination slip in an attempt to stall her escape and keep her out of the woods. He didn't want her running through swamps, tangling with dense underbrush and the assortment of wildlife that called them home. Hell, he wanted to teach her caution, not kill her.

"So while you play shadow, we will gather what we need."

Straightened away from his knees, Xavian rolled his shoulders, stretching stiff muscles. "Take only what we require to get through the winter. And only from those who can afford to have their carts and purses lightened."

Cristobal snorted. "Assassins with a conscience."

"Ex-assassins," he said, well aware of the inherent duplicity in his plan. He wanted a new life, one built on integrity, not theft. But with Afina in the fold, the promise of Vladimir's coin dried up along with the ability to buy provisions for Drachaven. His newfound standards would have to wait. The lads in his care needed to eat this winter along with everyone else in his new keep.

"*Ex*...past tense," Cristobal murmured, the low rumble of his voice tinged with more than simple agreement.

He glanced sideways at his friend, recognizing the emotion in his tone. Xavian felt it too. Gratefulness. A profound sense of gratitude mere words could never express.

With a slow indrawn breath, Xavian tipped his head back, searching for solace in the give and take of the oak's great canopy. Tree limbs swayed, their gentle murmur a cozy haven for the birds above. They chattered, talking to one another just as the silence engulfing him and Cristobal spoke, telling stories, reminding them both of what had been.

After a time, the painful hush grew too great, and Xavian broke through the quiet. "'Twill be on the morrow. She's quick and will use the crowded marketplace to cover her tracks."

"Mayhap." Cristobal cleared his throat then raised a brow. "Care to wager?"

"'Tisn't a game, my friend," he said, his voice soft with warning. His comrade's gaze narrowed on him, no doubt wondering why he refused to take the bet. He and Cristobal always wagered. 'Twas their habit, one they both enjoyed, but Xavian didn't want to play this time. It didn't sit well with him. He disliked making sport of Afina, trivializing what would cause her pain. "She will suffer before she accepts us and her new life."

Cristobal's brow rose a fraction, his silence as deafening as the clash of wooden swords in front of them. Unease pricked Xavian's spine, senses honed by years of stealth and death balking at the thorough examination. He understood the calculated hush well. His friend wanted an explanation—wished to know why he cared about Afina's feelings. He stayed silent. How could he explain what he didn't understand himself?

His friend straightened away from the oak. "I will inform everyone of the plan."

"Cristobal." He glanced away from the basswood block and met his friend's gaze. "Stay sharp. The closer we come to Drachaven, the greater the danger."

Cristobal cursed. "Halál."

"Aye. He's sent two, and failed twice."

Frowning, Xavian turned the figurine over in his hand and cut the outline of a leg along its flank. A canny old goat, Halál had the instincts of a raptor—a bird of prey so vicious it took apart its prey while still alive. He refused to become his next meal, regardless of the power that sat behind the old man. The Teutonic Knights could go to hell, along with Al Pacii, the covert death squad they financed.

"The next will be more skilled and better prepared."

"No doubt," his friend said, sighing as he tipped his head back. "Henrik, mayhap?"

Jesu, he hoped not. " 'Tis possible."

"We'll be ready."

Xavian nodded but said naught, the idea of fighting Henrik riding him hard. Of equal skill, the fight would be difficult in more ways than one. His heart wouldn't be in it.

Hell, 'twas an understatement.

He had no desire to kill a man he considered his brother. But reality came knocking. Halál wanted him dead for deserting Al Pacii. The old man hated the fact he hadn't broken him, couldn't control him. The defeat signaled weakness, something Halál never accepted. The bastard would send assassin after assassin until they accomplished their mission—took his head and those of his men.

His brow furrowed, Cristobal crouched and picked up an acorn. Staring at the nut, he rolled it on the pads of his fingertips. "One other thing…'tis about the woman."

"She is not to be touched."

"Your interest has been noted. None of the men will bother her." Balanced on the balls of his feet, a smile tugged the corners of his friend's mouth. He lobbed the acorn over a shrub and into the forest. "The question then becomes…will you?"

The traitor in Xavian's trews twitched, relishing the suggestion.

The tip of his knife stilled against wood and his attention strayed to Afina. Jesu, he would love to bother her, each morning and every night. He swallowed, an image of her under him, legs wrapped around his waist, spine bowed in supplication while he suckled her nipples ripped through his mind. A fine tremor rolled through him, his arousal so strong he ached to lay her down and love her into oblivion. Taking a deep breath, he tore his gaze from the beauty across the clearing and, reaching for self-mastery, drilled Cristobal with a glare.

"Why not, Ram?" he asked, his brow raised in challenge. "You deserve happiness."

He shook his head. Nay, he didn't. No one knew that better than Cristobal. They shared the same curse, the one that blotted the soul, leaving a stain so dark 'twas impenetrable. Too much blood had been spilled, and no amount of wishing would wash his hands clean. Afina deserved better than a man God would never forgive.

"Xavian," Cristobal said, his quiet tone pushing for an answer.

"Happiness belongs to other men. 'Tis too late for that...for me."

"*Ma rahat.* That's yak shit, and you know it." Dark eyes intent, Cristobal pushed to his feet, his attention on Afina. He watched her stir the pot perched over the fire, helping Qabil prepare their meal. "If you will not do it for yourself then consider this...take a woman of your own and the men will follow suit. Drachaven needs families, not assassin-monks if it is to become what you want. Lead by example, my friend, and the rest will follow."

Xavian tensed as the comment struck. Jesu, a direct hit. He wanted Drachaven to be something different...something more. He longed for a home; a place where children played and laughed. Where they were safe, not brutalized by war, tortured by others, or forced to kill to survive.

He raked a hand through his hair, struggling to banish the memories. One by one, he forced taut muscles to unlock, vowing to make his dream a reality.

Cristobal was wrong. The men would do as he said, not as he did.

It wouldn't be difficult to persuade them to take women of their own and raise their families at Drachaven. He could have what he wanted without visiting his sins on a lass and any child they created together. Leadership meant directing others, giving them a greater purpose, not abandoning what he knew to be right. He needed his convictions. They kept him strong, and he refused to relinquish his beliefs for a lass who stirred his blood.

Now all he needed to do was hold firm to the plan and stay the hell out of Afina's bed.

◈✟◈

The knife in his hand stopped Afina cold. Her eyes on the wicked six-inch blade, she swallowed hard, trying to understand…

Why was Xavian always armed to the teeth?

It was unseemly. They were camped, for the goddess's sake… in the middle of nowhere, far from anyone or anything, mean-looking men and a forest surrounding them. Did the man never rest? Let his guard down a bit?

No, of course not. That would make her approach too easy.

His strategy wasn't subtle. It was outright obvious—bold in a way only Xavian could manage. He wanted her off balance. Comfortable enough to settle in, afraid enough to pull what little confidence she possessed from its moorings.

Afina smoothed out a frown. But worse than all that? His tactics were working, making doubt seep between the cracks of her resolve.

Using her eyelashes to shield her gaze, she studied him from her position fireside. Beautiful man. So unfair: his handsome looks, the soothing timbre of his voice, his decadent smell, and the alluring strength of his body. Too bad the lovely package hid a steely determination more deadly than the blades on his back.

Well, there was naught for it. The warm comfort he wove around her could go hang itself. She must hold tight to the plan.

Wiping her damp palms on her skirt, Afina gathered her healing satchel. She wished there was another choice. Some other way, but wishing for another path wouldn't supply the answers she needed.

But, goddess help her. Getting anywhere near Xavian wasn't a good idea. She didn't want to touch him—or feel the flutter his proximity provoked—but tending his arm presented an opportunity. One she couldn't forego. Besides, it was useless to fight her sister's legacy. Bianca had done her job well, instilling her with a healing spirit. And now? The dratted thing wouldn't let her leave alone. Not until she tended his wound and made sure Xavian healed without complication.

She squeezed Qabil's shoulder and pushed to her feet. Wooden spoon in hand, he stopped stirring and turned big brown eyes on her. He raised both brows.

She patted him and raised her bag. "The healer calls."

"Aye, my lady," he said, his voice soft, his gaze flicking in Xavian's direction. "My thanks for your help."

Afina nodded, resisting the need to sweep the curl from his forehead. He was a sweet boy; a gentle soul on the cusp of manhood. But in his eyes she recognized the ravages of horror, a banked fear she felt herself and yearned to heal. Her brow puckered as she wondered about his wariness. Boys his age should be happy and carefree. Qabil, for all his gentleness, was neither of those things.

After a moment she gave in to the urge, reached out, and smoothed his hair back. Color swept his high cheekbones, but he allowed her touch. Leaned in the way a cat would when scratched behind the ears, almost as though he craved the tender contact.

She swallowed the lump in her throat. "I'll return in a bit."

His chin dipped and, head low, the shyness he wore like a cloak returned. The submissive position knocked at her heart, and of a sudden she knew what had been done to him. He'd been beaten down...stripped of dignity and worth. Of all the things that made a person strong, told them who they were and what they would become.

Her hand clenched, working on the leather satchel as she watched him turn back to the stew. A deep sorrow filled the space between her ribs, circling her heart, before she slung the strap over her shoulder and headed toward the lip of the clearing.

Was Xavian responsible for the boy's condition? She hoped not, couldn't imagine him being cruel. He'd been so patient with her, had accepted her resistance with a gentleness that both startled and lured. So different from her mother, from the force and drag of her keen temper and vicious ways.

The memory slapped.

Afina flinched inside, fighting to hold the awfulness at bay. But like the rising sun, the blinding light came, reminding her of her time in the Order and the terrible expectations that had ground her into dust. She was not so different from Qabil, knew the cost of clawing her way back to the surface after being dragged under.

That her mother had been responsible for her drowning— the one person Afina should have been able to trust not to hurt her—was unbearable. Forcing one foot in front of the other, she crossed the dell, fighting through the ice coating her insides. She would never do that to Sabine, would never hold her in so little regard. A mother nurtured, protected, stood firm for her child. 'Twas another truth her sister had taught her. The lesson was deep and abiding, even though Afina knew she would never measure up.

She stood flawed, a poor imitation of Bianca: an abysmal substitute for Sabine, for their situation and for the man who believed she held a healer's skills.

She should be here. Bianca, not me. Never me.

An ache took root at the base of her skull, the loss so heavy Afina struggled to carry it. She didn't want to talk to anyone, least of all Xavian. He was too astute for her to hide her restless urges and wounded spirit. What would he do when he learned of her lie? How could she prevent him from discovering her secrets?

Answers escaped her as she came to the point of no return. She couldn't turn tail and run now. Xavian had spotted her, and now that he had, pride wouldn't let her retreat.

Black birds with red-tipped wings swooped overhead, flitting from branch to branch. Afina followed their progress, letting their cheerful song lead the way to the man seated on the moss-covered log.

Xavian's gaze swept her face. "What troubles you, *draga*?"

Searing pain struck, arcing across her chest. The need to blurt the truth warred with common sense. She wanted to tell him so badly. But the words wouldn't come. She couldn't allow it and hope to survive. No soul baring would happen here. No communion of heart and mind. Instead she dropped her bag at his feet, and between one breath and the next? Turned the tide, easing into a stream of questions designed to unearth his motives. For her and Sabine. All the true reasons behind their kidnapping.

"What did you do to that boy?"

"Qabil?" His tone was quiet yet somehow deafening at the same time. It took up all the space inside her head and...Hmm, she loved his voice. The deep timbre never failed to warm her. If only...

Afina cut the thought off at the knees. "If onlys" weren't permitted today—or any other day for that matter. Scrambling to control her reaction to him, she took refuge in irritation and glared at him.

His lips twitched. "Naught."

"Am I the only one to be honest here?" she asked, plunking her hands on her hips. "He is afraid."

"He told you that?"

"No, but a blind man could see—"

"'Twill take time for him to feel safe, Afina. He has been with me but weeks." Holding her gaze, he studied her, something intangible—something gentle—thawing the ice chips in his eyes. 'Twas like being caressed; a nonphysical touch that stroked her in places she'd never been touched before.

"Oh, I..." She paused as the urge to touch him in return shimmered through her, sending a silent call. Her body rippled, begging her to answer, to curl into his warmth and let him melt the ice encasing her heart. "What happened to him?"

"You've no wish to know."

Yes, she did. "Has he no family?"

"His family sold him to the highest bidder...into hell," he said, his voice so low she barely heard him. But she didn't need the words to see his anger. He gripped the hilt of his blade so tight, his knuckles turned white. "Calm your healer's heart, Afina. He will recover."

She stared at him. He seemed so certain. A desperate urge rolled through her. The heavy weight pressed down on her chest, suffocating her with the need to know. How would he heal? How did one recover from brutality? She wanted to know for Qabil. But most of all, she wanted to ask for herself. How did he *know*?

His expression sharpened, his eyes so pale they became almost colorless. Locked inside his intensity, her windpipe contracted and she couldn't force the question past her throat. He held her there, time ticking, allowing her to wonder before he said, "Because I did, lass. That's how."

A broken breath rushed from her lungs. The goddess be saved. Who had dared to hurt *him*?

The tightness banding her chest eased and empathy moved in, infecting her with the need to soothe him. Ridiculous as far as impulses went. He was too tough to ever need her compassion. Her soft heart was like a rampaging disease: painful, unwanted, debilitating. And she needed to find a cure before it killed her.

Well, that, and the nearest escape route.

She must get away from him. Now. Before all that crippling emotion took over and left her a willing captive.

Willing.

The word clanged inside her head. Blessed goddess give her strength. 'Twould be so easy to give in, to let him take care of her, protect her, give her a home. He was so strong in all the right ways. His strength of spirit drew her, planting ideas she couldn't allow to flourish. Vladimir wanted her, enough to kill anyone standing between him and the throne. Enough to pay well and bring death to any who aided her.

With bone-deep certainty, Afina knew she was better off on her own. Alone. Insulated. Safe from all those who craved the coin and would betray her to gain it. No matter how much Drachaven's thick walls appealed to her, she refused to bring that kind of trouble to Xavian's gate. There were other boys involved…innocent ones. Qabil had told her so. The very reason they planned to stop at the bazaar, to gather supplies for the winter months.

Where would she be, Afina wondered, when the bitter cold and snow let loose? Snug and warm with a roof over her head or frozen in a barren field? Her heart dropped, the familiar worry churning her stomach until she felt sick.

Afina swallowed the burn, taking solace in her strategy. Blessed be, she hoped it worked, that Qabil's slip of the tongue— and the sure knowledge it provided—would give her the advantage on the morrow. The marketplace at the base of the mountains was the perfect place to make her escape. With so many people thronging the vendors, the men would be occupied trading for goods and packing supplies. Their distraction would equal her freedom. A freedom that included distance from Xavian and all the safety he provided.

Her bottom lip trembled a little.

Xavian reached out. He caught her chin on the tips of his fingers. With a gentle nudge, he turned her face to his. "What?"

Afina swallowed past thump in her throat. "Nothing."

"Liar," he said, his thumb drifting over the curve of her jaw.

The soft stroke sent a wave of heat through her, soothing tense muscles and her sore heart. With a frown, she pulled away from his touch. She couldn't accept his comfort. It was weakness come to life and the surest way to become snared in his net. "I am tired. That is all."

He arched a brow, laying her deceit bare with a look.

Her eyes narrowed, she warned him with a look. The message was clear...*leave me be*. "How is your arm?"

He studied her for a moment longer, his gaze probing. Silence stretched as he fingered the knife hilt, turning it over in his hand. "Fine."

Afina rolled her eyes. "Have you changed the dressing?"

He shrugged.

"You haven't changed it?"

"You are the healer," he said, something light and altogether untrustworthy in his tone. "'Tis your duty, not mine."

Confounded man. His wound was no doubt infected, and he was teasing her. She grabbed her satchel. "It will not heal if you ignore it, Xavian."

With a flick of his wrist, he sent the blade deep into the dirt between his feet and tilted his forearm for her inspection. She grumbled. He smiled, his mouth kicking up at the corners. The enticing display caused muscles low in her belly to flutter. Wretched stomach. She really must get a handle on that. Otherwise the unruly flock winging its way across her abdomen might fly her right into hot water.

For some reason, her imagination took flight, supplying a mental picture rife with possibilities. Bathtubs and scented oils… and Xavian. Heat prickled across her cheekbones and, clambering to cover her reaction, she knelt beside him, making certain to stay clear of his thigh. The last thing she needed was more contact. Desire already sped through her veins, kicking her heart into a gallop, and she'd barely touched him.

Keeping her face averted, she attacked the knot just below his elbow. Her hands brushed his skin. She suppressed a shiver laced with wonder. By the goddess, he was well-made. So powerful. All heat and hard muscle. She bit her bottom lip, tried not to notice, and forced her hands to move.

End over end, she unwound the thin strip until she reached his wrist. With a flick, she tossed the bandage aside. He caught it in midair. She flinched, startled by his speed, and watched him lay the linen over one of his thighs, transfixed by the long, graceful lines of his hands.

Beautifully masculine hands. Strong hands, capable of protecting, comforting…and pleasuring. Afina blinked. Pleasuring? All things goodness and light, what was the matter with her?

Xavian shifted, nudging her with the outside of his thigh. Her gaze leapt to his face. A crease between his brows, he frowned at his injury.

Releasing a breath in a slow rush, she turned her attention to the gash on his forearm. She scowled at him. "It's inflamed."

"Not badly." He flexed his fist, stretching the stitches.

"Stop that," she said, her tone snappish. "You will only make it worse."

Both brows rose, but he obeyed and uncurled his fingers. "As you wish."

Afina wasn't fooled by his quick compliance. The dolt found her reaction amusing, but she couldn't find anything to laugh about. He was fighting an infection. The sort of thing that could get out of hand quickly should she apply the wrong elixir or if the last batch of salve proved ineffective. What if she hadn't made the balm strong enough and the poison seeped from the wound into his blood?

And wasn't that just what she needed; another failure to add to the pile.

Pressure banded around Afina's chest as dread linked with concern. Bianca's words drifted through her mind. *Stay focused. Determine the damage. Treat the infection then stay the course.* Giving herself a mental nod, she followed her sister's advice and, with a gentle touch, pressed her thumb and forefinger on either side of the cut. No seepage. A good sign. She bit the inside of her cheek and shuffled on her knees, changing her angle to check each stitch. Warmth slid across the nape of her neck. Intent on the wound, it took her a moment to realize the heat came from Xavian's palm.

She stiffened, the unexpected touch forcing her retreat. His grip firmed, holding her in place. The blue flame of his eyes caught hers, and his hand moved, massaging the tension from her stiff muscles.

"'Twill be all right, lass." His palm warm against her nape, he delved into her hair, the pleasing rub of his fingers difficult to resist. "I have had much worse and recovered without difficulty."

"What happened in the past is not at issue." With a long sigh, she leaned into the stroking, even as she chastened herself for allowing it. She shouldn't welcome his touch, should tell him to leave her alone and move away. The problem? She enjoyed it too much to stop him. It was so nice to be touched without expectation…without worry of reprisal. In this moment, he meant nothing more than to soothe her. He was safe and, like it or not, she found that enthralling. "You were not in my care then."

"Fair enough," he said, his low tone alive with approval before he withdrew his hand.

A chill replaced his warmth at the base of her neck then washed out in a wave of goose bumps along her spine. She blinked, feeling lost for a moment, at sea with her lifeline drifting out of reach. Panic closed in, making her want to follow his retreat. Afina drew away instead, breaking the spell surrounding them.

Diving into her satchel, she pretended to dig, searching for the vial already in her hand. A buffer. She needed one, needed space between them before she did something stupid. Like lean in and thank him for his kindness with a kiss.

Her gaze drifted back to his lips. Good goddess. He was temptation and sin, male in a way that defied description. But she couldn't do it. Couldn't trade the hope of her future—and his life at the hands of her enemies—for a moment in his arms. She wasn't foolish, or mayhap brave enough.

With a frown, she put the witch hazel and a linen square to work. Silence dripped from the tree limbs above while she cleaned the wound, the hush so complete the wind was still, giving the leaves a momentary reprieve from the constant push and pull.

As the stillness folded in around them, she found herself falling into his rhythm: the easy in and out of his breathing, the murmur of leather and the special blend of spice that made up Xavian. It was a little hypnotic, like the Order's temple mass: the echo and incense and murmuring chant. String by taut string, Afina unwound and let herself drift into a place she used to know but hadn't visited in years. It felt good, as though she were sinking into a cushion of clouds or—

"From where do you hail, Afina?"

The question jarred her and she jumped, even though his voice had been soft. He was digging, using their proximity to find the whys and wherefores of her circumstance before his interference. Drat. She was supposed to be doing that. But somehow the tables had turned, and now she found herself on the wrong side of the question. "Severin…where you found me."

"Your accent is Transylvanian."

"Is it?"

"Aye. What took you so far from your home?" He paused then leaned forward and settled his uninjured forearm on his knee. The movement brought his head even with her own, and his heat rolled into her shoulder. "Sabine's sire, mayhap?"

Her hand paused in mid-dab.

A violent splash of memory washed in around her. Her chest went tight as the mental torrent picked her up and took her with it. As colorful as the paintings on the temple walls, pictures of Bianca surfaced and she remembered: the bright eyes and flushed cheeks, the lightness of spirit, her sister dancing across their tiny cottage each time Bianca returned from meeting her lover. Each time. Every time. The hope and happy glow that made Afina love her sister all the more for her courage, for her trust and generous heart.

"Or mayhap not for love at all. Mayhap you fled with naught but the clothes on your back…to keep yourself and Sabine safe." He plucked at the sleeve of her gown, giving weight to his theory by scratching at a thread-barren patch in the wool. "Which is it, *draga*? Love or self-preservation?"

She swallowed. What did Xavian know? Had Vladimir finally crumbled, cast aside his pride, and sent messengers far and wide to ensure her capture? What crime had he accused her of? Was there a price on her head now? But the bigger question, the one that truly mattered…was the promise of Transylvanian gold enough to tempt Xavian?

Afina chewed on the inside of her lip. She should have listened to her instincts and changed her name, cut her hair… something. Anything.

Goddess. Another mistake. More to add to her ever-growing tally.

She was foolish. So stupid to not have played the game in full measure. Now her daughter's life along with her own was in danger again. All because she'd clung to convention and the past.

But it was too late now. She could give up. Or give in. *No surrender.* She'd come too far, must hold the line and keep her secrets. "That is none of your—"

"What does Vladimir want with you?"

Afina felt her core temperature drop, the chill inside her chest expanding by the moment. With a jerk, she yanked her arm from beneath Xavian's fingers. Lightning quick, he turned his hand and shackled her wrist.

Trapped. Unable to retreat, she twisted her hand, fighting his grip. "Don't!"

Xavian didn't let go. Instead he leaned in, using his size as another form of intimidation. "What do you possess that has Barbu frothing at the mouth?"

That name sent shards of terror splintering like glass, ripping her apart. She'd never spoken it out loud, not since her mother's death. Sure, she'd cursed him silently. Had railed against fate and the raging sea of circumstance she'd been tossed into, but she had never allowed the name into the light of day. A surname of shadows, brutality swirled in each syllable, without the possibility of mercy, and to hear Xavian...to hear him say...Oh, no. She wanted to press her hands to her ears and scream at the injustice, to admonish the goddess for leaving her so alone.

Not that she could. The deity she served wasn't here to protect her. She must do that herself. "Nothing. I don't even know who that is."

"I grow impatient with your lies."

"I am not lying."

"Nay?"

"No," she said, throwing the conviction she didn't feel into her denial. Giving him a pointed look, she tugged at her wrist. Her strategy was simple. Waylay his suspicions by discounting each and every one.

Xavian was a bloodhound with the truth. He took his cues from her body as much as her words, weighing her responses, tracking her tension. To divert him she needed to relax and feign indifference. And so she did, letting her mouth curve, pulling away a little at a time, asking without words to be released.

His eyes narrowed.

She widened hers, the picture of innocence. *Please, oh, please, let him be fooled.*

"A word to the wise, love…" he trailed off, tone full of warning.

She pulled on her arm again. His grip loosened. Her heart in her throat, she turned her wrist, twisting away from his hand.

As her skin slid from beneath his, he murmured, "Be honest with me."

"Honest?" Really. Sir Skirts-the-Truth wanted *her* to be honest with him? Afina gave him a pointed look then turned her attention back to his injury and dumped more witch hazel onto the linen. Jamming the stopper on the vial, she flipped it into her satchel and went at his arm. He grunted. She lessened the pressure, gentling her touch, hoping to distract him. "I am your captive, Xavian, nothing more. There is no mystery to solve. No one is after me…and it isn't any surprise, I'm sure, that I choose not to share my past with the man responsible for my kidnapping."

"Liberation."

Hah. Right. There he went again…twisting the truth.

If her "liberation" was to be freeing, why did she feel trapped, tense, in danger of doing something foolish? Like fall in with the thief and forget all about duty. Her pledge to Bianca—to the Order—meant something. A whole kingdom was counting on her, whether they knew it or not. The fact she was ready to toss it aside for safety in the guise of a handsome face and hard body was disgusting.

Afina dabbed at his stitches, making certain the witch hazel reached every bit of inflamed skin. And how absurd was that? He caused her pain, made her falter until her convictions ended in a messy pile at her feet. And yet she remained gentle, seeing to his injury as though he was beloved, of such value she offered all her meager skill to ensure his recovery.

She fumbled with the linen in her hand, twisting it to find a clean spot. The clumsy movement screamed of ineptitude, reminding her she was unfit for both her duty and her sister's calling. Even so, she continued to rearrange the cloth, trying to deny that in this moment she valued him more than she did herself. But the proof lay in her actions: in the precision of her hands, the focus of her mind, and the heat in her heart.

"Afina," he said, his tone just shy of a growl.

She swiped at the corner of her eye, wanting to growl back. But her voice didn't come when called and she stayed silent, erecting barriers, shoring up defenses to cushion the blows from the battering ram he hammered against the brittle doors of her inner sanctum.

"*Draga*, I…" He cleared his throat, his attention trained on Kazim and Sabine across the clearing. "I cannot protect you if you will not let me."

"Be quiet!" She tried to sound strong, but her voice wavered, giving her away. He opened his mouth. But she'd had enough, was stretched way too thin. And before he spoke, Afina pointed at him, put her index finger right in his face. "Unless you wish to tend this yourself…*be quiet*."

Blue eyes narrowed on her, his mouth snapped shut.

An ache throbbed through her limbs, as though she'd been bruised from the inside out. Yet even as she suffered the pain Afina kept her gaze steady, her finger even with his nose to ensure he stayed silent. A muscle jumped along his jaw, and although he didn't look away, he didn't say another word.

Thank the goddess.

She didn't want to talk anymore.

Tears pricking the corners of her eyes, Afina lowered her hand and glanced away. The coming winter be damned. She needed to get away from Xavian before her courage crumbled... before the urge to stay and accept his protection overcame good sense and death came to claim them all.

CHAPTER SIX

The elusive son of a bitch was good. The best, really…if he took himself out of the equation. Henrik couldn't help but admire Ram's efficiency. He'd gotten to her first. Had tracked and taken Vladimir's prize, mayhap less than a day ago.

Henrik's gaze shifted from the scarred tabletop to the rickety stools then to the dirt floor. He followed the swirling pattern left by the fingers of a broom, the curling strokes as old as the ash in the hearth. One corner of his mouth turned up. Neat. Clean. Not a trace of the person who had occupied the sweet little hovel. He fingered one of the hooks nailed into the support beam. He'd even taken the hammock. His admiration widened into a smile.

Christ, he'd always liked Ram, even when they'd been trading fists.

With one last sweep of the one-room shack, Henrik slipped out the door and latched it behind him. His attention on the ground, he tracked east toward the large beech trees. Beneath fall's splendor, faint grooves marked the earth, hidden by fallen leaves and windblown vegetation. He stopped beneath one of the canopies. Thick tree limbs swayed above his head, rustling in the gloom. A storm was coming, a violent one that thickened the air and blackened the sky as he crouched to study the impressions.

Someone had lain here. The woman?

He frowned. Had she struggled against capture? Henrik snorted, hoping she'd given Ram all the trouble the bastard deserved. He didn't trust anything that came too easy. 'Twas the reason he wanted to kill that damned priest. Gutless, yellow-bellied arse.

With a soft growl, he pushed to his feet, fighting the urge to go back and give Father Marion his due. He was a priest, for Christ's sake. Yet, one look from him and the good father had lost all faith and betrayed the lass—pointing him in her direction like a Transylvanian hunting hound. Goddamn, he hated cowards. Their kind made his belly turn, and the fact the milksop wet his robes on Henrik's way out was only a small consolation.

He shook his head and snapped his fingers. The soft sound called Tabi to attention. The bay roan he favored lifted her head and, with a light step, followed him into the forest. He shifted through the shadows on the trail, careful not to step on the recent boot marks, Tabi moving quietly in his wake, until he reached a small clearing. A stream, mayhap five feet in width, skirted the edge of the small dell, meandering through twisted tree trunks and over rocks. Eager for a drink, his mount nudged him with the side of her head.

With a gentle hand, he stroked her soft muzzle. "'Tis safe enough. Go, Tabi…drink your fill."

She snorted, the sound friendly, and bumped him again before heading to the water's edge. Henrik watched her for a moment then turned his attention to the dark earth. Smaller boot impressions joined the larger ones surrounded by eight sets of distinct hoof prints. A sixth traveled with Ram and the famed four who followed him. Henrik grunted. A boy or an apprentice mayhap?

No matter. Their mistake would be his advantage.

A lad would be easier to track. Without an assassin's skill, the boy would lack the ability to blend into the shadows and disappear in crowded places. As good as a red flag waved in front of a maddened bull. The woman's presence would aid too. Not many missed a pretty face.

Afina Lazar.

He envied her the last name. Envied Ram too. How had he managed to keep his surname? In the shadowed halls of Al Pacii, no one had been permitted the right. Halál preferred the anonymous, enjoyed stripping every pupil of their identity until naught remained but a hollow husk...a fraction of what they'd been upon arrival at Grey Keep.

One session with Halál and all abandoned the name given them at birth. None withstood the bright light and sharp blades of the old man. None but Ram. He'd never surrendered his birthright, no matter how many times Halál had strapped him to that damned slab.

Images of his own initiation, wrists and ankles shackled, arms and legs spread wide on the blue stone, streamed into Henrik's head. He still felt the chill and bite of the blade against his skin. Sometimes he woke from a dead sleep on a silent scream, scraping at his chest, feeling his blood run hot against cold steel. How the hell had Ram endured it time and again?

Tough bastard.

Truth? He respected the hell out of Ram, but that didn't mean he wouldn't track him. Fate turned, spinning full circle. There was a certain symmetry in the circumstances. The best hunter becoming the hunted. The wronged seeking the right. No matter their closeness in Al Pacii and Grey Keep, he would hold his former comrade accountable for his crimes. As in all things,

Halál would have his due, the lass would be retrieved, and Ram would get what he deserved for his desertion.

Efficiency, precision, and a challenge. Henrik relished them all, and as he pushed to his feet and called Tabi from the stream, restless anticipation boiled in his gut. He could hardly wait to catch the traitor.

The bazaar at Ismal was a great ravening beast. All teeth and talon with the attitude to match. Thank Christ. 'Twas about time. Xavian required a distraction, one the busy marketplace would provide. The seething underbelly of humanity teemed with the unscrupulous. Thieves and well-armed merchants together in a swell of depravity where all looked out for themselves and tried to swindle each other.

'Twas perfect: the bread to his stew.

Drawing rein, Xavian absorbed the swill of aggression until it filled the void in his chest. He needed a fight, a vicious, bloody one. A knuckle-bruising, body-crunching brawl before he did the unthinkable.

Like force Afina to spill every detail. Force her to admit her time with Bodgan meant naught and that her heart remained untouched, ready to be given without reservation.

La dracu. He was a fool.

He wanted to spar with her again, if only to see her hazel eyes flash. Jesu, there was something wrong with him. He adored her temper. All that passion. The spark of her fury had lit the fuse on his arousal and made him hard, ready to take her, to dominate. He wanted to use his body to rock hers into submission, to ease the anger with pleasure while he showed her how a man claimed his woman and tunneled into her soul.

Everywhere he looked he saw a place to lay her down. Atop his horse, in the long field grass, in a hidden grove along the trail they'd ridden to reach the marketplace. He craved her warmth. The instant she'd stuck her finger in his face and told him to *be quiet*, the desire simmering beneath his surface had exploded. A raging wildfire that burned him from the inside out. Hell, his skin was practically steaming.

Had the ache been naught but physical, he could have ignored the twitch, buried it along with all the other *have nots*—all the things taken from him in his life. Conditioned for pain, he excelled at denial, thrived on the challenge of self-imposed limitation. He determined the course, his body obeyed. But not with her. Her strength of spirit unhinged him, opening a great yawning hole in his breastbone.

And *rahat*, it hurt.

No one spoke to him like that. Not even Halál had dared. But she had, eyes full of heat, all those soft curves tense as she pressed for a fight. A wee scrapper. Aye, 'twas what she was, and what he needed—wanted—with a yearning that cut so deep he bled more than lust. He bled for connection: for closeness and affection and trust.

Trust.

Christ, he wanted hers. Wanted her to lay her life's story open like a book and trust him to keep her safe. Wanted to slit Barbu's throat and watch his essence drain until naught but emptiness reflected in the bastard's eyes. But more than anything, he wanted to mark her with his possession until every man who saw her knew she belonged to him.

And wasn't that the height of witlessness?

She was not his, and never would be, but that didn't stop the images of her spread beneath him, of her stroking his body and murmuring softly in the aftermath.

"*Rahat.*" Easing his grip on the reins, Xavian settled his warhorse.

"Tight...you're wound far too tight," Cristobal murmured, bringing his big gelding alongside. One brow raised, his friend tossed him a look of inquiry. "Planning to kill someone here?"

"God willing."

Cristobal snorted. "Falling short of the *ex-assassin* you claim to be, aren't you?"

Xavian growled.

"Skip the fight...bed her instead."

"Hell," he muttered as temptation struck him with the force of an assailant's fist.

Xavian almost buckled beneath the blow...almost gave in to the urge to look over his shoulder. Afina was there, behind Andrei, to the left. Like a witch's fork tuned to water, he was drawn to her source. Be damned, he swore he could smell her, that light, diabolical fragrance that was all woman. His knees tightened on Mayhem's sides. The warhorse protested, shying sideways until he bumped into Cristobal.

His friend's smirk widened to a grin. "What has the devil to do with it?"

Shifting in the saddle, Xavian brought his mount under control while debating the merits of knocking the smug expression off Cristobal's face. 'Twould feel good, and at the very least his comrade would give him a good fight, unlike some inept merchant or oily criminal.

He tossed a nasty look in Cristobal's direction. "'Tis whose company you will be keeping if you do not stop pestering me."

"She is no maiden," his friend said, pushing the issue while taking one step closer to the fiery pit.

Feeling as though he already had one foot in the flames, Xavian broke into a cold sweat. He clenched his teeth, struggling to hide the fact Cristobal had hit his mark. His friend knew he never went anywhere near virgins. He was sullied, black deep inside, not fit to touch their snowy white innocence. Aye, Afina might not be a maiden, but...

Rahat. Was she any less pure?

His conscience stretched, awakening with a firm nay. The problem? Her lack of maidenhead blurred the line between right and wrong, putting her firmly in the field of possibility. Fair game for the likes of him.

Which, of course, roused the carnal side of his nature.

"Take her, Ram." His expression serious, Cristobal urged him in the direction his body ached to go. " 'Twill give you the ease you seek and save some fool from your fists."

"I am permitted but one?" Xavian glared at his friend before nudging Mayhem toward the stable they stood alongside.

"Mayhap a dozen, but then our healer will be forced to see to your wounds, in which case you will end where you should have begun. At her tender mercy," Cristobal said, his argument gaining ground by the moment. " 'Tis a vicious circle, my friend. One that will only lead back to her."

Xavian scowled and dismounted in front of the double-wide stable doors. Unseeing, he stared at the rough grey boards of the barn, wondering why the meddlesome arse he called friend always made good sense. 'Twas irritating to forever be on the receiving end of a well-launched argument. "Bugger off, Cristobal."

Flipping his leg over the horn, Cristobal's feet hit the dark earth beside him without making a sound. "Nay, 'tis what you should be doing...with our little healer."

The comment pushed Xavian over the edge.

With a snarl, he clipped Cristobal on the shoulder, warning him to assume a fighting stance. Cristobal countered with a growl and, crouching low, spun to deliver a solid kick to his ribs. He absorbed the pain, welcomed the familiar and entered the ring: an assassin, a fighter, a taker of lives. These things he knew, could navigate without difficulty or defeat. The feelings Afina stirred were foreign, a force he didn't know how to fight. 'Twas a weakness he couldn't abide.

But here, trading fists with Cristobal felt right and good and as satisfying as hell.

With a quick shift, he slammed his elbow into the side of his friend's head. Cristobal hit one knee. A woman shouted in dismay. His men bellowed their encouragement. Xavian took no notice and, balling his fist, swung, catching Cristobal's chin with a knuckle-crunching uppercut. As his comrade's head snapped back, he planted his foot in the center of his chest and pushed, sending him sprawling in the dirt. Cristobal laughed, rolled, and, flipping to his feet, assumed the ready position.

"Stop," a woman yelled, her voice close yet somehow far away. "Stop it!"

Focus absolute, power pounded through Xavian's veins, pushing all but the here and now from his mind. He growled. As the satisfying sound bubbled up his throat, he bared his teeth and circled left, countering Cristobal.

Small hands with cold fingers grabbed his upper arm.

Xavian snarled, temper wild as he whirled to dislodge the intruder. She hung on, arms roped around him, chest pressed flush to his right bicep. Hazel eyes wide with fear and confusion met his rage.

"Stop. Please, Xavian…stop."

Afina.

Her name rang in his head as she repeated her appeal. The soft plea broke through, washed over him, and turned his aggression into another kind of heat. His growl ended on a groan. Burned raw by her touch—by the concern in her gaze—his control slipped, sliding into the inferno blazing inside his chest. Lost, beyond redemption, he sank into need, picked her up, and carried her through the stable doors and into shadow.

CHAPTER SEVEN

The desperate gleam in Xavian's eyes scared her to death. The hard press of muscle locked around her and his pace didn't help much either. Each long stride took Afina further from safety, into the cool shadows of the stable and closer to full-blown panic.

Had she overstepped her bounds? Was he angry with her for interfering?

She bit the inside of her cheek and looked up into his face.

He didn't seem to be. Anger no longer lined his features. But then, nothing did. And his contained expression frightened her more than his fury would have. Something churned just before the surface, suppressed emotion she couldn't see but knew was there.

"Xavian?" She kept her voice soft as she looped her arms around his neck. Startling him wasn't a good idea. He was wound too tight, and she was too vulnerable…within striking distance. Not that she thought he would hurt her. But honestly? Better to be safe than sorry. "Please, stop."

He slowed, the echo of his footfalls fading as he halted in the middle of the aisle. She held her breath, listening to the thump of his heart as he tightened his grip under her knees and turned his face into her hair. Each one of his breaths whispered over her temple, the hot rush sweet with a hint of mint.

Not knowing what else to do, her hand stole to the nape of his neck, seeking, stroking to ease his tension. He murmured, pressed closer, curling around her as though he needed her touch as much as he needed to breathe. A small pang echoed in the center of her chest. Something was terribly wrong. He was hurting. The strong, brave warrior was in pain, and she couldn't stand it. Couldn't let it continue. The healer in her wouldn't allow it.

"Please, tell me what is wrong," she whispered, fingers playing in his hair, sifting through the thickness. Good goddess, it was a wonder, the softness. She'd never imagined a man could have such beautiful hair. Not that she was noticing. No, not really. She touched to reassure, not to—

Drat. Now she was lying to herself.

She ordered her wayward hands to still. When neither listened, she returned her attention to Xavian. "Let me help you."

A fine tremor racked his large frame.

She tightened her grip. "Put me down so I can help."

"Nay," he said, his voice half-growl, half-groan before he shuddered and moved forward, continuing into the interior of the stable. "You're mine."

Mine? Or rather, *his*? What the devil did that mean?

"Ah, Xavian, I think mayhap..." She trailed off, catching a glimpse of movement in her periphery. Three stable lads, pitchforks hanging from limp hands, gaped at them, mouths wide open. Wonderful. Now they had an audience. She glanced at Xavian, knowing he wouldn't approve. He was having some sort of breakdown, and no man worth his weight would relish witnesses for that.

Afina hung on as he took a sharp right at the end of the aisle. Two strides later, and he'd walked them through a doorway and into the tack room beyond. Sacks of grain occupied one corner, fat companions to the array of bridles hanging on the chamber walls. The long leather strips hovered above saddle horses, some in use, some patiently awaiting the weight of their next charge. With little room to maneuver, Xavian stopped in the center of the room and, one arm still around her, dropped her feet to the floor.

As she found her balance, he murmured, "*La dracu,* you feel good…so warm."

The whispered words tickled the side of her neck then rolled like a dark wave down her spine. His voice was decadent. The resonance one of perfect pitch; deep enough to tie her up, light enough to make her want to relax and trust and give. But two years of running—of Vladimir—had ruined any chance of that.

Her hands flat against his chest, she pushed, needing distance. He tightened his grip, shackling her against him while he inhaled, burrowing deep to press his lips to her pulse point.

The contact—mouth to neck, skin to skin—hit her like a thunderstorm, and heat gathered with an alarming rumble. "I, ah…Are you all right?"

"I'm so cold inside…so cold."

Cold? Afina frowned and rubbed his upper arms. Odd, he didn't feel chilled. He radiated heat, a pleasant warmth that roped hard muscle and enlivened the surface of his skin. A fever mayhap? That would explain his strange behavior. She'd seen it many times. The crazed look in glazed-over eyes, the chill deep inside a person even though they burned with sickness. A terrible fear gripped her. Was Xavian's infection out of hand? Was this the beginning of the blood disease that so frightened her?

If he suffered from the ailment, she needed to know…right now. Her healing satchel was woefully in need of restocking, and without the proper herbs he would suffer before the poison ran its course and his body fought it off or—

No, she refused to think like that. He was strong. She wouldn't allow him to die…refused to fail him like she'd done her sister.

"Xavian, look at me," she said, her tone tight.

One arm nestled against her back, he buried his free hand in her unbound hair, pulling her flush against him. Her fingers curled, and finding the edge of his sleeveless tunic, she shook him. He raised his head, blue eyes glowing with heat that had nothing to do with a fever. Afina froze. She felt her eyes widen and heard her lips part on a strangled gasp. Could he be…what… Good goddess, was he—

"Don't be afraid. I won't hurt you." He cupped her cheek with a warrior-rough palm. Holding her there, his gaze half-searched, half-pleaded as he leaned in and kissed her, whisper-soft. "Please, *draga*. Warm me…make me forget the cold for a while."

Afina's breath got tangled up in the back of her throat. Wonder nipped at her, drowning out the little voice that whispered a warning. Somewhere deep inside she knew she should listen, heed the kernel of fear coiling low in her belly. But the fact he wanted her—the way a man did a woman—trumped good sense, spinning her into a world filled with new possibilities.

She wanted them all, craved the moment of freedom. Longed to let loose, and just once, do what she wanted instead of pleasing someone else.

And Xavian? His desire was the perfect foil.

Without shame or seduction, he asked, leaving the outcome up to her. But what to do…accept his touch or deny her yearning? Ignoring the lust-filled ache would be safer, but curiosity was a powerful thing. And as she stared into his eyes, blue as the Danube, warm as a hot spring, she remembered Bianca.

Ever since her sister had danced across their small cottage, Afina had wondered about her secret meetings with Bodgan. Her enjoyment had been obvious, a curious splendor that had left Afina dissatisfied with her own life.

The restlessness hit her full force. It wasn't fair that everyone knew joy except her. Life had dealt her a series of denials, but not today. Today was about her, about what she needed—what she wanted—and for once, she followed desire, titled her chin up and invited his kiss.

Xavian struggled to draw a full breath. Holy hell, Afina was going to let him. Allow him to lay her down and touch her soft skin, love her the way he wanted—needed—to. He could tell by the way she moved, that subtle shift in weight that brought her a wee bit closer, and the color...Jesu help him, the color. The sweet wave of crimson washed over her cheekbones, a hot rush of feminine arousal that almost leveled him where he stood.

Held fast by her physical response, he swallowed as her eyes dropped, shielding her thoughts behind her lashes. The downward sweep of her gaze branded him, the invisible caress making him squirm while her fingers played across his already too-hot skin.

He was going to come. Right now. In his leathers before he ever got the chance to touch her.

The decadent dreams that plagued his nights front and center in his mind, Xavian pictured her splayed beneath him, wrapped around him, spine arched, mouth open as she screamed in ecstasy. *Rahat.* He needed to pull himself together. If he didn't, he'd never get to hear that scream. He'd be finished so fast he'd cut her pleasure short. And he craved her bliss as much as his own, yearned to give her every bit of what he'd imagined her capable of beneath him. Or atop him. Hell, he didn't care. He'd give her whatever she asked, however she wanted, just as long as he ended up deep inside her.

Just the thought…of her…of him…

A wicked rush swept through him. Xavian groaned, his whole body straining against his fast-slipping control.

"Shh, 'tis all right," she said, the husky tenor of her voice stringing him even tighter. "Here. Let me warm you."

And just like that, the dam broke.

His control split wide open, leaving nothing but need in its wake. The rush rolled over him, and before he knew what hit him he was inside her mouth. Kissing her deep, his tongue stroked along her teeth and…Jesu. She tasted better than he'd imagined, a feast of delight without end. And he wanted more. Wanted to savor every bit of her until he glutted himself and left her weak with satiation.

Full of fire, the heat in his veins boiled over as his hands roamed. He explored every curve, caressing her in long, sweeping strokes, unable to decide what he liked best: her sweetly rounded ass, the nip at her waist, or the bounty of her breasts. Hell, he loved every part of her, but settled on the last, slipping his hand between their bodies to cup one of the pair. With a gasp, she twisted against him. He let go of her mouth, eager to watch her as he played with the tightly furled nipple.

She arched and, eyes closed, threw her head back. Unable to resist the invitation, Xavian lowered his head, kissing the curve of her neck as he cupped the lush curve of her behind. Her moan joined his groan, and walking her backward, he headed for the large grain sacks piled in the corner of the chamber. He couldn't wait to lie her down, to get at her soft skin and the wet heat between her thighs.

But not like this. Not while he was armed to the teeth and fully clothed.

With a flick, he undid the buckle securing his sword harness and slipped free of the twin blades. As they hit the floor beside the burlap sacks, he returned to her mouth, hungry for more as he attacked the side lacing of his tunic. The instant he was free, he raised his head. Afina whimpered, tightening her grip in his hair as if protesting his departure. He smiled a little, lighter of heart than he'd ever remembered being, then returned, nipping her softly before sliding his tongue between her lips. She sighed, the sound so arousing his shaft throbbed, impatient for the feel of her.

God, she wanted him. 'Twas a miracle, a precious gift that tugged at the tight knot always riding in the center of his chest. He felt himself unravel, slip from gentle to greedy in a heartbeat. Ferocious with need, he cupped her shoulders, released her mouth, and gave her a push. As she tumbled back against the bags of grain, he lifted the leather tunic over his head and tossed it aside.

Landing in a delicious sprawl, color high, hazel eyes wide, she stared up at him.

"Unlace for me, *draga*," he said, aware his tone was more plea than command. "Give yourself to me."

Surprise flared in her eyes. Afina blinked, and Xavian prayed she understood what he was asking. He needed to know she was certain, willing to take him all the way without regret or reprisal. Doubt held no place between them. If she harbored any second thoughts, he had to know now...while he was still able to walk away. Once he touched her, there would be no going back.

She hesitated, her attention straying to his bare chest. He held his breath, forcing himself to endure her scrutiny without moving. After what seemed an eternity, she brought her hands to the lacing running down the front of her gown. The tidy bow sitting atop her breasts gave way and his knees almost followed suit. He locked them to remain standing and watched as she drew the folds wide then toyed with the string holding her chemise closed. The corners of her mouth curved, her focus steady on him, she played, wrapping the tie around her fingertip and pulled...a wee bit, but not enough to expose what lay hidden beneath.

Xavian raised a brow, relishing the playful taunt. "Enjoy teasing, do you?"

"Mayhap..." Her tongue peeked out, leaving a moist trail on her bottom lip. "With you."

He inhaled hard, loving her response. She understood both her power and appeal. And was prepared to torture him with both. The realization cranked him higher and, unable to hold back, he unlaced his trews and joined her on their makeshift bed. She sighed, burying her hand in his hair, arching against him, bringing him flush into her. As he groaned and settled against her, Xavian murmured to her, praising her welcome, her softness, her desire for him.

Afina hummed and tipped her chin, begging for his kiss. But as much as he wanted to taste her again, Xavian needed something else more. He wanted to see her, touch her, hold the soft, warm weight of her in his hands. So instead of kissing her, he did what she hadn't and released the tie holding her chemise. His heart hammering like he'd run flat out for a mile, he pushed the linen wide.

Sweet Jesu. She was perfect.

The most beautiful thing he'd ever had the privilege to lay eyes upon.

"Afina," he murmured, awe in his tone, hand sliding beneath the folds of linen.

Her breath caught as he cupped her, covering her pretty pink nipple with the heat of his palm. The bud furled tighter at the contact, and she twisted a little, as if shocked…as though unaccustomed to being touched. The reaction told him plainly she didn't accept men with ease—or very often.

His heart went loose in his chest and a burning rush of tenderness lit him up from the inside out. Precious. She was precious. Someone to be cherished and cared for. Someone for his warrior soul to shield and protect. The depth of emotion startled him a bit, but he took no notice, his happiness that she had chosen him to please her too strong to deny.

Dipping his head, he set his mouth to the soft place between her breasts then turned to kiss the tight bud of her nipple. She started, twitching before arching beneath him, begging for more. He hummed, the sound one of satisfaction, and licked the pebbled peak. Her hands flexed in his hair, drawing him closer as he sucked, lightly. God, she was sensitive, exquisitely so. "Been a while, hasn't it, *draga*?"

She whispered his name.

The husky entreaty unleashed him, washing every thought from his head. With a growl, he shoved her skirt up, pushed her legs wide, and settled between their spread. Hitching her knee around his hip, he caressed the inside of her thigh on a steady upward slide. The instant he found her heat, his shaft thumped in his trews.

God give him strength. She was so wet, so soft, so unbelievably hot. He couldn't wait. She was ready, and his greed, out of
control. He needed inside. Now.

Stroking the nub at the top of her sex, he waited until she
caught his rhythm then set himself to her entrance and thrust,
embedding himself to the hilt. She stiffened, a wild cry rippling
from her throat. Xavian froze. What the hell? He'd hurt her. That
terrible whimper was one of pain, not pleasure.

He reared, concern stilling his heart until the only noise he
heard was the hitching sob of her breath. He cupped her face,
smoothed the furrow between her brows with his thumb and
tried to think. What had he done wrong? Desperate to soothe
her, he brushed the hair away from her face and adjusted his
position in hopes of easing her.

As she quieted, he replayed his entry. He shook his head. Nay,
'twas not possible. She…she was…she had a child, for Christ's
sake. But the physical evidence overrode what he believed to be
true. He'd felt the membrane tear, the one that confirmed she
was untouched.

La dracu. A virgin.

Regret and a strange sense of pride battled, fighting for
supremacy. Disappointment and the razor-sharp edge of betrayal
won, hitting him gut level. He dropped his chin to his chest and,
head low, fought the dull ache punching through to his heart.
She'd lied to him…about everything.

Pain. She hadn't expected so much pain. A sting, yes. A pinch,
certainly. But not…Afina swallowed…*this.*

The burn broke from her body and entered her mind. Agony expanded, opening a door to somewhere else. She was fracturing, being torn apart inside by an outside force that had nothing to do with Xavian. Red mist seethed through the cracks, bubbling between the jagged seams to wash in behind her eyes. The haze grew, turning gold then white, an expansive sensation that unlocked a floodgate. Images flowed in a river of fire: great winged beasts and smoke, cauldrons and incense, the blood-red glow in the Chamber of Whispers.

Voices, a thousand strong, murmured inside her head... begging her to accept something she didn't understand. What was happening? Apart from the pain, the pressure and heat—the vivid pictures in her mind—didn't seem, well, normal. Was every woman's first time like this, or was there something wrong with her?

Whatever the case—right, wrong, or somewhere in between—Afina knew that it was all her fault. It always was, but she couldn't dwell on that now. She was in serious trouble, in way over her head with Xavian.

Inhaling hard, she shifted beneath him. The movement helped, and the fog in her mind receded, a slow retreat that dimmed the pain enough for her to open her eyes. Xavian's face came into sharp focus. She lost the air she so desperately needed. The chill in his expression sucked it right out of her lungs. Gasping, the ache still fierce enough to make her flinch, fear coalesced into a giant ball in the center of her chest. She wiggled, pushing against his shoulders while digging one heel into a grain sack, hoping he would let her go.

Eyes of ice blue drilled into her. One big hand clamped on her hip, he planted the other beside her head, locking her in place as a muscle jumped along his jaw. His throat worked before he unclenched his teeth and growled, "Do. Not. Move."

Was he insane? Anger burned in his gaze and bled from his pores, and he wanted her to stay put? Not in this lifetime. Her will to survive was too strong for that.

"Y-you are h-hurting me." Afina blinked back tears, hating the wispy stutter in her voice.

Xavian cursed and shifted, easing the pressure between her thighs, only to come back. She stiffened, a desperate sound exploding from her throat as he tilted her hips into his, widened her legs a little more. The angle pushed him deeper. The pinch intensified, shooting stinging barbs up her spine.

"P-please." Her bottom lip trembled.

Good goddess. Now she was begging, something she'd experienced too often at her mother's hand and in the temple. Weak. She was weak, so foolish to have given into the yearning and welcomed his possession. But she had wanted him with a fierceness that broke all the rules and, truth be told, still did. But not like this. Not with fury on his handsome face and in the hard lines of his body. The vulnerability that held her trapped beneath him was too much for her to handle.

"Please...I c-cannot breathe."

"*Draga*, be easy." His voice came to her on a soft exhale. Tears in her eyes, she watched the anger fade in his as he held her gaze. "The first time is always difficult, but the pain will go."

"W-when?"

"Soon."

Soon? How soon? Afina needed to know. She didn't think she could take much more.

Closing her eyes, she tipped her head back, twisting a little beneath him. He answered her movement, coming down on his forearms to cup her head between his large palms. The caress eased the throb between her temples, and grateful for the reprieve, Afina turned her face into his hand.

With a low murmur, he kissed her collarbone and settled deeper between the spread of her thighs. The breath she'd managed to capture sped out in a rush.

"It still h-hurts. M-mayhap...mayhap you should let me go."

He muttered something she didn't quite catch. A moment later he nodded and, with a rough exhale, shifted to leave her. Something unnatural roared inside her head, sending denial pounding through her veins. On a gasp, against her will, she locked her calf around his hip and arched to keep him deep.

His hand flexed on her hip. *"Rahat."*

What was wrong with her? She shouldn't be resisting—wanted to release him—but something hungry and aggressive took over, refusing to let him go.

Panic welled inside her chest. "S-sorry, I cannot...I don't mean to—"

"Jesu, do that again," he rasped, his breath hot against the side of her throat. "God, you feel so good. So good, and I...Christ."

The breathy quality of his voice caught her attention. He sounded like he was being tortured while loving the abuse. Afina's lips parted in wonder as his spine arched and his head came up. Color rode the ridge of his high cheekbones, and she drew in a soft breath as something close to bliss winged across his features. Do *what* again? By the goddess, she'd do anything to see delight return to his beautiful face.

"Squeeze me tight...with your muscles deep inside," he said, answering her silent query as though she'd spoken it out loud.

She did, and her eyes flew wide. What was *that*? She did it again, tightening around him. The contraction dragged a guttural groan from him and a startled gasp from her. The goddess preserve her...the pain was gone and the pleasure returning, pulled to the surface when Xavian circled his hips.

"Oh. That's...O-ooh!"

Sliding his hand between their bodies, his fingers found the top of her sex, just above where they were joined. He played with the nubbin, stroking her lightly. She bucked, the maelstrom of sensation tearing a low moan from her throat.

"Aye, like that, love." Xavian pressed a little harder, caressing her with his body as well as his hand. "I'll make it good for you. I'll make it good."

Bliss threw her head back and churned her hips, and in that moment, Afina didn't doubt him. No matter how they'd started, *this* was unbelievably good. The feel of his hot skin beneath her hands and between her legs, the rocking of his hips and hardness deep inside was everything she'd imagined. Everything she'd dreamed of sitting beneath the summer moon, star gazing, hoping to someday find a man of her own. One who was gentle with her body and kind to her heart.

Xavian, with all his strength and quiet ways, fit. Mayhap she was wrong to leave him. Mayhap she should give him a chance, tell him all her troubles and let him help fight the battles instinct warned her were coming. He was a warrior: hard, capable, honorable. The kind of man she needed, wanted—yearned for.

The evidence was in his patience, in the way he moved and watched her from above, gauging her pleasure then adjusting to give her more. He was splendor in every form. Fashioned for her...only for her.

"Xavian!"

"Hmm, almost there, love. You're almost there." He hummed, the soft purr so full of satisfaction it catapulted Afina to a whole new level of awareness. To the place where ecstasy lived and oblivion ruled. "Come for me, Afina. Scream for me."

He backed the command by lowering his head to her breast. His gaze trained on her face, he curled his tongue around her nipple then bathed her in the heat of his mouth and suckled... hard. The suction drew her up, arched her spine, sent her flying, and she did as he asked. She screamed his name, cresting on a wave so intense she knew she would never be the same.

Locked in a free fall, spiraling out into space, she felt him quicken, riding hard. The wild rhythm turned her inside out, and with a moan she wrapped her legs around his hips and rode with him into another round of oblivion.

Adrift on wonder, the red mist faded to the back of Afina's mind. One hand buried in the soft curls at his nape, she left the other to play along Xavian's spine. Umm, he was amazing, his body relaxed yet so solid at the same time. She loved his weight, the way he smelled, forest musk woven into the fabric of masculine scent that was as much a part of him as the width of his shoulders and the strength in his limbs.

He'd given her a gift. One of splendor and light.

The urge to hug him tight and kiss the cove behind his ear—to thank him—warred with the need to stay precisely as they were; tucked against one another, skin to hot skin, safe from the world and all its troubles. It was silly, the need to stay hidden, and she sighed when he shifted, hating to lose his warmth when he withdrew and pushed to his feet.

Too sated to move, she lay supine, legs curled, gown unlaced and soft against her thighs. She watched him set his trews to rights and felt a momentary twinge of regret. Next time. He would undress for her next time, and she for him. Her heart thumped a little faster at the thought, but as he turned to pick up his leather tunic, Afina frowned. He was being awfully quiet. Why? Was there something wrong or was this how all couplings ended? Without cuddles or kisses, without aid from the other as each of them dressed?

She pushed onto one elbow. "Xavian?"

His head turned, showing her his profile. The small muscle—the one that liked to jump along his jaw—twitched. Afina swallowed. He was back to being angry. It showed in the set of his shoulders and in the tight, straight line of his spine. Each movement controlled, he slipped the leather tunic over his head, tied the side laces, and reached for his swords.

Afina drew the sides of her gown closed, covering her breasts behind wool worn by time and faded by use. She shivered, the chill in the small chamber unbearable as shame reared its ugly head.

Her voice a mere shadow of its former self, she asked, "Why are you angry?"

At last he pivoted, the rasp of his boots sounding loud on the compact earth. Deadly serious, his eyes burned with a dangerous intensity that drilled a hole in her breastbone and took her breath away. "Has everything you told me been a lie?"

Afina shook her head, hurt sloshing around inside her. "I—"

"Have you been honest with me once? Do you even know how to tell the truth?"

She opened her mouth to answer.

He slashed his big hand through the air, the motion one of fury as he stepped toward her. "I warned you I value truth, yet you lie to me at every turn."

"What are you accusing me of...what crime?"

"You are not Sabine's mother," he said, tone harsh, expression fierce.

"Yes, I am! I may not have birthed her," she said, her voice as hard as his, "but she is mine in every way that truly matters."

"Bullshit."

His harsh denial lit the fuse on a temper Afina hadn't known she possessed. *Dolt.* What was his problem? True, she hadn't warned him. Had bedded him knowing full well he expected her to be a woman of experience. Regardless, the lie paled in comparison to what she'd given him—her innocence. Most men would have been thrilled with her gift. Afina chewed on her bottom lip. Wouldn't they?

Ice in his gaze, Xavian opened his mouth, no doubt to hurl some other unpleasantry in her direction.

"You insufferable ass," she said, cutting him off. "Lie or no, you lay with me and it is too late for regrets. You cannot take it back and...by the goddess, all this because I chose *you*...gifted *you* with my maidenhead."

"'Twas not a gift, but a curse. Jesu, I...*Rahat.*" He shook his head and took a step back. Away from her. Away from what they had done together. Anger coupled with something intangible—something approaching pain—flashed across his face. With another expletive, he tunneled both hands through his hair and headed for the exit. Hammering the wooden lock free, he wrenched the door open and snarled over his shoulder, "Put yourself to rights and meet me outside. I have business to see to and no more time to waste."

The door slammed closed, the sound as hollow as the hope dying in her heart. *A curse.* He'd called her innocence a curse. He abhorred what they'd shared. And hated her for not telling him...for her duplicity.

Yes, he valued honesty, but not her. Never her.

Betrayal.

He felt it, and now she did too. But more than that, she suffered from the shame in knowing the man she'd made love to didn't consider it so. It had been naught more than a quick tumble for him. An unimportant event to slake his lust with the woman nearest to hand.

And she thought to stay with him, to trust him with all her secrets…with her life? When had she become such a fool?

The red mist returned and heat prickled, clouding her vision pink.

Afina covered her mouth with her hand to stifle a sob. She would not cry. *She would not.* Xavian was not worth her tears.

She repeated that over and over, forcing herself to believe it as she stood. Spotting a water bucket in the corner, she limped to the table and reached for the ladle. Her eyes burned, and her chest tightened until it hurt to breathe. She swiped at her cheek, told herself she wasn't weeping, but another droplet fell, joining the first. A choking noise filled her ears, the sound raw as she picked up a thin piece of linen. As the cool cloth brushed flesh too tender to touch, she washed Xavian from her body, all the while wishing she could wash him from her mind. Mayhap then she'd feel whole again.

Vladimir fisted his hand, crushing the precious parchment. Christ, could the timing be any worse? He scowled at the vellum then tossed the wretched thing into the hearth. Flame flared, devouring it with ravenous teeth as he headed for the sideboard across the chamber.

He needed a drink. More than one, truth be told.

The white-robed, ruddy-cheeked bastard. What the hell was the Grand Master of the Teutonic Knights doing traveling so close to Castle Raul?

'Twas a mystery. One Vladimir didn't want to unravel.

But what else could he do? The grand bastard had requested his escort, safe passage into the Carpathians. Something as acting voivode Vladimir couldn't deny. News spread like piss on dry ground. Any slight to Grand Master Stein would reach King Charles. Shit, word would travel so fast the corners of the missive would still be smoking as the royal arse cracked the seal.

"Damnation," he muttered, pouring himself a goblet of wine. Raising his hand, he took a fortifying sip and pivoted to sit on the edge of the sideboard. He stared at the fire across the room, mind churning to form a plan.

He didn't have time to pander to the self-important idiot. He was needed at home. Unrest swirled, infecting the common man like disease did a well-used whore. Some were even asking questions, challenging his authority, demanding to know why the High Priestess of Orm stayed cloistered behind the walls of the White Temple. Soon word of her disappearance would leak out and the people would rebel, turning to King Charles for help to displace him.

Vladimir tightened his grip on the mug. The little bitch could ruin everything.

A hesitant knock sounded on the door.

Turning his head, he glared at the well-oiled panels. "Come."

The latch clicked, and Anton, his manservant, stumbled into the chamber. Red-eyed from too much drink, the imbecile swayed, blinking hard against the light coming through the high windows. His head swung left then right, passing over Vladimir without registering his presence.

"Over here, you idiot."

Anton blinked again, the movement wide and rapid like a startled owl. "Oh, m'lord...didn't see ye there."

"Obviously." He sighed, accustomed to Anton's idiocy if not yet resigned to it. Honestly, the man was good for naught but shoveling horse shit.

"Yer horse is rigged out, m'lord," he said, words slurred, leaning forward as if to impart some great pearl of wisdom.

Vladimir gritted his teeth. Even from across the room, he could smell the homemade whiskey. The rank odor wafted around Anton, a swirling trail of inebriation that for once Vladimir wished he could fall headlong into. But today was not the day. He had the grand bastard to coddle.

Grabbing his cloak, he swung it around his shoulders and strode toward the door. As Anton scurried out of the way, he vowed to use his time in the saddle well. A side trip was in order. Henrik hadn't delivered. Ramir was a ghost. And instinct told him he couldn't trust either one.

'Twas time to take measures into his own hands. He'd tried to avoid to it—his kingdom and the people in it needed constant supervision—but clearly paying another to do his dirty work wasn't working. Unreliable bastards would no doubt double cross him.

If they hadn't already.

He hit the stairs, taking them two at a time. Aye, 'twas time to do some hunting, and Drachaven was as good a place as any to start.

CHAPTER EIGHT

A virgin. *Rahat.* How could he have predicted that? She was a mother, for the love of Christ, which naturally made for certain assumptions. But then, naught about Afina rang true. Hell, she had enjoyed his touch, acted a wee bit surprised mayhap, but her kiss and sweet curves...

Xavian's fingers curled. Such heat. The scorching intensity still blazed in his veins, under his skin, stoking his fire higher. He wanted to roar at the unfairness. Wanted to shake Afina until her teeth rattled. Wanted to lay her down and love her again.

He snorted. 'Twas rank stupidity.

What the hell was the matter with him?

She had lied to him. *Lied.* This time about something so important it—

Her betrayal tore him wide open. Everything he thought he knew about her was tainted by deceit. The ugliness almost brought him to his knees, along with the double-edged sword of regret.

He'd taken her maidenhead—a gift that had not been his to claim. Now his vow lay shattered, the shards as deadly and sharp as the blades strapped to his back. With sure, even strokes, they stabbed at his conscience, bleeding him dry...reminding him of his reasons.

He hadn't taken the oath without thought. Armed with the knowledge of his kind, he'd made it with single-minded purpose.

A good lass expected good things;, deserved the best of them. He couldn't provide a woman of worth aught but brutality. He was an assassin, so dark inside his soul bled black. He'd tortured and killed in the name of Al Pacii. For Halál, until blood ran in rivulets, staining his hands, destroying any chance of absolution.

Secrets weren't meant to be kept, least of all his.

Sooner or later, any woman he took as his own would learn the truth—about who and what he was. And sure rejection would follow. He refused to set himself up for that kind of fall, for the pain as he watched her recoil with disgust in her eyes. But now he was waist deep and sinking fast.

An honorable man would do the right thing, marry Afina, slay her dragons, and give her a solid home. The dragons he could handle, mayhap even the home, but he couldn't make her his. His stamp of ownership didn't belong anywhere near her lovely skin. She deserved better, more than he could give in a hundred lifetimes of trying.

The proof lay in his behavior after he'd loved her—in the hurt in her eyes and the look of horror on her beautiful face. He'd done that: put the shame in her expression, shoved it deep until he saw her choke on it. Jesu, he was a beast. A first-rate brute not fit to talk to her, never mind touch her. Or wish for permanency that would destroy them both in the end.

Nay, 'twould be whores for him from now on. Like before. No more assumptions. No more mistakes. And no more touching Afina.

'Twas the decent thing to do. Aye, the right decision, the only decision.

Why then did he feel hollow inside? As though something important had just slipped through his fingertips?

Xavian shook his head and put the thought away. He needed to stay sharp. Danger always lurked in the marketplace and anger blunted the senses. No matter how furious at Afina, he must mute its intensity for now. He'd promised to keep her safe, and with both her and Sabine an arm's length behind him, he refused to place them at risk. They had a ways to go yet to reach the shop he sought.

Already the vendors lining the wide, rutted streets of Ismal eyed Afina more than he liked. Women were always of interest. A pretty one could start street brawls. But Afina? There was no doubt into which category she fell. Beautiful didn't begin to describe her.

Xavian locked onto a particularly bold merchant. Dressed in a purple tunic, the bastard stood beneath a thatched overhang, watching from his place in the shadows. He played with the curled tip of his mustache, his potbelly protruding above spindly legs and knobby knees. But it was his eyes that drew Xavian tight. Bright with calculation, his gaze ran Afina's length before shifting to assess Sabine.

A slaver. Though why the flesh peddler was so far from Constantinople was anyone's guess. Had he delivered his goods already or were the men, women, and children the bastard considered merchandise chained somewhere nearby?

He clenched his teeth on a curse and schooled his features, refusing to allow even a flicker of emotion to crease his face.

'Twas a man like this who had taken his family.

He'd been so young, just seven years old. And Nadia? They'd celebrated her fifth birthday the day before. The thought unlocked the memories. Images and sounds swamped him, swimming like poison through his mind. The feel of rough hands wrenching him from his bed, the fear and confusion, his sister crying, his mother's pleas then sobs while his father roared in agony. The smell of smoke and blood and sweat. The sight of his parents lying face down, crumbled like dolls on the cottage floor before men set torches to the roof. Bound and gagged, they'd made him watch, helpless as his parents' bodies burned along with his home. Now he could barely remember them—couldn't recall their faces or the color of his mother's eyes.

A low growl—half-pain, half-rage—rolled up his throat. He wanted to kill the flesh monger, lay him low where he stood. For looking at Afina, for weighing her worth with coins in his eyes.

Just as that scum had done to Nadia.

Instead he leveled him with a look, using his gaze to effect, and slowed his pace, reeling Afina in. He wanted her close, a breath away so the slaver understood. She belonged to his circle and any who attempted to touch her would die...screaming.

A little slow on the uptake, Afina bumped into him. Her gasp of surprise brushed the exposed skin of his shoulder. Uncaring of the reason for her proximity, lust unfurled, speeding heat through his veins. He ignored the arousal she stirred with a touch and stood his ground, intent on the slaver and their surroundings.

The bastard wasn't alone. His kind never was.

Hired henchmen always circled, watching for the signal. The one that identified their master's prey. Once received, the band of thugs would close the loop, blocking all avenues of escape to take their target. Xavian bared his teeth, hoping they made that mistake with him. He would slit every one of their throats.

One brow raised, he held the flesh monger's gaze, daring him to set the attack in motion. The bastard blinked and, red-faced, glanced away, shoulders rounding as he slid further into the shadows and retreated.

Not so brave after all. But then, slavers weren't stupid. A canny bunch, the majority stayed ahead of their enemies by out-thinking them. Add the fact that most only challenged those they outnumbered ten to one, and the life of a flesh peddler had the potential to be a long, prosperous one.

With a sigh, Xavian glanced over his shoulder. Two sets of eyes stared back, one beguiling hazel, the other, mismatched green and blue.

Sabine grinned around her thumb. "X."

"What's wrong?" Afina asked, voice soft, her question coming on top of the little one's greeting.

Xavian tamped down an unexpected spike of admiration. He had to give her credit. She didn't miss much. Had read his body cues and taken them to mean danger. Smart lass. "Naught you need worry about. Stay close."

He held her gaze, waiting for her to acknowledge his command. When she nodded, he unlocked his body's protective shield and moved forward, leading them into the heart of the marketplace. Senses alive and searching, he wove a trail through the thickening crowd, around carts piled high with goods pulled by oxen. The beasts snorted and heaved, thick horns curled against their ears as though protesting the noisy chatter of vendors, the scrape of tanners' blades, and the high-pitched clank of a blacksmith's anvil.

The farther they walked the more the air thickened, and the smell of roasted nuts, warm apple cider, and oven-baked bread joined the sights and sounds of the Ring. An enormous circle at the market's center, everything rippled out from it, the streets taking its shape and form. The less affluent vendors occupied the curved avenues banding the hub, while those who could afford to paid the higher rents to set up on the Ring's edge.

Colorful awnings graced the fronts of most shops. The light fabric undulated in the early morning sun, a light breeze teasing their ample underbellies. One-half of the circle contained pens for livestock, the sounds of cattle, pigs, and goats joining the enthusiastic cries of the onlookers gathered at the other end. Heading in that direction, his gaze skipped over the multitude of street performers that delighted crowds on a daily basis.

Xavian's mood lifted a little. He enjoyed the performers' antics. And more often than not indulged in a bag of roasted nuts and a cup of cider whenever he ventured into Ismal. He skirted a group swaying on stilts, an admiring eye on the knives they juggled. Not for the first time, he wondered how sharp they kept the long, thin blades.

Caught up in the gleam and flash of metal, he paused to admire their skill, but got distracted by the soft body at his back. Xavian flinched. He'd told her to stay close, but…not so close she touched him at every turn. The sweet curves brushing him made him remember the wild rush when he'd had her beneath him. He inhaled hard and exhaled smooth, struggling to contain his reaction.

Refusing to retreat, he waited for her to step away. She didn't. Xavian swallowed a curse. What was she trying to do, set him ablaze where he stood?

He glanced over his shoulder, intending to tell her to back the hell off. He didn't get that far. Instead he got tangled up by the wonder in her expression. And hell, she wasn't even looking at him. Flicking his gaze over wooden stalls and the assortment of jugglers, he found the source of her fascination.

Heedless to his body's tension, his lips twitched. "Fire eaters."

She blinked. "W-what?"

"Fire eaters."

One arm curled around Sabine, her gaze jumped from their torches to the streams of flame blazing from their mouths then back again. "How are they doing that?"

"Turpentine."

"They put it in their mouths?"

"Aye."

"Isn't that dangerous?"

"Very. Many scorch their lungs and suffocate before they master the trick." Unable to look away, Xavian watched emotion play across the fine contours of her face. Astonishment, curiosity, and horror all made a pass. But the most prominent was bafflement, as though she struggled to understand why someone would risk himself in such a way. "'Tis a popular spectacle and earns them coin enough to live."

She shook her head, her attention bouncing to the next performer. Her jaw dropped as she watched the man insert a long, thin sword down his throat.

"A metal tube," he said, biting back a grin.

In a heartbeat, he killed the amusement, smoothing his expression. He didn't want to laugh with her. 'Twas common ground he could ill afford if he held any chance of keeping his oath. Anger and indifference would serve him better. The first he possessed in abundance. The second? He was carrying the short end of the stick. But even as he acknowledged the weakness and told himself to ignore her, the urge to assuage her curiosity proved stronger. "He swallowed it."

She threw him an incredulous look. "Like a scabbard in his throat?"

Xavian nodded. He didn't trust himself to answer the question. Not without his mouth giving into a smile.

"That's insane."

"Mayhap," he said, unwilling to agree. 'Twas another point of camaraderie he couldn't afford. If he allowed himself closeness of any kind, he would fail to keep his hands off her. "Stay on my heels in this crowd. We're almost there."

"Where is *there*?"

"You'll know when we arrive," he said, refusing to give her a clue.

He required an edge, the advantage of surprise. If he gave her any forewarning, he wouldn't get what he needed to douse the slow burn. The blaze of lust. The clawing need. His obsession with Afina. A dangerous combination. One he needed to slay then bury six feet under. The only way to do that was to provoke her. Make her hate him enough to stay away.

And God forgive him, he could hardly wait for the fight.

The smell of warmed wool and peat moss drifted from the dark interior. The comforting blend tickled her nose, reminding Afina of home. She wanted to take solace in the scent. To dive into the past and remember the good times. She caught herself at the last moment. Before she made another mistake and let her guard slip. Now was not the time to lose focus.

Xavian was up to something.

She knew it deep down, in the same way she'd known that danger stood in front of them as they entered the marketplace. The tension holding his body taut had told her so then, just as it did now. Except his rigidity here was different. Afina couldn't put her finger on the reason, but something—the strange red mist mayhap—warned her to be wary.

Adjusting the sling around her shoulder, she tucked Sabine tighter against her side. Almost time for her morning nap, her cherub nestled in, the suck-suck-sucking sound of Sabine's thumb soft comfort as Afina followed Xavian inside. He stopped in the middle of the room, and as her eyes adjusted she understood why the scent of wool had rolled out into the street.

Stacked from floor to timber-beamed ceiling, rolls of fabric sat piled, one on top of the other. The mounds were everywhere, taking every available space along the long wall opposite the door. Afina nibbled on her lower lip and turned to look behind her. Make that *every* wall, except the one the hearth called home.

A tailor's shop?

Well, the man must have an army of seamstresses. Either that or a fixation for fabric. She'd never seen so many different kinds in one place. Even in the living quarters at the temple, where coin never lacked, their seamstresses had never been given so much choice. Here every color imaginable shimmered in the low light. Yellows and golds, vibrant reds and rich blues, purples, and so many different greens. Wool, linen, and silk together in a kaleidoscope of color that made Afina's eyes round with wonder. Spools of thread, one to match each shade, sat lumped in shallow-sided wooden boxes, awaiting their turns in the needle.

She shook her head, her gaze bouncing, unable to stay in one place long enough to give each item the attention it deserved. The shop was a veritable treasure trove, a thick-spun oasis in the middle of the clamoring marketplace.

Afina frowned. The shop didn't seem like one of Xavian's usual haunts. Not that he wasn't refined enough, it was just, well...the mill was a woman's place. Not a man's.

The thought brought her up short. Suspicion formed, slithering through her mind like a venomous snake. As it reared its ugly head, Afina chanced a quick peek in his direction.

Standing still as death, he watched her from his position by the door. Besides the fact he blocked her path to the exit, a few other things registered. His stance, for one, was all wrong. Arms crossed, chin angled down, he looked as if he anticipated an attack. But more damning than those telltale signs was his silence. He was too quiet. Far too quiet.

Intuition gave her a nudge. "Why are we here?"

"Why do you think?"

Afina's eyes narrowed. Oblivious to her tension Sabine burrowed into her collarbone with a sleepy murmur. Rubbing her daughter's back, she met Xavian's gaze head-on. "Let's pretend I'm a little slow this morrow and you tell me instead."

He raised a brow and ran his eyes over her. The message was clear; he found her lacking. Every bit of her...along with her attire. And without him saying a word, she knew what he intended.

A thick ball of dread congealed in the pit of her stomach. She fought the nauseating lump and kept her chin level, unwilling to show him how much his opinion hurt. Yes, she'd lied to him, but did she truly deserve *this*? To be treated no better than a...like a...oh, goddess, no...a whore on sale to the highest bidder?

But the hard lines in his face said it all. He'd brought her here—to the most exquisite shop she'd ever seen—as payment for their intimacy. He would provide her with a new gown. Mayhap even a warm cloak to compensate her for the fact he'd taken her maidenhead. As if that would repair the damage—soothe her suffering over his rejection.

Afina curled her free hand into a fist and straightened until her spine cracked. Reaching deep, she dredged the bottom of her soul, looking for anger. Shame surfaced instead.

She wanted to be furious. She really did. But fury was a difficult animal. A disobedient wretch that never came when called. Pain, though—pain was a different story. Predictable, trustworthy, it always arrived without the barest whisper of warning. Now she throbbed with it, the pressure in her chest so heavy she struggled to draw a full breath.

She cleared her throat. "I don't want anything from you."

"The decision is not yours to make."

"I won't wear them."

"You will," he said, his quiet tone so chilly goose bumps erupted on Afina's skin. His eyes followed suit, freezing her in place until she swore frost gathered between her shoulder blades. "Or I will put them on you myself...and enjoy the doing."

Afina clenched her teeth to keep them from chattering and looked away, unable to handle the directness of his gaze. Shelves stacked high with rolls of wool and folded linen, the ones she found so beautiful, blurred. She swallowed. Hadn't she promised not to do this? Hadn't she told herself he wasn't worth her sorrow? Hah. Barely an hour later, and she was already breaking her word. Pitiful.

"Afina."

The hard thread in his voice was as good as any threat. Like a knife wielded by an expert hand, it cut deep, warning if she didn't obey he'd make her sorry. She understood the underlying message, but refused to listen, even though it meant getting sliced again. Yes, it might sting, but she'd live. If she looked at him now, something told her she wouldn't survive. The cold was too intense. Her heart would suffer, freeze into a solid block inside her chest and stop beating.

He sighed, exasperation and more expelled on a single rush of air. "We head into the mountains on the morrow. Both you and Sabine will need the added warmth to survive the cool nights and bitter winds. The new gowns will provide that, along with a thick cloak and good boots."

The wretch.

With the ease of a smooth-tongued swindler, he tossed Sabine into the mix. He hacked at her pride, scraping her raw with the fact she couldn't provide her daughter the basic necessities. Afina's stomach cramped, guilt rolling like thunder in her belly. How could she refute him? He was right. She was a terrible mother, unable to give what her baby needed to stay safe and warm.

"One gown each," she said, agreeing under duress and a cart-load of self-reproach. But pride wouldn't let her leave it at that. "But I'll pay you back."

"With what?"

Heat hit her cheeks then washed up until the tips of her ears burned. "I-I'll—"

"Forget I said that." One hand clenched into a fist, he ran the other through his hair. "Consider it an advancement."

"An advancement?" Shaking her head, Afina blinked away the threat of tears. "I d-don't understand."

"You are my healer, Afina," he said. "There are many in my home that will require your skills. As your master, it is my duty to provide for you."

Her master. Right.

She held no more importance to him beyond that. Naught more than an underling. A bit of rot to be scraped off the bottom of his boot and forgotten just as fast. Self-preservation told her to remember that fact. But pride wanted her to shout a denial. Afina settled for ignoring both and, cradling Sabine, moved closer to the fire. Mayhap if she got close enough, the frozen lump burning its way up her throat would melt and give her ease.

"My lord."

The softly spoken address brought Afina's head up. *My lord?*

Spinning on her heels, Afina turned toward the other side of the room. A woman stood in an open doorway, her focus on Xavian, warm welcome on her face. She stared, unable to help herself. Afina had never seen anything like her. Not only had the woman called Xavian *my lord*, but she was brown from head to toe. Brown eyes, brown hair, and the most beautiful dark brown skin Afina had ever seen.

But worse? She was beautiful, a vision in green silk.

"Sherene," Xavian said, honey in his tone. His lips tipped up at the corners, his eyes traveled, moving over the woman with approval, and something more. Afina swallowed, recognizing the mix of emotion—admiration and affection. Unlike her, he respected Sherene. "'Tis good to see you."

The dark beauty smiled and, in a quiet voice, asked, "How fare you, my lord?"

"Well enough. And Dharr?"

"A mischief maker. Always up to no good." Sherene laughed, the tinkling sound a warm gift before her chin dipped and humor faded. A soft veil clouding her features, she bowed low. "Thank you once more, my lord, for his safe return."

"You need not thank me, Sherene."

"I must," she said, disagreement in her wide, expressive eyes. "I do not know what I would have done if...if..."

" 'Tis over, and he is safe." Xavian shifted as though uncomfortable with the topic.

Afina's instincts went on high alert.

What were they talking about? Something important... monumental, in fact, if Sherene's anxious expression was anything to go on. Her gaze bounced between the two as Afina ran through the possibilities, formulating questions and building theories. Each of them came to the same conclusion. The woman was Xavian's lover. She had to be. The subtle connection permeated the air like a fragrance, radiating around the chamber with such strength it knocked Afina off balance, and right into...

What exactly?

Confusion? Disappointment? Anger and disgust?

And all with herself.

She should have known. Should have been better prepared for the eventuality. Xavian wasn't celibate. He was a man with needs. Her experience with him in the stable had shown her that, so why was she surprised? Why did she feel the overwhelming urge to place herself in front of him and stake her claim?

Lunacy. Pure, unadulterated witlessness.

She held no claim on him. His reaction in the aftermath, once the pleasure had faded, told her all she needed to know. He didn't want her beyond the pleasure her body could give him. Beyond the one tryst they'd shared. But that didn't stop the craving, the soul-deep ache that wanted the affection he so easily gave to Sherene for herself.

"What brings you to my shop, my lord?"

The sultry hum in the exotic beauty's voice rubbed Afina raw, making her want to root through her healing satchel in search of her salve. Instead she stood stock-still, hoping the floor would open up and swallow her whole.

"I am in need of your talents."

Afina snorted. Hah. No doubt. Too bad she was standing between him and his lover. Otherwise she was certain he would have tossed Sherene onto the nearest table and—

Xavian cleared his throat. He raised a brow, throwing her a strange look. She glanced away, unable to look him in the eye. If she did, he might see the yearning she kept buried in her heart and believe he was the reason.

CHAPTER NINE

"I am glad he brought you to me."

Busy watching Xavian's retreat, the softly spoken comment threw Afina. The door closed with a *thunk*, leaving her inside with his lover and him out of bashing range. She glared at the wooden planks, resisting the urge to stomp her feet like a child, and tossed Sherene a look that said she was insane. Unhinged. Totally deranged. What other explanation could there be? The welcome she extended must be contrived. No woman worth her salt would accept a rival with so much warmth.

Sherene raised both hands, flipping them palms up. "Truly."

Afina's eyes narrowed.

"And before you ask," she said, lips twitching, a gleam in her dark eyes. "No, we are not."

"Not what?" Afina asked, hurling another imaginary fireball at the door. Too bad she couldn't conjure a real one. Maybe if she could, the flames would eat through the wood and singe the dolt no doubt standing guard on the other side.

"Lovers."

The admission whipped Afina's head around. She stared at Sherene, mouth wide open. "But you seemed so...Then he was, well...You're not...really?"

"Yes, really." Picking up a measuring tape from inside a metal tin, Sherene fiddled with the leather end, winding the strip around her index finger. "Although there was a time I would not have said no to Xavian, I am grateful he pushed me in Ivan's direction instead."

"Who?"

"My husband." Sherene's mouth curved up at the corners. "For almost a year now."

"Oh. I...Forgive me," Afina said, combating the heat in her face.

"It is nothing." Sherene waved her hand, brushing the apology along with her awkwardness aside. "It is good you feel as you do. Your possessiveness shows you have spirit. A necessary thing when dealing with bullheaded men. No?"

Spirit...as in courage? No, not really.

Bianca had been the one with cartloads of courage, leading the way, making all the difficult decisions. A little like Sherene in some ways. Afina chewed the inside of her lip, wishing she'd inherited some of those traits. Then again, boldness had never been an option with her mother, and dreaming didn't make things so.

"Truthfully," she said, feeling as much a toadstool next to Sherene as she had with her sister, "I haven't the first idea about men or how to deal with them."

"You will learn, as I did." Her head tilted, the seamstress stopped in front of Afina. A soft expression on her face, she reached out and brushed golden strands from Sabine's brow. Afina's daughter sighed and put her thumb back to work, and Sherene smiled. "She is beautiful, your little one."

With a murmured "thank you," Afina kissed the top of her cherub's head. Silence stretched and time expanded as she stood with Sherene. Unmoving. Content in the moment to watch her daughter fall into slumber as the fire cracked and a plan formed.

A good one, and with Xavian gone? Out of sight. Out of earshot. Out of mind.

Now presented the best chance for escape.

Nodding to the seamstress, Afina skirted a pile of linen and headed for the nearest shelf. Implements of all kinds lay scattered on the wooden surface: wood and metal, round and straight, short and long, sharp and dull. There seemed an unending supply, but what held her attention most were thin strips of trim on the shelf below them. If she could manage to—

"Mistress?"

Afina glanced over her shoulder, half turning toward the door. A dark-haired girl stood on the threshold, a wooden platter in her hands. The scent of honeyed biscuits and apples drifted into the chamber, pulling her gaze to the pitcher and two glasses sitting on the tray. Sweet cider. Thank the goddess. It was just want she needed, even better than what she'd planned.

"Ah, Basima. Good," Sherene said, waving the girl into the chamber, toward the work surface in the center of the room. "You may place our refreshment on the table and go. I will not require your aid with Lady Afina."

Lady?

Afina almost sighed. The title sounded so good with her name. A little taste of respect and home; one that had been denied her for two very long years. But she couldn't allow the assumption to go uncontested. Part of her disguise required she pass as a commoner. Having everyone believe she held no importance above her healing skills kept Vladimir from picking up her scent. But Xavian knew. Somehow he knew the swine hunted her—his demand that she tell him why while they had argued in the dell made that all too clear.

She frowned at the coiled measuring tapes. How did he know the bastard was after her? Had Vladimir's frustration boiled over, causing him to make her disappearance public knowledge?

She examined the possibility then discarded the idea. News traveled fast, and the fact Transylvania's new high priestess was not where she needed to be would have started the gossip hounds howling and a widespread search. With merchants and laymen moving from village to village, word would have reached her by now...forewarned her of the increased threat.

No such warning had come.

Not a murmur from her enemy, even though Afina knew he still searched for her. The swine would never give up. He couldn't claim the throne or the Transylvanian coffers without her.

So the bigger question became...what was Xavian's objective?

Afina played with a thimble, scraping her nail against its stippled edge as she examined all the facts. The puzzle pieces slowly came together, and with a curse, she tossed the trinket onto the shelf. Xavian knew because he was involved. Had somehow gained inside information. The kind that could only come from Vladimir.

By the goddess, she was an imbecile. How could she have missed that?

Distraction was no excuse, exhaustion less so. No matter how tired of running, she should never have stayed so long in Severin. Foolish and weak, and a whole host of other—

"My lady?"

"Do not call me that, Sherene," she said, her voice so low she barely recognized it. On a slow spin, Afina turned into the room, determined to throw the woman off her trail. "I am no lady."

"You are." Sherene's gaze narrowed while speculation played across her face. "I am accustomed to dealing with the wealthy and titled. Though you may not look it, I know you belong in that circle. It is in the way you hold yourself…in your manner and speech."

"You are mistaken. I but mimic my betters, no more."

"You will need to do better than that if you wish to fool me— or Xavian, for that matter." The seamstress shook her head, her voice even as though she instructed a child. "He does not tolerate lies. But I suspect you are already aware of his fondness for honesty."

Right. *Honesty.* Afina curled her hand into a fist. Xavian… the dishonest cheat. And he had the gall to call her a liar? "He lies as much as any."

"Now you are the one mistaken, *fetita.* I know him," Sherene said, her quiet tone undercut with steel and just as sharp as she called Afina *little girl.* "Like my Ivan, he has endured much for very little in return. Too many lies, too much death. Truth is the only thing his kind trusts. Give him that, and his loyalty has no end. If you do not? He will cut you to the quick and leave you where you lie."

His kind. What did that mean? And why did she care?

She shouldn't, but Afina wanted to ask anyway. To delve into why Sherene spoke as though her husband and Xavian were a breed apart, a dangerous one. But anger stopped her. She didn't want to know any more about him or *his kind.* She knew all she needed to. The lying, two-faced jackal was in league with her enemy. He held her life in the balance, playing cat to her mouse.

And goddess keep her. She'd slept with him. Made love to him while the entire time he intended to do her harm. Her stomach rolled, wanting to heave. She swallowed the burn and turned her attention back to Sherene. The sooner they finished, the sooner she could flee. Time wasn't on her side. Xavian wouldn't stay outside long, and she refused to be anywhere near Sherene and her shop when he came to collect her.

"Do you need to measure me?"

"Only for length." Sherene's dark eyes narrowed on her face.

Afina wiped her expression clean, refusing to give away her plan. Or the advantage. No matter how nice, Sherene wasn't her ally. The moment the seamstress guessed her intent, she'd run straight to Xavian.

Loosening the strap at her shoulder, Afina asked, "Where may I put Sabine?"

"There." A frown puckering her brow, Sherene searched Afina's face as she pointed to a pile of linen beside the hearth. "She will be safe enough while I see to your fitting. I have ones ready made that should suit."

Afina nodded, grateful for Sherene's efficiency and, flipping the sling's strap over her head, set Sabine down gently on the makeshift bed. As she arranged the dark wool around her daughter she tamped down her guilt. What she planned wasn't wrong. Unkind, mayhap, but not wrong. Sherene didn't deserve it, but Xavian did. He'd taken her against her will—scared her half to death in her own home—for the bastard who stalked her. No doubt for a wagonload of coin.

The fact she intended to take the warm clothes and run before he came back didn't qualify as dishonest. It was simply fair play. Well earned, and not half of what he deserved.

Straightening away from Sabine, she moved toward the refreshments as Sherene flipped open the lid of a large trunk in the far corner of the chamber. As the seamstress rooted through the contents, Afina palmed a small vial from her healing satchel before lifting it over her head. She propped the leather bag against the table leg, sent a silent prayer heavenward, and asked, "May I pour you some cider, mistress?"

"Yes, please do." Head half buried in the trunk, Sherene's elbows bobbed as she dug, tossing fabric hither and yon. "We will partake before I fit you."

Thank the goddess. Had Sherene refused she didn't know what she would have…Well, it didn't bear thinking about.

A slight tremor in her hands, Afina poured two cups of sweet cider and threw a quick glance in Sherene's direction. Still elbow deep in the trunk, the seamstress mumbled, eliminating one gown after another, giving Afina time to wiggle the vial's stopper free. Her conscience reared its ugly head. She shoved it back down. The seriousness of the circumstance dictated the path. Sabine needed her to be strong. Bianca, bless her soul, was counting on her, along with the Transylvanian people.

'Twas life or death, more than just hers.

With a "dear goddess, forgive me," she flicked her wrist and upended the entire contents into Sherene's cup. The clear elixir made a plunking sound. Afina froze, waiting for Sherene to catch on, accuse her, and call for Xavian. When nothing but muttering came from that side of the chamber, she released a slow breath and swirled the amber liquid in the mug. The cider circled, playing at the rim while a whirlpool sucked at its center. After a few rotations, when she was sure the stirring masked the tonic's taste, she put the tainted cup down to pick up her own.

"Ah-ha. This one will do well with your coloring." Sherene nodded as though satisfied, tossing a butter yellow chemise over one arm followed by a dark amber gown. Over the other, she carried a smaller set, both the deepest hue of indigo. "And these we will put on your little one. They should fit without any altering."

Drawn to the sensual color Sherene had chosen for her, Afina's fingers curled, wanting to touch the fabric and see if it was as soft as it looked. Bolder than anything she'd ever worn, the weave simmered in the low light, as though gold threads had been woven into the wool. She bit the inside of her cheek. It wasn't fair. She planned to drug and leave the woman senseless, and what was Sherene's most pressing concern? That the gown's color complemented Afina.

Guilt hit her like a closed fist. She fidgeted, detesting the feeling as the woman hauled out two sets of boots with matching mantles. Both fur-lined. For pity's sake, how much worse could it get? Not that she didn't want the boots. The added warmth would serve them well over the coming months; protect them against the snow and bitter cold. But how could she do what needed to be done in the face of Sherene's generosity?

Afina almost changed her mind, feigned clumsiness, and tipped the drugged cider over. She wanted to, but in the end, self-preservation forced her to toast the seamstress's choice.

"It is a beautiful color. Thank you."

A pleased gleam in her eyes, Sherene accepted the cider. As custom held, she clinked her cup to Afina's then drank. Relief mingled with regret, and Afina berated herself as she drained her own mug. When both cups stood empty, she unlaced the frayed ties of her gown, inviting Sherene without words to begin the fitting. The faster she got into the new gown, the better. With the tonic flowing through her veins, it wouldn't take long for Sherene to feel sleepy and then succumb to the drug altogether.

The soft chemise and amber gown settled against her like a caress, reminding her once more of home and the family that no longer lived there. Her mother, sister, and brother were all gone. Dead and buried, each one taken from her too early by unjust cause. Now all the memories lay tarnished along with her integrity.

As Afina laced up the fur-lined boots, Sherene swayed, forcing her to face how very low she had sunk. Reduced to drugging an innocent woman. She wanted to cry, to scream at the heavens, chasten the Gods for the unfairness of it all.

Instead she cupped Sherene's shoulders and, with a kind touch, coaxed her into the cushioned armchair near the hearth. Her chest tight, she brushed the dark hair from the exotic beauty's face and whispered, "I am sorry. Someday I pray you'll find it in your heart to forgive me."

Her brows furrowed, Sherene murmured. Her eyelashes flickered once and then a second time before she succumbed and sank deep into the world of dreams.

Turning away, Afina gathered the small bundle meant for Sabine. With quick hands, she dressed her sleeping child, making certain not to disturb her slumber, then buckled on the new fur-lined mantle. The sling with Sabine settled on her shoulders, she crossed the chamber. Her heart heavy, Afina slipped through the door opposite the one she knew Xavian guarded.

All without a backward glance.

In the alley between Sherene's and a kilim shop, where shadows grew thickest, Xavian settled in to wait. His twin blades scraped uneven stone as he shifted, rechecking his sight lines. From his vantage point, he had an unobstructed view of both doors, the ones through which Afina would attempt to escape.

She was an easy read, her anger an excellent impetus. Right now she possessed enough to burn Ismal to the ground. But then, he did too. 'Twas a volatile mixture, his fury combined with hers. An unsafe one, and he needed to calm himself before dealing with her again.

If he didn't, she wouldn't like the outcome. And neither would he.

Taking a cleansing breath, Xavian filled his lungs to capacity. He counted to seven before releasing the air slowly on a measured exhalation. Hidden away in his niche, he repeated the process again and again, willing his muscles and mind to ease.

Just as he evened into some semblance of peace, he caught movement out of the corner of his eye.

Afina.

He shook his head, unable to stop his lips from curving. Such a bold lass; courageous with spirit to spare. Fortunately for him—and, however, unfortunate for her—that boldness came with a healthy dose of predictability.

Perched in the doorway's deep alcove, she paused to check both ends of the alley, and his admiration spiked. Bold and smart. 'Twas a deadly enough combination. But add those traits to her beauty and the most fetching gown he'd ever seen, and well, a man could find himself in a serious amount of trouble. The trouble became painfully obvious when, oblivious to his will, his body reacted, hardening for the wild claiming it wanted to deliver. Xavian ignored the call and shifted when she did, moving from dense shadow into shades of grey as she skirted a pile of debris and made for the other end of the alleyway.

Attuned to her tension, he followed at a distance, making certain to stay out of sight. He still planned to let her run for a while. Mayhap as far as the market's edge before he brought her back. No matter how hot his anger, he refused to let her go. His reasons remained the same. The fact he'd violated his oath and slept with her changed little. Vladimir was after her, and the mystery of why still stoked his interest. Add to that he needed a healer, and all the rationale he required fell neatly into place.

Crouched behind the wooden slats of a lean-to, he paused when she rounded the corner of the building and stopped. Frozen in place, she stood stone still, and although he couldn't see her face, he felt her fear.

What the hell? Had the busyness of the marketplace startled her?

No sooner had the question entered his mind than the fine hairs on the back of his neck lifted. He spotted the merchant a moment later. Dressed in the same purple tunic, the slaver backed her away from the street and into the alley.

Rahat. He should have finished the bastard when he'd had the chance.

Xavian unsheathed the blades on his back in twin arcs of movement. The steel cleared his scabbards, the scathing sound aggressive and sure. Just as the custom hilts settled like home in his hands, four men stepped into the mouth of the alley behind him. Two more stepped around the flesh peddler toward Afina.

A raw sound escaped her throat.

He secured his grip, preparing for the attack. "Afina. Get back to the shop."

Wide-eyed, she swung his way and hesitated, uncertainty on her face. Xavian's eyes narrowed. Jesu, that look. 'Twas as though she was as much afraid of him as the bastards slithering toward her. What had Sherene told her?

With no time to wonder, Xavian barked, "Afina, move."

The harshness of his tone made her flinch and got her feet moving. But it was too late. The vermin closed ranks, grabbed hold, and shoved her in the direction of the slave merchant.

Cut off from her, Xavian drilled the slaver with a glare. "Take her, and you die."

The warning drifted, held high by the promise of violence. The flesh peddler stilled. His hand hovered a breath away from Afina. The merchant eyed him, measuring his skill before he smirked, reached out, and grabbed her upper arm.

Teeth bared, she rounded on the slaver. Shielding Sabine with her body, Afina fisted her hand and swung at his head. Bigger and stronger, the merchant shackled her wrist.

"Xavian!"

Her terror ringing in his ears, Xavian snarled at the six circling him. Rage bled through his pores, lathering his skin as the slaver dragged Afina from his sight and the safety he provided.

With a howl, he unleashed violence and consummate skill. Blades flashing, he painted the alleyway with their blood, fear for Afina in each arc and slice of steel. If the slaver hurt one hair on her head...left so much as a mark on her soft skin...

Damn the bastard to hell.

He would carve the swine's heart out with a spoon. Pop his eyes from their sockets. Make the bastard scream for touching her...for daring to take what belonged to him.

The lad sat on a crate beside the stable doors, a curved blade in his hands. The motion he used to sharpen it was natural and smooth, but the knife didn't belong to him. The telltale steel of the Al Pacii dagger was too long for his hands, the hilt too thick. Were he a betting man, Henrik would wager Ram's initials sat near the base of the blade, carved with care by Henrik's own hand.

The dagger had been the first—and last—gift he'd ever given.

He'd thought Ram worthy of it at the time. Hell, mayhap he still was, but none of that mattered anymore.

Crouched in shadow across from the stable, he watched the dark-skinned boy, trying to decide. Was the lad worth the trouble? How much had Ram told him? Very little, no doubt. 'Twas safer that way. Ignorance made him less of a target.

Ram knew it, and so did Henrik. It was the way of their kind: keep the details hidden until no other choice existed but to share them. The lack of trust worked well—both insulating them from potential threat and protecting those around them.

Henrik slid from the shadows and turned to go. Questioning the boy would do naught but waste time. Something he couldn't afford if he wanted to catch Ram. The realization—along with relief—settled deep. He didn't like hurting children. 'Twas a flaw he couldn't help. The one time he'd been forced to...

He swallowed. The memory of the lass's face, of the pain in her eyes, burned like a hot iron in the back of his mind.

With a curse, Henrik swept the image aside. Naught but pain would come from revisiting the past, and today he didn't need the distraction. Ismal seethed around him; a virulent cesspool of humanity.

Ignoring the noxious smell, he wove a trail around oxen and carts, vendors and fortunetelling Gypsies, darks eyes lined with kohl, lips with red paint. Women called to him, offering their bodies for free, and the men looked away, fearing his attention. 'Twas always this way: fear and attraction a tedious mix that left a bad taste in his mouth.

Henrik quickened his pace, wanting out of the crowded marketplace. He cursed Ram for bringing him here. What was he doing in Ismal? How the hell could his former friend stand it?

The scent of human waste and garbage, the hard press of bodies and noise made Henrik's head pound and his stomach turn.

Holding his breath, he passed in front of a tanner-cum-butcher's shop and turned down a narrow alley. At its mouth, he pressed his back to the wooden wall, palm on his dagger, and scanned the open area. Circular in shape, the Ring boasted the more expensive shops on its edge and an auction for livestock in its center. At one end, street performers dazzled a thinning crowd as daylight faded into dusk.

Excellent. Enough of a crowd left to point him in the right direction with few people sober enough to remember his presence.

A few well-placed questions led him to a tailor's shop. He studied the bright blue door from across the square then crossed the Ring toward the yellow awning perched atop it. A light breeze ruffled its tasseled edge as he passed beneath, continuing on to the alleyway. With a quick glance over his shoulder, he slid across into the narrow opening. Shadows closed in, the damp darkness a welcome reprieve from the toss and swell of the marketplace.

An instant later, he was through the side entrance, twin daggers drawn, feet soundless on the flagstone floor. He heard a man talking, tone soft with a hint of worry. Henrik followed the voice. Was Ram still here? Was he that foolish? Had the woman caused his comrade to make a mistake?

His heart picked up a beat then another, eager anticipation in each thump. He came through the doorway with seamless aggression, mind and body ready to strike. Bent over a chair by the hearth, a man murmured, hands stroking a woman's hair as though trying to rouse her.

"What the hell, Ivan?" The tips of his knives dipped as Henrik dropped his guard.

Jet black eyes lifted away from the woman. Ivan scowled at him. "Henrik."

"Where is he?"

With skilled precision, Ivan shifted to protect the unconscious woman, placing himself in front of her. "Not here."

"You lie."

"Mayhap," Ivan said as he shrugged, beefy hands at the ready. "Care to test it?"

Henrik sheathed both blades. "Shit."

The curse was all the warning he gave Ivan. His former comrade didn't need much more. With stunning speed, he blocked Henrik's first thrust then parried, slamming his fist into his gut. The blow lifted Henrik an inch off the floor. Years of training took hold and he countered, launching an assault that cracked Ivan's ribs. Next he blooded his comrade's nose, loosening a few of his teeth in the process.

Spitting blood, Ivan spun low, making one last attempt to bring him down. Aggression and a lifetime of fury let loose, and Henrik hammered him in the temple. Ivan reeled. Without mercy, Henrik circled in behind and delivered a blow to the small of his comrade's back. The instant Ivan hit his knees, he locked him in a chokehold. Henrik twisted, the need to snap the assassin's neck almost too difficult to resist.

"Where?"

"Fuck you."

Henrik tightened his hold, cutting off Ivan's air supply a little at a time.

A moment before he snapped his neck, Ivan rasped, "Don't hurt her."

Henrik closed his eyes. Christ, he was about to die and all Ivan could think about was the dark-haired woman in the chair?

What the hell was wrong with him? Such selfless loyalty didn't belong in an assassin. 'Twas a weakness that would make Halál rage and reach for his knives.

Ivan whispered the entreaty again.

Henrik's grip loosened.

He couldn't do it. After escaping the hell of Grey Keep, Ivan had found happiness, a rarity among their kind. He couldn't take it from him on a whim. Goddamn, he held no quarrel with the man—connection to Ram aside—and Ivan didn't deserve to die for that.

With a silent curse, he changed his hand position, adjusting the pressure on the side of Ivan's neck. The big bastard went boneless, losing consciousness between one heartbeat and the next. Henrik shook his head. There was something wrong with him. A year ago he would have killed Ivan and not felt a thing. Now he couldn't seem to stop *feeling*. The excess emotion bothered the hell out of him. He should be able to control it, bend it to his will, but—

Glass shattered, spilling across the floor from the open doorway.

He shifted, positioning Ivan's body between him and the door then glared at the intruder from beneath his brows. A lass stood frozen on the threshold, a tray and broken crockery at her feet, dark eyes so round they nearly swallowed her small face. She twitched, feet shuffling on flagstone, ready to flee like a doe that had just scented a wolf.

"Don't run." He lowered Ivan to the floor. "You will not enjoy my reaction."

A tremor racked her slight frame, working its way up until her bottom lip quivered.

He took pity. "My quarrel is not with you, lass."

Her gaze slid to Ivan.

Henrik stepped over him, blocking the sprawl of his comrade's body, and moved toward the girl. Her shaking became so violent he heard her teeth chatter as he stopped in front of her. She shrank from him, trying to make herself small. With a fingertip, he tipped her chin up, conveying his intent with a gentle touch.

"Answer my questions and I will leave you in peace," he said, making sure to keep his voice soft. "I have no wish to harm you."

She took a stuttered breath, chin wobbling against his hand, and nodded.

"What is your name?"

"B-basim-ma," she said, the name barely audible.

"Ivan is not dead, Basima. Give him time, and he will rouse." Air puffed between her lips, and her tension eased, though not enough to bring her any true comfort. He dropped his hand from her face. "Xavian Ramir…he was here, aye?"

"He followed the woman into the alley."

Henrik raised a brow.

"The dark-haired one." She bit her bottom lip, no doubt uncertain she should continue.

"'Tis all right." He shifted, creating more distance between them. He didn't need to threaten her with his size any longer. She'd submitted; now was the time to reassure. 'Twas the only way he'd get the information he sought without breaking his word…without hurting her. "You can tell me, lass."

"She went out the side door…away from…my lord X-Xavian," she said, then paused.

My lord. So the rumors were true. Lucky bastard. Ram owned land and had a new home. "And?"

"The others came…the ones that work for the man in purple. A slaver, some say." She met his eyes then shied, shuffling sideways. "T-there was a fight and…they took her."

"The slave merchant?"

Basima nodded, the movement jerky. "Lord Xavian, he…he k-killed them all. The ones who tried to s-stop him and…w-went after her."

"Ivan cleaned it up?"

"He h-hid the bodies."

"Many thanks, Basima," he said and turned to leave.

Something stopped him halfway down the narrow corridor. He glanced over his shoulder. She stood statue-still, no doubt afraid to move…afraid the slightest noise would bring him back. Vise-like pressure banded around his chest. Without thinking, he reached into the pouch at his waist. Coming away with a coin, he flipped the gold in her direction and was out the door before it hit the floor between her feet.

CHAPTER TEN

It was getting cold. So very cold. And no matter how fast Afina rubbed her arms and back, Sabine continued to shiver. Wrapped in the fur-lined mantle, she cuddled her daughter closer, lending as much body heat as she could, and peered through the metal bars. The setting sun bobbed, its rhythm following the jump and sway of the wagon that held them captive.

Or rather, the lion's cage.

That's what the man in purple had called it. He'd laughed, calling her his new lioness as he'd shoved her through the jaws of wood and iron and slammed the door shut behind her. The hinges had screeched, the high-pitched scream almost as bad as the click of the padlock. Afina shivered, her gaze on the forest and the deepening shadows on either side of the road.

They would stop to make camp soon. The men were talking. She could hear the creak of leather as they shifted in their saddles, complaining of stiff limbs and sore arses.

So much for escape. True to form, her attempt had only made things worse.

Even Xavian and his plan to hand her over to Vladimir was better than this. At least with him, she held some hope of surviving. The swine needed her alive, after all. These men, the ones surrounding her like a steel trap, didn't care whether she lived to see Constantinople. It was a long journey; a boring one filled with an endless supply of women to replace her if she didn't live long enough to stand on the auction block.

Slavers. She understood that now.

Twenty strong, they were nothing but a bunch of thugs. A band ruled by the bastard who'd dragged her out of the alleyway. Away from Xavian.

Afina tightened her arms around Sabine. Was he dead? Lying in the dirt with his throat slashed or a sword through his belly? The thought made her stomach roll. No matter his intensions, she didn't want…couldn't imagine…

He couldn't be dead. He was too vibrant a man—too strong—to be cut down.

Her knuckles went white against the brown edges of her cloak. If he'd been killed, it was her fault. Had she stayed with Sherene…had she just—

By the goddess. No matter how much she wanted to she couldn't go back. It was done. Over. And regret was now starting to elbow shock out of the way. It sank deep, like thorny barbs, razor-sharp tips tearing at her.

Afina closed her eyes and pictured Xavian. Twin swords raised, muscled arms flexing, he stood strong, eyes flashing. Yes, she would remember him like that. Hold onto that image like a candle in the dark. She needed it, to soothe her heart as the guilt ate her alive.

The wagon rocked from side to side, bumping over a deep rut in the road. She opened her eyes. Unwelcome ones trapped her own, the leer as much a threat as the daggers Xavian carried. She recoiled, hugging Sabine closer. The thug smiled, yellow teeth flashing from where he rode alongside her prison. Her stomach revolted, but Afina swallowed the burn. The moment she showed fear, he won.

Tucking her lips inside the folds of her clock to hide her chin wobble, she met his gaze. One corner of his mouth curved up. His unkempt beard bristled as his gaze swept her, cruel intent sifting through his dark eyes.

"I'm going to make you scream." He smirked then glanced at the darkening sky. "Soon, pussycat. Very soon."

Afina swallowed, tasting bile, and watched him spur his mount to the front of the procession.

"They'll each take a turn, you know."

The raspy voice brought Afina's head around. Her attention landed on the other captive. The one she'd been trying to talk to since the cage door slammed shut behind her. Little more than a scruffy ball in the back corner, the woman rocked—back and forth—one bruised shoulder peeking between the broken threads of her dirty gown.

Afina longed for her healing satchel. She had salve that would soothe the girl's wounds and tonic that would ease her pain. The agony was no doubt the reason she rocked, trying to comfort herself the only way she knew how. But her bag was gone, taken by the thugs who would rape them both the instant they stopped for the night.

Her mind shied away from the thought, but her body understood and her muscles tightened, preparing for flight. But escape wasn't an option. Not while locked inside the cage. Even if she managed to break free, she couldn't run without her satchel. No matter how much she hated it, she couldn't leave the amulet behind. The stupid thing was her birthright, the only leverage she held to keep herself and the people of Transylvania safe.

As though in answer, the amulet pulsed like a heartbeat. The throb slid across the nape of her neck: searching, stroking, soothing. Afina stilled and stared at the wooden wall at the front of the wagon. She knew the amulet lay just beyond, probably nestled under the bench seat beneath the driver. But how did she know that? She'd never felt it before—not even when she'd touched the dratted thing.

So what was happening? Was she so distressed her brain played tricks on her, imagining things that couldn't be real?

Another strange sensation rolled through her, followed by the red mist. Afina squirmed against the hard wagon bed, trying to quash the tingle working its way from fingertips to her shoulders. She flexed her hands, curling and uncurling them in her cloak. Had she been sitting in the same position too long? Were her limbs falling asleep?

It didn't feel like it, but the explanation made sense. Mayhap the cold combined with confinement had—

"If you wish to live, don't fight," the girl said, her haunted gaze darting to Afina then away again. "Just do what they want."

The tingle settled, drawing a soft circle on the small of her back. Afina sucked in a shaky breath and glanced at the ugly welts on the girl's skin. "You didn't."

The split in her bottom lip trembled. "Don't fight. They'll hurt you worse."

As if understanding the message, Sabine whimpered. The sound of distress bumped along Afina's spine. The strangle prickle spiked, hitting the base of her skull as she rubbed a gentle circle on her cherub's back. Moisture threatened in the corners of her eyes. She pushed the tears away. She must stay calm. The more afraid she became, the more terrified her daughter would become.

"How long have you been..." Afina almost said *with them*. But she knew that wasn't right. No one, least of all a woman, would be *with* this group, not by choice. "Here?"

"T-three days."

"Is there anyone who—"

"No one." Were it possible, the girl became even smaller, curling in on herself like an opossum, nose tucked to belly. "They k-killed my father to take me."

Just like they had killed Xavian.

Afina's vision blurred before she caught herself. A picture of him sprawled face down in a pool of his own blood surfaced and despair settled like a rock in the pit of her stomach. She picked up the weight and tossed it aside, grabbing for the image she'd created earlier. Twin swords, she reminded herself...*twin swords* carried by big, strong hands.

"I'm sorry."

"Not nearly as much as me," the girl said, her thread-barren voice raw with pain.

Silence settled as they waited for the day to fade into dusk. The sway and bump of the wagon, the leering threat of men, the red mist, the tingle and setting sun constant things around her, she finally said, "I am Afina."

Matching her tone, the girl whispered back, "Maiya."

Afina nodded, feeling a certain triumph at having discovered the girl's name. The sharp taste of victory faded, however, when the thugs turned off the road. As the wagon thumped down a hill toward the small dell beyond, the eerie prickle drew her tight. A scrolling list of *if onlys* raced through her mind, but it was too late.

She'd done this to herself. And no one was going to save her.

❖✣❖

The one with the beard would be the first to die. The mangy bastard had looked at Afina one too many times. Had said something as well, and although Xavian wasn't close enough to hear he knew from her reaction that it had scared her.

He didn't like her fear, but he was too angry to care much why. The why of the thing would have to wait. The how of things he had all worked out.

The slavers didn't know he followed, hunting them from a distance. No one ever did...until he struck. Then the blood flowed. Always in silence as he gave his prey no chance to scream. This time would be different. He wanted to hear them squeal like stuck pigs. To beg for their lives even as they realized no quarter would be given. Mercy wasn't in the cards. Only brutality would do; would satisfy the howl of possessiveness inside his head.

'Twas their punishment for touching her. For frightening her and the little one she protected.

The caravan veered right, heading for a copse of pale trees. His gaze left the scum riding alongside the wagon to touch Afina. Curled around Sabine, the child's blond hair barely visible beneath her cloak, she looked composed enough. But Xavian knew better. Even at a distance, he saw the strain in her expression. And she was breathing too fast. Thin clouds rushed between her lips, coming one on top of the other, frosting the cold air that descended with the gloom of twilight.

The prison cart slowed then stopped, swaying in the dimness. With the slash of his hand, he signaled to his men and dismounted. As he moved on silent feet through the underbrush, his focus shifted back to the one with the beard. The bastard unlocked the wagon door. He swung the barrier wide and crooked his finger at Afina.

Stone-cold aggression slid through his veins. The killer deep inside him—the one he kept leashed—seethed, begging for freedom. Focused on his prey, Xavian unsheathed his knives and let the monster loose.

CHAPTER ELEVEN

Iron hinges creaked as the cage door swung wide, leaving the thug framed in the open doorway. Freedom lay just beyond him, but Afina knew she would never make it to the forest. He blocked the exit too well and his companions were too many. Even if she got past him, the others would run her to ground like a fox chased by a pack of hounds.

"Get out." Bearded chin tipped down, he stared at her from beneath his brows, fingers flexing as if he couldn't wait to get his hands on her. "And leave the cub, pussycat."

Maiya moved, her crab-like shuffle painful to watch as she approached the opening. A low whimper came on each rasp of breath, and as the girl passed, she brushed the toe of Afina's foot. She drew her legs in, giving Maiya the room she needed to reach the door.

Head low, Maiya shot her a furtive glance. "D-don't."

Afina almost told her to go to the devil. Unkind, she knew, but she didn't care. All she wanted to do was fight: to lift her booted foot, slam it into the thug's bushy face, and flatten his nose. If she got lucky, she might drive the bone straight into his brain. Not that he had much of one. What little he possessed no doubt ran on one track—the one where pain and the anticipation of delivering it rode—and unfortunately for her? She was planted between the rails.

Collision inevitable.

Drawing in a shallow breath, she kissed Sabine's temple then the tip of her nose as she undid the tie holding her cloak in place. Her daughter would need the added warmth. As Afina lifted Sabine from her lap, she arranged the soft fur around her, praying it would shield her as well. She didn't want her cherub to witness...or see...

Tears burned her throat. An impatient growl came from the end of the wagon, and with quick hands, Afina tucked Sabine's blond curls behind her ears and the cloak around her wee head.

Her daughter stared at her, eyes huge in her small face. "Mama."

"Sabine, love, stay here," she said, her voice little more than a hoarse whisper. "Mama will be right back."

"Move it, woman."

Little hands grabbed at her. "Mama...no go."

"It's all right, cherub." Afina faked a smile, pulled the fur tighter around her daughter then shuffled backward toward the door. The rough wood of the wagon bed scraped her knees, but she kept her gaze steady on Sabine, trying to keep her calm. "Mama will be right back."

As soon as she reached striking distance, a large hand grabbed her upper arm and hauled her sideways through the door. She kicked against the rough frame, trying to stay clear of the metal stairs. Her left foot dragged and caught, pulling her leg straight as it slid between two stair treads. The thug yanked. Afina screamed as her knee twisted, agony driving a spike deep before it clawed her from ankle to hip.

"Mama!" Sabine's high-pitched wail scraped Afina raw. "Mama! No go...Mama!"

The slaver laughed. "Told you I'd make you scream."

Holding onto the back of her calf with one hand, Afina shoved at the thug with the other. He grabbed a handful of hair and, bending her sideways, bashed her head against the side of the wagon. Stars exploded before the twinkling turned and black spots swam in her vision.

"Bastard!"

Blood seeped from her temple then oozed across her cheekbone. He sneered and wrenched on her boot, releasing her foot from the tread's hold. Air rushed from her lungs, agony along with it as he fisted his hand in her gown and hauled her to her feet. Pulled in his wake around the end of the cage, Afina hopped on her right foot, dragging her injured one behind her.

Sabine's screaming sobs echoed in the crisp air, rebounding around the clearing.

The thug cursed.

The amulet growled, a silent protest that pounded between Afina's temples as he shoved her against the solid wood at the front of the wagon. "Make the little bitch stop."

"C-can't." Afina wheezed, fear and pain making her breaths come short and fast. "Needs me."

He grabbed her throat, squeezed, and lifted. The toe of her right boot barely touching the ground, she wrapped both hands around his wrist to loosen his hold as the air in her lungs became thinner and thinner.

"Then she'll scream, but you do exactly what I want or..." He trailed off and pressed her harder against the wood at her back. He leaned in, foul breath tracing her mouth before he glanced to his left. "Your cub gets cut. Right, Bruno?"

Afina turned her head, straining against the grip on her throat. A dark man, just as scruffy as the brute holding her, stood with a dagger in his hand. He tested the tip for sharpness then ran the blade along the bars. Metal grazed metal, the soft clink as ominous as her daughter's wails mere feet from where Bruno stood.

"Right," Bruno said, his eyes cold as he stared at Sabine.

Afina closed her own. The canny bastard. With a few well-placed words, he'd stripped her of the right to fight. No matter how much she wanted to, she couldn't. Not now. She wouldn't risk Sabine. She could endure anything—*anything*—as long as her daughter remained untouched.

He shook her, thumping her head against wood. "Whatever I want, pussycat."

Bile threatened her throat. "W-whatever you w-want."

"Good." A smile beneath the beard, he dropped his hand from her throat to grab her breast. As his fingers bit into her flesh, Afina turned her face away. He chuckled, tightened his already fierce grip and fisted his free hand in her skirt, thigh level. Cool air hit her calves as he raised the wool. "Let's see what treasures lie beneath. Time for the first ride, pussycat."

She clenched her teeth, trying to keep them from chattering as she retreated—mind, body and soul—to a time and place she felt safe. Xavian's face surfaced. She swam toward it, needing him and his steady strength to see her through. To help her block out Sabine: the relentless wailing, the horror of the foul-smelling thug, and the reality of what was about to happen.

Something warm splashed across her cheek.

Her captor's grip went lax. Afina opened her eyes and looked into his dark ones. Surprise drained from his gaze until nothing but emptiness remained, and he listed sideways. Her attention jumped to his neck. The tip of a black dagger protruded from one side of his throat, the hilt flush against skin on the other. As the thug went down, he took her with him, but not before she saw

Xavian across the clearing, a knife in one hand, nothing in the other.

❀✛❀

Xavian pinwheeled, unsheathing his twin swords midspin. The failing light glinted off the blades, forewarning, challenging, inciting those closing ranks to come closer. The first swing struck full force. Teeth rattled and blood splattered, painting the turf crimson as the slaver's head hit the ground. He barely noticed, too intent on reaching Afina. She'd gone down, pulled sideways by the bastard as he fell.

Jesu, she wasn't moving. He couldn't see her moving.

Sabine's screams throbbed through the clearing. Like a winch pulling cable, each wail drew him tighter, and control became a distant memory. Teeth bared, he whirled and sliced, cleaving flesh from bone, delivering death with each blow. Men dropped at his feet. He stepped over them, sweat trickling between his shoulder blades, single-minded focus on Afina and Sabine.

The little one stopped howling.

The silence pressed against Xavian's breastbone, boring deep as the clang of steel and gasps of dying men filled the void. Christ, was the baby—

He sidestepped, moving left to avoid an enemy's blade. With a thrust, he pierced the bastard's heart and looked toward the wagon.

Empty. Naught but the crumpled shell of the cloak sat on the wagon bed.

Xavian's heart stopped inside his chest. *Rahat.* Where the—

"Got her!" Andrei's voice rose above the clash of swords and curse of men.

The shout accompanied a whirl of movement from the other side of the cart. One arm around Sabine, Andrei tucked her tight against his hip. She pressed her wee face into his shoulder as he shifted to shield her from attack. Two slavers closed in, trying to pin him against the side of the wagon. Xavian saw a blur of black and a flash of steel. One man jerked, face gone blank as Andrei spun left. With a flick of his blade, he decapitated the second man before the first hit the ground.

He met Andrei's gaze through a gap in the metal bars. "Go!"

Andrei pivoted, holding Sabine, and ran for the horses concealed in the woods.

Xavian watched his retreat then swung right to engage the three poised to strike. Cristobal mirrored him, settling into a fight triangle that was one man short. Trained in the same unit, they caught the other's rhythm, each swing timed with precision and edged by grace. The smell of blood and urine in the air, men screamed and fell, littering the path as Xavian cut his way toward Afina.

Halfway to his target, the bearded bastard moved. Xavian clenched his teeth, praying that the slaver was dead. Logic told him he was—that his dagger had flown straight and true—but he couldn't shake the feeling that it hadn't. What if he'd missed... been an inch off target? A man could live with a spike through his neck, at least for a while.

What if the bastard had his hands wrapped around Afina's throat?

Rahat. Let her be alive.

He fought harder. Spun with dizzying speed. Taking enemy heads and limbs without mercy or regret. He needed to reach her—had given his word to protect her, and he would keep it, even if it killed him.

CHAPTER TWELVE

Sabine was screaming; a terror-filled wail that left tiny pieces of Afina's heart scattered inside her rib cage. The shards jabbed, sharp edges digging into flesh until all she wanted to do was give agony a voice and scream herself. She planted her hands and pushed instead, fingers tearing at the tunic of the bastard bleeding all over her.

The goddess help her, she needed to get out from under him. Bruno had a knife. He was hurting her cherub and she couldn't get free to stop him.

"Please, help me." The prayer was more sob than plea. Twisting her hands in the linen at the dead man shoulders, she closed her eyes, reaching deep to find a faith long forgotten. "Great goddess of the moon, of shadow and light, hear me now. Help me."

The amulet pulsed, sending shockwaves arcing before it started to sing. The trill tripped into sorrowfulness as though adding its appeal to Afina's, and heat pooled in her fingertips.

Afina shoved again. The corpse rolled, spinning with astonishing speed in the opposite direction. She stared at it a moment, surprise an empty echo in her mind.

The amulet hummed, and a voice whispered, "*Welcome, daughter.*"

She barely registered the soft words. And didn't have time to wonder. Her daughter was—

Sabine stopped screaming.

The silence sliced, cutting Afina wide open, shattering her ability to move. One moment ticked into another before she shook herself, fighting through fear to grab the edge of the wagon bed. She needed to make sure her baby was still there...still whole and breathing. The air felt flat, too thin to breathe as she hauled hard, pulling to her feet. Her ankle gave out, and pain shot in a blistering streak up her leg only to slam into her hipbone. She fell sideways, a strangled cry in her throat as her knee folded.

A man shouted, his voice carrying over the clash of steel. Another answered.

Through the blur, Afina recognized the voices. Andrei? Xavian? Did they have Sabine?

Dear goddess, please...please, please, please.

On her knees in the dirt, she tried to focus...to hear over the screaming horses and cursing men. A black flash brought her head around. Andrei. Sword raised, he sprinted toward the edge of the forest, a golden-haired bundle in his arms.

"Run!" The force of Afina's scream came out whisper-thin. The sounds of death and the smell of blood swallowed it whole, but she didn't care. Her baby was safe, each of Andrei's long strides taking her farther from the heart-wrenching violence.

A tear rolled over her bottom lash. Even knowing he couldn't hear her, she rasped, "Run."

"Afina!" Xavian's snarl snapped her attention left.

Twin swords flashing, he spun, severing a slaver's head with the ease of scissors on thread. Blood flew, splattering the man beside the dead one with crimson. With a bellow, the thug turned, eyes wild, retreat in the lines of his face, searching for the quickest escape. His hunted look turned to one of determination when it landed on her.

Her heart went loose inside her chest.

"*Retreat*," the strange voice said. "*Retreat to safety, child.*"

Xavian echoed the sentiment and, slashing another slaver, roared, "Move!"

Damp earth pushing between her fingers, Afina scuttled backward. Under the wagon now, she pivoted on her knees and crawled toward the opposite side. The horses reared. The cart lurched and went sideways. Old leaves hit her in the face as the wheels bit, mounding dirt against the rounded wells. The one next to her dug a trench, sliding closer as the horses bucked against the wedge locking them in place.

The beasts protested, high-pitched shrieks snaking through the air. Blood rushed in her ears and into her muscles, giving her the strength to keep moving. She was almost there. Just a little farther, and—

Someone grabbed her from behind.

She yanked on her skirt. The bastard's grip held then tugged, trying to drag her from beneath the cart. Her teeth clenched, Afina flipped onto her back, planted the heel of her uninjured foot in the ground, and kicked with the other. She bashed the back of the slaver's hand. His curse echoed her own as pain shot up from her ankle.

His arm arched, swiping at her. Musty leaves and the scent of fear all around her, Afina scurried for the other side. She could hear him behind her, felt his breath on her neck as he pursued her farther under the wagon. Panting with exertion, she whispered Xavian's name over and over to borrow his strength. She could do it, escape the man after her. Xavian was fighting his way toward her. All he needed was time…just moments more.

Rolling free of the wheels, she crawled over a dead man. She tried not to look at his wide, blank eyes, too intent on the wicked-looking hatchet in his limp hand. A weapon. She needed one, something sharp to hold the bastard slithering behind her at bay.

Concentration set on the handle, she reached, stretching hard to gain it. Just as she grasped the leather-wrapped hilt, a big hand seized her thigh. He laughed, hot breath puffing out like a call to victory. With a hiss, Afina turned, hatchet raised high, and swung, aiming for his wrist. The razor-sharp blade bit, slicing through flesh to find the bone. The slaver jerked, a horrific howl in his throat, and flailed backward.

Afina lost her grip.

The weapon went skyward. She watched it spin, head over handle, until it landed with a thud six feet away. Glancing from it to the slaver, now clutching his arm in white-faced disbelief, Afina experienced the same bewilderment. Had she done that? It didn't seem real, but the blood running from his almost-severed wrist told a different tale. No matter how much he deserved it, she couldn't...

Dear goddess. The urge to apologize, to find her satchel and tend the wound hit her full force.

Cristobal rounded the end of the wagon, the tips of both swords running red. "Afina, are you—"

A woman's scream split the air.

Afina's head whipped around so fast it nearly fell off her shoulders. Oh, no...Maiya.

A knife in each hand, the man in purple held a blade to the girl's throat. Pressing another against her abdomen, he backed them toward a roped enclosure. Horses paced inside, the scent of blood whipping them into a frenzy. The goddess preserve her, the bastard was getting away.

"*Ma rahat.*"

The curse told Afina all she needed to know. Cristobal was too far away to stop the slaver's flight. And Xavian...where the devil was he? Was he...had they—

"No," Afina said, voice soft with gathering fury. "No."

She couldn't allow it. He was the cause of it all. Had the bastard left them alone, Sabine would never have been in danger. Maiya would not have been brutalized. And Xavian wouldn't be...he wouldn't be...dead.

Red mist washed in behind her eyes. Afina glanced toward the hatchet. She needed to reach it and stop the slaver's escape. If only she could...

Her vision dimmed, narrowing on the back of his tunic.

An echo in her mind, the voice murmured, *"Concentrate, child. See it, and so it shall be."*

She painted a picture in her mind's eye. Envisioned her hand around the handle. Felt its weight and her strength as she threw it. Oh, if only she had the strength to throw it.

One moment the image was nothing more than a thought, and the next? The hatchet was flying end over end through the air. It struck with a thunk, dead center, cutting through flesh and bone to split the slaver's head in two. Blood spilled in a river, flowing down the back of his head as he fell.

The amulet chirped as though it approved.

Belly down in the dirt, Afina stared, teetering on the rim of coherence.

What was happening to her? The red mist and headaches, the swirling heat in her fingertips and strange voice...none of it made sense or felt familiar. That ill-advised moment with Xavian had fractured more than her maidenhead. It had somehow touched her soul. Now she lay broken, perched on the edge of a chasm into the unknown.

CHAPTER THIRTEEN

Afina couldn't take another moment. She was going to be sick. The motion of the horse beneath her—the blur of tree limbs and the cruel slap of frosty air—turned her inside out, sending her stomach into a freefall. She gagged and clung to the saddle horn to keep her perch.

Xavian was inhuman. How could he travel at such an unrelenting pace?

They'd been riding for over an hour: on narrow trails, up hills, around twists and turns, cutting through a forest no sane person would ever have entered. Were she brave enough, she would throw something at the back of his head, rein in, and rail at him until her throat hurt. The problem? She couldn't find the courage. Was too afraid he would yell back.

She didn't want his fury, even though she deserved it. Her escape had put them all at risk. Sabine could have been killed, along with his men, and Afina knew they would never forgive her.

Such foolishness. She hadn't gained a thing. Except mayhap Xavian's disgust.

He hated her now, couldn't wait to be rid of her. Even without him saying so, she knew what he planned. He was riding hellbent to Castle Raul, intent on dumping her in Vladimir's lap. It was the only explanation—particularly since he'd tossed her in the saddle and ordered Cristobal to take Maiya in a different direction.

Two years spent running…for what? To end up back where she started? Only this time she didn't have her sister to shield her. Bianca was dead, and how was Afina going to honor her memory? By breaking her vow and leaving Sabine to grow up without a mother's love to hold her.

Goddess forgive her, she'd failed them all.

Afina closed her eyes to hold the tears at bay. The slow swing of inevitability pulled her off balance, making her head spin and stomach churn. One hand pressed over her mouth, she swallowed the burn, determined to stay on the horse and keep what little remained of her pride. The beast had other ideas and, tossing its head, sidestepped. She lost her grip and slid in the opposite direction. The ground rose to meet her, and she landed with a bone-jarring thump.

Dead leaves and dirt flew up, surrounding her in a cloud of dust. She ignored her aches and pains, more concerned with her stomach as she crawled toward the edge of the trail. Unable to control it, she heaved, bringing up nothing but air and bile.

"*Rahat.*"

Horse's hooves pivoted then galloped back toward her. On her knees amid small bushes and damp turf, Afina threw up again. Xavian's boots touched down a few feet away. Flicking the reins over his horse's neck, he knelt, coming to his haunches at her side.

"Afina," he said, his voice sounding far away.

"Go…away."

"Nay." With gentle hands, he drew her back until she sat on one hip, both legs curled beneath her. Her ankle throbbed in time with her heart as he looped her hair around one hand and brought a flask to her mouth with the other. "Drink."

She jerked and turned her face away.

"Easy, *draga*...be easy." He released her hair to cup the nape of her neck. His fingers shifting through her hair, he stroked at her sore muscles.

Better than a soothing balm, his touch unlocked the tension. With a sigh, Afina curled into him, needing his warmth more than the water. His arms tightening around her, he murmured and tucked her head beneath his chin. The red mist receded, sweeping aside the jumbled mess inside her head along with the nausea.

"Apologies, love. Had I realized how bad—"

"My fault...not yours." She snuggled closer, searching for his scent beneath the smell of blood and death. "I shouldn't have run. Should have known I'd never make it, but I had to try."

He coaxed her to take a sip. Cool liquid trickled down her throat, soothing the soreness as he asked, "Why then?"

She shook her head. "How much longer do I have?"

Xavian drew away to look at her, a clear question in his eyes.

"Before you deliver me to Vladimir."

"Afina, I'm not—"

"Promise me you'll look after her." Afina clutched at his arm, fear for her daughter binding her heart. Sabine's future was more important than hers. Despite what he intended, she knew if Xavian gave his word he would keep it. "Promise me."

"Who, love?"

"Sabine." Tears filled her eyes then spilled over her lashes to nest in her hairline. "Please...she cannot come with me. He'll hurt her. Please, keep her safe. Give her a good home after I'm gone."

"Jesu, Afina." Expression set, he scooped her off the ground and stood. Strides long and even, he crossed the trail toward a huge beech tree. Spread like a fan above them, the canopy swayed, pushed by the soundless rhythm of the wind. Afina swallowed as he set her down on a moss-covered log. His knees hit the ground on either side of her, caging her with his strong thighs and big body.

She shivered. "I don't blame you."

"For what?"

"For needing the coin," she said, her voice so soft she barely heard it. Pressing her hands between her knees, she tried to chase the chill in her blood—in her heart—away. "Vladimir is wealthy and willing to pay, but—"

"Stop." He framed her face with his hands and, wiping at her tears, forced her to meet his gaze. "I'm not taking you to the bastard."

"I don't understand. I thought...you said...how..."

"Vladimir approached me...offered me coin to track you."

"But you don't intend to—"

"I told him I would find you. I never said I'd bring you back."

She frowned, confusion warring with relief. "But you sent Cristobal away. If you aren't taking me to...where are we going?"

"The hot springs. You need a bath, and the warm water will help with the pain." He brushed another tear away and released her. Settling back on his heels, he cupped her calf and set her injured foot on the top of his thigh.

Agony came calling, licking up her leg like fire. Afina bit down on a whimper and tried to keep her bottom from walking along the log.

"Hurts?"

Unable to answer through clenched teeth, she nodded then squirmed when he flipped her skirt above her knee.

"Relax, *draga*," he murmured, sweeping gentle circles up the back of her calf.

Magic in his fingertips, he increased the pressure, massaging to ease the muscle. Each stroke lessened the pain, drew comfort a little closer, and slowed her heartbeat until her eyelids felt too heavy. Eyes drifting closed, Afina fell into his rhythm, let the heat in his hands lull her into relaxation.

Cool air touched her thigh. Afina twitched then sighed when Xavian's hands followed. Calloused and warm, one circled her knee while the other traveled, cupping the back of her thigh. He stayed there a moment then shifted to massage the top of her leg on an upward glide. Alarm bells sounded somewhere inside her head. Afina ignored them. The stroke and release of his hands felt too good to stop. The terrible throb was almost gone.

A warm rush of air brushed her before Xavian's mouth touched down. His whiskers pricked her skin as he drew a heated trail down the top of her thigh. Afina opened her eyes. Xavian nuzzled the inside of her knee and raised his head.

"Better?"

"Ah-huh."

"Good." A wicked gleam in his eyes, his hands continued to play, massaging in wide circles as he dipped his head again. Afina held her breath as he planted a gentle kiss on her knee. "Now tell me. Why is Vladimir after you?"

His tone was quiet, the question delivered with an innocent lilt designed to coax an answer. Still Afina hesitated. Could she trust him with her secret? It was the ultimate question, one she had struggled with since he'd taken her from Severin. A number of things stood in his favor—the fact he didn't intend to give her to Vladimir chief among them. But in the end, it all came down to one thing. Anyone who helped her would always be in danger.

If she told him the truth of her heritage—all the awful things that always happened because of it—she put him in jeopardy. Drachaven wouldn't be safe from Vladimir. The swine would lay siege to Xavian's home and kill everyone in it. The only chance she held was to hide, to stay one step ahead of him.

"You need to let me go," she said, hearing the panic in her voice. "He won't stop. Ever. He'll—"

"Stop protecting everyone but yourself and tell me."

Afina chewed on her bottom lip. He held her gaze, hands skimming her skin, waiting for her to obey. A new plan took shape. Mayhap the truth was the only way. If he knew her history—the terrible legacy given to her at birth—he would turn away.

Between one heartbeat and the next, she told him…everything. She didn't make it look pretty. Didn't cover up her mother's viciousness or gloss over Bianca's death. Even went so far and told him what he had unleashed by his possession in the stables. No, she didn't understand it—wasn't sure what it meant or even what she was now capable of—but she refused to tell him that. She wanted him to run…for him to take her to Sabine and let them both go.

"A high priestess," he said, so low Afina barely heard him.

"Yes," she whispered back, accepting her legacy even as she wished to erase it.

"He will hunt me to the ends of this world to take the throne." Afina gripped his forearms, willing him to understand. "It would be safer…better for you and Drachaven…if you let me go."

"I told you once, now I'll say it again. You belong to my circle. Mine." His gaze bore into hers, his determination unmistakable. "Accept it, *draga*. Vladimir will never take you from me."

"Xavian," she said, gratefulness and fear a mixed-up mess inside her chest. "I know you mean well, but—"

"Christ, don't move."

Afina tensed, her focus on the hard planes of his face. "W-what?"

"Do. Not. Move." He shifted, the movement measured and slow, his attention on something over her left shoulder. Unsheathing a blade from his boot, he rotated the weapon until the hilt sat in the palm of his hand.

A hiss came from behind her head.

She twitched.

Xavian cursed as his arm shot forward, knife at the ready.

A dark brown head flew, end over end, to land in the dust a foot from her own. Air left her lungs on a rush. A northern viper. By the goddess, had—

Afina turned to Xavian. "Were you bitten?"

He grimaced and rotated his wrist. "'Tis nothing."

"Were you bitten!" She grabbed his arm.

Two small puncture wounds, the skin already red around them, marred the flesh of his forearm. He tried to pull away. She held firm and shoved, putting him on his backside. No doubt shocked by the move, he sat unmoving as she lowered her head and set her mouth over the bite.

"Afina."

She sucked then spit, repeating the process before coming up for air. "Be quiet. I have to get the poison out."

"We have to move." He twisted his wrist, breaking her hold. "The spring is not far. We cannot stay in the open."

"But—"

Fisting his hand in the front of her gown, he hauled her to her feet and, with a low whistle, called the horses to attention.

Aches and pains gone in the face of his peril, Afina didn't complain when Xavian tossed her into his saddle, mounted behind her, and set his heels to his warhorse's flank. She needed him to hurry. No matter how strong, Xavian couldn't withstand the viper's venom for long. If she didn't treat the bite fast, he would slip away before she got the chance to save him.

CHAPTER FOURTEEN

It was time to end the game. The visions grew bolder, but even without them, Halál knew it deep inside. Just to be certain, he rattled the bones in the cup and tossed them again. Sure enough, the small white sticks taken from a child's hand landed in the same scattered position on the low table.

A new beginning. The bones demanded one.

He was more than eager to do his part. Thus far, he'd done nothing but play, sending those of lesser skill after the *Betrayer*. Not that many equaled the artistry of his former pupil. Xavian was an exquisite killer, the best he'd ever trained. Now, however, came the turn and hollow, the point at which he could no longer afford to expend so much effort in one direction.

Halál sighed. Using the tip of his index finger, he stroked the grooves in the bones. Such a shame. He so enjoyed pitting one assassin against another. Particularly if they had any fondness for each other. The torment was highest then, a grand match where one must bleed the other to survive. Death. The pleasure of it came in so many interesting forms, but his amusement must end.

He'd received word.

Grand Master Stein of the Teutonic Knights would arrive soon. And all loose ends needed to be tied off. Stein disliked disorder as much as Halál enjoyed chaos. Not that the difference bothered him. Each to his own, and so long as the grand master paid the coin to retain Al Pacii's services, Halál would allow him to keep his preferences.

A bell tolled. Four counts, announcing the fight hour.

The ringing echoed, bouncing off the barren stone walls with a ripple that filled Halál with purpose. Reaching across the low table, he palmed the thin roll of parchment. Three inches wide and twice as long, the strip had been painted with a waxy film, giving it the necessary durability. He rubbed the corner between his thumb and forefinger, comparing the paper's slippery quality to the alluring feel of Beauty's scales.

He would visit her now, up on the roof while the sun warmed her and he assessed the new arrivals.

Slipping the parchment inside his robe pocket, he crossed to the circular staircase in the corner of the chamber. His gait smooth and unhurried, he climbed, soft eagerness guiding each step. Fresh blood. The Pit always hummed with more potency when the new ones were brought in. The more accomplished relished the chance to return the brutality they had received their first time around. The game would turn bloody, though not deadly.

At least not this day.

The purpose lay in the method. He needed to know which of the fledglings held the greatest potential for the academy and which the least. Al Pacii was only as strong as its weakest link. Perseverance in the Pit was key, as important as physical prowess. The ability to defend and deliver wrenching violence with cold efficiency were traits without equal. Something at which Xavian excelled.

The sunlight caressed Halál's face as he came out onto the rooftop, the warmth doing little to assuage his disappointment. He imagined his former pupil in the Pit, blades raised, face expressionless as he spilled fledgling blood. Such a pity. Such wasted potential. But then, had Xavian not deserted Al Pacii, Halál would never have entered the game he now played. And truth? He was enjoying himself more than he had in months... years, in fact. Nothing was better—or more satisfying—than a worthy opponent.

The smell of sweat and leather teased his senses before he heard the whisper of movement. A boot scraped against stone. Without turning, he said, "Shay. Why are you not in the Pit?"

"Master, I bring news."

"What sort?" Halál stepped up to the cage. Thin metal bars, an inch apart, crisscrossed, keeping Beauty in even as they allowed her to see out. The viper raised her sleek head, uncoiled her length from around a sun-warmed rock, and hissed in greeting.

"Bodgan failed. He is dead."

"Are you certain?"

"Yes." Shay shuffled, shifting his weight from one foot to the other. "A carrier pigeon arrived with a note, written in Xavian's hand."

Halál smiled softly and, unlatching the lock, flipped the cage door open. Beauty rose on her belly, chin down, ready to strike. With sleight of hand, he distracted her, and she hesitated, giving him the second he needed to grab her by the throat. Fangs bared, she fought, black body bucking before settling enough for him to pull her from confinement.

He stroked the underside of the viper's chin, murmuring just loud enough for her to hear, "Skilled, just like you. He makes me proud, Beauty. Indeed, he does."

"Master?"

"Unleash The Three, Shay." Silence met his pronouncement. Halál hummed, relishing the scent of his apprentice's uncertainty. One brow raised, he pivoted, Beauty coiled around his forearm. "You question me?"

"Nay, master," Shay said, chin low. "But they are mad... uncontrollable. How do I ensure their obedience?"

Withdrawing the rolled parchment and a key from his robes, Halál tossed both between Shay's feet. "Give them this as you release them from the cave. They will obey and leave for the hunt."

"Of course, master," he said, bending to retrieve the paper.

Halál turned toward the lip of the roof as a scream echoed up from the Pit. The sound unfurled in his stomach like a soothing tonic as he reached the low wall of the roof's edge. Three deep, his men ringed the fighting circle, watching the action at its center. Sharp metal flashed in the sunlight, the knife sure in the hands of one of his more accomplished killers. The fledgling's blood flowed in rivulets of red, his movements clumsy, his steps uneven.

He shook his head. Weak. The newcomer was weak, without the innate skill needed to create a great assassin. He needed more like Xavian for Al Pacii to thrive. Why could he not find more?

Lowering his head, he brushed his mouth to the back of Beauty's skull. She hissed. His apprentice shifted.

Halál glanced over his shoulder. "That is all."

With a bow, Shay made for the stairs. Halál watched him go, aware it would be the last time he saw him alive.

◆✦◆

Shadows lingered, clinging to crooked tree trunks along the dirt path Shay traveled. Thick canopies overhead turned down, frowning at him, the leaves so dark their jagged edges appeared almost black in the dim light. Despite their disapproval, he walked on, reins of his warhorse wrapped around his fist, ignoring the rasp of Tia's breath coming from behind him. She clung to the saddle horn, knuckles white as he led her farther into the gloom.

"How much farther?" she asked, the clicking sounds of her teeth interrupting the question.

"Almost there."

"Alls I got to do is turn the key, right?"

"Aye." He kept his voice low in the hopes of calming her.

"And the paper?" She shifted in the saddle, the movement as frayed as her nerves must be. "The paper will protect me?"

Shay nodded.

"Then I'm free, right? To go where I please."

"As free as a bird, Tia," he said, tempting her with the one thing he knew she couldn't resist. A whore to the men of Al Pacii, she was well used, willing or not. It was sad and also the reason he never slept with any of the women brought into the fold. He refused to take from them what had been taken from him—the right to choose their own path. "You may even take the horse."

He didn't add—if she survived.

He hoped she would; had taken pains to research The Three and their preferences. Women were not among them. The book of history locked away in the master's study had told him that much. Aye, they might feed on human flesh, but Halál kept them well fed and always with the blood of men.

Stopping half a league from the cave, he released Curio's reins and turned to look up at the girl. Her brown eyes were huge in her pale face as he palmed her waist and lifted her down. She stiffened, hands fluttering against his biceps, and guilt hit him hard.

She didn't like his touch, and he didn't blame her. The rough sport Al Pacii played with their female captives wasn't pleasant.

As soon as her feet touched the ground, he let go and stepped back. "This way. It isn't far now."

She nodded.

With a hand gesture, he instructed Curio to stay. He liked his warhorse too much to risk him; didn't want him anywhere near the cave when the beasts took flight. Turning on the little-used trail, he listened to Tia's light footsteps behind him as he tracked north toward The Three's prison. The climb grew more difficult the farther they went, but he didn't turn to help the girl. She would no doubt refuse his hand, not wanting to endure his touch again.

They reached the entrance just as twilight fell, the sun nothing but a soft glow in the western sky. His back to Tia, Shay stood on the lip of the cave, staring into the black hole, knowing Halál had meant to serve him up as The Three's next meal. The bastard. No wonder Xavian had left Al Pacii. The old man's depravity knew no bounds…disloyal to the core.

Unclenching his hand, he lifted the flap on the satchel slung across his shoulder and dug out the small piece of parchment and a skeleton key. The dark grey metal sucked at the shadows, the grime in the nicks at its throat as pronounced as the demons feeding on Shay's soul.

He was about to deliver a young girl—an abused one—into the jaws of death. All to save his own skin. What kind of man did that make him?

Not a very good one.

Killing the sudden surge of conscience, he pivoted to face Tia. She was as pale as ever, but a determined light had replaced the frightened one in her dark eyes.

He held out the key and slim piece of paper. "Toss the parchment to the floor inside the bars, unlock the gate, and put your back to the wall. Stay low, stay silent. Understood?"

Her chin dipped as she took his offerings. "Thank you for choosing me, Master Shay."

Shay closed his eyes. *Shit.* Gratitude. He hadn't expected that, and for a moment—a rare one colored by honor—he almost called her back. But his voice failed, and instead of stopping her he watched her slim silhouette disappear into the black. When he couldn't see her anymore, he found a foothold in the cliff face and climbed to the ledge high above the cave's entrance. There, hidden by shadow and rock, he waited.

The girl screamed.

The terrible sound of feeding ensued, drifting up to surround him.

Shay hung his head and watched three winged shapes fly from the cave's mouth. Contrary to the book and its predictions, the beasts enjoyed female blood as much as any man's.

God forgive him.

CHAPTER FIFTEEN

Xavian wiped the sweat from his eyes as they crested the last rise. The sting blurred his vision, but he could see enough. His destination lay just beyond the circle of standing stones guarding the cave's entrance. He needed to reach it. Full night was almost upon them, and Afina would be vulnerable without him to protect her.

For some reason, her welfare was more important than his own. Foolishness, no doubt, but he couldn't fight it. His reaction was more primal than rational. Even in his weakened state, he knew it. He just didn't care.

Feeling himself sway, Xavian stopped at the mouth of the cavern and slid from the saddle. He dragged Afina after him.

The wolves would be here soon. He heard them baying in the distance, forewarning in each howl. The beasts would pick up their scent and come, but he refused to give them the advantage. A fire needed to be built in the circle of stones. It would shield the entrance and keep predators away with the added benefit of keeping Afina warm through the night.

But first he needed to start the damn thing.

"Afina." He gripped her shoulder, using her to steady himself. "Get the horses inside."

"After. Let me tend you first." She wrapped an arm around his back, trying to steer him toward the cave.

He tightened his grip and, using precious strength, shrugged out of her hold. "Get moving. We've not much time."

With a push, he shoved her toward Mayhem. Her bad ankle gave out, and she stumbled before regaining her balance. Xavian shrugged aside his regret. He didn't have time to feel bad. She would understand once the wolves started circling.

He sank to his knees beside a fire pit. Thank God for foresight. He often stopped here, maintaining the underground passage that led to his mountain home. The woodpile sat just as he had left it, the dry tinder and long logs all he required to keep a blaze going for days.

Double vision struck.

Xavian shook his head and set the firewood before reaching into the pouch at his waist. Almost blind now, he found the flint by touch and struck a spark. And then another until a small flame took hold. He smelled the smoke and felt the heat an instant before his legs gave out. Pressure banding around his chest, he crumpled, coming to rest on his back against cold earth.

Cool hands touched his forehead. Xavian cracked his eyelids open. Hazel eyes full of concern, she flipped the strap of her healing satchel over her head and settled beside him.

"At dawn," he whispered, taking a sip from the vial she brought to his mouth. Sweet mint combined with something bitter flowed over his tongue. He swallowed and took a shallow breath. "Take the...underground...passage...at the back of the cave. Leave me...and go."

She forced more liquid down his throat. "No."

"Mayhem...knows the way."

"I'm not leaving you."

He gripped her hand, trying to make her understand. She couldn't stay here. It wasn't safe. "Afina."

"Be quiet and drink."

Too weak to fight, Xavian obeyed. His vision went wavy. He struggled to find focus, tried to memorize her face before the light winked out, and he fell headlong into the darkness.

The fire needed another log, but Afina couldn't make herself move. Yellow eyes, ever watchful, stared from beyond the circle of stones. Razor-sharp teeth no doubt sat beneath the feral gazes, awaiting a taste of her blood. She tightened her grip on Xavian's dagger. The leather-bound hilt bit into her palm, making her hand ache. She rotated her wrist to release the tension, her gaze jumping from shadow to flickering shadow.

She couldn't stay here, crouched in the cave entrance. If the flames grew any smaller, she would lose her opportunity, but...

The wolves.

What if her movement made them bold, and they leapt over the standing stones? If she died, Xavian wouldn't stand a chance.

A full day had come and gone, and still he lay unconscious. No matter what she tried, his fever raged and the nightmares came. Her heart broke each time he lashed out, cursing her attempts to comfort him as he fought demons Afina couldn't see, much less imagine. Were they real or was the venom inventing stories? Either way, he was suffering, and none of her medicine was working.

Afina swiped at her eyes. She needed help, but that wasn't going to happen. Xavian's men were miles away, and Ismal wasn't an option. She'd never make it back to the marketplace. Her sense of direction wasn't, well, truth be told, she didn't have one.

Could hardly tell the hind-end of a horse from a fetlock, never mind point the beast in the right direction.

No, she couldn't go back. The only choice was to move forward.

Her legs shook as she pushed to her feet. She took a moment to still the trembling. It wouldn't do. Animals sensed a person's unease, counting it as weakness. If the pack felt her fear, they would tear her apart then turn on Xavian. She must protect him—had promised not to leave him, and death was simply another form of abandonment.

"Get ready, you mangy mongrels." The strength in her voice steadied her, allowing her to step from the cave, into the firelight.

A snarl came from her left.

Afina stilled, spotting the beast from the corner of her eye. Almost completely white, he stood at the cornerstone: head low, ears back, fangs bared. She met his yellow gaze from beneath her brows. If she gave an inch, he would pounce and bring the others with him.

Staying low, she set her balance and, dagger raised, moved toward the fire pit.

A vicious growl came from between his teeth.

She shook her head. "Not today, my friend. Go find your meal elsewhere."

He blinked and, nose twitching, angled his head to the side. *Goliath.*

The name whispered through her mind. Afina's heart shuddered. The voice again. Who was that? She wanted to look over her shoulder—to check if a woman stood behind her—but didn't dare. Real or imagined, the voice could wait. Every moment counted. One wrong move would seal her fate.

The pack leader inched forward, around the tall stone column.

"Goliath," she said, uncaring whether the name was a figment of her imagination. It suited him; made him seem more like a pet and less like a beast. Tame, she could handle. Wild and unmanageable, she could not. "I know you are hungry, but you cannot have me or the one I protect."

He snorted and, muzzle crinkled, took a step back. Then another.

Her jaw went slack. Impossible. He was retreating, inch by precious inch.

Dagger at the ready, she scuttled sideways until she reached the pit. A branch, free of fire at one end, pointed heavenward, as though begging for divine intervention. Afina echoed the sentiment, grabbed the stub, and swung left, placing the flames between her and the wolf.

Panting now, he stared at her, ears forward, a perplexed look on his furry face. Perplexed? Good goddess. Her imagination was definitely getting the best of her.

Slow and steady, she set the burning branch on the ground between them. "Off you go, then. The moon is high, Goliath. You still have time to hunt tonight."

Goliath made a sound she thought might be disgust.

Afina bit her bottom lip. She shouldn't feel like laughing. The wolf could still come over the rocks and tear her apart. But she didn't think he would. They had come to an understanding... insane as that seemed. But then, she refused to quibble. Crazy sounded better than dead.

The wolf pivoted, took two steps, and swung back. A death grip on the knife, Afina held her breath and waited. Goliath gazed at her, head tilted. Time hung like smoke in the air before he dipped his snout and yipped.

Instinct guiding her, she whispered back, "Good-bye."

White fur became a silhouette then passed from shadow into nothingness. Clawed feet scraped against stone as the pack followed Goliath's retreat. Muscles gone liquid, Afina's knees gave out. She landed on her behind with a bump. The bone-deep chill came next, blowing through her like an ice storm. Releasing the knife, she held out her hands. Her fingertips trembled, casting long shadows on the dirt.

She should be stronger than this. Shouldn't be so afraid, especially after...

What was happening to her? The whole mind-throwing-the-hatchet incident along with the headaches and strange voice were terrible enough. Now she talked to animals. And they understood. How was that possible?

Sorcery.

The dark word slithered up her spine, dragging a shiver in its wake. Her mother had often spoken of black magic. She'd been adamant—obsessed—telling the awful stories with relish, as a warning to her and Bianca. What had her mother known but not shared? Had she tested the darkness she loved to lecture about and been drawn too deep? It would explain the violent outbursts at the end, along with her mistake. No one in her right mind would believe Vladimir fit to rule Transylvania.

So many questions.

Her mother's love of secrecy had left her ill prepared. She wanted to believe her new skills were expected of a high priestess, desired even. But the opposite side of the equation must be examined. Good could not exist without evil.

"Well done, lass." The deep voice came from the shadows, just beyond the circle of stones. "I have a liking for wolves and had no wish to destroy him."

With a gasp, Afina reached for the knife and shot to her feet. Her bruised ankle protested, upsetting her balance. Right boot planted to compensate, she recovered from the wobble and spun to face the intruder. He paused at the cornerstone, a bow notched with an arrow in one hand, the reins of his horse in the other.

Dagger raised, Afina stepped right, placing herself between the stranger and the cave entrance. "Stay back."

Stepping into the light, he frowned, his focus straying to her leg. "Are you hurt?"

"Do I look injured?" Afina adjusted her stance. Pain ghosted up her calf. She ignored it, refusing to show weakness. This man was more dangerous than the wolves. He bled power, the same kind Xavian and his men did. Was he one of them?

Afina toyed with the possibility. He looked like them: dark hair cropped short, dressed in black, his muscular build and towering height, the directness of his gaze, and the amount of weaponry. All spoke to an aggression they wore like armor. She bit the inside of her cheek. Could she trust him? Xavian lay helpless just behind her. If she made the wrong decision, he would never wake up.

"Be at ease, *sora*."

Sora? Had he just called her sister? Afina didn't know much, but one thing was certain, she didn't look like a nun. Not in a ripped gown and covered in day-old blood. She tightened her grip on the knife and turned the blade sideways, warning him she wasn't a weakling.

Tugging on the reins, he brought his warhorse forward to tuck his weapon into a quiver behind the saddle. Hands free, he held them out to the side, palms up. "See? I've no intention of hurting you."

"And Xavian?"

His gaze sharpened. "Ram is here?"

"Who are you?" She wasn't a fool. His bow might be stowed, but the daggers sheathed on his chest were within easy reach and his big hands were no doubt lethal. "One of his men?"

"Henrik, at your service."

Afina breathed a little easier. He knew Xavian. Even so, she needed more information before she dropped her guard. "What brings you here?"

One corner of his mouth curved up. "You do not trust easily."

"Answer the question."

"'Tis one of our hidey-holes, lass. A place to rest before continuing on to Drachaven."

She stared at him. He wasn't lying—exactly—but something wasn't quite, well...right.

"Take a look around." He swept one hand out to the side. "Do you think the wood piled itself? Or the pallets inside and the trunks filled with foodstuffs appeared by magic?"

Afina huffed. He was teasing her. The dolt. Of course she'd seen the supplies. She'd been using them to treat Xavian and feed herself.

"You've naught to fear," he said, taking a step closer. His horse followed, frosting the air over his shoulder. "Not from me or anyone else who comes here. 'Tis a hidden place, one that's secret is well-guarded."

What Henrik said made perfect sense. How would he know of the preparations inside the cave unless he helped maintain them? Afina lowered the dagger. She needed help, and holding Xavian's man at knifepoint wouldn't solve anything.

The warhorse bumped him with her nose. With a murmur, Henrik stroked the beast's muzzle. "What is your name?"

"Afina."

Henrik nodded and looked away. The horse nudged him again. He patted his steed one last time and unbuckled the halter before moving to the belly strap. Metal rattled as he lifted the saddle from the beast's back and set it down beside the fire.

The strain of the last day pushed tears into her eyes. With a helpless shrug, Afina gestured with the knife. "Sorry about before, but...it's just...Xavian is ill and I—"

"Ill?" Henrik glanced away from his saddlebags and raised a brow.

"Snakebite." A pang hit her chest level, making her heart feel hollow. It was her fault. He wouldn't be sick if she hadn't taken a fall. "He was protecting me."

"A viper?"

"H-how—"

"They are common in this area."

"I am treating him, but it's been a full day and he's yet to awaken." She kicked at the dirt, making a hole with the toe of her boot.

Crouched beside the pit, Henrik selected an enormous log and reset the fire. "If the venom went deep, 'twill take more than a day."

To what? Kill him or for his body to expel the poison? Afina swallowed, praying it wasn't the former. If Xavian died, she couldn't...

No, she refused to acknowledge the possibility. He was strong and the medicine would work. It *had* to. Besides, Henrik was here now, and he would protect them.

❋✛❋

Halál plucked the scrap of paper from the dead girl's hand. Two fingers were missing, the ragged ends little more than shriveled stubs. The stench of human decay a living thing, she lay supine, eyes wide open, the horror in their vacant depths easy to read. His gaze drifted to the bars anchored in the cave walls. Twisted, the gate hung from one hinge, a visual reminder of the monsters it had imprisoned for almost twenty years.

Magnificent creatures. If only they would obey him. If only…

Halál returned his attention to the girl. He flicked at the shreds of her bodice. Dry blood drew interesting patterns on her skin, the gaping wounds astonishing even to him.

A day, mayhap two, since The Three had made a meal of her.

He shook his head and pushed from a crouch. Clever, clever Shay. He'd used the whore to save his own skin.

The realization lightened Halál's mood. It was a worthy play, one only a full-blooded assassin would make. The brutality of the girl's death was proof enough of that.

Halál ran his thumb over the piece of parchment. His skin stuck, blood and decay impeding its progress across the once-smooth surface. Using spit, he wiped the stickiness away to reveal the looping scrawl. Uneven words jumped into focus. Halál cursed. The handwriting was not his own; neither was the message.

He crushed the paper in his hand.

The bold bastard. Shay had altered the incantation. Now The Three were on the hunt and he was left with little choice.

Halál half-turned toward the cave entrance. "V."

"Aye, master?" Valmont shifted from his position near the lip of the cavern, his height throwing long shadows on the jagged stone walls.

"Castle Raul...do you know it?"

"Vladimir Barbu's keep."

"Yes." Halál smoothed the creases from the parchment. He would need it. Preserving the message was the only way to undo what Shay had set in motion. "Within his lands to the south lies the White Temple. Bring me the High Priestess of Orm."

Boots whispering over stone, Valmont turned to leave.

"One other thing."

Poised in the mouth of the cave, his new apprentice glanced over his shoulder.

"Choose six others to ride with you."

"Seven," Valmont murmured, quiet reverence in his voice.

Engrained in the hearts and minds of his men, the number seven symbolized the strength of their order. It was in everything: from the walled sides of the Pit and their crest to the number of daggers each wore, and the chronicles of Al Pacii. A mystic long ago had written about the group of seven...a divine force so brutal none could defeat them. Superstitious nonsense, mayhap, but Halál allowed his assassins their illusions.

Fear and rage only got a man so far. Faith and magic, however, drove men past their natural limits into the soulless places he wanted them to go. His assassin believed in the power of seven, and so he would use it. He must stop The Three before they found Xavian. Otherwise he would hold an advantage Al Pacii could ill afford.

CHAPTER SIXTEEN

On his haunches beside the pit, Henrik stirred the fire with a thin stick. Sparks snapped, rising to greet a jet-black sky. He watched the embers float, lost in the whisper of tree limbs and night sounds. Afina's voice drifted from the cavern, tone soothing as she tended Ram. Henrik glanced over his shoulder at the cave entrance. When would she be finished?

He had so many questions. Useless wonderings. The sum of which didn't amount to much.

Deep down, he already knew the answer to the most important one. Bianca was dead. He'd felt the fragile bond he shared with his twin sister snap nearly two years ago. While he'd been in Poland, doing Halál's bidding.

With a silent curse he jabbed at the coals. The logs shifted and flame roared, sucking air in and spewing smoke out as it fed on the wood. He wished he could do the same: explode and find some small measure of relief.

Damn the old man and his infernal ways.

Had he been at Grey Keep, he would have heard of the trouble, and Bianca would still be alive. But then, Halál knew of his attachments and used them to effect. His sisters were the bastard's only leverage. A way to keep him in the fold after he reached maturity and Al Pacii could no longer contain him.

If not for Halál's promise to leave Bianca and Afina untouched in return for his service, he would never have stayed.

"Henrik?"

He pivoted on the balls of his feet. Afina stood in the mouth of the cave, bucket in hand, the firelight casting shadows on her face. Christ, she looked so much like their mother. The only true difference was her coloring. Mother had been blond and fair, like Bianca. Afina shared his dark hair and hazel eyes, though hers were touched with green and his, with gold.

He stood, pushing memories of his mother's betrayal to the back of his mind. Like ghosts rising from the ruins, they rushed back, grabbing at him with greedy hands. Goddamn, he'd only been eight years old, but that hadn't stopped her. He'd been naught more than an abomination; a male born in a place where only females were accepted.

Afina took a step back as he approached.

Henrik tucked the fury deep and stopped a few feet away. The last thing he wanted was to frighten her. Fear didn't belong in families. Honesty, however, did. But truth wasn't his forte. Deception fit him better. With a history like that, how could he dispel his mother's lies and make Afina believe him—treat him like a brother instead of a stranger?

She thought him dead, he knew that; just like he knew she would be better off if he left her alone. Problem was, he couldn't. Despite everything, she was his sister, and blood ties were too important to ignore.

He cleared his throat. "More water?"

"If you don't mind."

He held out his hand to take the pail. "How is he?"

"Better...cooler." After relinquishing the bucket, she pressed her fingertips above her eye then shifted to rub her temple.

His grip tightened around the rope handle. "You need to sleep."

"I know, but—"

"You will be no good to him if you exhaust yourself."

"Arrogant, aren't you?" She huffed. The small sound mixed with laughter, lightening his heart a little. "You and Xavian are cut from the same cloth."

"Mayhap, but we are often right."

"So you believe," she said, tone full of exasperation. "I need to mix more medicine before I rest. One more dose, and mayhap…I'm hoping it will help him wake."

He nodded and, with a wave, motioned Afina back inside the cave…to heal his former friend. What the hell was he doing? Ram was defenseless, and yet here he stood, ready to fetch and carry. He should be in there helping him die, not aiding his little sister while she tended him.

Henrik glared at the fire. Life or Death. Kill or be killed.

It wasn't that simple anymore. Afina cared for Ram. Mayhap strongly enough to call it love. He could see it in her eyes, in her determination to see him healed. Did he have the right to take that from her? From either of them?

The code by which he lived said aye. But then, he no longer needed to appease Halál or walk a fine line with Al Pacii. The bastard had lost his leverage. For the first time in his life, Henrik was free to make his own choices. The realization tugged at the tight knot in the center of his chest as he took the path toward the stream.

Reaching the river's edge, Henrik filled the bucket. Water spilled over the edge, washing the rest of his tension away as he retraced his steps. The future seemed brighter somehow. Al Pacii was a thing of the past. Now all he had to do was keep his sister safe.

What was Ram up to? Did he still intend to hand Afina over to Vladimir? Or had he changed his plans—his feelings for Afina dictating a new path?

Half of him hoped not. No matter how much he wanted to see his sister happy, he couldn't forgive Ram. His betrayal stung too much. Loyalty mattered. And years of training—of believing revenge was everything—were hard to ignore.

The urge to unsheathe his dagger and bury it hilt-deep in Ram's chest pressed in, making his head ache. Henrik shook it off. He needed to be patient. Accidents happened all the time, and what Afina didn't know wouldn't hurt her.

Xavian dreamt of hazel eyes and a soft, lilting voice. It pulled him toward the light, away from the violence and bitter cold. The warmth came next, drifting over his shoulders and chest. Wispy strokes, barely there, yet combined with the scent of mint and woman.

Hmm, paradise.

Years of training told him to deny the pleasure and reach for a weapon. Instinct softened by the haze of slumber stilled his hand. The heat and gentle touch played on the fringes, present but not quite there. 'Twas like lying in the long field grass, arms and legs stretched wide as the sun's fingers drew warm patterns on his skin. With a sigh, he settled into the rhythm. A moment more, just to drift and enjoy, then he would...

The stroking moved south over his rib cage and across his abdomen. Xavian murmured, lifting his hips to keep contact a little longer.

"Xavian?"

The voice rushed over him, husky warm and sable rich. His eyelashes flickered. Afina. He should have known. No one else sounded like that, naughty and innocent at the same time. He whispered her name and let his eyes drift closed again, clinging to his dream. If he woke, she would disappear. And he needed her to stay.

"Hello." Something brushed across his temple then twirled gently in his hair. "Open your eyes for me again."

He frowned. Did he have to? The dream was heaven, a cocoon so real he swore she was actually touching him. If he refused, would she stop? The possibility was too much to risk. Fighting through the fog blanketing his mind, he cracked his eyelids.

A soft smile played at the corners of Afina's mouth. She caressed him again. He turned into the touch, a rumble of satisfaction in his throat. Jesu, he wished every night came and went like this...deep in the land of slumber with her hands in his hair and her warmth all around him.

"Come now, wake up for me."

"Nay."

"Please?" Water sloshed and dripped before something cool drifted over his brow.

He shifted his arms and legs. Mayhap if he moved, his mind would follow. Sharp pain settled into discomfort as he pushed onto his elbows and forced his eyes open again.

The sheen of tears in her own, Afina whispered, "Welcome back."

Xavian blinked and squinted hard, trying to bring her face into better focus. Back? From where? He opened his mouth to ask. His tongue got stuck to the roof of his mouth.

"Here." She brought a cup to his mouth. "Drink."

Cool water trickled over his tongue and down his throat. Afina moved the mug away. He grabbed her wrist, needing more. She brought it back, one hand supporting his neck as she helped him drink his fill.

"Not a dream," he said, thankful for her support even as his pride chafed at the weakness. Why did he feel so sick? What... *Rahat*, the viper. Keeping hold of her wrist, he rotated his free arm and looked for the puncture wounds. Linen strips, wrapped end over end, obstructed his view. She'd tended him, placed him above her own safety and...Jesu.

"You stayed."

"Of course." Nibbling on her bottom lip, she looked away.

Xavian stared at her, unable to believe her audacity. She'd disobeyed and...stayed when no one else would have. Of a sudden, his rib cage felt too small for his lungs. He wanted to be furious. Wanted to turn her over his knee and paddle some sense into her. But that tight knot in the center of his chest got in the way.

He coughed to cover his reaction. "You shouldn't have."

"I promised not to leave you, and I won't." Brow furrowed, she tossed the cloth into the bucket. The linen square made a plopping sound then sank, just like his heart. She shouldn't want to be with him. And he shouldn't like it so much that she did.

She fished the cloth from the water, wrung it out, and brought it to his face. Xavian watched her from behind his lashes, relishing each cool glide as Afina washed his face and circled around to the nape of his neck.

"How do you feel?"

"Like shit."

"Understandable." He sensed more than saw her smile. "Viper venom is nothing to trifle with."

He grunted then held his breath as she drifted over the top of his shoulder. He should tell her to stop—that he could look after himself—but didn't want to. Her touch felt so good. No one had ever tended him before. 'Twas the truth; none had cared enough to wish him well. But Afina? Xavian swallowed. She cared. He saw it in her eyes, felt it in her hands, each gentle sweep like an undertow, trying to suck him out to sea.

A droplet trickled down his chest. Xavian wanted her to chase it with her tongue. Follow that bastard until…

Memories of them locked together in the stable blindsided him. Exhaling hard, he refocused on her face. She was so lovely: the shape of her hazel-green eyes and all that dark, flowing—

"What happened to your hair?"

Her gaze swung up to meet his. "N-nothing."

Before she could protest he buried his fingers in her topknot. With a twist, her raven locks tumbled around her shoulders. "Better. I like it loose."

"You like…Xavian, you are suffering delusions. You've been very ill and…"

She kept talking.

Xavian didn't hear a word. Weak as he was from the venom, her dark tresses distracted him, and drawing in a quick breath, he explored. The lengths curled around his fingers and played in the valleys between. Incredible. So soft and thick and…He should let her go. He knew that, knew as sure as he knew he wasn't going to. Right or wrong, he needed a wee touch and a little taste. Surely a few moments wouldn't matter.

Tightening his hold, he rolled, reversing their positions. With an "oomph," she landed beneath him on the pallet. The blanket tangled around his hips, he took advantage of her surprise and settled, hands in her hair, one thigh buried between her own.

"By the...What are you doing?"

He nuzzled the underside of her chin. "A wee sip, *draga*, 'tis all I need."

"B-but—"

"Mercy, Afina."

Xavian heard her breath catch and held his own. 'Twasn't rational, this need to forge a connection, to seek her acceptance and trust. He could make excuses, pretend the urge to reaffirm life after his brush with death made him turn to her—made him want to take his fill for no other reason than to feel. The truth was far more damning.

He craved her, with more than just his body. No matter how hard he fought the pull, it all came down to one thing. Possession. Nothing would do but that he make her submit. He held back, refusing to overwhelm her as he had in the stable. Accept him or nay, 'twas her choice. She deserved better than a soulless romp, but...Christ, he had naught else to offer. He didn't match up, not to Afina with her high bloodlines and lofty purpose.

So he handed her the power to decide: pull him close or push him away.

His face pressed to her throat, Xavian waited, every one of his senses focused on her. On a shaky exhale she relaxed beneath him. Gratitude spiraled into lust, sucking him down until nothing mattered but her. Naught but the scent of her skin, the shape of each curve, and the heat of her hands as they drifted over his shoulders. She clutched at him, asking for more of his weight. With a groan, he wrapped her closer, reveling in each soft sigh and gentle touch. Wild sensation skittered down his spine and around to his groin. Xavian lifted his head and cupped her face to capture her gaze. Not shy now, she stared back, her eyes more green than hazel, welcome in their shimmering depths.

He shook his head. How could she want him? How could she possibly—

Afina tipped her chin up and offered him her mouth. His heart stumbled, flipping over in his chest as he lowered his head. She met him halfway, lips brushing his, fingers playing in his hair. He wanted to go slow, but need took hold, made him impatient and sent his tongue deep. With a gasp, she opened wide, matching him stroke for heated stroke.

Dizziness hit him. His brain went sideways inside his head. Jesu, he was going to...

He lifted his mouth from Afina's. Short of breath, his chest heaved as he placed his hand, palm down, on the pallet to stop the spinning.

Afina steadied him. "What?"

"'Tis..." he broke off, his stomach taking the battle to his throat. "I'm not..."

"Here." She smoothed her hand over his hair, massaging in circles. Reaching the nape of his neck, she applied gentle pressure and brought his head down. He exhaled as his cheek touched down on her breastbone. "Rest a moment."

Without the strength to argue, Xavian settled into her softness. Her hands were magic. Each stroke and release evened him out, chased the spinning away until the pitch and roll of nausea followed its retreat. His conscience murmured, told him to pull away as he nestled in, trying to get closer.

"Better?"

He nodded, unraveling a thread at a time deep inside. The result was a messy pile of confusion. She turned him inside out. "Thank you for staying."

"Thank you for saving my life."

"So we're even now?"

"Not even close." The devil in her tone, she trailed her fingertips down his spine. He shivered, stretching like a cat beneath his master's hand. "You still owe me for Severin."

"Wench," he murmured, rubbing his cheek against her. Snared by his whiskers, her gown shifted and the wool slipped to her upper arm. A small mark sat on the curve of her shoulder. He stroked his thumb over it. Not a bruise at all, but a birthmark; a crescent moon with a tiny star nestled inside it. Unable to resist, he traced the outline, savoring her softness as a memory rose. He recognized the mark. Had seen it before, but…where?

Too tired to search for the answer, he tucked the mystery away. He would solve it another time. Right now Afina was beneath him, white skin exposed. Needing another taste, he flicked her with his tongue and almost groaned. God, she was sweet.

"Xavian," she said, warning him.

Jesu, even with that tone he loved the way she said his name. Foolishness, no doubt, but he couldn't help it. She wasn't afraid of him like all the others. But then, she didn't have much to fear. He was as weak as a babe and just as manageable.

With a grumble, he raised his head, making sure he kept the movement slow and even. An ache pounded between his temples, but his stomach stayed true, only pitching a little. Shadows flickered against the cave wall. Good, she'd kept the fire going.

Afina placed her hand against his forehead. "Does your head hurt?"

"'Twill pass," he said, not wanting her to worry.

Propped on one elbow, he settled his free hand at her waist and scanned the back of the cavern, looking for Mayhem. He stilled and counted again. Three horses, not two. His grip on Afina tightened. *"Draga—"*

"Goddamn!"

The roar came from outside the cavern. A scrape and claw and hiss echoed, the reverberation against stone walls loud in semi-darkness. The zing of twin blades split the air as ash and the smell of sulfur billowed into the cave.

The hair on the back of Xavian's neck stood on end. "Afina, where are—"

She pushed against his shoulders and rolled. He landed on his arse and reached for her. *Rahat.* She was already out of range, heading hell-bent toward the entrance.

What did she think she was doing? Fool woman. She should be cowering behind him, not running headlong into danger.

Metal clanged against metal.

Something unearthly growled. Another round of smoke rolled in, clouding the entrance.

Xavian gritted his teeth and, using the uneven stone wall for leverage, lurched to his feet. The blanket hit the floor, taking his heat with it. He swayed and glanced down. Good Christ, she'd stripped him to the skin. With a curse, he ignored the pile of clothes and grabbed his swords. His trews would have to wait. He needed to reach Afina before whatever was out there killed her.

CHAPTER SEVENTEEN

Thick yellow smoke burned Afina's eyes. Tears welled, combating the sting like water dousing fire on a thatched roof. She swiped at the moisture and ran toward the mouth of the cave. Her senses reeled. The sharp stab of intuition made her head ache, and reaching deep, Afina struggled to decipher its message. The meaning floated just out of reach, close enough to taunt, far enough away to deny her the answer.

What was out there? Why the smoke and now the silence?

The question snapped, crackling in the air around her. Foreboding brushed the nape of her neck, urging her to retreat. The idea was seductive. Save herself and live to see another sunrise. But Afina refused to run away. Henrik was out there... somewhere. She couldn't leave him to the mercy of the beast.

Beast.

The word rang inside her head and awareness expanded, pushing outward until it struck the inside of her skull like a smithy's hammer. Dizziness rose in a sickly wave. Afina shook her head to clear her vision and forced one foot in front of the other.

She couldn't quit now. Something was out there. Something familiar and unfriendly and in need of...what? Taming? Like Goliath and his pack of wolves?

She came through the wall of smoke. The haze went from yellow to white then grey. Fine wisps curled around her forearms, pulling at her, begging her to flee. With a jerk, she sliced them aside, followed instinct, and moved left. A hiss slithered through the fog, wrapping her in a chill so complete an involuntary shiver rolled down her spine. Afina stopped short, aware now the thing stood just beyond the circle of stones. She inched forward, fear and curiosity a morbid mix that weighed like a stone in the center of her chest.

Where was Henrik? Was he dead? Is that why—

A blast of cold air hit her full force as something shifted. Something...big.

"Priestess-ssss."

Afina's mouth went dry. "H-hello?"

A guttural snarl swirled in the mist. Menace lived in the sound, pulling the fine hair on her arms upright. The scent of brimstone assaulted her, a harsh accompaniment to the rush of wind that cleared the air enough for her to see over the standing stones.

She saw the huge wing first.

Unfurled, it stretched from one side of the pit to the other. Band after band tightened around her rib cage, squeezing until she couldn't breathe. Spun between disbelief and fascination, she stared, her heart an empty echo inside her chest. The appendage folded, the indigo webbing retreating foot by unbelievable foot until the wing met the side of a body.

Iridescent scales gleamed in the low light. Deep-hued purples moved into blues, the color coming alive as muscle undulated along its flank. A paw, tipped with razor-sharp claws, gripped the top of a boulder, and the jagged spines down the center of its back rippled as it raised its head. Afina tipped her own back and watched it rise, her gaze bouncing from the horns atop its skull to the fangs sitting just below.

Was that a...Blessed mother, creator of all things. It couldn't be. Dragons didn't exist. The stuff of legends, they belonged in the imaginations of the storytellers. Not in Transylvania or the mountains surrounding it.

The beast in front of her clearly didn't agree. Larger than life, it stared at her, hunger in its eyes.

Her muscles quivered.

"Don't run," she said under her breath, trying to convince her feet to stay put. The pair shuffled, itching to bolt for safer ground.

She killed the urge and stayed stock-still. Running wasn't an option. Predators liked to chase. A sudden movement might prompt it to attack, and honestly? Being eaten by a fire-breathing dragon wasn't high on her list of priorities.

Horned head tilted, it shifted sideways, like a snake before the first strike and...

Afina saw it. The size of a man's fist, the medallion rested at the base of the beast's throat. Suspended around its neck by gold links, the disc's center boasted a blood crystal. Tiny lights swirled in the gemstone's center. Afina fell into its spin, relaxing into the downward spiral. Her eyelids grew heavy and she swayed, wanting to touch the pendant so badly her fingertips tingled.

The dragon snorted.

Afina flinched, dragging her focus back to the beast. Twin wisps of smoke curled up from its nostrils and a cloud of sulfur rolled into her face. Her nose twitched and she held her breath, trying to stave off the inevitable. It didn't help. The sneeze shot out like an arrow leaving a bow. The dragon surged, bringing half its body over the high monoliths. Spine and head aligned, it stopped, on the verge of attack.

Her breath coming in shallow drifts, Afina locked her knees to stay standing and prayed. Instead of divine intervention, a curse, followed by a grunt, drifted from behind the beast. One eye on the dragon, she shuffled sideways to improve her view. Held fast in its back talon, Henrik struck the thing's foot, hammering it with his fist.

Good goddess. Was he insane? What the devil did he think he was doing?

No doubt asking the same question, the dragon swung its head around to glare at Henrik. He kept at it, alternating between punching the beast and trying to pry himself out of its grip. It retaliated, shaking Henrik so hard she heard his teeth rattle.

"Let him go." The words escaped before she could stop them. Afina took a step back as the dragon's head swung around to her again. She swallowed, working moisture back into her mouth. "Please."

Violet eyes with oval pupils narrowed on her. "No."

No. No? Heaven help her, the thing could talk.

"Goddamn it, woman...run!" Henrik snarled and kicked out, thumping the dragon in the side. Attention trained on her, the beast lowered its foot. Afina cringed as it pinned Henrik to the ground beneath its claw.

She watched Henrik struggle for a moment, torn between following his advice and standing her ground. Courage didn't come naturally to her. She'd been running and hiding all her life, but the last week had taught her something. Running only made things worse.

"I am Afina, High Priestess of Orm," she said, feet planted, shoulders squared. Forget Henrik and his idiot command.

She knew the beast somehow. Not that they'd ever met. The certainty was instinctual; a truth buried deep, banked but alive in her blood. "By my command, release him."

"You hold no power over us-sss."

"Christ, Afina…go," Henrik rasped, struggling to breathe.

Afina closed her mind to his plea, more concerned by the dragon's use of *us*. "Where are the others?"

Hot breath fanned the back of her neck. "Here."

Shivers chased the warm air, whispering over her skin in a wave of gooseflesh. Keeping the movement slow, she glanced over her shoulder. Little more than ten feet away, a second dragon, the color of fire, stood between the cave wall and smooth surface of the cornerstone. Green eyes narrowed, its lip curled, no doubt fantasizing about eating her.

"And here." The smell of smoke came from above, carrying a third voice.

Oh, no, an ambush…three strong.

She was surrounded and as good as dead if she couldn't bring them around. The fact she believed she could surprised her. But as implausible as it seemed, she saw the truth in it. The proof lay in the conversation and the lead dragon's willingness to engage in one. He could kill her without effort, yet here he stood, talking.

There must be a reason. He was obviously an intelligent creature. The key was to find out what he wanted and give it to him in return for their lives.

Taking a deep breath, she waded into uncertain waters. "What is your name?"

The dragon drew his head back. A look of consternation in his eyes, he studied her, the silence so thick it pulled her muscles tight. *Please answer.* The silent plea drifted through her mind an instant before—

"Tareek," the one behind her said, shifting closer. Firelight flickered, casting eerie patterns on his red-tipped scales.

Violet Eyes snarled at his companion, knifelike teeth gleaming in the low light.

"What matters a name..." Tareek's forked tongue licked over one of his fangs, "when she will not live to repeat it?"

Lovely. Mayhap the belief she could turn them to her side was based more in wishful thinking than reality. Where was that voice when she needed it? Guidance, a strategy, the last rites... anything at all would be welcome.

Not knowing what else to do, she lied. "The goddess will not be happy if I am harmed."

Wings flapped as the third adjusted his perch, watching like a vulture from above. "What care we?"

"Remember the White Temple, dragon, and your duty."

Violet Eyes snorted, smoke rising from his nostrils. "Unwise to remind us from whence you come, Priestess-sss...and of the bitch who whelped you."

She looked him square in the eyes. A truth shone in their violet depths. Here was her clue. The inkling—intangible but real—rose from deep inside her. It dragged a memory with it... of a girl-child playing hide-and-seek with a fanged beast. "You serve me and my house."

"No longer." The whispered growl carried pain in each syllable; of great loss and wrenching sorrow.

The sadness swirled in the space between them and her heart ached. He had suffered a terrible hurt, one so intense he couldn't see past his anger. Afina had suffered the same and understood, but now was not the time for weakness. Like it or not, the dragon would strike. It was only a matter of time until he did.

"I have no wish to hurt you," she said, having no idea whether she could. It was so much bravado. The strategy, however, was simple: make the enemy believe you held the upper hand and thereby the power. Her mother, at least, had taught her that. "Release Henrik and be on your way."

Tareek hissed. "We come for the male...the other."

The leader raised his hind claw and tossed Henrik over the standing stones. He landed with a thump and rolled to a stop beside her feet. Stepping forward and left, she placed herself in front of Xavian's man, giving him a moment to recover his breath.

"Where is Xavian?" One paw spread wide beside the fire pit, the dragon closed the distance between them. "I smell him on you."

"You cannot have him." Afina fisted her hands as something dark—something dangerous—seethed inside her. Red mist washed in behind her eyes, pulling aggression along with it. What right did they have to demand Xavian? He belonged with her, not them. "He is mine."

"Afina—"

"Protect Xavian," she snarled at Henrik, chin tipped down, magic throbbing in her fingertips.

"Where?" The roar echoed, bouncing off stone until pebbles tumbled down the rock face.

"Here." Edged by violence, Xavian's voice rolled in around her.

Afina pivoted toward the cave entrance. She wanted to weep when she saw him. He stood warrior strong, sword in hand, belying the illness that had ravaged him. But she knew better. The venom had taken its toll. He was too weak to fight.

"Xavian, don't."

He bared his teeth in answer. "Leave her…I am here. Come and get me."

Tareek reached for him, claws spread wide. Xavian rotated the sword hilt in his hand and brought the tip up. His death flashed in her mind's eye. Half-crazed by the image, Afina screamed, threw her hands up and out, pushing into thin air an instant before the dragon struck. A gust of wind swept the ground, hit Tareek like a battering ram, and tossed him over the standing stones. Dust and debris flew, clouding the air as he struck the ground on the other side.

The dragon above inhaled, a long, slow draw.

The centers of her palms throbbing, Afina growled, "Henrik, go! Take Xavian and go."

With a curse, Henrik scrambled to obey.

"*Rahat.*" Xavian lunged toward her. With a flying leap, Henrik tackled him, sending them both tumbling backward though the mouth of the cave. "Afina, nay!"

Launched from its perch, the fireball descended, the blaze a thin-tailed inferno. The scent of brimstone licked the inside of her nose. Relying on instinct, she imagined a dome and raised her hands. The flame collided with an invisible barrier then curled, contouring the vault she held in her mind. Black residue stuck to the curved surface, scorched ash floating just above it.

Violet Eyes swung his huge paw, claws tucked under like a fist, spiked tail flying overhead. Settled into her stance, she shifted to meet him, protecting the cave entrance. Henrik needed more time to reach safety. The entrance to the underground tunnel was at the back of the cavern, a long way for him to go if Xavian struggled. She must hold out a while longer or they wouldn't stand a chance.

Scaled knuckles closed the distance. Feet planted and eyes wide, she waited for the blow, for the crippling pain and the agonizing death that would follow. A hollow clang sounded, rippling out in all directions. The dragon howled and recoiled, pulling his claw in tight as though he'd hit something hard.

Afina exhaled in a rush. The shield was holding. But for how long? Already exhaustion tugged at her, fraying the edge of her peripheral vision.

"*Well done, daughter,*" the voice said. "*Now...run.*"

Had she been able think, Afina would have cursed the stupid voice. Asked it all kinds of questions like...where the devil have you been? Instead she took its advice, turned tail, and sprinted for the cave. The beasts would no doubt regroup. She didn't want to be anywhere near them when they did.

CHAPTER EIGHTEEN

Afina's eyes were still glowing. 'Twas not as intense as when she'd blasted the dragon, but...Jesu. Xavian ran a hand through his hair.

Dragons.

Had he not seen them with his own eyes, he never would have believed it. They were the stuff of legends and the only clear memory he had of his father. He remembered the elaborate tales told after the supper hour. Cross-legged, he and Nadia had always settled in front of the hearth, eager for the storytelling to begin. He had a vague picture of his mother sewing, of his father whittling arrow shafts while he talked of great winged beasts and their friendship with mankind.

His father had gotten it all wrong. There wasn't a friendly thing about them.

Proof enough sat huddled inside her cloak a few feet away. Silent since their narrow escape into the underground passageway, Afina could hardly put one foot in front of the other. He knew, because he'd dragged her most of the way. Now they sat amongst the brambles, in the small clearing at its heart. Several leagues from the mouth of the tunnel, it was the best place to rest and regroup. The prickly shrubs would shield them on all sides and from above, hiding them from view if the beasts flew overhead.

Aye, they were safe for the moment, but Afina...

She looked so small, curled in on herself like that. Knees tucked in tight with her arms wrapped around both, she rocked back and forth. The movement was slight, barely a rock at all and all the more heartbreaking for it. Xavian wished he could see her face. Mayhap then he would know what to do.

She needed ease. Anyone with eyes could see that, but... would he make it better or worse if he offered comfort?

In that moment, he wanted to be anyone but himself. A whole man—one with a normal upbringing—would know how to help her. But he wasn't normal. He was brutal and didn't know the first thing about soothing another.

Her clenched hands started to shake. She pressed her legs even closer, and he leaned forward, instinct urging him to hold her.

Still, he hesitated.

She could hurt him if she wanted—use the power she possessed to toss him over the brambles and out into the open. So much strength in such a wee package. The thought was strangely arousing, and of a sudden, the front of his leathers felt too tight. Xavian shifted, hoping to halt his unholy reaction. It didn't work. All he could think of was Afina; of the glow in her eyes and the determination on her face as she'd sent that dragon tumbling. She'd done it to protect him; something no one else had ever done.

Another round of sensation stirred below his waist. *Rahat.* He was lower than low. Afina was suffering and here he sat, a full-fledged erection in his trews. Adjusting the traitor, he took a calming breath.

The chill of midnight seeped into his lungs and made him cough. The sound was hollow, a remnant of the viper venom, along with shivers. Tucked into his fur-lined cloak, Xavian cursed his weakness and looked to the sky. Moonlight spilled, casting shadows amid tumbling branches with thorny teeth. The silvery glow reached deep into the thicket, illuminating the rabbit warren and its many trails. His gaze drifted back to Afina.

La dracu. He couldn't fight it anymore.

"Afina."

"Christ, 'tis about time."

Xavian glanced toward the opposite side of the clearing. "Speaking to me now, are you?"

Henrik shrugged. "She needs help."

His eyes narrowed on his comrade. He tried to hide it, but concern shone in Henrik's eyes. Xavian's territorial instinct tightened. The sentiment didn't become his former friend. A brilliant strategist, Henrik never did anything without reason, and his interest in Afina was cause for worry. Now, however, was not the time to push for an answer. Now was for the lass coming apart at the seams.

Inching toward her, Xavian stopped an arm's length away. *"Draga?"*

She flinched.

Careful to keep his touch gentle, he brushed the dark tresses away from the side of her face. The tendrils clung to his fingertips as through trying to keep him in place, and Afina swayed. Xavian shuffled closer. As though drawn, she leaned in his direction.

"That's it, love," he said, tone so soft he almost crooned. "Let me help...let me—"

She raised her head. Her eyes glimmered softly, the green glow hiding the hazel. "There is something wrong with me."

"Not true." Xavian brushed the pad of his thumb across her temple. "You are as you should be."

Tears trembled on her lower lashes. "Where is Sabine?"

"Safe at Drachaven by now."

"I need to hold her."

"I know, but until you can...hold on to me instead."

He cupped the nape of her neck and waited. The embrace had to be her decision. He couldn't give her comfort unless she wanted it. Moments ticked into more before she bridged the gulf between them. She settled like home in his arms, coming to him with such trust Xavian didn't know what to do first: thank God or hug her close.

He settled for both at the same time.

It felt like a miracle. He was soothing her, bringing her the ease she needed. Pride nudged him as he sat back and pulled her into his lap. Like a kitten, she nestled deep, head tucked beneath his chin, her body supported by his. He stroked his hand along her spine, encouraging her to relax. Small animals rustled through the thicket and an owl called, the night sounds as natural as having her in his arms.

In time, her tension ebbed, flowing out of her and into him. He took it all, aware of the strange current ghosting between them. It pricked his skin, raising the fine hair on the nape of his neck and forearms.

With a frown, he shifted to brush the heavy hair away from her nape. His gaze on her face, he massaged the top of her shoulder. A wee sound, more purr than moan, escaped her. He kept at it, working the tense muscle with sweeping circles. The more relaxed she became the more the current intensified, rushing out of her like water from a broken dam. As she went boneless, he channeled the flow, siphoning the sizzle until none remained.

Inhaling through his nose, he blew the breath out through his mouth. Warm for the first time since he'd been bitten, strength swept back into his limbs, dispelling the weakness as though it had never existed. Xavian rolled his shoulders. Christ, he felt as though he'd been placed on a rack and stretched to the limit.

What the hell had just happened?

He glanced down at Afina. Her head bobbed against his chest.

"Afina?" He cupped her cheek and tipped her chin up.

Her eyelashes flickered. "Hmm."

"Let her sleep," Henrik said, tone soft with warning.

Xavian's attention snapped right. *Rahat.* He'd forgotten about Henrik. 'Twas understandable but not acceptable. No matter his absorption with Afina, he couldn't afford to lose sight of an enemy.

A whetstone in one hand, his blade in the other, Henrik slid steel against stone. The rasp of each swipe disturbed nearby wildlife. Twigs snapped and the brambles rustled as rabbits sped away from danger.

"What's your angle?" Body tense, Xavian shifted the precious bundle in his lap, preparing to move fast if Henrik attacked. Evenly matched, he refused to give his former friend the upper hand. If he died, Afina would be left on her own. "Did Halál send you?"

In answer, Henrik slid his dagger into a sheath high on his chest, pushed to his feet, and tossed him a leather pouch. Xavian caught it in midair. His gaze never leaving his comrade, he turned it over in his hand, recognizing it by feel alone. Hell, a trail pack. Filled with dried figs, nuts, and berries, the small sack was what Al Pacii assassins ate while in the saddle and on the hunt.

"Eat and grow strong. I do not kill weaklings." Pivoting toward a break in the brambles, Henrik glanced over his shoulder. "Get some rest. I'll take the first watch."

Afina in one hand, the trail pack in the other, Xavian watched his comrade retreat. Shadows shifted from shades of grey to black until his tunic became one with the night. Senses twitching, he listened, tracking Henrik's movement through the thorny shrubs. Clouds covered the moon and a tree limb creaked. Xavian's lips curved. His friend had opted for high ground, no doubt in the large beech at the edge of the thicket. 'Twas a good spot to keep watch and an even better one to launch an ambush.

Though Xavian doubted he would.

Henrik thought him weak from his clash with the viper. No challenge lay in killing an ill opponent, and slitting a man's throat while he slept wasn't Henrik's style. He liked the fight too much, needed the challenge and the danger and the satisfaction of a clean victory. No one would ever accuse Henrik of being a coward.

Nay, the bastard wouldn't attack tonight. Tomorrow, however, was a new day.

Being away from Castle Raul was bothersome. Vile, actually. Vladimir hated everything about it: the uncomfortable saddles and stiff muscles, the chilly nights and grey days, the absence of soft beds, hot meals, and sweet wine. As it was, he had to settle for ale. Foul brew. But most of all, he hated pissing in the forest. There was something uncouth about it.

His lip curled, Vladimir refastened his trews then ducked. Damnation, the insects were bigger than minted coins out here. Batting the bug away, he started toward camp, dodging swaying tree limbs and overgrown ferns. Some might find the lush greenery beautiful. He found it annoying. 'Twas yet another stark reminder of a good strategy gone awry.

The fact it had all gone so horribly wrong confounded him. A good planner, he'd spent hours looking for holes in his scheme until he dreamed of nothing but the steps needed to be taken. Yet victory stood miles away. Up in the mountains with a bunch of thieving assassins.

How could Afina prefer that whoreson to him? She was too pure for the likes of Ramir and his ilk.

With a growl, Vladimir unsheathed his dagger and swiped at a fern stock. The leafy top flipped, tumbling end over end, then hit the ground, much as a head would after decapitation. Ramir would suffer a similar fate. The bastard had stolen what belonged to him, and if he had sullied her...dared to touch her—

"Damnation." Vladimir slashed at an old oak, sending his knifepoint deep into the bark as he passed.

Afina's maidenhead had better be intact. He owned her virginity along with everything else about her. She was his mate. *His.*

The truth had come to Afina's mother in a dream, foretelling his destiny as ruler of Transylvania. As such, Ylenia had explained the mating ritual. The coupling of a high priestess and her mate was a powerful thing. It ignited the magic in her blood and forged a connection that would bind them together for all time. Therein lay a high priestess's greatest weakness. For once the bonding took hold, she needed her mate close—his touch and attention—to drain the excess magic in her veins. Or she would slowly go insane.

Vladimir thought about bedding her every day: how he would do it, what she would feel like, and where he would take her. In truth, the where of it was the least important detail.

He would tup her in the dirt with his men watching so long as he bound her to him. He needed that connection. If he controlled Afina, he held the keys to the kingdom—the power to dominate one of the most powerful creatures in Christendom.

A shiver of anticipation swept through him as he entered the camp. Black birds with red-tipped wings flitted from branch to branch, watching him with tilted heads and beady eyes. He ignored the inspection and swept the clearing with a glance, looking for Stein. Not that he wanted to see the bastard. Christ, he couldn't wait until the morrow when they reached the mountain pass. The grand master would turn north toward Grey Keep and Halál, while he continued west into the teeth of the Carpathians.

The terrain would grow rough and his men would grumble. Vladimir didn't care. Drachaven Castle lay within striking distance. Two weeks at best, three at worst and he would claim Afina and, through her, the Transylvanian crown. The ceremony was already planned. The priest and people primed. Now all he required was the priestess's legs wrapped around his waist and her blessing.

When he possessed those, he would have everything he deserved.

CHAPTER NINETEEN

Hazy tendrils of sleep loosened their grip one finger at a time. Afina drifted up and out of the fog, ascending through layer upon lazy layer. Something told her to get up and get moving, but she swept the impulse aside. She wanted to stay a while, to float amid warm blankets and no worries. It was self-indulgent, but for once she didn't care. Sometimes it was good to think of oneself instead of another. Not that it happened often. She served the people, and their needs were more important than her own.

Besides, Bianca would come soon. She always arrived after the bells tolled, giving Afina the extra time to sleep. She smiled, burrowed into the blankets, and waited for the telltale creak. Her sister was sneaky and always opened the door—

The thought jarred her, and awareness struck like a slap in the face.

The dream had been so vivid...so welcome. Afina blinked, refusing to cry. She'd shed too many tears already, a whole river full. Now it was time to wake up and greet the morning along with the truth.

But goddess help her, she didn't want to face it. Not the magic or the fact she could barely control it. All she wanted to do was hide. Well, that and give it all back. Nothing about her new abilities suited her. Her sister would have been the better choice. Why hadn't the goddess chosen Bianca instead? Afina shifted under the wool blanket. She'd asked that question count-less times, searching for answers, desperate to understand. As always, the reasons eluded her. But fact was fact. The mark of the goddess marred her skin, and no matter how much she scrubbed it wouldn't come off.

Soft sounds, clinking metal, rustling leaves, and light foot-falls caught her attention. The smell of wood smoke reached her next. Afina planted her hand on the rough weave of the pallet and pushed herself upright. Her muscles squawked, protesting the shift. With a groan, she rolled her shoulders, trying to allevi-ate the stiffness.

"Finally."

The deep rumble flowed over her, rich with a hint of sweet-ness…like the honey she'd favored so much at home. She sighed, let it carry and soothe her for a moment, then opened her eyes. Xavian. Crouched by the fire, wooden spoon in hand, he stirred the contents of a small stew pot, looking decadent and far too tempting.

"Good morrow."

"Eventide, actually." His gaze on hers, he tapped the spoon against the iron edge. "You've slept the day away."

"Oh." Afina bit her bottom lip. She'd been more selfish than she realized. "I guess I was tired."

He set the spoon aside, leaving it to balance on the pot's rim. "Feeling better?"

She nodded. "You?"

"Good as new."

Afina ran her gaze over him, searching for any remnant of weakness. His illness had been severe, but as she studied him she realized none of it showed. The effects of the viper venom were gone. In their place was an intensity that made her squirm.

She glanced away. Not in the brambles anymore, large beech trees and big oaks towered above smaller shrubs, blocking out the setting sun. The orange glow of the day's final moments peeked through the leaves, throwing odd-shaped patterns on the forest floor. They'd traveled while she slept. How much ground had they covered? Had he held her close while riding, cradled her in his lap like he had in the thicket?

Wickedly insistent, sensation ghosted in a heated swirl across her belly. Afina shifted, tucked her legs in close, and chanced a peek at Xavian. He watched her still, a question in his eyes. She took a calming breath.

Whatever he wanted to know, she wouldn't have the answer. She never did.

"The stew is almost ready."

His voice lured, centering all of her awareness on him. In truth, it didn't want to be anywhere else. His appeal was lethal, more dangerous than an enemy's blade. At least with Vladimir she could run and hide. Xavian would never permit her the luxury. He was too good a hunter and, was she honest? She enjoyed being his prey.

"Hungry?"

Her hands tightened on the blanket. Goodness, yes, she was hungry...for him. A picture of them entwined—of her desperate and clingy—entered her mind. Heat rushed to her cheeks, and she cleared her throat. "A little."

Xavian's gaze sharpened. "What is wrong?"

Well, so much for skirting the issue. "I..."

"What?"

She rubbed her knuckles against her mouth and felt his touch; the warm sweep of his hands as he'd soothed her in the brambles. She didn't understand how, but he'd taken the pain and turned it into peace. He deserved her thanks for that—for his kindness and patience. The problem? In thanking him, she would remind him of her foolishness, of the weakness that had sent her into his arms.

Just thinking about her behavior made her cringe. He must think her unbalanced. She was a high priestess, for heaven's sake. She ought to be able to handle dragons, flying hatchets, all the chaos pulling her apart inside.

He stood and stepped around the jagged stones circling the fire pit. Afina dropped the blanket and scrambled to her feet. Xavian didn't need the advantage. Like any self-respecting bit of prey, she refused to sit while he loomed over her. The ability to evade was key. At least until she was ready to be caught.

And she would need to be…soon. No matter her discomfort, he wouldn't tolerate her silence much longer. She saw it in the planes of his face, in the way he moved: quiet, deliberate, danger-ous in his approach.

He halted an arm's length away. "Why the unease?"

Afina wanted to tell him. She did. But uncertainty got in the way. Something strange was happening between them. He calmed her in ways she didn't understand. It was becoming an addiction: the draw and pull, the desire to touch and be touched driving her from right straight into wrong. It was selfish. If she gave in to the compulsion, where would that leave her? And those at Drachaven?

In turmoil. Fighting for their lives while Xavian tried to pro-tect his home. She was misery wrapped up in a small package. An illusion at its most lethal. Xavian deserved better and so did the people inside his keep.

She heard him move before she felt his touch. Butterfly soft, he smoothed the crease between her brows then drifted, tracing the curve of her eyebrow, the hollow of her cheek until he reached her jaw. He stroked the sensitive skin beneath, raising her chin as he turned her face toward him.

Well, there was nothing for it. She must tell him something, and a half-truth was better than nothing at all. "Thank you...for the other night...in the brambles."

"Look at me when you thank me."

Drat. She'd been hoping to avoid that. Looking at him made it more personal. Why did he have to make everything so difficult? Was a simple "you're welcome" too much to expect? Out of the realm of possibility? Probably. Just like escape right now. Xavian wouldn't let her go until she gave him what he wanted.

No doubt 'twould be easier that way. Mayhap faster too. And faster was good...very, very good.

Bracing herself, she raised her gaze and fell headlong into his. She tried to resist the tumble and back away until the entire clearing stood between them, but that pull was seductive. Like the ocean tide it crept in, eroding her will one wave at a time until the inevitability of her downfall became just that...inevitable.

Without any urging from him, she leaned into his touch. As he turned his hand to cup her cheek, she whispered, "Thank you."

"'Twas naught," he said, tone so quiet she barely heard him.

"Not true," she said, borrowing his expression even as she wondered what possessed her. Clearly her mouth was miles ahead of her brain. He'd given her an opportunity to escape. Why hadn't she taken it?

He shifted, bringing his body flush with hers. Like a light in a dark place, his heat reached out, drew her in until she took the last step. He murmured as she settled against him: cheek cushioned on his chest, arms around him, her will to resist obliterated.

One hand pressed to the small of her back, he stroked her hair with the other. "I do not like to see you distressed."

"Oh, well, I am better now." And there went her mouth again. By the goddess, would her brain ever catch up? She was tired of sounding like an idiot.

"Good." He gave her a little squeeze.

Someone cleared his throat.

Afina nearly jumped out of her skin. Controlled and smooth, Xavian pivoted, placing her behind his back. She grabbed his tunic and peered around his shoulder. Oh, it was only Henrik. Damp hair gleaming in the fading light, he stood at the edge of the clearing, even with a copse of small trees.

"The river's free," he said, gaze leveled on Xavian. A linen towel slung over his bare shoulder, he crossed the clearing and dropped a leather satchel next to the fire. "Cold as hell, but free."

A river. Praise the lord. That meant she could have a bath. A bath! Afina smiled, resisting the urge to do a jig. After everything she'd suffered—the slavers, the viper, those blasted dragons—the grime on her skin must be an inch thick by now.

As excited as a child at Michaelmas, Afina sidestepped. Xavian's arm shot out, blocking her path, keeping her behind him. She froze, catching his tension. Focused on Henrik, the chill in his eyes sent shivers down her spine. A storm was brewing and aggression rolled like thunder, clouding the space between the two men.

Afina glanced from Xavian to Henrik then back again. What the devil was going on? These two were friends. Not that it looked that way at the moment. Both were as taut as bowstrings. "Is everything all right?"

"Aye," they both said at once.

Afina started, the force of that single word almost knocking her flat.

"Take the satchel behind me, Afina." Without looking at her, Xavian widened his stance, making himself bigger as she glanced over her shoulder. The leather pouch sat beside his saddlebags, not far from the horses. "Inside you will find all you need for your bath. The clothes are Qabil's, but they will do until we reach Drachaven."

The goddess love him…clean clothes. Afina almost sat down and wept. Tattered and stained, her gown was a mess. Sherene would no doubt wail if she could see it. "It seems I can do nothing but thank you today."

Xavian's mouth curved. The delicious shift made his eyes sparkle, and triumph swirled in the depths of her heart. He'd smiled…for her.

"Go, *draga*."

With a nod, she backtracked to grab the satchel. Slinging it over her shoulder, she picked up her own as well. She needed her healing salve to take the sting from her muscles and soothe a few scrapes. As she reached the edge of the clearing, instinct whispered a warning. She turned back. Two sets of eyes bored into her, both men watching as though they couldn't wait to be rid of her.

Expressions set, bodies tense, they were acting like recalcitrant children. Giving them a hard look, she pointed first at Xavian then Henrik. "Behave. Both of you."

Henrik blinked.

Xavian frowned.

Afina retreated, taking the path toward the river. They were grown men, for pity's sake. Surely they could get along…at least for the time it took to have her bath.

❦✠❦

Beauty took so many forms. But it was best, the most potent, with death as a companion. A brother-in-arms so to speak. A dark angel casting shadow on the ground and up into the heavens.

The Carpathian Mountains were like that; splendid yet cruel to the point of evisceration.

Shay felt the twist in his gut even now. The mental disembowelment came with a view. Stretched out for miles in front of him, the peaks and valleys connected ridges and lakes and plateaus alike. The beast of it waited in those hollows, sure with jagged teeth, deep crevices, and slippery slopes. Were he lucky, he might lose his footing and fall into one like Curio had almost done.

His warhorse snorted. The weak sound made Shay squeeze his eyes shut. He couldn't wait much longer. It was selfish to do so, but—

Shit. He couldn't bear to kill his horse. Curio was his only friend.

His eyes burned as he swept the landscape, trying to find the courage. Drachaven lay to the east, nestled amid sheer cliffs and solid rock. Ram had chosen his roost well. From what he'd heard from the villagers below, the fortress was carved into the mountainside, right into the belly of the beast. Probably had the temperament and teeth to match.

Shay didn't care. Death was inevitable. A sure bet that made him twitch with impatience.

It wouldn't be long now. A week, no more, and he would be crouched in Drachaven's shadow. Camped like a wraith on Ram's doorstep.

Rock clicked against stone, scrambling one ahead of the other in a quick tumble down the path he'd just climbed. He glanced over his shoulder. His stomach clenched, fisting up tight. Curio was trying to get up.

With a silent curse, he jumped from his perch onto the path below. The warhorse kicked out with his broken fetlock, rocking his powerful body to shift from his supine position. Curio screamed but tried again. The sound of agony ripped Shay in two. He shouldn't have waited. It was the height of cruelty to leave a friend to suffer and one the code did not allow.

Screw the code. This was his friend and comrade. And selfish or nay, he'd needed some time to say good-bye, to send his trusted companion off into the ether with more than a slice to the neck.

Rock scale crunched beneath his knees, biting through his leathers as he knelt beside Curio. He put his hand on his shoulder, on the soft pelt he would never touch again. "Stay down, boy. Stay down."

Shay stroked him gently, murmuring reassurances. Like a good soldier, the warhorse laid his head back down, trusting him to do the right thing. But he never had. Didn't have the first clue about right and wrong. Or which was which. Halál was responsible for that along with Al Pacii.

The anger inside him burned a hole in his heart. How different his life could have been if only—

Curio shifted, and the bone shard protruding from his slim leg trembled. High-pitched but soft, he whinnied while the wind whispered against the back of Shay's neck.

It was time.

Dipping his head, he laid his cheek against Curio's neck. The heat and nap of his fine coat tunneled deep, opening gaps until he felt like naught but a hard shell with an empty inside. "I am sorry, my friend. I never should have brought you here...through this passage on this journey. It was mine alone to take. Not yours… never yours."

A breathy gust left Curio.

Forgiveness? Shay wanted to believe it was, but absolution lay through the mountains. Action must accompany words. Otherwise they meant little or naught at all. "My pledge to you, Curio. I go to my death to right this wrong."

The warhorse made one last attempt to get up.

He unsheathed the blade high on his chest and held him down. "You cannot come with me."

Curio snorted but lay accepting, heavy muscle flickering in a rolling tremble along his flank. Resting the knife against Curio's flesh, Shay pressed in, made a clean slice, and watched his friend's blood flow. It ran red, marring the beauty of his black hide, and dripped onto the grey rock below. He sent his steed into the afterlife with a soft stroke, a gentle murmur, and a heavy weight in his heart.

One life for another.

He had taken an innocent girl's. Now the universe had claimed his friend. Balance. In all things, there must be balance.

Light and dark. Soft and hard. Right and wrong.

Each complemented the other, painting a clear picture.

He knew the way forward, just as he had in front of that cave. He must finish what he started. Ram needed to be warned of The Three, of what he'd let loose upon the earth and the incantation. Otherwise he wouldn't be able to use them, and Halál would win.

Stroking Curio one last time, Shay pushed to his feet. After wiping the blade clean, he set it back in its sheath, wishing it was his heart. The damn thing hurt and the ache wasn't likely to stop anytime soon.

A beautiful death. It was what he wished for above all else.

He only hoped Ram would be merciful. Just as he had been with Curio.

CHAPTER TWENTY

Mercy wasn't part of the plan. Flying fists that ended in broken bones and spilled blood? Now that had a serious amount of potential. Though he should probably wait until Henrik started it.

Afina had told him to *behave*.

Xavian cranked his fists in tight. The muscles along the column of his spine flexed as he followed her retreat through a break in the trees. She paused on the path to glance at him over her shoulder. Even from there he saw the warning in her gaze.

Aye, no doubt about it. Waiting was absolutely the best strategy. That way when she came back to find Henrik lying face down on the turf he wouldn't have to lie. He'd have an excuse... self-defense.

Dishonesty was never acceptable. Hedging, manipulating, or even omitting certain facts?—always, but outright lies held no place between them. And though he hadn't promised her a thing, the idea of disappointing her didn't sit well. Jesu, he was going to have to sort that out. Going soft for a priestess with a gentle touch and giving nature put him in lunatic territory. One shade shy of an asylum.

Regardless, the urge to please her was too strong to deny. No chance in hell he would strike first. Henrik would have to come to him.

"Feathering your love nest, are you?" With great interest, Henrik traced Afina's retreat. Silence swirled like poison before he returned his attention to Xavian, his gaze full of speculation. "Any room for a third?"

Rahat. He would do more than kill the bastard. He would skin him alive.

But not until Henrik engaged.

His comrade was fishing. Xavian smelled the trap, knew bait when he saw it. Afina sat perched on the hook, a provocation Henrik had cast out for a reason.

"She's pretty, if a bit thin." Turning sideways, Henrik flicked the towel from his shoulder.

Xavian tensed, instincts coming alive. Their kind never turned away from an enemy. To give their back or side left them open to attack. And vulnerable was never where an assassin wanted to be. The fact his comrade had committed that sin was worthy of note.

What the hell was Henrik hiding? What sat on his chest that he didn't want Xavian to see? Thinking back he realized Henrik had never gone without a tunic at Grey Keep. Or in an Al Pacii camp. Not while training or in the midst of others. Xavian shifted right, trying to get a clear view.

In a rush, Henrik reached for his clothes. Before Xavian could get a glimpse, he tossed his leather tunic over his head. "I like my women plump, but an exception can always be made."

A direct hit.

Xavian clenched his teeth. Christ, this silent shit was getting old. But the more Henrik talked, the better his ability to ferret out the facts. His comrade wanted something. Something that had little if anything to do with the old man. Halál had ordered his execution on sight, and if Henrik were here for that purpose he would already have tried to take his head.

"What say you?" Henrik pulled the lacing on the side of his tunic tight. "In the mood to share the wench?"

Hearing Afina called a "wench" almost sent Xavian over the edge. He locked his muscles, refusing to move. He couldn't stop the growl, however. It broke through, rolled up his throat, giving sound to his rage. Black birds in the tree above him scattered, taking flight as they perceived a predator in their midst.

"Hmm, guess not." One corner of his mouth jacked up, Henrik sheathed his blades and pivoted to face him. Xavian frowned. Something other than amusement gleamed in his comrade's eyes. Was that relief he spotted? "A bit possessive of her, aren't you, Ram?"

"Very," he said, his territorial nature getting the better of him. Didn't matter. 'Twas time to end the game. If Henrik needed a declaration to start the fight, he was more than happy to provide one. "Touch her and you die."

Henrik nodded and broke eye contact. Xavian's gaze narrowed. Aye, 'twas definitely relief on his comrade's face.

"Time to tell me why you are here, brother."

In answer, Henrik unsheathed a dagger and let it fly.

Without moving his feet, Xavian tipped his head to the side, felt the wind, heard the blade whistle by his ear before it hit the tree trunk behind him. The *twang* rippled through the clearing as the steel settled into its temporary home.

Dropping his arm to his side, Henrik raised a brow. "Clear enough?"

Well, well, well. The bastard had clearly started something, hadn't he? Xavian bared his teeth and started forward. In agreement with the plan, Henrik settled into a fighting stance.

Finally. He would get what he needed. The satisfaction of a bone-crushing brawl while he beat the truth out of Henrik. And really, who could deny such a gift as that?

❊❖❊

Blood ran from Henrik's left temple. The trickle just missed the outside corner of his eye as he blocked the right hook with his forearm. Ram countered with a quick jab to his rib cage. Tucking his elbow in tight, Henrik absorbed the blow and spun. Loose turf churning beneath his boots, he delivered an uppercut, unwrapping the punch like a present beneath Ram's chin.

A shock wave rippled through his fist.

Ram cursed.

Henrik grinned. Goddamn, he loved a skilled opponent. And one as fast as Ram never failed to please.

"That all you got?" Ram stepped back and circled left.

"Not even close." Henrik moved right, mirroring his friend. "I learned a few things in Poland."

"Prepared to share?"

" 'Tis the least I can do."

Ram snorted.

Henrik attacked, hammering his friend with all the skill he'd gained from the savages in the North. Someone needed to pay for the loss of his sister, for her senseless death and his pain. It might as well be Ram. He could take it, shape it, give him the release he needed.

Christ, he hadn't felt this good in months.

Fighting with Ram was like manna from heaven. Inspired in a hallelujah kind of way.

His comrade smiled around his split lip, dropped into a crouch, and pinwheeled. The bastard's boot caught his ankles and sent him flying. Henrik landed with a thud beside the fire pit and, planting his hand in the dirt, rolled in the opposite direction.

"*Rahat.*" Ram leapt skyward, trying to clear his body as it hurtled toward his legs.

As he passed underneath him, Henrik reached up, caught the toe of Ram's boot, and pulled. His friend went topsy-turvy, landing in a heap a few feet away.

"Nice." On his back in the dirt, Ram jackknifed to his feet. Rotating his arm in a backward circle, he closed the distance between them, coming at him like a sidewinder. "Impressive, H."

He reset his stance. "I aim to please."

"Since when?"

Henrik shook his head. Trust Ram to want to chat while in the midst of a good fight. It was surprising, actually. In the heart of Al Pacii, Ram had been quiet, keeping to himself more often than not. But then, he'd been the same way, and like recognized like. 'Twas the reason he'd spent most of his time with Ram, almost all of it passing in companionable silence.

But his friend wasn't silent now. Something had changed. Henrik suspected Afina was to blame.

It didn't seem possible, but seeing them together forced him to admit the truth. Ram was perfect for her. The bastard could love and protect her at the same time. Something he'd been unable to do on his best day. What did that make him? Weak? Inept? A terrible brother?

The roar of denial started soul deep. The vibration rattled through him, ripping him wide open. Rage spilled out, giving way to a war cry as he lunged at his friend. Halfway to his target,

Henrik realized his error. But it was too late to stop. The narrow alleyway to his heart was already open, and Ram would use it without mercy.

Henrik saw the flash of a blade and almost smiled. Relief was but moments away. His death would wipe the slate clean—bring justice to those he'd killed, to the murdered lass with pleading eyes that still haunted his dreams.

He could go now.

His sister was safe with a man he trusted, no matter how badly it had gone in the end. 'Twas the last piece of his puzzle, and as it slid home to complete the picture, steel nicked his skin. Instinct threw his hands out to block the thrust. Ram twisted his wrist and brought the dagger up, slicing through the lacing on the side of his tunic.

Henrik grabbed for his belly, searching for the wound. His hands came away clean. No blood. No guts. No torn flesh.

Time defied logic and slowed until every moment lasted an eternity. Henrik frowned and met Ram's icy gaze. The bastard kicked his feet out from under him, slamming him back-first into the turf. The numbness left and feeling came back in a rush. The tingle worked its way to his fingertips as Ram planted one boot on his biceps, the other on the opposite thigh, and ripped his tunic aside.

His friend's gaze landed on his chest—on the proof of his shared blood with Afina. Both marked by the moon-star, the goddess's brand sat over his heart. Christ, what a fallacy. He hated the goddess. She'd destroyed his family. Cut them apart like a butcher's knife separating muscle from bone.

And now Ram had made the connection. Henrik could see it in his eyes.

"Jesu. I knew you were hiding something. I knew, but…" The tip of his knife dipped as Ram's gaze left the moon-star to meet his. Surprise and something more moved in the depths of his pale eyes.

Henrik recognized it for what it was…compassion. A rare understanding that made him want to gag. The bitter taste sat like a boil on his tongue, oozing poison. The bastard. What right did he have to pity him? Grey Keep wasn't a place anyone went to by choice. Whatever Ram's history, it couldn't be any better than his.

Grabbing Ram's calf, he shoved. "Back the hell off."

A crease between his dark brows, Ram stepped back. "You are related."

Pulling his tunic closed, he hid the mark that shamed him and rolled to his feet. Ram stood six feet away, ready but quiet, ever patient as was his nature. Normally he respected that about his friend. Today he wanted to kill him for it.

The silence was too much, opening a fissure into the past. It made him remember what he needed to forget: that his mother and the goddess of all things had never wanted him. And no matter how many times he told himself it didn't matter, the hurt shattered his well-constructed illusion.

His rib cage contracted around his lungs. He breathed deep to combat the squeeze and reached for a distraction. He wouldn't best Ram if he lost control again.

"Shit," he said, glancing down at the loopholes of his damaged tunic. "You owe me new laces."

"Screw the laces." Sheathing his dagger, Ram gave him a hard look, refusing to allow his evasion. "Afina's your sister, isn't she?"

The question wasn't a question at all, but a statement of fact. Henrik waited for the panic, for the closed in feeling he always got when caged. It never came. Instead the truth embraced him like a thick mantle in the dead of winter. Goddamn, it felt good. He didn't have to hide it anymore. "We are blood kin...of the same line."

"Sweet Christ, H," Ram said, tone edged by fury. "What the hell have you been doing? She needed you...your protection and strength. You could have...You are her family, for shit's sake."

His hands cranked into fists, he surged toward Ram. "Do not pretend gallantry. You are no better than I."

"I did not abandon my kin." His guard up, Ram pivoted on one foot, matching him step for step.

"The hell you didn't." Henrik bared his teeth and struck, cranking his knuckles into Ram's ribs. Ever ready, his friend absorbed the blow, brought his elbow up, and slammed it against the side of his head. Off balance, Henrik dodged a well-aimed jab and circled left as Ram went right.

"Who did I betray? Halál?" Pale eyes almost glowing, Ram said, "I owe that butcher nothing. Not my loyalty or my skill."

"You bastard," Henrik said, hearing the ache in his own voice. He hated the weakness, but naught could stop the wound from opening. Even after all this time, it was still fresh. Deep-seated pain threw his fists out in a volley meant to maim.

Ram blocked each thrust, turning them aside without attacking in return. "Who, Henrik?"

"Goddamn it..." Henrik's throat closed around a lump so big he couldn't swallow. How could Ram not know? How could he not see his mistake?

He threw another punch. Ram caught his fist in the cup of his hand, held on, and reeled him in. Nose to nose, his friend locked him in place. Henrik refused to retreat. He would have his say before he slit Ram's throat. Naught would do but that he die with the truth of his crime ringing inside his head.

"Tell me, brother."

"Me!" His eyes burned as the truth exploded, geyser high. "You betrayed me!"

Ram's hand tightened around his fist. "Nay. Never. I—"

"You left me there...with that bastard," he said, the accusation whisper-thin as his voice gave out. "You took the others... and left me! You left me..."

"Jesu, Henrik. You were in Poland."

"You could have gotten word to me." He thumped Ram on the shoulder with his free hand. "Instead you gathered the others and—"

"I did not! They followed, H. They followed!" Ram grabbed the side of his neck with his free hand and hung on. "I left alone. Scaled the north cliffs in the dead of night to escape Grey Keep and Halál."

Henrik shook his head, struggling to understand. A moment passed before comprehension hit. The band around his chest loosened a little. Drawing back as much as Ram's hold would allow, he wiped his eyes.

Christ, the north cliffs. Ram must have been half mad to have risked his life like that.

"I stopped at Ismal to return the boy...to Sherene," Ram said as his grip tightened.

"Ivan's woman?"

He nodded. "Cristobal and the others tracked me through the mountains into the marketplace."

"Goddamn Cristobal." Henrik closed his eyes, no longer fighting Ram's touch. Had he not been a man, he might have cried. His friend hadn't chosen the others above him. Hadn't meant to leave him behind. Relief came with that knowledge, and struggling for control, he said, "The son of a bitch always was the best tracker."

"I thought they'd been sent to kill me, but—"

"They wished to join you instead."

"Aye."

"And Drachaven?"

"The keep and land were given to me by the Wallachian ruler, Basarab...for services rendered."

So the rumors were true. No surprise there. A credit to their kind, Ram was brutal when it came to battle and ambushes. "The decimation of the Hungarian army in the mountain pass."

"We killed many, forcing King Charles into negotiations with Basarab," Ram said, loosening his grip a little. "Wallachia is now a free country, and I have a home."

Henrik straightened, putting more space between them. "Lucky bastard."

"Very." His expression serious, Ram released Henrik's fist to rest his hand on his shoulder. Locked together by touch and truth, he said, "I did not want to leave you, brother, or the others, but I couldn't stay. Not a moment longer."

Foolish or not, Henrik believed him. Ram never lied. 'Twas a flaw he didn't understand, but one he appreciated. The truth was a strange animal. It washed all things clean. Forgiveness didn't come easy, but for the moment, letting go of the anger felt better than holding onto it.

Henrik rolled his shoulder, knocking his friend's hand free. "You're taking Afina to Drachaven?"

"Aye." Releasing his nape, Ram stepped back, resetting the boundaries between them. His gaze slid to the head of the trail, toward the river and Afina. "Vladimir Barbu's wolves hunt her. Until I find and kill him, 'tis the safest place for her to be."

"I know where to find him," Henrik said, inspecting his bruised knuckles.

"How's that?"

"I'm inside the enemy camp...a hunter hired to track Barbu's prey." He shrugged when Ram raised a brow. "I needed information to track Afina...her last known location. The bastard provided that."

"He paid you?"

"In gold."

The corners of Ram's mouth curved. "Well done."

Henrik dipped his chin in a mock bow and straightened with a grin. His enjoyment faded, however, when Ram stepped in close again and offered his hand.

Still as death, his comrade waited for him to accept the peace offering. "Will you make your home with us, brother? Drachaven is strong, but 'twill be stronger with you among us. You have a place with us, H...if you want it."

His heart stumbled then picked up its beat. A home. A true one he could come back to with friends inside instead of rivals. It took an instant to decide, and as his palm met Ram's the pieces of another puzzle clicked into place. "Do you have a priest at Drachaven?"

Ram shook his head. "Why? You going to need the last rites anytime soon?"

"Nay. But you will..." Henrik trailed off, using the pause to effect. "If you don't do right by Afina."

"'Tisn't that simple. I—"

"She is my sister." He tightened his grip on his friend. "My *sister*."

"Christ."

"Do not make me regret my forgiveness." Meeting his gaze head-on, Henrik put a warning in his own. "Wed her, brother, and you will have no quarrel with me. Abandon her and I will take you apart...piece by bloody piece."

CHAPTER TWENTY-ONE

The trews were a revelation. The clean skin a blessing. And the two came together as though meant to be...like wings on a bird.

Afina smoothed her hand over the leather encasing her thigh then kicked out with her foot. Her mouth curved. Good goddess, the freedom was nothing short of amazing. She could move so quickly. No heavy fabric to twitch aside or lift, just...light-as-air leather. She did a little jig. The trews slipped, falling down her hips an inch at a time.

She grabbed for the waistband and reached for the lacing. Each tug pulled the leather tighter, molded it to her curves until she bit her bottom lip. Glancing over her shoulder, she took a gander at her behind.

Well. The trews certainty fit...umm, adequately.

Her gaze swung to the head of the path. Xavian was going to have a seizure when he saw her outfit. Then again, he was the one to suggest it, so...

"Never mind him," she said, tying a bow to secure the trews. With a wiggle, she adjusted the lacing below her belly button and reached for a long linen strip. "As if his opinion matters."

The instant she said it Afina recognized it for what it was—a lie.

She sighed. Drat Xavian and his love of honesty. She'd caught his disease. Now it spread like some rampant infection, disrupting her ability to avoid the truth. Afina smoothed her thumb over the fraying ends of the linen binding and wondered if there was a cure. An elixir, mayhap, that would return the capacity to delude herself.

Maybe then she could stop what was happening. Stop the ache and the need and the—

No. She refused to call it love. She didn't *love* Xavian. How could she? He'd kidnapped her, for heaven's sake. Scared and harassed and...protected her at every turn. Made her feel important and cherished, as though she mattered to someone.

A delusion. She needed one right now. Otherwise she would remember the way he made her toes curl when he touched her, and that wouldn't be good for anyone.

Afina tucked the linen strip beneath her arm and wound the first length underneath both breasts. How could she fix this? How could she defend against something she didn't understand? The walls she'd spent most of her life building were failing. With the efficiency of a siege engine, Xavian had hammered a hole in her defenses. Now the ramparts were crumbling, opening a fissure into a world of hurt. Sooner or later she would lose her footing and fall in. And how did one recover from a tumble like that?

She glanced toward the trailhead, picturing his rugged beauty and steady strength. It would be so easy to take that leap, to push off and let herself fly. But Xavian had made it clear he didn't want to catch her. Not that he'd said as much. It was more a feeling; a deep truth that festered like a sore on her soul.

He didn't want her. At least, not in a way that mattered...in a way that lasted.

Her brows drawn tight, Afina stared at the roots of the huge oak beside her. A family of black ants worked between its gnarled feet. She watched one drag an impossible load and yanked on the linen strip, pulling the cloth tight around her rib cage. With quick hands, she wound the linen over her breasts until nothing but a small bump sat on her chest. Qabil's tunic was too thin to go without binding. Bottom-hugging trews aside, her nipples didn't need to make an appearance. She would die—simply *die*— if the pair peeked when Xavian laid eyes on her. He had that effect. And while keeling over might fix her problem with him, she refused to leave Sabine.

After tossing on her tunic, she laced up her boots. Double knotting the last bow, she—

The amulet chirped.

Afina glanced at her satchel. She frowned as it trilled again. While taking her bath, she'd heard it a number of times, each chirp longer than the last. It was almost as if the white crystal searched for her, calling out in the hopes she might come. Ridiculous mayhap, but the whisper pull her forward until she stood beside the leather pouch.

Birds twittered, balancing on the branch above her. Afina watched them for a moment, uncertainty drawing her stomach tight. With a sigh, she pivoted to sit on a smooth-faced rock. Her gaze drifted to the bag beside her feet. She really didn't have time for this. She needed to return to the clearing. Xavian and Henrik were up to something. And it wasn't anything good. They had acted like a couple of rabid dogs, gazes trained on each other, just short of snarling.

She rubbed her damp palms on her leather-clad thighs. Mayhap she should wait. The amulet wasn't going anywhere and—

Afina flinched as the satchel shifted to touch the side of her boot. The amulet squawked again, the piercing sound insistent. All right, so maybe waiting wasn't the best thing to do. But honestly, she didn't want to touch the thing. It reminded her too much of her mother.

"Mama's dead," she whispered to make herself feel better. "She cannot hurt you anymore."

Logically, Afina knew that. Her mother was long gone, but the memories persisted. Images of her mother's eyes filled with fury, of a raised hand and the amulet's bright flash against her breastbone came with unrelenting regularity.

But that flash.

Afina squeezed her eyes shut and pressed her hand over her mouth. The crystal twittered again, this time softly, as though it understood. Releasing a pent-up breath, she reached for the satchel. Worn by time, the leather settled against her palm as she lifted the bag into her lap. It was time to stopping running. She hadn't run from the dragons, and now she must stop fleeing her legacy.

With a flick, she split its mouth wide and looked inside. Clean and straight, the stitches sat as she had left them with nary a lump to indicate the amulet lay hidden behind fold after fold of leather. Afina traced each one then palmed her healing knife. Often used to lance abscesses, the small blade made quick work, cutting through each thread to unearth an infection of a different kind.

The crystal winked in the low light.

About the size of her palm, the gemstone was a perfect circle. Cut with a precision seldom seen, the gemstone sat in a bed of gold, the lip of which curled around it to form a quarter-inch band. Afina traced the inscription engraved on the golden face with her fingertip. Each letter looped into the next, forming an intricate message that looked more like scrollwork than words.

The engraving was written in an ancient language. One Afina couldn't read. Her mother had never bothered to teach her.

Her hand poised above it, she stared at the thing then reached in. She cringed as the pendant slid into her palm, expecting to see her mother's face, hear her voice and the terrible things she'd always said. Ghosting warmth wrapped around her forearm instead. The heat dove beneath the surface of her skin, and a wave of contentment wound its way around her heart. The amulet pulsed then hummed a welcome.

Put me on, it seemed to say. As though only the skin around her neck would do.

She fingered the gold links. After a moment, she dipped her head and looped the chain over it. As the pendant settled against her heart, she sighed. By the goddess, it felt like coming home.

"And so you are," the voice said as white light flashed on the riverbank. "Welcome, daughter."

Afina yelped and shot to her feet. Twin fists at the ready, she raised them as she'd seen Xavian do and spun toward the water's edge. A woman stood six feet away. Dressed in an emerald gown, the sparkling folds flowed around her long limbs and graceful lines. A jeweled crown perched amid auburn hair that flowed in a wave to her ankles. Afina traced the golden aura surrounding the woman's body, felt her power, and knew awe for the first time in her life.

The goddess: keeper of light and shadow. Mother of all things.

At a complete loss for words, she stood stock-still and stared. The goddess gazed back, a soft smile on her face, no doubt waiting for her to return the greeting. But...what did one say to a goddess?

Probably something polite and respectful.

Lowering her fists, Afina ran through the possibilities. Just as she settled on one, her mouth ran away with her brain, and she blurted, "Where the devil have you been?"

The goddess laughed. The tinkling sound circled, wrapping Afina in a warm embrace. "I can see why the male desires you, child. Your spirit is commendable."

Taking a shallow breath, Afina fought the hollowness rising like a starburst inside her. A burn with sharp teeth and bitter disposition, it scorched her, begging for freedom. How dare the goddess *praise* her? The all-powerful being had stood by and done nothing while her family suffered.

"Why did you never help?" Afina took a step toward her, muscles so tight they shrieked in protest. "Why? Bianca is dead! And my brother, he—"

"Will come back to you…in time."

In time? What did that mean? Afina paced to the opposite side of the clearing. It was either that or scream and hurl a tree branch at the deity's head.

"Patience, Afina." The goddess drew her elegant hands from inside the wide sleeves of her gown. "All things happen for a reason. Destiny takes each on their own journey. Bianca's life was meant to be powerful but never long. You have her memory to comfort you. Be satisfied with that."

"Satisfied…" Afina fisted her hand in her tunic, right over her heart. The ache was unbearable. An empty hole inside her that grew by the day. How was she to fill it? What would stop the hurt?

She stared at the rippling surface of the river, struggling to understand. No matter how hard she tried, she couldn't. It was senseless, the pain and suffering so unnecessary. "You could have saved her. You could have…"

Her green eyes filled with what Afina wanted to believe was sorrow, the goddess shook her head. "Nay, child. Things are as they should be, and you are the stronger for it."

"It isn't fair."

"Not many things are. But know this…you are the chosen. The bridge from the past into our future."

"I don't understand. Not any of it."

Gentle fingers touched her chin. Afina raised her head and stared across the expanse between them. The goddess hadn't moved, but she felt the brush of her hand. Her chin perched on invisible fingers, Afina watched the goddess shimmer in the evening light.

Brushing the hair away from Afina's temple, she said, "Daughter, I have waited so many moons for you to be ready. Very soon our work will begin. Until then, stay close to your male. We will speak again when you are safely housed within his fortress."

"But—"

"Look to the sky, Afina." The goddess tapped the tip of her nose, glanced at the setting sun, then disappeared on a wave of sparkling light.

The last of her instructions came through on a whisper. *"Look to the sky, child."*

A ripple of unease rolled through Afina. Unable to ignore the warning, she glanced up and heard a faint undulation of large wings. Heaven help her.

Grabbing both satchels on the fly, Afina tore toward the trail and Xavian. She needed to reach him before they did.

❈✛❈

For the first time in his life, Xavian was afraid. Not of Henrik or his threats, but of himself. The ultimatum his friend had delivered wasn't the problem. He could deal with the consequences of denying Henrik. Delivering death to preserve his life was a part of him—so familiar he called it friend most days. Instinct wasn't a bad thing. It kept him strong, but now it ran contrary to his will.

Wed Afina.

La dracu. Temptation nearly brought him to his knees. What he wouldn't give to wake up with her each morning and love her every night. To have her time and attention, to share the moments in his day, both large and small. To have someone love him for more than what he could do with a blade.

But then that was the problem, wasn't it?

All he knew—all he was—started and ended in a fight. Without a sword in his hand, he didn't amount to much. Aye, Afina would give him all he needed, everything he craved, but what did he have to give her in return? Naught. He was a brutal man with a brutal way of life. Her gentle soul and loving heart wouldn't survive him. Without meaning to he would take her apart, one piece at a time until he destroyed what he loved about her.

Xavian rubbed a hand over the back of his neck. He couldn't let that happen. She was too precious, too pure to be touched again by him.

"What say you?"

He glanced at Henrik. Crouched by the fire pit, his friend's gaze drilled him. The persistent bastard wasn't going to drop the issue. He wanted an answer—his promise—and as Xavian watched him stir the fire with a thin stick, he searched for the right response. Something to appease his comrade and buy himself more time.

When he didn't answer, Henrik's eyes narrowed on him. Xavian ignored the warning and walked past him to reach his saddlebags. Flipping the leather flap open, he palmed a small packet. As he turned, he tossed the bundle at his friend. Henrik caught it in midair.

"New laces." Closing the bag, he straightened and glanced toward the path. The small break in the trees stood empty, but it wouldn't for long. Afina was coming up the trail.

'Twas the strangest thing, but he could feel her like a heartbeat. He needed the conversation to end...now, before she entered the dell. The last thing he wanted was for her to overhear—he wouldn't dishonor her with false promises.

He dragged his focus from the path and approached the pit. Stepping over a moss-covered log, he sat and met Henrik's gaze head-on. "All will be settled at Drachaven."

"With a priest?"

"I'll find one," he said, feeling like a cad for misleading his friend. It wasn't a lie, exactly. He would keep his word. Drachaven needed a priest and his people, a good father's guidance. Others would be married by the man even if Xavian never used his services.

"Good." Henrik dropped the stick and picked up the wooden spoon. He stirred the stew then sipped, tasting the broth. "'Tis ready. Do we wait for Afina or—"

"Xavian!" Afina tore into the clearing, both satchels flapping behind her.

The urgency in her voice elevated his pulse. Xavian shot to his feet. He scanned the woods behind her. Was someone after her? Had she been hurt? Bandits sometimes roamed the forest, outcasts waiting for unsuspecting travelers. They'd always given him a wide berth, but...

He unsheathed the daggers high on his chest and heard Henrik do the same.

After searching the tree line, his attention slid back to Afina. He ran his gaze over her, fearing an injury, and stopped short. Not a bruise or a scratch, but...sweet Jesu. Xavian swallowed, unable to take his eyes away from the trews. From all the lovely curves encased in leather.

God help him. Her legs were so long.

He relived the feel of them wrapped around his hips. The memory gathered speed until coherent thought left his head. The mass exodus took the blood with it, sending a rush below his waist. As the traitor in his own trews stirred, Xavian started at her boots and worked his way up, memorizing the slim line of her calves and sweetly rounded thighs. The hollow between almost did him in, but more than anything he wanted her to turn around. He hadn't seen her bottom during their loving in the stables. If only she'd—

"Xavian." Out of breath, she doubled over, planting both hands on her knees. "We need to go."

The urge to move around behind her and enjoy the view grabbed hold. He started toward her. She straightened, and frustration got the better of him until he met her gaze. Fear shone in her eyes, a true panic that returned him to proper working order.

Shoving lust back into its drawer, he sheathed one blade and reached for her. Her skin whispered against his palm as he cupped the side of her neck. "What?"

"We need to leave...right now." She grabbed his forearm with both hands.

Henrik stepped up beside them, his focus on the trees. "Why?"

She turned wide eyes on her brother. "They're coming. I can hear them...they're coming."

Xavian didn't need to ask, he knew. "H, put out the fire. I'll saddle the horses."

With a nod, his friend pivoted toward the fire pit and their evening meal.

"What can I do?"

"Gather our things, Afina. Make sure they are well packed and the ties well knotted." Xavian gave her shoulder a gentle squeeze, hating the fact he could do naught more to reassure her. If what she sensed held true, the dragons weren't far off. He refused to risk Afina again, to test her abilities a second time. The pain she'd experienced after their first attack told him all he needed to know. She might not survive another. "We ride hard and fast for Drachaven."

She clung to his arm. "But—"

"Go," he said, putting the harshness of command in his tone. Without time for regret, he gave her a little push as he released her. "We're going to outrun the bastards."

CHAPTER TWENTY-TWO

A winged shadow drifted over the ground, blocking out the setting sun. Hunched over the saddle horn, Afina followed Xavian's lead. She didn't need to look to know Henrik rode hell-bent behind her. She could almost feel his horse's breath on the back of her neck.

A second silhouette joined the first, turning the brown dirt of the forest floor black.

The dark stain banked right, circling behind them, and sweat trickled between her shoulder blades. A chill swept through her, chasing the droplets down her spine. With the reins sliding between her numb fingers, she waited for the third shadow.

Violet Eyes hadn't flown over yet.

The magical trace he left in his wake was different than the others—a unique signature she knew as sure as the moon-star on her shoulder. He was older, filled with a cosmic vibration Afina recognized without knowing why. The fact he was absent didn't feel right.

Why had he sent Tareek and the younger dragon ahead?

Another mile thundered past, her heartbeat keeping time with the horses' hooves, her mind chewing on the question while tree trunks blurred together. The fury of it made Afina imagine the forest was taking cover—as though each tree knew what flew above and had picked up its roots to flee in the opposite direction. The thinning woods gave credence to the thought. They were running out of trail, galloping straight into the teeth of the Carpathians.

Afina flinched. That was it...the reason they hadn't moved in for the kill.

The canny beasts were waiting for them to reach the mountains, a dragon's natural hunting ground. Violet Eyes was no doubt perched in a deep crevice while the others herded them toward him like cattle.

Mother Mary. She needed to warn Xavian. Now. Before he charged into a trap.

Afraid to yell and alert Tareek, Afina urged her horse to greater speed. With a snort, the beast surged forward then faltered—ears flat, sides heaving—exhaustion from the extended run taking hold. If she pushed the gelding any harder he would stumble, and she would fall.

Tight bands of pressure squeezed her rib cage as she watched the gap between her horse and Xavian's grow. Well, there was nothing for it. Xavian would no doubt throttle her, but what other choice did she have?

Tam-tam drums pounding in her temples, Afina eased her grip on the reins, slowing the horse to a canter. Henrik thundered past her. She heard him curse then whistle softly. Xavian glanced over his shoulder. She was already slipping from the saddle. With a yank, she loosened the belly cinch, grabbed the reins, and led her horse off the trail.

She stopped in a small break in the bracken. Huge oaks held court, shielding them from the sky and the predators who owned it. She took a fortifying breath, planted her feet, and waited for Xavian.

She didn't wait long.

With soundless precision, he came through the high ferns, the devil in his eyes and a scowl on his face. A sliver of fear took root then grew, strangling her confidence. She held both hands out and took a step back. "Xavian…"

He vaulted from Mayhem's saddle.

"If you'll just listen for a moment, I can exp—"

Afina squeaked as his arms closed around her. Without losing stride, he hauled her beneath the oak's thick canopy and pinned her to its trunk. Sharp ridges of bark bit through the thin tunic into her back, but she didn't fight him. Instead she let him mold her as he slid his knee between her legs, caging her against his chest.

"Look, I just—"

"Be quiet. Don't move." He growled the order against her cheek.

The urge to bash him for his arrogance reared its ugly head. Afina squashed it and shut her mouth instead. His high-handed nature would be dealt with later. Not now. Not with dragons flying overhead and his hands all over her. If she put him in his place, one of two things would happen: he would strangle her or find a better way to keep her quiet. Her body hummed, voting for option two. Afina sighed. If only it were that easy—as effortless as the pleasure he gave her. But the price of oblivion was consequence, and that meant dealing with Xavian's anger after the bliss had faded and reality returned.

"Anything?" he whispered, his attention now on Henrik.

Under the neighboring oak, Henrik fisted three sets of reins, peering around leaves and twisted tree limbs. The horses shifted behind him, blowing hard, the toll of exertion flickering along their lathered flanks. With a murmur, he quieted them, expression intense as he searched the sky.

One moment tipped into the next until they piled up, one stacked on top the other. The silence pressed in on an eerie echo, hammering her temples with a persistent tattoo. She turned her face into Xavian's throat. As her skin touched his, he shifted, making space beneath his chin. Greedy, she nestled in, his woodsy scent and the steady beat of his heart more reassuring than the absence of winged shadows on the ground.

Henrik whistled, the sound mimicking the birds that sat above their heads. Catching movement out of the corner of her eye, Afina watched him tap his ear twice and shake his head.

Xavian nodded, accepting the silent message before he dipped his chin. Day-old whiskers rasped against her skin and heat swirled, raising her awareness along with a shiver. Afina burrowed a little deeper, needing more of his scent, more of his warmth, more of everything.

"What the hell were you thinking?" he asked, tone harsh, touch gentle. The paradox gave her pause. How could he sound so angry, yet hold her so gently at the same time?

Her hands flexed on his upper arms. "We need a new plan."

"What's wrong with the old one?" He drew back just enough to look at her.

"Everything." Seduced by the feel of him, desire ignored the danger and murmured. Her body warmed, and her gaze dropped to his mouth. A whisper away, the fullness of his lower lip looked like perfection. Hmm, his taste. It was temptation, a dark craving she longed to appease.

Afina flicked her tongue over her bottom lip, remembering his kiss in the cave. Surely one more sip wouldn't matter. She didn't sense the dragons nearby and—

"Stop it," he said, low and tight. The ache in his voice matched the heat in his eyes as he removed his thigh from between hers.

On a slow exhale, he stepped away, allowing cool air to ghost between them. "Start talking."

His withdrawal left her cold. Struggling to combat the chill, she wrapped her arms around herself. "Something's wrong. Violet Eyes isn't with the others. I can feel his absence."

"Who?"

"Leader of the dragons. The one with blue scales and violet eyes."

"Unbelievable," Henrik said from a few feet away.

Afina flinched. He moved like the wind. How the devil had Henrik gone from his oak to theirs without making a sound—and with the horses in tow?

He winked at her. "Trust a woman to notice eye color in the midst of battle."

Xavian threw him an annoyed look. "An ambush?"

"I think so," she said, rubbing her upper arms. "Dragons like to hunt in the mountains. 'Tis where they are most comfortable, in the high places."

Henrik raised a dark brow. "You sure about that?"

"Yes." Chewing on her lower lip, Afina looked for the evidence to support her certainty. But the memory was slippery, avoiding capture until it sank to the inky depths of her mind. She shook her head and frowned. "I don't know how I know...I just do."

Xavian tugged his cloak from behind the saddle and searched her face, hunting for any trace of doubt. Afina refused to show any. She knew the dragons somehow—*knew* their habits like a mother knew her children—and couldn't abandon the conviction now. If she did, she would fail not only herself, but Xavian as well.

With a flip, he draped his mantle around her shoulders. Soft fur brushed the nape of her neck and his scent drifted from the folds, enveloping her in warm comfort. She sighed, tension fading as he pulled the wool tight and pinned it in place.

Fiddling with the brooch, his eyes narrowed a fraction, and Afina saw the instant a new plan formed in his mind. "Do the beasts like water?"

It was scary, really. The man was brilliant. "No. They are weak swimmers."

"The river," Henrik said, catching on fast.

"The Jiu is our best option," Xavian said, reaching for Mayhem's reins. The warhorse stepped out, bumping Henrik out of the way with his nose. "'Tis wide and deep…the gorge is smooth sided."

Henrik patted Mayhem's flank, making him sidestep. "No place to perch."

"Exactly." Tossing the reins over his steed's neck, Xavian checked the saddlebags before reaching for Afina's horse. With a murmur, he ran his hands from shoulder to haunch, soothing the gelding before tightening the belly strap. "At night no one will see a swift-moving boat."

"How long to Drachaven that way?" Henrik asked, checking his own packs.

"A night to reach the cliffs, another on the river."

Wide-eyed, Afina looked from him to Henrik then back again. "But the horses—"

"Will come with us," he said, his gaze steady on Afina. He could almost see her mind working. Worry was alive in her eyes, inventing problems that had yet to arrive. "The ferrier's boat is large enough to hold them."

Leather creaked as Henrik swung into his saddle. "Any cover on board?"

"Awnings midship, port to starboard." With a frown, he watched Afina chew on her thumbnail. The nervous twitch was out of character, a shift in tension Xavian felt as well as saw. She moved on to the next finger, intent on massacring another nail. He grabbed her hand and, with a tug, brought her a step closer. The strange connection they shared flared as he tipped his chin, demanding an answer without asking.

"I don't like boats," she said, resorting to gnawing on her bottom lip.

"And the water?"

"Even less than boats."

The news brought him up short. Good Christ, the woman could toss a full-grown dragon over a megalith yet feared water? 'Twas baffling and…more than a bit endearing. Even with all her power, she needed him—was depending on him—and that made him feel so damned good he could hardly stand himself.

Lacing their fingers together, he murmured, "'Twill be all right, love. Trust me."

She nodded, and after giving her hand a squeeze, he got her moving. 'Twas dangerous to linger in one place for too long.

As he set her in the saddle, he rechecked her stirrups, concerned for her comfort. The day had been long. The night would be longer. He didn't want her falling from the saddle when exhaustion took hold. Already dark circles had crept beneath her eyes, giving her a bruised look. She needed a soft bed and a week of hearty meals, but that would have to wait a few more days.

Drachaven was close, but so were the beasts.

'Twould take all his considerable skill to see them through. Under normal circumstances, the prospect of besting a worthy opponent would have invigorated him. Not tonight. And as his gaze brushed over Afina one last time, he knew the reason why. He had her now and far too much to lose.

Crouched in shadow at the edge of the forest, Xavian stared across the open expanse toward the cliff edge. Moonlight spilled, greeting the night chill as a brisk breeze played in the short field grass. The gusts swept across the plain, rolling against each blade until the lea rippled like verdant water.

One hundred and fifty yards to the head of the path and no place to hide.

'Twas less than ideal. A true death trap, if the dragons found them before he was ready. But what other choice did he have?

The narrow trail was the only way down the cliffs and onto the beach. A short league and a half away, the cavern lay hidden by the jagged rock face. Deep water washed in through the cave's mouth, and only those brave enough to swim ever saw the inside. The ferrier's dock sat under the cover of the first cavern, and if the dragons refused to swim he would be one step closer to safety and Drachaven.

His senses wide open, Xavian listened but heard naught more than he expected: the leaves rustled above his head and the river murmured, rushing against the high cliffs as it snaked through stone on its way to mountain passes. The horses were calm. Henrik was ready. Afina was not.

He glanced over his shoulder at her. Still mounted, her hands clutched the reins as she waged an internal battle—run and hide or stay and fight. He was torn too. It wasn't the danger, but the fact he didn't want Afina anywhere near it.

Pushing to his feet, he crossed to her. As he slid his hand over her leather-clad thigh and gave her a gentle squeeze, he murmured, "*Draga*, look at me."

Lean muscle flickered under his palm as she dragged her attention away from the field stretched out in front of them. Her gaze met his, and the worry he saw there nearly ripped his heart out. "I d-don't think it's safe here."

"It isn't," he said, for once wishing he could lie. He wanted to reassure her but knew dishonesty wouldn't serve either of them. "Do you sense them?"

"Yes, but..." She glanced at the sky. A copse of blackwood trees obscured the moon, hiding them with thick limbs and flat leaves. Her knuckles went white against the reins. "I cannot...I don't know how close they are. Everything is hazy. It's as though there's a thin film between me and them."

"No doubt their doing," Henrik said, gravity in his gaze as he dismounted. His feet touched the ground without making a sound, and turning to his pack, he tugged open a saddlebag. "A decoy, Ram?"

"Do it." Xavian palmed Afina's waist. His grip light, he lifted her from the saddle. "Your clothes...your scent. The leader will try to take you out first."

Henrik snorted. "He didn't like me much."

"But he didn't kill you," Afina said, slipping her arms around Xavian's waist. Taken off guard, Xavian let her nestle in, cheek to his chest, head beneath his chin. Somehow his arms knew what to do and closed around her, adjusting their fit until she was snug against him. "Why? Violet Eyes could have killed us all with little effort."

"Not true." Giving into impulse, he stroked his hand over her hair. The raven tresses were soft with a hint of dampness, no doubt from her bath. "You kicked his arse."

Her mouth curved against his throat then smoothed out as she leaned away. Back to chewing on her lip, she caressed the tops of his shoulders, following the seam in the leather to his upper arms. "He was after you for some reason. He wanted you."

Xavian shook his head, tried to focus. Jesu, the woman had busy hands. The muscle roping his abdomen flexed as her fingertips played, leaving a heated trail on his skin. She stroked over his biceps. His palms itched, wanting to cup her bottom and lift her against him. Her fingers dipped, caressing the inside crease of his elbows. Xavian locked his knees, ordered the traitor in his trews to settle down, and palmed her waist. It was a sorry second to what he really wanted to touch, but close enough to keep him happy.

"Mayhap..." She peeked up at him through her lashes. "We should try and talk to him again. I could—"

"Nay." The force of his denial made her jump. He grabbed her hands—before she drove him mad with her touch—and held both of hers in one of his. "I'll not risk you like that. Not again."

"Agreed." Finished stuffing his extra trews with dead leaves, Henrik set to work on a tunic. Tucking the linen into the trews, he tied his mantle around the shoulders and stood. "What do you think?"

"Needs a head," Afina said, eying Henrik's makeshift man. "It won't fool them."

"Oh ye of little faith." Henrik propped the stuffed form against a tree trunk and unsheathed a blade. Grabbing a fistful of long weeds, he wound them around his forearm, cut them at the base, then went to work, bending them end over end. With quick hands, he wrapped twine around the bundle, stuffed the lot into the neck hole, and slammed a wide-brimmed hat on the impromptu head. "Better?"

"'Twill do." Xavian released Afina and reached for the decoy. Silence descended, leaving naught but the night sounds as he tied their diversion to Afina's saddle. After wrapping the reins around its wrists, he turned to Henrik. "H, arrows at the ready."

"Aye." Bow in hand, his friend slung a quiver full of poison-tipped arrows over his shoulder. He pulled the buckle in the center of his chest tight and said, "As soon as the gelding clears the long grass, make for the stones at the head of the trail. I'll be on your arse."

Xavian unsheathed one of his swords and shared a look with his friend. 'Twas strange to have him here, ready to charge into battle. Accustomed to hunting alone, he'd never imagined anyone would care enough to fight alongside him. Not until Cristobal and the others had followed. But now in the quiet moments before their flight, Xavian couldn't decide what he liked better. Having Henrik steady at his back or Afina to protect.

"No matter what happens, stay with me." He drilled Afina with a look and checked his knives. Looking pale but determined, she nodded. With a soundlessness born of his time in the saddle, he settled onto Mayhem's back and held out his free hand. She took it, hers fitting like a jewel in his palm as he swung her up behind him. "Hold on tight. 'Twill be a rough ride down the cliff's path to the beach below."

Her cheek against his back, she locked her arms around his waist, and something close to pride struck Xavian chest-level. She was incredible. Without training, she'd faced each challenge he'd thrown at her head-on. Hell, most men couldn't do that, but whether she knew it or not, Afina was a warrior. A lass of such fortitude she made his heart turn over.

"Ready?"

A feral light in his eyes, Henrik nodded, raised his bow, and brought it down across the gelding's rump. With a start, the horse lurched then bolted, jumping over the long grass into the open expanse beyond. His hooves hammered the hard ground and a roar rumbled up the cliff face. The dark shadow followed, wings spread, talons unfurled. The beast hung a moment, suspended in the moonlight, then shot forward.

Already moving, Xavian stayed close to the forest's edge and urged his warhorse into an all-out gallop. Mayhem didn't need any prompting. Even after the long night and extra weight, his legs flew over the short grass. A blast of heat rolled into his flank, and Xavian saw a stream of orange flame from the corner of his eye.

High-pitched and heart-wrenching, a scream ripped across the plain. The dragon had roasted the decoy and now the gelding...

Sweet Christ, nay.

Brimstone combined with the smell of burning flesh. His stomach fisting up tight, Xavian tore his gaze away from the fireball. He couldn't help the horse. He was gone. The only thing Xavian could do now was honor his sacrifice and get them to safety.

A second shadow came over the tops of the trees. Xavian swerved toward the cliff edge, racing for the trailhead as the beast came in low. Henrik crisscrossed, clearing his flank. Arrows whistled, one after the other as his friend let loose.

The blue dragon pitched and rolled, landing ten feet in front of them. Talons leaving deep furrows in the dirt, Violet Eyes sidestepped and, fangs bared, roared. The howl was unlike anything

Xavian had ever heard. Piercing in intensity, it rumbled through the air and across the ground, flattening the sweet grass until it hit them in a deafening wave. Pain streaked between his temples. Afina jerked as Mayhem reared, prancing backward on his hind legs.

With a curse, Xavian fought for control, praying Afina hung on. A death grip on his rib cage, she slid backward then recovered, butting up against him as he put his heels to Mayhem's sides. The warhorse lunged, returning to all fours as Henrik galloped past them. Circling around, his friend unleashed arrow after arrow, aiming for the dragon's vulnerable points: eyes, ears, and nose. The blue-scaled bastard took the volley, using his scales and teeth to deflect them.

The red dragon dove, coming at them from above. Teeth bared, Xavian wheeled Mayhem around and brought his sword up. Just as Tareek reached for Afina, his blade bit. Blood flew, an arcing bolt of black in the pale light.

Tareek shrieked and lost momentum, wobbling as he banked left. Ducking to avoid his wing, Xavian rotated his sword to sink the tip into the beast's soft underbelly. An instant before he struck, Tareek's back claw dipped low, catching Afina midswipe. Time slowed, and Xavian's heart stopped as he felt a tug then the loss of her warmth against his back. He cursed and tried to adjust, to stop her tumble as the red dragon went down.

The beast hit the ground hard, grinding a divot in the earth. One of his claws caught in the cloak, Tareek dragged Afina with him toward the edge of the cliff. Heels digging into the broken ground, she scrambled, clawing at the clasp Xavian had secured only hours before.

Christ, he'd killed her. Had he not given her his mantle…

Anguish a living thing inside his chest he leapt from Mayhem's back. If he could reach her in time, if only…

He roared her name as Tareek went over the edge, hauling Afina into the gorge beyond.

CHAPTER TWENTY-THREE

Freefalling to the river below, Tareek lay on his back, eyes closed and wings folded. Balanced in the center of the dragon's chest, Afina clung to his forepaw to keep from falling. The wind tore at her hair, whipping it around her head as blood rushed in her ears. Red scales slid under her boot treads, pitching her sideways. With a gasp, she grabbed the gold chain around Tareek's neck. The blood crystal flashed, lighting up the center of the medallion.

Her amulet pulsed in answer.

The beat throbbed against her breastbone, recognition blending with revulsion as the red mist washed in behind her eyes. Her vision narrowed and the moon went scarlet, turning the stars pink around it.

Afina pounded on the dragon's chest. "Tareek!"

One green eye cracked open.

"Fly, dragon!"

Tareek blinked once and unfurled his wings. Air caught in the webbing, slowing their descent. His gaze locked on her, he hissed, showing teeth along with temper. Afina snarled back. Idiot dragon. What did he think? That she would faint? Curl up and cry because he growled at her? Not in this lifetime. And not while plummeting headlong to her death.

A dangerous gleam in his eyes, Tareek grinned at her. Oh, dear goddess, no. The beast had no shame. She'd just saved his life and now he was about to—

"*La revedere*, Priestess-sss." Tareek flipped, extending his wings.

Tossed like a rotten apple, Afina hung motionless a moment: Tareek, a red streak above her, the Jiu, a ribbon of indigo below. The blood crystal's glow faded. She reached for it, stretching hard for the gold chain. Her hand caught and held as Tareek surged skyward. She followed his ascent, jerked up like a sturgeon on a fishing line.

The amulet thumped against her breastbone as Tareek banked hard. Flung wide, Afina gritted her teeth and hung on, cursing the goddess for her absence. Mother Mary, it never failed. She was about to freefall to her death, and where was the dratted deity?

Nowhere to be found.

Arm muscles straining, Afina sailed into Tareek's next turn. Fighting momentum, she reached up with her free hand. She needed a better grip, a secure one. Otherwise Tareek would shake her loose and laugh while he watched her fall.

The image gave her strength, and kicking her legs, she propelled herself upward. Just as her left hand grabbed hold, the dragon curled his head under and snorted. Sulfur hit her full force, singeing the inside of her nose. Her lungs seized and pressure built until pain crawled the inside of her chest. Unable to breathe, desperate to hold on, she brought her knees up and curled her body around the medallion.

The amulet's white crystal struck the medallion's red one. Lightning flashed, zigzagging across the night sky, striking so close Tareek flinched. The next strike lit Afina up from the inside out. Her heartbeat slowed. Her eyelids grew heavy and her body light. Blinking, she tried to stay with it and not drift. But a chill slipped through her, relaxing her muscles, forcing its way into her mind until...

She floated carefree and boneless into a pool of clear, bright light.

Invisible hands brushed her face, cupped her hands, pulling her through a blanket of fluffy white fog. Afina blinked to clear her vision. Had she lost her grip and fallen? Was this what dead felt like?

She put one hand to her chest and felt her heartbeat...along with cold metal. She glanced down. Cheek to cheek with the medallion, the amulet hummed, opening her senses wide. Afina found Tareek on the other side of the fog. He was still flying, still trying to shake her loose. Strange. Her body was still with him, but her mind was somewhere else.

Blood stirred, rushing in her ears. Afina listened to it. Heard the magic rise. Felt the burn as she flew into another time and place.

Movement caught her attention, and she glanced down.

Beech trees stretched up toward her, leaves full and green. Pushed by a gentle breeze, the branches swayed, parting enough for her see beneath the wide canopies. She frowned. Three men lay stretched out below, cushioned by soft turf and watched by blue skies. The scene looked peaceful enough. Nothing more than tired men resting after a long day's work.

Except...

Something was wrong.

Perhaps it was the rancid smell beneath the trees. Perhaps the stillness in the air, but somehow Afina knew their sleep was unnatural; not their choice at all, but a forced slumber induced by...what?

Her brows drawn, she floated above, searching for the answer.

Afina tensed as her mother stepped into view. Gold winked in the sunlight, drawing her focus to the three medallions clasped in her mother's hand. Black magic swirled around her as Ylenia strode toward the warriors lying like corpses beneath the trees. Halting at their feet, her mother raised her hands. Discs clinking together, she spread her arms wide and started to chant. The ancient language throbbed through the glade. It gathered speed until darkness came, obscuring the sun.

A bitter taste in her mouth, Afina flinched as her mother placed a medallion against each warrior's heart. Ylenia murmured an incantation. The thick chains fused behind their necks, imprisoning each in magic, and her mother smiled. The sight made Afina's stomach heave. How many times had she seen that satisfied smirk?

After every beating. After every humiliation. After every act of deceit.

Tears threatened, but Afina refused to let them fall. The warriors were in trouble, but there was little she could do to help them. She'd been drawn to a distant time by the medallion. Not to participate, but to watch, to bear witness to the past and her mother's perfidy.

Red light crept from each blood crystal, staining the men and the ground around them. With a cry, they awoke, features twisted, bodies arching as bones cracked and muscle grew, transforming each into their new form. Afina clenched her teeth on a cry of dismay and watched the dragons rise—docile, subdued by her mother and black magic.

Ylenia turned to the man across the dell. "I have kept my end of the bargain. Now your promise, assassin."

Eyes as black as the pit of hell, the man held out his hand. "The incantation needed to control them."

"Your promise first, Halál" her mother said, holding tight to the piece of parchment. "I will not release them until I have it."

Halál planted his boot on top of the boy at his feet. His gaze still on her mother, he raised his fist and slammed it into his captive's temple. "You will never see or hear from him again. My word."

Unable to stop herself, Afina's gaze dropped to the boy. Dark lashes forming half-moons on his cheeks, blood flowing from a crescent-shaped cut delivered by the assassin's strike. A memory stirred, and she was five years old again. Crouched behind the rose thicket, she and her brother hid from a red-haired warrior, playing hide and seek. It had been her favorite game, and as she looked at the boy Afina remembered his face, his laugh, and how well he'd thrown stink-balls from her window onto the unsuspecting guards below.

A terrible ache settled in the center of her chest. She blinked away her tears. Oh, goddess…Heny. Her brother wasn't dead—wasn't buried in the awful little cemetery behind the White Temple. He was across the clearing: bound, gagged, unconscious from the blow.

The funeral had been a lie. Naught but a ruse to hide her mother's sin.

"I will hold you to it," her mother said, giving Halál a pointed look.

The man bowed, tilting his head in reverence. "The paper."

"They are yours, as is he." Her gaze dropped to Heny, disgust alive in the angles of her face. The look was one Afina recognized;

one she'd been treated to time and time again. She covered her mouth with her palm, the horror of it more than she could bear as the parchment changed hands. "Use him well. Make him suffer."

"My specialty, Priestess."

Wrapping his hand in Heny's tunic, Halál dragged him toward his horse. Even knowing she was powerless to stop it, Afina lost control. She screamed and reached for her brother, striking out with all the loathing she felt for her mother. The spell inside Tareek's medallion recoiled, betraying its structure.

Afina latched on, hunting for the invisible threads. Like a spiderweb, thin bands crisscrossed inside the medallion. Black magic seethed in each connection; the evil a measure of her mother's madness. Afina could see her signature everywhere: in the slither and slide of each knot and the hatred written into the webbing. It was more than she could take. With a roar, she unleashed her magic and clawed at the network inside the blood crystal, turning the darkness to dust.

The chain holding the medallion unlocked. Gold rattled. Tareek snarled as the links slid against his scales. With a yank, magic hauled Afina out of the glade and through the fog. She slammed back into her body, jerking, gasping, breathing the night chill as it slapped against her face.

Oh, goddess. What the devil had she done?

The medallion was her only handhold. And now? The chain was slipping free and—

Tareek roared and twisted, arching as though in pain. Flipped by his momentum, Afina tumbled up and over him. His powerful wing came around, and she met his gaze over the webbing. Greens eyes wide, he reached for her. The heat of his claw encircled her wrist as the bones in his face shifted.

Afina heard the crack as he threw his head back on a shriek. An instant later, she was tangled up with a man instead of a dragon. Eyes the same hue as Tareek's, dark red hair blew around his head as he stared at her, awe deep in the planes of his face. Suspended in the moment, Afina stretched her hand toward him. She knew him. Had seen him before as a child. In the garden, playing hide and seek.

"I know you," she said, gripping his forearm.

He didn't answer, simply studied her as their bodies stopped traveling up and started to come back down.

"The goddess preserve me," she whispered as the stars spun and they dropped, falling without his wings to carry them.

Tightening his hold on her, he swung them full circle, putting his back to the ground.

"Tareek!"

"Relax, Priestess." Eyes crinkled at the corners, a slow grin spread across his face. He tugged her closer, brought his foot up, and planted it against her breastbone. His expression smoothed out, turning serious as he said, "Do not drop the medallion."

"No. Don't...d-don't—"

With a grunt, he kicked out, tossing her above him like a baton. Afina screamed as she shot upward. The medallion slipped against her sweat-slicked palms. She grabbed for it, catching the links with her fingertips.

Tareek transformed, shifting into the red dragon. Lightning quick, he plucked her out of thin air, his talon a firm weight around her rib cage. As he secured his hold and unfurled his wings, he tucked into a dive and headed for the cliff edge.

A death grip on his leg, Afina watched the ground approach. Tareek banked right, and she got a clear view of the field below them.

"Thank the goddess," she gasped, spotting Xavian.

Little more than a black blob on green grass, he stood back to back with Henrik. Swords protecting the other, they moved in concert, the dance as beautiful as it was deadly. The dragons shifted around them, scales gleaming in the moonlight, advancing with one goal in mind: separate the men, move in for the kill.

Afina hammered Tareek's foot with her fist. With a snort, he tossed her an annoyed look.

She hit him again. "Tell the others to back away."

Tareek ignored her and, wings spread wide, prepared to land. Afina bucked, screaming a warning as Violet Eyes circled around behind Xavian. Movements coordinated, the younger dragon drew Henrik's fire and raised his spiked tail. Green scales flashed as it flew overhead and slammed into the ground at the men's feet. Both jumped, trying to avoid the backlash when the dragon pivoted. Another scream locked in her throat, Afina watched helplessly as the huge spikes caught their boot heels and sent them tumbling.

Quick to recover, Xavian kicked to his feet, but it was too late. Violet Eyes was already moving. With a growl that sent shivers down her spine, he knocked Xavian down again. Talon unfurled, the blue dragon pinned him, razor-sharp claws on either side of his head. Henrik notched an arrow and took aim. Still twenty feet in the air, Afina focused on the arrowhead, willing a straight shot and a true target.

Before he could release the arrow, the green dragon engaged. Henrik turned to protect his flank, leaving Xavian without help. Afina's heart skipped a beat then thumped hard. Running on pure instinct, she threw her hand out. Air rushed to meet her palm then pushed out, roaring toward Violet Eyes. With a hiss, he shifted. And she missed. Dirt exploded, the air blast tearing a trench in the earth six feet wide beside him.

The spikes along his spine aligned, tail swishing like a cat's, Violet Eyes crouched above Xavian, his gaze following her descent.

She raised her hand again.

Tareek squeezed her rib cage. "Temper, temper, Priestess-sss."

"Tell Violet Eyes to let him go!"

With a grunt, Tareek touched down on his hind legs. He hopped once then dropped her. Afina landed hard, but ignored the pain and rolled, using her momentum to gain her feet. She needed to reach Xavian. If she got close enough, she could set up a shield and send Violet Eyes flying.

Constructing a barrier in her mind, she lengthened her stride, her gaze locked on Xavian. A growl sounded at her back. She zigzagged, praying Tareek missed. Luck wasn't with her as the dragon pounced, knocking her flat from behind.

Claws turned to fingers as he shifted into a man. Wrapping her hair around his fist, he hauled her up and back, away from Xavian.

"No!"

"Be silent." With a quick kick, her feet left the ground, and Tareek forced her to her knees.

Her back to him, she raised her hand to blast him. He brought the medallion up and wrapped it around her throat. Afina gagged as the blood crystal settled under her chin, searing her skin. Pain arced, and she screamed as the gemstone opened a doorway inside her, sucking the magic from her blood until she was nothing but a shell with an empty inside.

"A word to the wise, Priestess." His mouth against the curve of her ear, Tareek murmured, "Never allow a blood crystal near your throat. 'Tis as good as any noose, strangling the life from your magic."

She coughed and clawed at Tareek's forearms.

He twisted the chain, tightening it turn by turn until her back bowed. Leaning in, he met her gaze. "What...Didn't think you were invincible, did you?"

"But..." Unable to get enough air, she wheezed as the blood crystal pressed against her windpipe. The gemstone burned and magic rippled. Agonizing pain sank deep, eating at her. Afina fisted the amulet she wore. "How? I wear one...every day."

"White, not red." He shifted his hold on the chain, improving his grip. "Hristos, didn't that bitch teach you anything?"

Afina shook her head, hopelessness swelling inside her. She was so unprepared. Knew nothing about the role she was meant to play. She wanted to cry, but couldn't. Tears wouldn't change the outcome. Begging, however, might.

Her hands around the gold links, she tugged, needed some slack to speak.

Tareek retaliated, pulling on the chain until her spine arched. "Behave."

"Promise me...he won't be...hurt."

"I promise you nothing."

The tears she'd fought so hard not to shed spilled over her lashes. As the droplets streaked her cheeks, desperation took hold. She needed to make Tareek understand. Her family's crimes were not Xavian's. If they wanted blood, she would gladly give them hers to see Xavian safe.

"Tareek, please," she said, her voice a mere wisp. "I will pay... take the blame for my mother's crimes, but please, let Xavian go free."

A muscle jumping along his jaw, he looked way without answering.

Afina closed her eyes. The dragon shifter's hatred was absolute. He would give no quarter, and neither would the others.

CHAPTER TWENTY-FOUR

The talon pressed him into the ground, cutting off his air supply. Xavian twisted, wedging his hand between the massive claw and his chest. He needed some wiggle room. Not a lot. Just enough to reach the blade sheathed against his back. The thick scales were impenetrable, but he'd found a weakness…right between the bastard's toes.

Devoid of scales, his knife would sink deep into the dragon's flesh, ripping at muscle to reach the bone beneath. But first, he had to reach the christing thing.

Xavian slammed his fist against the beast's knuckle and shifted sideways. He didn't have much time. Though he couldn't see Afina, he could feel her. So much pain. The bastard was hurting her. And he was stuck: unable to reach her, unable to help her, unable to stop Tareek from…

He couldn't stand it. She was so close. So damn close.

Baring his teeth, he roared, "Afina!"

The blue dragon's eyes narrowed on him. "Quiet, human."

Xavian snarled in answer, shoved harder, grinding his back into the ground. His swords were gone, lost in battle among the field grass. But his double scabbards did their job, gouging the earth, digging a hole beneath him. The smell of dirt and turf clogged the air, mixing with the chill of midnight. He hammered the bastard again. Harder than stone, the scales split his knuckles wide open. He smelled blood. Knew it was his but didn't care.

"Hristos, so fucking stubborn." Violet Eyes lowered his head, bringing them nose-to-nose. "Cease, Xavian. You do yourself harm and little good. You cannot hurt me."

"Let her go."

"Or what?"

"I'll rip your head off."

The dragon snorted. Tendrils of smoke curled from his nostrils as he shook his horned head.

Steel clanged against scales. The echo rang in his ears as Xavian looked left. Christ, Henrik had engaged the green dragon. Twin blades flashing, he struck over and over, trying to drive the beast back into Violet Eyes. 'Twas a sound strategy. The dragons were too big to fight in close proximity. At least on the ground. One would eventually unbalance the other and—

The dragon holding him captive sidestepped, dragging Xavian with him. As he lifted his claw, a narrow sliver opened beneath Xavian's back. He stretched hard, fingers spread wide, and palmed the knife hilt. The grip felt like home as the metal edge rasped against leather. He brought his arm up and around. Moonlight touched steel an instant before he rammed the blade between the dragon's toes. It sank to the hilt in the webbing, finding vulnerable flesh.

The beast's eyes went wide. He sucked in a quick breath, the sharp sound momentary before his paw jerked, up and back. Xavian went flying. Twisting in midair, he came down feet first and rolled, eyes on the ground, searching for his weapons. Moments turned into an eternity. Where were they?

Steel peeked between tuffs of field grass.

Locked on, Xavian lunged, curling both hands around the hilts. As the leather grips settled in his palms, he kicked to his feet and raised both blades. Picked up by the night breeze, his war cry echoed across the field as he leveled his swords at Violet Eyes' head.

The dragon shook out his paw. Looking annoyed more than hurt, he said, "You are a pain in the ass."

"I aim to please." Xavian shifted right. He needed a way around the scaly bastard...that or a clear throwing lane. If he timed it right the redhead holding Afina wouldn't see the blade coming until it took his head off.

Afina whimpered.

The soft sound broke Xavian's concentration. He told himself not to look, to stay focused, but...

God help him. The bastard had her on her knees. Tears streaked down her cheeks as she fought for each breath, small hands pulling at the chain wrapped around her throat. Xavian's heart constricted. He lunged forward, desperate to reach her.

Head low, ready to strike, Violet Eyes stepped into his path. Xavian pinwheeled, twin blades flashing as he spun. The tips of the weapons scored the dragon's flank. Sparks flew. The beast reared, countering his blows, staying between him and Afina.

"Garren," the redhead yelled, his deep voice drifting like a ribbon on the wind. "I am ready."

Garren snapped at him, razor-sharp fangs clipping his steel before he hissed, "Cruz, leave Henrik and come. I will hold the humans at bay."

Green scales gleaming in the moonlight, Cruz glanced over his shoulder. Garren tipped his chin, motioning him toward Tareek. With a nod, Cruz glanced at Henrik and inhaled. Xavian shouted a warning. His friend leapt right as the fireball left the dragon's mouth. Flames exploded, eating a trail through the grass as the green beast retreated toward Afina.

Xavian's heart went loose inside his chest. He'd never reach her in time. The blue dragon stood in his path and Cruz was too fast. "Jesu, let her go. She has done naught wrong. Whatever it is you want—"

"I have what I want." Garren spread his claws, preparing for attack as Henrik rolled to his feet. "You."

The confirmation unhinged him, and with a howl, Xavian attacked. Twin swords blazing in the weak light, he thrust and slashed, meeting hard scales and wicked skill as the beast blocked every strike. He couldn't get through or past the bastard. He knew that, but didn't care. All that mattered was Afina. He needed to reach her...to stop her suffering. Had he done as she asked and left her alone, she wouldn't have a chain to her throat and a dragon who wanted her dead.

Chest heaving, he circled the beast. Henrik took the other side, sheathing his blades in favor of his bow. The green dragon stopped in front of Afina. Anguish hit, slicing Xavian wide open. God, nay. Not Afina. Whatever the price, he would pay it. Would accept the pain to spare her a thimbleful of hurt.

Lowering his blades, he stood vulnerable, without his swords to shield him. "Do not do this."

Garren hesitated, his gaze riveted on him.

"You want me then take me," Xavian said, hearing the agony in his own voice. He let the weakness lie. Afina was worth the blow to his pride. Hell, he would forsake it entirely to see her safe. "Do what you will, but leave Afina unharmed. She has done naught to deserve your anger or death. I will go willingly if you release her."

"You have feelings for the witch?"

Xavian bared his teeth. "Call her that again and I will cut your balls off."

Scaled brows drew in tight. "Hristos, you've done more than bed her. You've taken her to mate."

Long-standing habit told him to deny it. Instinct wouldn't let him. The bond he shared with Afina meant something to the dragon. Xavian could all but taste it. "She is mine."

"*Ce chin.*" Garren's lip curled, his disgust plain to see as he yelled over his shoulder, "Tareek...ease up. He's bonded with her."

"Shit." The redhead scowled. "Can nothing ever be easy?"

"Do it," Garren said, throwing Xavian a dark look.

With a curse, Tareek unwound the gold links from around his fists. Afina sucked in a desperate breath. Then another. Xavian breathed with her, willing air into her lungs. As the red gemstone left her skin, she gasped and pitched forward. Her hands hit the ground. Xavian surged toward her, needing to touch her so badly his fingertips throbbed.

Blue scales flashed in the low light. The spiked tail slammed into the ground then dragged, taking his feet out from under him. Xavian hit the turf shoulders first. The air in his lungs vanished, and he rolled onto his knees, struggling to breathe.

"Cruz, now." Garren glanced away from him toward Afina.

The sound of a bow being drawn snapped the dragon's head around. Wood whistled through the air. Catching the arrow shaft between his teeth, Garren snapped it like a toothpick.

Henrik notched another and pulled the bowstring tight. "Stay away from her."

The dragon eyed Henrik then his bow. "If you value your boy, Xavian, tell him to back off. We are bound to you and no other."

"Bound to...*Rahat*..." Xavian's chest spasmed as his lungs inflated. Eyes watering, he tried to make sense of the blue bastard's words. They couldn't be bound to him. He held no natural ties to the dragons. Other than the stories told by his father, he knew naught about them. But the fact Garren hadn't killed him—hell, after all the fighting he'd come out with naught more than a bruise or two. "What—"

White light flashed in his periphery. It lit up the night sky and sent shock waves through him. His hands flexing around his sword hilts, Xavian pushed to his feet, trying to see through the glow.

"Relax, warrior," Garren said, putting his big body between him and Afina. "She but frees Cruz. Allow her to complete the spell."

"H!"

"Go!" Henrik pivoted and loosed an arrow.

Garren cursed and turned his head to meet his friend's volley.

With no way around the beast, Xavian went at him head-on. Arms and legs pumping, he took the high road, planted his foot on the dragon's knee and launched himself up and over. He rotated full circle, the spikes along Garren's spine mere inches from his head. Coming over the other side, he sighted the ground and took a deep breath. He landed and rolled, commanding his legs to support his weight as he cycled onto his feet.

Lightning cracked across the sky. Green scales shimmered and Afina murmured, her voice echoing like thunder across the flatlands to the cliffs. Another flash, a rush of air then a cracking pop. The snap rippled, flattening the grass like the sweep of a hand.

Xavian slowed as the light faded. Good Christ. The green dragon was gone. In his place stood a lad with black hair. With eyes almost as dark, the boy stared at Afina. Astonishment on his face, he sank to his knees before her.

"Priestess…" Tears in his eyes, the lad held out shaking hands, palms to the ground. He turned them over as though he'd never see them before and looked back at Afina. "The pain, Priestess…it's gone."

Dropping the medallion, Afina reached out to cup Cruz's cheek. "You are free."

"Get your hands off her," Xavian snarled from six feet away.

'Twas an unreasonable demand. The lad wasn't touching her—'twas the other way around—but the distinction was lost on Xavian. Something territorial had taken hold, snaking through him like poison. Afina belonged to him. No one—neither man nor beast—was permitted to touch her.

Baring his teeth, Xavian raised his swords. Cruz scrambled, backing away so fast his heels left divots in the grass. Garren growled behind him. Blades ready, Xavian spun, planting himself in front of Afina.

"Xavian…" Afina rasped behind him. "It's all right. I'm all right."

The words were meant to reassure him. They only drew Xavian tighter. She was anything but *all right*. He could hear the truth in her voice. Tareek had hurt her. Whatever they were forcing her to do with the medallions was killing her. No matter what she said, he wouldn't allow them near her again.

Tipping his chin down, he rotated the blades in his hands. As he met Garren's gaze, he growled a warning.

"Hristo, Garren." Tareek circled around to his left. "He's lost it."

"Can you blame him? We threaten his female." Like a sidewinder, Garren's head shifted right. His clawed feet followed, crossing one over the other.

"No. Please, d-don't hurt him, Garren," Afina whispered. Xavian heard rustling and knew she was trying to get up. "He d-doesn't understand. Let m-me—"

"S-shh, Priestess," Tareek said, his tone as untrustworthy as the rest of him.

Xavian held his ground, refusing to take the bait when Tareek slithered from view. He caught a flash of red hair in his peripheral vision. The bastard was trying to draw him away from Afina. Garren wanted a shot at her. That wasn't going to happen. Not as long as he had breath in his body.

"Warrior..." Using his torso to shield it, Garren cranked his hind claw back. "Catch."

He expected a fireball. What he got was a face full of Henrik.

Tossed like a stone, Henrik tumbled through the air. Widening his stance, Xavian dropped his shoulder then his sword tips to avoid slicing his friend. Henrik hit him like a runaway horse. The blow knocked him off his feet, and they went down in a tangle of arms and legs. Xavian landed on the bottom, taking the brunt of the fall. It took him an instant to realize his friend wasn't moving.

He shoved at Henrik. His friend rolled, head bobbing as his back touched the ground. Xavian sucked in a quick breath. Blood was everywhere: covering half of Henrik's face, matting his hair, pooling in the hollow at the base of his throat. An ache roared to life in the center of his chest. Jesu, they'd killed his brother. The beasts had—

A flash lit up the night sky. The glow spread, obliterating the stars as the sound of snapping bones exploded across the field.

Years of training dragged Xavian to his feet. Securing his weapons, he pivoted, searching for Afina. He found her halfway across the clearing, on her feet now, a medallion dangled from her fingertips. A strange man stood beside her. Dark hair streaked with blue, he rolled his shoulders, tipped his head back, and snarled at the night sky.

The sound hit Xavian like a battering ram, propelling him forward. The man's head snapped around and violet eyes narrowed on him. Garren. Even in human form, he recognized the bastard.

Six feet from his target, Xavian growled, "Back the hell away from her."

"Sheath your weapons, warrior. We are no longer a threat..." Fists cranked in tight, Garren stared at him from beneath dark brows. "And you cannot catch her with your hands full."

Afina swayed on her feet. Dark eyelashes flickering, her head lolled on her shoulders. Xavian cursed and, with a flip, stowed one blade as she listed sideways. Garren stepped away and let her fall, his gaze locked on Xavian. She hit the ground before he reached her, gold chain rattling in her lax hand.

Xavian's heart fractured inside his chest. "Nay...nay. Afina!"

Whispering her name over and over, he knelt beside her. She lay like a broken doll: ashen skin, limbs askew, lips blue...barely breathing. Xavian dropped his sword to free both hands and gathered her to his chest. Clutching her, he pressed his mouth to her temple, her cheek, her mouth.

"*Draga*, come back." He stroked her hair, rocking her in his arms. "Please, come back to me."

She didn't move.

He went numb inside. She was dying and so was he. A quiver started soul deep then spread until Xavian felt himself grow cold. 'Twas his fault she lay lifeless in a barren field. 'Twas his fault she would never open her eyes again and see the light of day.

Agony tumbled into despair, and after each painful thump of his heart he cursed it. He wanted it to stop beating. But it defied his will, kept beating until the only thing left inside him was fury: a soul-deep rage that turned everything black. A violent shudder racked him as Xavian pressed his cheek to hers. He whispered against her soft skin, apologizing, asking for forgiveness, saying good-bye all in the same tortured breath.

Kissing her one last time, he set her down with gentle hands. Naught mattered anymore. Naught except revenge.

He met Garren's gaze over Afina's supine body. Tears in his eyes, he palmed his weapon and stood. A life for a life. The whoreson would lose his to pay for Afina's. But first, Xavian was going to rip the bastard's face off his skull.

CHAPTER TWENTY-FIVE

Xavian struck with force, slamming his fist into Garren's temple. The delivery was perfect. The bastard's head snapped to the side. Blood welled from a gash beside his eyebrow as Garren reset his stance and blocked a left hook. Xavian countered with an upper-cut. *Rahat*, it felt good to hit the whoreson. Each strike drove him further into himself, away from the grief, away from the agony of losing Afina.

He caught a glimpse of her as he pivoted. Lifeless, she lay in the grass, her hair a dark stain on muted green. His heart cracked then fell apart as pain rippled through him. He would make the bastard pay. Would rip him apart with his bare hands. Using a blade wasn't personal enough. 'Twould be too quick. He wanted to get bloody on this one.

Xavian's feet skimmed over the grass. He threw a quick jab. The points of his knuckles grazed Garren's cheekbone.

"Tell me, warrior," Garren said, hands moving like quick-silver, deflecting the next strike. "Is taking my life worth your mate's?"

Xavian bared his teeth in answer.

Keeping his guard high, he planted one foot and kicked with the other. His boot connected with Garren's rib cage. The whore-son grunted, tucked his elbow in tight, and twisted sideways to avoid the next blow.

Too late. Xavian was already moving through the opening in his defense.

He grabbed Garren by the throat. Pressing his thumb beneath the sharp edge of the bastard's jawbone, he forced his head back. With one clean kick, Xavian took his feet from beneath him and slammed his back into the ground.

Victory a moment away, he planted his knee on his opponent's chest. Before Xavian wrapped his hand around his throat, Garren grabbed the leather edge of his tunic and heaved. His strength combined with a quick turn tossed Xavian up and over him. He landed shoulder first and, rolling to his feet, reset his stance.

"Clever move, dragon."

"Like your opinion means shit." Garren raised his guard and dropped his right foot, preparing for another round. "And I'm as human as you are, *fratele*."

"I am not your brother," Xavian said, denying any connection between them. Human, his arse. Aye, he might look the part at the moment, but Garren wasn't a man. He'd seen him, scales and all. "The only one I claim you killed."

Violet eyes glittering, Garren's gaze shifted to Afina. "She suffers without you."

Xavian's heart clenched and the pain he fought to suppress surged. Like a disease, it spread, eating him from the inside out. It made his skin shrink until his bones felt too big for his body. He itched to rip it off, but naught would ease the awful ache. Afina was gone, and naught he did would bring her back.

"She is already dead."

"Not dead…just weak."

Moisture gathered in the corners of Xavian's eyes, blurring his vision. "You lie."

"I would not." The blue streaks of hair at his temples rippled as Garren shook his head and stepped back. After a moment he dropped his fists, leaving himself open to attack. "I am bound to you by blood oath and parchment. This is sacred to our kind and cannot be broken. I kill her...I hurt you. This I would never willingly do, Xavian."

Unable to prevent it, hope welled then poured through him. His gaze strayed to Afina. His heart picked up a beat then another. His fingers curled, betraying his need to touch her—to discover if Garren spoke true.

"Go." Backing away, Garren gave Xavian room to reach her. "I will not interfere. You have my word."

His chest heaving, he studied Garren. The bastard was clever. He'd proven it time and again. What if he was playing him—giving him all the rope he needed to hang himself? If he turned his back to help Afina, would the whoreson attack?

Xavian swallowed, realizing it didn't matter. Wily trick or nay, he couldn't risk her dying if the smallest chance of her living existed. He ached to see her smile again. To have her hale and whole.

He backed up a step then another until he stood over her. His eyes burned as he knelt and pushed his arms beneath her back. Her head lolled on her shoulders. He sat back and pulled her into his lap. Dampness and chill sank through his leather trews. He settled on his arse anyway, hardly aware of the discomfort, and curled himself around her.

"Afina. Breathe, love." He stroked her hair, hands shaking. "Please...take a breath, *draga*."

Naught happened.

He nestled his cheek against hers. Kissed the corner of her mouth. Caressed her back, the curve of her hip, the top of her thigh.

Setting his lips against her pulse point, he hugged her close, the pain inside him unbearable. "Her heart isn't beating."

"It is…faintly," Garren said from somewhere nearby.

Xavian looked up to find him six feet away. Cruz stood behind him, concern in his dark eyes. Ignoring them both, he tucked her head beneath his chin and rocked her gently. Where was the current—the one he'd felt in the brambles when he'd helped her the first time?

"I cannot feel it, Garren. I cannot—"

"Close your eyes and listen, warrior. You will hear it." Planting his elbows on his knees, the man-dragon solidified his crouch. "You are a bonded male…she is an echo in your blood."

Xavian hesitated. True, Garren was keeping his word. But that didn't mean he would for much longer. The bastard might attack the instant he lost sight of him. Giving him that advantage was foolhardy. But then, what choice did he have? Afina needed him.

He closed his eyes.

A quiet throb echoed through the back of his mind. His brow puckered, Xavian held his breath and listened harder. The faint beat sounded again. He counted the moments between them then exhaled in a rush. Though barely there, the soft thumps were quickening, coming one after the other.

"Feel it?"

"Aye." He shifted Afina, kissing her temple as he cupped her cheek. "If not for me, you would have killed her."

"Yes."

"Why?"

A muscle jumped along Garren's jaw. "She is the High Priestess of Orm and cannot be trusted."

Xavian stroked a hand along Afina's back, his gaze riveted to the man-dragon. Something was off—in truth, a great many things were...like the existence of dragons and magic and God only knew what else. But 'twas Garren's anger and the truth that interested him now. "She freed you. You have no reason to hate her."

"Her kind imprisoned us in dragon form," he said, the fury in his eyes telling.

Her kind? Xavian's eyes narrowed. Were there more like her? "'Twas not Afina's doing though, was it, dragon?"

Garren looked away, expression tight, his huge hands curled into fists.

His arms wrapped tight around Afina, Xavian prepared to move. He needed to get her out of range if Garren lost control. His anger was so great it swirled in the air around him. Xavian understood that kind of rage; felt it himself for Halál. But Afina didn't deserve it. Instinct told him she'd had naught to do with what happened to Garren and his comrades.

"Hristo." His expression fierce, Tareek knelt beside Henrik.

Xavian palmed the dagger high on his chest. If the bastard made another move toward his friend he would be wearing a blade on the side of his head instead of an ear.

"Relax, Xavian," the redhead said without looking away from Henrik. "I wish to inspect his wound, nothing more."

The blade perched between Xavian's fingertips wobbled. "He isn't—"

"No." With gentle hands, Tareek tilted his friend's head to inspect the gash on his temple. "Shit, Garren. Did you have to hit the lad so hard?"

"He isn't a lad anymore, Tareek." Garren threw the redhead an annoyed look.

Tareek prodded the cut then lifted one of Henrik's eyelids. "Jesus...a sleeping spell too?"

Garren shrugged. "He was trying to kill me."

"Still..." Tareek scowled. "Didn't need to hit him so hard."

"Old habits die hard." Returning his attention to Xavian, Garren tilted his head in the redhead's direction. "Tareek was Henrik's boyhood guard. He is still rather protective."

Breathing in through his nose, Xavian exhaled through his mouth, gratitude and relief a mixed bag inside his head. Henrik was alive and...

His gaze narrowed on Garren. The picture of innocence, the wily bastard met his gaze and the suspicion in it head-on. Xavian gritted his teeth. Jesu, they were trying to distract him. Tareek's interruption had been too well timed.

"Well done, dragon. 'Twas a good diversion, but not nearly clever enough." Xavian stroked his hand along Afina's thigh. A soft puff of air wafted across the base of his throat. He held his breath and waited, praying he wasn't imagining it. Her chest moved a wee bit, and the strange current he'd felt in the brambles sizzled to life. 'Twas faint, but the more he caressed her, the stronger it became until the hairs on his forearms stirred. The tangle around his heart loosened as he siphoned the flow, taking all Afina gave him.

His hand in her hair, he massaged the nape of her neck. He tipped his chin in Garren's direction. "Going to answer my question?"

"Which one?"

"Who is to blame, Garren?"

Stone-faced, the man-dragon shook his head. The twin streaks at his temples glinted blue in the weak light.

"Tell me the truth," Xavian said, pushing for an answer. Afina couldn't be responsible. She was too gentle. Even when she'd used her magic to protect him, she hadn't hurt Tareek, merely tossed him out of the way. "Are there others like Afina?"

"Not anymore."

"Then who?"

"Her mother...Ylenia." Garren spat the name like poison through clenched teeth and a mouthful of distaste. "We are half-human, Xavian...each of us born to a human female. Aye, we change form at will, but we have always been human on the inside. We feel the same things you do. Have the same emotions. Feel the same pain.

"Being in dragon form too long robs us of that...of our humanity. We were made to do things to others...to innocents and...you cannot imagine...Have you any idea how painful it is to be trapped and unable to change back?"

"You cannot blame Afina for another's crime," Xavian said, understanding Garren's pain and the misery that came with it. He'd been forced to do all kinds of things he'd rather forget, but he needed to make his point. 'Twas vital Garren accept the truth. If he didn't, Afina would never be safe. "You wish to make your home with me? Let it go and start anew."

"As you have done with Halál?"

"Christ." The name crawled up Xavian's spine. His hands stilled on Afina, and he glared at Garren from beneath his brows.

His gaze steady, Garren plucked a blade of grass from its root. "Turnabout is fair play."

Fair play. Hell, there was naught *fair* about the old man. "You serve me now, true?"

"Yes."

"Then I will have your promise you will treat her with respect. And…" He paused for effect, his gaze boring into a violet one. "You will protect her when I cannot."

"Shit."

"Your word."

With a flick of his wrist, Garren tossed the blade of grass aside. "You have it."

Even though the pledge was growled, Xavian believed him. Garren might not like it, but he would respect his wishes and make the others do the same.

"She is still pale." Cupping Afina's cheek, he tipped her chin up to study her face. The current hummed between them now. Her heartbeat was stronger too. Still, he wasn't satisfied. He wouldn't be until she opened her eyes. "Tell me what else I can do to help her."

"'Twould be better if you were skin to skin." A frown in his voice, Garren looked to the sky. Thunder rumbled, a threatening growl to the north. "We need to get you to shelter so you may service her properly."

Xavian's brows collided. Service her? Hell, no chance that would happen. If Garren thought he'd bed Afina while she lay unconscious, he had miscalculated…badly. Even so, the comment gave him an idea. Shifting Afina in his arms, he dragged the cloak from beneath her bottom. Still boneless, she sagged against his chest while he wrenched the tunic from her trews. His hand found the soft skin along her spine. Her muscles twitched. He curled his arm around her, pressing his skin to hers as his palm cupped her rib cage. Her chest rose, each breath fuller than the last.

"Your exit strategy?" Garren asked, pushing to his feet, his eyes still on the sky. Thick clouds were blowing in, reducing the moon to a faint glow. Stars blinked, playing hide-and-seek behind the billowy edges.

"A boat," Xavian said, rearranging his mantle around Afina. "The ferrier's dock lies inside the cavern at the end of the beach."

"Any swimming involved?"

"Some."

Tareek cursed.

Garren grimaced.

"I will go," Cruz said, joining the conversation at last. Garren threw him a measured look. The lad tossed a perturbed one back. "What? I am a better swimmer than either of you."

"True enough." With a nod, Garren slapped the lad's shoulder. "Go. We will follow on foot."

Cruz retreated until he stood twenty feet away. He took a deep breath and, between one heartbeat and the next, transformed. Green scales gleamed, appearing black without the light of the moon as the dragon unfurled his wings and leapt skyward.

Xavian went tense around Afina. "Jesu."

"You'll become accustomed to it…" Garren trailed off, his tone more wary than amused, "…in time."

On his feet now with Afina cradled in his arms, Xavian tipped his chin at Tareek. "You carrying Henrik?"

In answer, the redhead slung Henrik over his shoulder and stood. Xavian shook his head. Jesus, the added weight barely fazed the man-dragon.

"Got the horses," Garren said from behind him.

Xavian nodded, uneasiness riding him like a whore. Afina was still so weak. Ice cold against him, her heartbeat flickered, a slow, sluggish pulse that made his go still. He needed to get her to safety, somewhere he could have her skin to skin. He only prayed Garren spoke true and his nearness would save her.

CHAPTER TWENTY-SIX

The smell of dead fish was the first thing Afina noticed. Well, that and the fact her head hurt. The throb hammered the back of her skull, urging her to go back to sleep. She tried then gave up. The idiot birds were arguing again.

More of a caw than a twitter.

She breathed in through her nose and out through her mouth. Repeated the process then cracked her eyelids. Sunlight nailed her between the eyes. With a gasp, she rolled her face into something soft. A fur throw? She didn't know and refused to look. She wasn't brave enough. The pain from her first attempt was still radiating between her temples.

Cool air drifted over the curve of her shoulder. With a shiver, she pulled her knees in tight, battling the chill. The plush surface she lay on pitched to one side then rolled to the other, the movement more a lullaby than a jig as something flapped overhead.

"*Draga?*" Warm and deep, the voice drew her like a bathtub full of hot suds. "You awake?"

Afina brought her knees in a little closer. Why was it so cold? Another case of shivers attacked an instant before something warm brushed over her shoulder. She followed it, wiggling backward until the source gloved her spine. Oh, the heat was lovely. Better than anything she'd ever felt.

"Love?"

A gentle nudge rolled her onto her back. She cracked her lids, moaned, and shut them again. But the brief glimpse was enough to clue her in. "Xavian?"

"Aye." Calloused fingers drifted: over her temple, along her jaw, across her bottom lip only to stop at her chin. Gentle but sure, they tipped her face up. "Look at me."

"No." She grimaced. Her voice wasn't working any better than her eyes.

"Come on, love." His tone coaxed. His hand massaged, drawing warm circles on the curve of her hip. "Open for me."

"Hurts."

"I know. 'Twill for a while, but I need to see their color."

With a grumble, she cracked her lids. Sunlight blazed, piercing through to the back of her brain. Afina turned her face away, fighting him and the pain, wishing both would leave her in peace.

"Easy," Xavian murmured as he brought her back. She pushed at his shoulders. He cupped her face and, ignoring her halfhearted struggle, set his thumbs at the corners of her eyes. Applying gentle pressure, he coaxed her into opening them.

She blinked, struggling to find focus.

"Thank Christ…hazel." After a rough exhale, he leaned in to kiss her eyelids. His mouth was gentle, his breath warm, and Afina sighed as he murmured, "You are much better."

Better? Afina frowned. It didn't feel any better. "Where?"

"On a boat."

"Don't like boats," she croaked, wrinkling her nose. Well, that explained the awful smell and the urge to throw up. Boats rocked, and rocking didn't agree with her.

"I know." His eyes crinkled at the corners. "You told me, remember?"

Afina grumbled, wanting to smack him for laughing at her. But her arms weren't on board with the plan, so she switched focus, retreating into her mind. A memory tugged at her. Vague at first, it gathered speed until a clear image floated through the mist.

Her breath caught. Swallowing past her sore throat, she said, "Are they all right...the dragons?"

Xavian stroked her temples, massaging with the pads of his thumbs. She groaned. His hands were magic, releasing the tension one string at a time. He kept at it until the last thread loosened and she went boneless in his arms.

"The dragon-shifters are fine. Henrik too," he said, kissing the tip of her nose.

As he lifted his head, her lips curved all by themselves. It was sweet, really, him kissing her nose: platonic, unthreatening, soothing. He was such a good man—a gentle one despite his aggressive nature and terrible skill with a blade.

"They've gone now?" Forcing strength into her limbs, she raised her hand to set her fingertips to his mouth. She followed the bottom curve, marveling at its softness.

He nipped at the tips. "Nay. You were right. They were after me."

"B-but—"

"'Tis all right." Blue eyes glinting beneath his lashes, he dipped his head. His whiskers brushed over her skin, making her shiver, making her want more as his mouth burned a path along her collarbone. "They are no longer a threat. They are sworn to protect me...bound by some sort of spell on parchment."

Like hot cider on a cold day, his voice sank deep, warming her from the inside out. Tendrils of desire stirred, awakening the memory of them in the stables. She wanted to feel that again. Let him take her back to that place where nothing mattered but the two of them.

Shifting beneath him, she kissed his shoulder, tasting his skin. "What parchment?"

"Don't know," he murmured against her throat. With a flick, he laved her pulse point then suckled, drawing gently on her skin. "Don't care right now."

Bliss swirled, telling her not to care either. But something wasn't right. With the information...not with Xavian. He was incredible. Hard and strong and so hot he...Good goddess, she really needed to stay focused. What had he said? Oh, yes. Something about a spell on parchment. The combination of words popped the top off a memory and—

Xavian cupped the back of her knee and lifted, up and to the side. He pressed in, sliding his thigh between her own, spreading her legs until hard muscle touched her core. She gasped, overwhelmed by sensation as her breasts brushed his chest. With a groan, he gathered her closer, teasing her nipples until she ached for more of his touch. For the heat of his mouth.

"Ah, Xavian?"

"Uh-hmm."

"Something's not right...with the dragons."

"You think?"

"I just...I'm not sure, o-oh..." she trailed off as Xavian moved south: hot mouth on her skin, calloused hand stroking the curve of her behind. "Can you trust them? I mean, really?"

"Aye." He kissed the hollow between her breasts. "It's all good, love."

"Promise me you'll be careful." She smoothed her hand over his shoulders. "With the dragons. I don't know who sent them or if you can trust them."

"'Twill be fine, love," he said, kissing the crease between her brows.

"Promise me."

He held her gaze a moment then nodded. She breathed out in relief as his focus shifted away from her face. It touched down on the moon-star that marred the curve of her shoulder. He traced it with his fingertip. "So pretty."

Afina blinked. Pretty? Really? She'd always thought of it as an ugly stain—something she wanted to scrub off, a great shame that needed to be hidden from view. But as his mouth brushed over her birthmark, she forced herself to see it through his eyes. It wasn't so bad if she looked at it that way. She would never think it was "pretty," but if nothing else, the mark symbolized something greater than herself. It made her take stock and reevaluate. It made her believe she had a choice. She wasn't doomed to be like her mother—freeing the dragons had taught her that. She could decide what she wanted to be and fate would follow.

The realization lightened her heart, and grateful for the man in her arms as much as the lesson, she turned into Xavian. His whiskers pricked her and sensation spiraled as she curled her arms around his neck. He murmured, kissed the moon-star again, and hugged her back.

Unable to help herself, her hands found the curling ends at the nape of his neck. She loved his hair: the color, its softness, how the thick strands played between her fingers. Afina set her mouth to the corner of his and whispered, "You're all right? Not hurt?"

He shook his head and accepted her kiss, eyes glinting beneath dark lashes. "You are the one who was hurt, Afina."

"I'll recover," she said, knowing it was true. Each kiss—each of his caresses—eased the burden. The stiffness in her muscles was fading and her headache, though still present, didn't seem so terrible.

"You had better."

She huffed, enjoying his rough tone and the threat in it. It told her plainly he cared for her. Had been worried, and for some reason, she liked his concern almost as much as his body against hers.

"Are you laughing at me?"

"A little." She smiled, daring him to retaliate for her audacity.

"Wench," he whispered, wielding the word like an endearment.

Dipping his head, he nipped her upper lip, demanding entrance. She opened, welcoming him in with a sigh. He tasted like moonbeams and shadows; a dark decadence that nourished even as it stripped her of pride. Had he demanded it, she would have begged for him, brought herself low for the simple pleasure of holding him, heart to heart and skin to skin.

The fact she was naked beneath the blanket should have shocked her. After all, good girls didn't wake up bare bottomed in a man's bed. At least not without the benefit of a marriage ceremony. But Afina was tired of being good. In truth, the only *good* thing she wanted at the moment was to be very, very bad with Xavian.

The imp in her roared with approval and set about making a plan.

"Ah, question for you." She drew away a little, following her imp's advice. The need to tease him—the way a woman did a man—was too much to resist.

"Hmm?" Denied the pleasure of her mouth, he changed direction, finding the sensitive spot behind her ear.

Her breath hitched, and she gave in to a shiver. "Any reason I haven't got a stitch on?"

"Same reason I don't."

"Which is?"

"I needed to be skin to skin with you."

His hand slid down to cup her bottom, caressed with a light touch, making her pay for teasing him. Pleasure hummed, and without shame she wrapped her calf over his hip and rolled against the hard muscle between her thighs. He returned to her mouth, delving deep, tangling their tongues, delivering his taste one delicious stroke at a time. Taking all he gave her, she anchored her hands in his hair and opened wide to appease him.

"Jesu," he said against her mouth.

Cords of muscle bunched beneath her hands. Afina caught her breath. The sheer strength in his arms, the hard flex of his shoulders, the ripple of his chest…Goddess, it made her head spin. But even as she reveled in the feel of him, he retreated, straightening his arms to break away from her. She tried to hold on, to bring him back, but he locked his elbows, hovering above her. Twin flames flickered in his eyes, half desire, half desperation.

She stroked his biceps, keeping the touch light, coaxing. "What?"

A tremor rolled though him. "Afina, love, I didn't intend… shouldn't have started…"

Tracing his collarbone with one hand, her other jumped to his jaw. She ran her fingertips over his whiskers, trying to soothe him while she waited for him to explain. It was hard to be patient. She wanted him so much. Needed his touch like a starving child needed food. But he struggled with something so powerful it furrowed his brow and brought regret into his incredible eyes.

Afina cupped his cheek, not understanding. "What is wrong?"

"We cannot do this. Not now." Taking her hand from his face, he turned his mouth into her palm. "We should get dressed and…talk."

Oh, goddess. She was losing him. His retreat was more than physical. It was emotional too. He was taking away what she needed most. But she refused to let him go. He belonged to her whether he wanted to or not. It was too late to go back, for either of them.

She had to make him see it. Had to make him realize how much he meant to her, that she was too far gone to bring her heart back into line. The love had grown with each gentle touch and soft murmur and heated look.

He cared for her too. The truth was in his eyes and the strong hands that stroked her. It was in the way their mouths met and their gazes held and their hearts beat. And as she looked up into his gorgeous face, she needed to make him believe in their connection. Part of that was having him make love to her…here and now, regardless of the consequences.

"Later." Propped up on her elbow, she kissed the hollow at the base of his throat. He inhaled so sharply his chest jumped. She continued her assault, hands stroking over skin and hard muscle. A fine tremor rolled through him as she caressed his nape and whispered, "We'll talk after, I promise."

"Nay."

She clenched her teeth on his denial, trying to contain the pain. She couldn't. No matter how hard she fought, it bubbled up from deep inside, coming through on a whimper.

As the anguished sound spilled out, he groaned and one of his arms came around her, supporting her weight as he rolled.

The lambskin murmured as they touched down on their sides, facing each other. Afraid he would pull away, she clutched his shoulders. But instead of setting her aside, he drew her in, surrounding her body with his larger one.

Brushing her hair away from her face, he forced her to meet his gaze. "There are things I haven't told you...things you need to know about me."

"I know enough."

He shook his head.

Determination took hold. Afina tipped her chin up, offering her mouth. His gaze betrayed him, straying to her lips. She parted them. He dipped his head. Their mouths met, but instead of the open-mouth kiss she craved, he gave her a gentle one. She pressed forward, flicked him with her tongue, needing him deep inside her. But he kept the caress light, each brush designed to soothe rather than arouse.

Well, she was way past that. She was hot and wet, so needy she ached from the inside out. And he wasn't going to relent and let her have her way. She could see it in his eyes, in the controlled way he touched her and the set of his jaw. His restraint pushed her past determined into downright desperate, and she made the only play she had left. She used his concern for her against him.

"Xavian, my head still hurts and your touch helps...I need you right now."

"Afina," he said, tone soft with regret. He stroked the outside of her thigh, trying to soothe the way for his denial. "It isn't that I don't want you...Jesu, I would kill to be inside you, but 'twould be better if—"

"If you stopped talking and touched me...the way I want you to."

"*Rahat*, you do not fight fair."

She hitched her calf over his thigh and pushed into his embrace. "Finish what you started."

"I am trying to do right by you. If you will just—"

"Do you want me to beg?"

His breath caught as he went statue still beside her. She studied his face, watched his nostrils flare, his eyes narrow, and saw the truth. The thought of her begging excited him...unbearably. It should have shocked her, but it didn't. Somehow it made perfect sense. Dominant by nature, he liked control, wanted to push her over the edge while she pleaded for him to take her.

She licked her bottom lip and whispered, "Please."

"Nay..." His tone beyond desperate, he rasped, "Don't."

"Please, Xavian."

He shoved out of her embrace and backed away, sliding on one knee.

Deciding it was all or nothing, she turned onto her back and arched. His breathing became rougher when she spread her thighs and ran a fingertip down her throat. Eyes veiled by her lashes, she moved lower, watching him as he watched her hand trail between her breasts. Already hard, her nipples tingled as his gaze swept over her.

He slid back another foot.

"Please, touch me."

"Jesu." His throat worked as he swallowed.

Cupping one breast, her other hand continued its descent. Her heart tumbled as she circled her belly button, touch lazy and light. Watching him watch her, she shifted on the lambskin throw, enticing him one undulation at a time.

"Don't do that." His hands curled into fists, he growled, "Play fair, Afina."

"No." Her thumb brushed over her nipple, and oh…that felt good.

With a soft moan, she tipped her head back, breaking eye contact with Xavian. She heard him shift closer as her other hand slid into the curls between her thighs. She'd never touched herself before, but had overhead the women she'd tended talk about it. And Xavian had stroked her there once when she'd been beneath him. She wanted to feel him again, the stroke of his fingers and the pleasure and—

"Sweet Christ." Xavian's hand skimmed over her hip.

Afina bit down on her bottom lip to keep from smiling. She'd won. He'd crumbled, and as he slid between her legs and pushed her knees wider she didn't resist. Simply opened and waited for his touch, for the magic in his fingertips.

Except something hot and wet touched her instead.

Xavian growled. Her eyes flew open on a sharp inhale. He settled, his shoulders between her thighs, his mouth…

He was…he was…Oh, yes. His tongue was so hot, so insistent and—

Afina whimpered. He showed no mercy and licked her again. Her eyes rolled back in her head. Goddess, and she thought his fingers were good. His tongue was better, pure delight in every stroke.

The pressure built and she twisted as he licked deeper, spreading her with his fingers to reach a sensitive spot high on her sex. He flicked her lightly, sweeping around the nubbin, testing her response. With a keening cry, she surged against him. He held her down, one hand flat on her belly as his tongue explored her folds.

Lost in the bliss, she threw her head back, moving her hips, following his rhythm, wanting more. He didn't deny her.

Settling deep, he sent her higher, knowing just where to touch and how much pressure to apply. But he wasn't playing fair. He was making her pay for pushing him. The cost was pleasure: mind-blowing, gut-wrenching pleasure that never spilled into release.

On edge, held high without the promise of rapture, she grabbed fistfuls of his hair, demanding he give her what she needed. "Xavian! I c-can't...Oh, Gods!"

He lifted his mouth and set his chin on her curls.

"No! Don't...go. Don't—"

"Beg...beg me to let you come." His eyes narrowed on her face, he nipped the inside of her thigh while tracing her folds with a fingertip. Her muscles clenched. He hummed, the sound delicious and wicked and ruthless. "You wanted it this way. Now beg. Make me believe you need me."

As far as payback went, it was diabolical. But her pride was already long gone. "Please."

"Please, what?"

"Make me come."

He murmured in approval and slid one finger inside her. She moaned and rolled her hips, happy to have any part of him. He retreated then came back, stretching her with gentle strokes. But gentle wasn't what she wanted. "More. I need more!"

"What do you say?"

"Please...please...yes, please!"

Without mercy, he thrust a second finger deep as his mouth moved over her again. He worked her hard: suckling, licking, plucking, his hand moving faster. Sweat slick and needy, she followed his rhythm, pleading with him to let her finish. He nipped her gently. She sobbed his name. He sucked harder. Her spine bowed off the furs: nipples tight, legs spread, the fire in her veins more than she could handle. She couldn't take anymore...she couldn't—

"So good...you taste so damn good."

His words accompanied one last, lingering lick. Then he latched on, put his mouth right over her nub and sucked until she crested on hard pleasure. Multicolored sparks set off the explosion, devastating her from the inside out.

She came down slowly: panting, boneless, so full of bliss she couldn't remember her own name.

"Afina?"

Oh, right. That was it.

Something warm tugged on her nipple. She cracked her lids. Xavian's tongue lapped her again, suckled a moment then turned to lavish its mate. She arched into the wet heat as his hips settled between her thighs. "Hmm...your turn."

He groaned, the sound full of anticipation as he lifted his head from her breast. Afina met his ascent with her mouth, tasting herself as she tangled their tongues together. The kiss was slow and sweet, a gentle fusing as he cupped her bottom and adjusted their fit.

Afina gave an impatient wiggle. She couldn't wait to have him inside her. To be picked up and carried away again by his rhythm and the long, hard length of him. She wanted his scent all over her: in her lungs, on her skin, deep inside her.

Poised to give her all she wanted, Xavian tensed and broke from the kiss. Still as death against her, he looked left, eyes narrowed, head tilted. Gripping the heavy muscle of his shoulders, she started to ask—

Wood shifted, cracked, then hit the deck.

Afina flinched as the horrendous sound shattered the quiet around them.

With a curse, Xavian rolled, reaching under the lambskin above her head. He came away with a dagger. She scrambled as he pivoted into a crouch, placing himself in front of her. White knuckling the blanket, Afina pressed the wool to her chest and held her breath. Her heart paused mid-beat as she peeked around him.

The boat pitched gently and the awning snapped overhead, the smell of bruised fruit drifting as a shadow separated from the edge of the main mast.

Unfazed by his nakedness, Xavian stood to face the intruder.

"I'm looking for a priest," Henrik said, tone tight, sunlight flashing across the hard planes of his face. "Seen one around here?"

CHAPTER TWENTY-SEVEN

Xavian's gaze narrowed on the rope behind Henrik's head. Threaded through the edge of the awning, the cord went taut as the faded red canvas sailed high, rolling like a wave overhead. He eyed the end knotted to the main mast, calculating how long it would take him to cut the rope, wrap it around Henrik's neck, and toss the entire mess—friend and all—overboard.

To the count of thirty...tops.

Quick. Clean. Satisfying. Exactly the way he liked a problem solved.

Henrik eyed the line then gave him a level look. "Don't even think about it."

"Leave."

He shook his head. "Not going to happen."

Rahat, the bastard was asking for it. But then, so was he.

Xavian ran his hand over the back of his neck. What the hell was he doing? They were on a ship full of men. It didn't matter that most aboard were scared of him. He never should have touched Afina in such a public place. Unclothing her had been necessary to help her recover. Keeping her that way had not been part of the plan. No matter how much he craved her soft skin against his, he should have shoved her into her trews the moment she woke up and done what he'd wanted to do from the start. Talk.

But the feel of her against him...the sight of her: back arched, thighs spread, and fingers playing...

God. Xavian swallowed.

Seeing her splayed out like that had emptied his head. In truth, there wasn't much between his ears even now. Hell, all his blood was still below his waist, throbbing with an insistence that made him want to kill something.

"Goddamn it, Ram," his friend growled, toeing an apple away from his foot. The fruit rolled, bumping against one of the broken crates between them. "We spoke of this."

"And I agreed."

"Agreed, my arse. 'Twas a well-executed sidestep, naught more. You have no intention—"

"Things have changed."

"Have they?" Henrik raised a dark brow. "Then you won't mind waiting for the priest."

Christ.

His friend was like a dog with a bone. He wouldn't let it go, and Xavian couldn't help but like him all the more for it. Afina deserved better. The best, in fact, and he was naught close to what she needed. He wasn't gentle or kind. His black heart was buried beneath muscle and bone, stained by death, cheapened by deceit, ruined by what he had done and been and still was. His eyes on the tip of his blade, he tightened his grip on the hilt. The steel was heavy, a silent reminder of the filth beneath his skin. Hell, every time he touched Afina some of that stink rubbed off on her; infected and brought her lower...down to his level.

He was a selfish bastard.

To know what he was and still not be able to back away—to do the right thing by her—was a curse he couldn't deny. The pain of that weakness stung like a son of a bitch.

"Get gone, H." His voice sounded raw, wounded without the possibility of recovery. He cleared his throat, tossed the blade onto a sheepskin, and reached for his trews. "Afina needs privacy to dress."

"Not a chance." Henrik crossed his arms over his chest, widening his stance as the boat rolled to starboard then came back to its keel. "The moment I turn my back, you'll be on her again."

Xavian gritted his teeth, knowing it was true. Given half a chance, he'd have her beneath him again in a heartbeat. And she wouldn't stop him. He knew it with certainty…in the same way she'd known that begging would send him over the edge.

He rubbed the back of his hand over his mouth. God, he could still taste her on his tongue and down the back of his throat. She was sweetness and light. And he wanted more. 'Twas more than just two bodies coming together. Aye, the sex was good—best he'd ever had—but the need for connection came along with it. And as much as he wanted to deny it, being with her physically wasn't enough. It was all or naught. He wanted every single piece of her.

And that just pissed him off.

A soft rustle came from behind him and he tensed, shoulders bunching up hard as he thrust his legs into his leathers.

"Xavian?"

Jesu, her voice. Edged with passion, the husky whisper touched him like a prayer. The concern in it sucked him dry, made him crave her tongue and the heat of her mouth. Yanking his trews over his arse, Xavian braced himself before glancing at Afina over his shoulder.

Oh, Christ.

She looked…delicious. Good enough to eat.

Again.

Cheeks flushed with passion, dark hair a decadent tumble around her face, she met his stare head-on. He came unhinged inside and half turned toward her: wanting, needing, yearning. Henrik grumbled. Xavian ignored him, drinking her in, absorbing her scent, reliving the feel of her beneath his hands. Unable to help himself, his gaze dipped to her mouth. He bit back a groan. Her lips were still swollen from his kisses and…God, he'd just been there, had but moments ago tasted that sweetness in all its glory. His shaft jerked upright, straining against unlaced leather.

Grabbing hold of the ties, he closed the opening with a vicious pull. By way of punishment, it didn't do much. The bastard behind the lacing leapt forward, happy for the attention. And Afina wasn't helping matters. She was eating him with her eyes, her hazel-green gaze almost glowing as it drifted across his chest then south of his waistband. Her imaginary touch made his balls fist up so tight he started to pant. He breathed through it, taking shots of air as he tied off his lacing. His fingers shook. Xavian frowned at them, inhaled again, and willed his heart to slow. Little by little, the self-discipline he'd spent a lifetime perfecting kicked in, saving Henrik from a swim in the Jiu.

His focus still fixed on Afina, he exhaled slowly. "Get dressed, *draga*."

"Not with him watching."

"Turn around." Violence rolled like thunder, blanketing him with the need to pummel his friend. The bastard stood little more than six feet away, and Afina was all but naked. It didn't matter that Henrik was her brother. The territorial need to protect what belonged to him was stronger than reason. "Now."

Henrik's eyes narrowed. "Ram—"

"Now." Rolling his shoulders, he cranked his fists in tight, wanting to hit Henrik so badly it took all he had to stay still. "Or you take a swim."

"Goddamn it." With a scowl, Henrik pivoted, giving them his back.

Xavian exhaled slowly as Afina stepped behind him. He widened his stance, made himself bigger to shield her. It felt good to protect her, to provide what she needed when she needed it. One eye on Henrik, he glanced over his shoulder, the urge to look at her too much to resist.

She dropped the blanket.

His breath caught, stalling in his throat like he'd been punched in the chest. She was so damned beautiful—all round curves and lean limbs and soft skin. Xavian snapped his head around. Looking at her was a bad idea. It only intensified the ache and elevated his frustration past what was safe.

Linen rustled and leather snapped as he listened to her dress. Needing a distraction, he grabbed his tunic, jammed it over his head, and did up the side lacing. His boots came next, and as he stomped the second one on he sheathed his daggers, sliding each one home before reaching for his twin scabbards. With care, he adjusted the harness over his chest, crisscrossing the leather straps, aware of the slip and slide behind him as Afina laced up her boots.

As he secured the last buckle, she came up behind him. Still using him as a shield, she set her small hand on his shoulder. He closed his eyes. Shivers chased a tremor down his spine as her warmth seeped into him.

"What's going on?" The question, quietly spoken, held an edge of uncertainty that made his stomach ache.

He tried to ignore the urge, but the need to reassure her hung on and he murmured, "'Tis all right, love."

Chewing on her bottom lip, her focus shifted to Henrik. "Why is he so angry?"

Xavian inhaled, filling his lungs to capacity. Thank Christ…a distraction in its purest form; the kind he needed to keep his hands off Afina. And it came with an added bonus—retribution. Though Xavian couldn't help but admire Henrik's methods. Knocking over the crate had been a stroke of genius. Still, he wasn't feeling magnanimous. The need to do his friend a little damage was too much to resist.

"You going to tell her, H? Or am I?"

"Not now."

"Here. Now."

Henrik scrubbed his hand over the back of his head. "Shit."

Good at waiting, Xavian stayed quiet. His gaze steady on his friend, he reached for Afina's hand. Little shocks grabbed at his forearms as he made contact and pulled her out from behind his back. As soon as she stood alongside him, he let go. She held on, slipping her pinky between his index and middle fingers. Her palm met his. His heart kicked at his chest as she leaned into him—body against his, her cheek against his upper arm.

Henrik turned to face them, something desperate in his eyes.

Xavian almost felt bad. Almost. But his friend deserved what he got. If he hadn't wanted to be messed with, he should have left well enough alone. He tipped his chin in Henrik's direction, prompting him.

"Afina, I, ah…" Henrik frowned and glanced away. He stared out to the cliff face rising out of the river, concentrating hard on the rough wall. "I tried to tell you…at the cave, but…"

"Tell me what?" Afina gripped Xavian's hand harder.

Xavian squeezed back, not liking her fear. Hell, mayhap he shouldn't have pushed it. Mayhap forcing Henrik to spill his secret wasn't the best idea. Mayhap Afina wouldn't welcome the news she had a brother. She'd been through so much in such a short time. Had nearly died and—

"Please tell me…what is so wrong?"

"Naught is wrong," Xavian said, giving her hand another pump. "H, mayhap—"

"We are kin, Afina," Henrik blurted, his chest rising and falling in fast bursts. "I…I am your brother."

Afina jerked then went stiff against him. Her mouth opened once, twice, a third time as she stared at Henrik. The tears, though, were terrible, and unable to stop himself, Xavian hooked his arm around her back, offering comfort with his body. She didn't take it. He tightened his hold, willing her to relax, to breathe and lean on him.

"Draga—"

She shook free of his hold, planted her palms on his chest, and pushed. Xavian sucked in a quick breath and unlocked his arms. It almost killed him to let her go, but he refused to draw her back. He couldn't protect her from the truth.

"Show me," she said, voice unsteady.

Henrik went rigid, the muscles in his arms and neck standing out in relief. "Listen, 'tis—"

"I won't believe you unless you show me. I want to see it."

"Christ." Henrik hesitated a heartbeat, dark brows drawn, face expressionless before his hands went to the lacing on his tunic. Yanking the knot free, he loosened the ties, pull by slow pull. His jaw clenched, he lifted the leather over his head in one strong movement.

Afina's hand flew over her mouth.

Xavian went stock still, his eyes on his friend's chest. The moon-star was still there—the same size, shape, and color as Afina's mark. The difference? Afina's sat on the front curve of her shoulder. Henrik's was stamped directly over his heart.

Why his friend had tried so hard to hide it, Xavian didn't know, but—

"Hell," Xavian murmured, understanding hitting him sideways.

It had never been about Henrik, but something more important.

His gaze left the birthmark to meet Henrik's. The truth lay in his friend's eyes: the reason he'd stay with Al Pacii, all the times he'd done Halál's bidding without complaint, why he'd never fought being strapped to the blue stone or the old man's knife.

Henrik had been protecting his family.

The noble sacrifice made Xavian feel even dirtier. Henrik was lily white—a killer with righteous cause. Xavian couldn't say the same. He'd killed and maimed not to protect a loved one, but to shield himself. And that kind of selfishness came at a cost.

What he'd done in the name of Al Pacii couldn't be undone. The blood on his hands couldn't be washed off. The stain inside him would never come clean. Aye, he flirted with absolution and saved as many boys as he could, but that would never be enough. 'Twas his penance—a cross he bore to ensure each lad had a childhood—but an equal amount was about revenge. About depriving Al Pacii of the fresh blood it needed to replenish its numbers and continue. About his hatred for Halál.

He wasn't an altar boy with a pure motive. Didn't go to church or pray or expect God to look upon him with favor. 'Twas too late for forgiveness.

The realization tore him in two, and as he listened to Afina sob, watched her launch herself at her brother and Henrik embrace her in return, he realized he couldn't do it. Couldn't take her before a priest and contaminate her with his filth. He was less than half the man Afina needed him to be, and as his hungry gaze devoured her he knew what he had to do.

He had to let her go.

No matter how much it hurt, he needed to find another capable of easing her when the magic became too much and…find the strength to let her go.

If he didn't, he would kill her spirit as surely as Halál had killed his.

A cold draft blew through the long, narrow chamber. Chased by a chill, the wind batted at the candle flames and the light wavered. Oddly shaped shadows flickered across the face of Halál's page. Drawing his hand over the text, he smoothed the parchment flat before adjusting the wolf pelt around his shoulders. The fur blocked out the cold, protecting old bones from the bitter mountain air.

Fat candles, seven strong and grouped in a half-circle, bent sideways as another gust found its way around the leather covering stretched over the sole window and swirled into the room. Two went out, their black wicks standing like skeletons in liquid pools as the scent of beeswax suffused the air around him. Picking up a thin stick, he relit the tapers and returned to the tome.

A gift from his men, the leather-bound book was a prized possession. Like the many scattered across the wooden surface of the table and discarded on the floor at his feet, its value lay in its content. The topic dipped into the darkness, into the fascinating world of the occult.

This one, though, was special.

Stamped into black leather, its face bore the image of a goat's head. Horns twisted up from its skull almost touching the thick circle surrounding it. Halál didn't know why, but he loved the emblem. There was something about it…something otherworldly, almost alive as its eyes stared out from the leather.

But more than all that, it was the book's origin that gave him a thrill. Taken from the Vatican, the ancient text belonged to the pope—or rather, had. No longer. One of his assassins had stolen it from a locked vault deep beneath the walled city. No doubt the arrogant bastard had thought it obscene. To most, it would be, but not to Halál. To him, it was a thing of beauty, to be protected from those who would destroy it and all the knowledge it contained.

His lips curved as he flipped a page. The soft rustle and smell of old parchment rose as he read through another spell. He shook his head. No, that one wouldn't do. He needed something stronger—specific—to break the incantation.

Shay—that clever bastard—had made sure the spell would hold. The only way to regain control of The Three was to get close enough to counteract it. But he needed the right incantation, and time was running out.

The beasts were exceptional hunters. Exquisite killers with single-minded purpose—find Xavian and see their duty done. Once sworn, the spell would bind them to Xavian for all time. The melding would be irrevocable and they would not only kill to protect him, but do his bidding without question.

That kind of firepower would tip the scales in Xavian's favor. Make him bolder and his goals bigger. And Al Pacii would be his number one target.

Not that Grey Keep was in any danger. The enchanted wards buried deep beneath the ancient castle would keep the beasts at bay, but Xavian could do serious damage to his assassins once they stepped outside the circle the wards provided. In truth, he had already done damage, intercepting some of the lads he required to replenish the Al Pacii ranks. Even Qabil, his next apprentice, hadn't been safe from Xavian.

All of a sudden, the game he played didn't seem so amusing.

Halál sat back against the thickly cushioned armchair. Ruffling the tome's parchment, he flicked the page corner with the tip of his finger then flipped the heavy volume closed. The thump echoed in the cavernous chamber, nothing but vaulted ceilings, stone walls, and rows of wooden shelves to muffle the sound.

The door creaked open at the far end of the chamber. Halál's gaze narrowed on the opening, displeasure a cold void inside his chest. A thick shadow loomed on the threshold.

"What?" His voice was soft, like Beauty's hiss and just as deadly as her poison.

"I knocked, master," Valmont said, tone hesitant, his body backlit by the torchlight streaming in from the corridor. "When you did not answer, I..."

As the assassin trailed off, Halál smiled. He smelled Valmont's fear. The reaction appeased him enough to let the disrespectful entrance slide. For now. Later, when he had finished his report, Halál would make him pay for his sin. The blue stone hadn't been used today, and he was itching to take out his knives.

He flicked his fingers, and Valmont came forward. He stopped on the other side of the table and, no more than three feet away, bowed, laying the back of his neck vulnerable to a blade. Halál wanted to unsheathe his, but stilled the need. He would get to play soon enough.

"The high priestess?"

"Gone, master."

Halál's hand curled into a fist on top of the goat head. The witch had been his last hope. His precious tomes had yielded little. He needed stronger magic to bring The Three home, but without the high priestess…

He uncurled his hand and laid it flat against the tome's face. The cool leather calmed him. Rage would gain him nothing. It was a weak emotion, a precursor to defeat. A quick mind required a still spirit…A good plan was only possible with both. "What else?"

"Ylenia is dead and her daughters are gone," Valmont said, words rushing one over the other like water over river rock. "The Blessed have abandoned the temple. No one has been seen there for almost two years."

Interesting. The Blessed were rumored to be servants of the goddess. Led by the high priestess, they observed the ancient traditions, performing the rituals that brought balance to the earth. Not that he believed in such things. But for them to have abandoned their station an event close to cataclysmic had taken place.

Halál ran a fingertip over one of the goat horns, following the twisted lines.

"There is more, master," he said, shuffling his feet. His boots rasped against the stone floor as Halál's gaze left the tome and returned to Valmont. "Vladimir Barbu is not at Castle Raul. He left with a full contingent, some flying the grand master's colors."

"Stein?" When Valmont nodded, he almost smiled. Those two had a long history. Stein liked young boys and Barbu had once been one. "Anything else?"

"Rumor has it Barbu hunts the young high priestess."

"Of course," he murmured, the piece of the puzzle falling into place nicely. The ambitious bastard wanted to be voivode of Transylvania, but without the high priestess's blessing he couldn't claim the throne.

Eyes narrowed, he turned the new information over in his mind. Power-hungry men were useful. Perhaps he should enter the fray. Find Ylenia's whelp and extract a heavy price from Barbu. Mayhap it was time to call Henrik home. He'd been in Poland long enough, and Halál enjoyed a tragic twist. It was poetic, really. Imagine, sending a brother out to hunt his sister only to deliver her into the hands of the enemy.

His spirit lifted at the thought, but that was for another time. First things first. He must deal with Xavian.

Another gust washed over the candles. Halál watched the flames battle to stay alive, a plan forming as the seven righted themselves. "I have another task for you, Valmont."

"Anything, master."

"Our next shipment..." Unable to stop himself, his hand made another pass over the goat's head. "When are the lads due to arrive?"

"At the end of next month."

Halál nodded, his hands still caressing black leather. "Send word out they will be here sooner...within the next fortnight."

"But—"

"Be sure to tell all we are transporting them via the north mountain trail." Halál reached for another of his treasures and, pulling it into his lap, opened the thick volume. Leather creaked as the smell of musty parchment rushed into his face. He thumbed the edges of the vellum. "Xavian likes to steal Al Pacii boys. We will bait the trap and reel him in."

"An ambush?"

He inclined his head. "Take the six plus twenty-one more. I want the *betrayer* dead before the next full moon."

A gleam in his dark eyes, Valmont bowed. "With pleasure, master."

Halál couldn't help but approve. The blue stone and his knives would have to wait. His assassin needed to be strong for the mission ahead.

CHAPTER TWENTY-EIGHT

Two weeks at Drachaven and Afina wanted to tie Xavian to the nearest tree. Not that there were many around the great stone fortress. Still, if it meant keeping him in one place long enough to talk to him she would find one. At least then he wouldn't be able to avoid her.

Avoid. Now there was a word with resonance.

She'd explored its meaning at length, turned it over in her mind, trying to understand why Xavian stayed away. She felt his gaze often—responded to the yearning as it stroked over her—but never saw him. He was a ghost, drifting around the castle, using Drachaven's clever layout and its many rock ledges to hide from her.

And that was before she even entered the keep.

Inside the fortress was a complex warren, a rabbit hole of connecting tunnels and large chambers. Carved into solid rock, the castle's facade hung like a portrait on the mountainside. Yet most rooms had natural light, small slits in the rock face in stairwells, larger windows in the third-level bedchambers, at least on the south side overlooking the cliffs. It was an impressive place, half the structure inside the mountain, half out, almost as though the mountain gods had swallowed a portion and left the rest to the elements.

Crossing the courtyard, she scanned the thick outer walls, looking for any sign of Xavian. Nothing. Only the guards and… Cruz. Afina smiled a little. The lad loved high places. But then, that was no great surprise. He was half-dragon, after all. Despite that, she couldn't help but like him. The other two *shifters* she would have gladly tossed into the Jiu River, but Cruz?

Well, he was special. In spite of everything, he accepted her without question.

As if sensing her presence, he shifted and glanced down. One hand shielding her eyes from the morning sun, she waved at him with the other. He tipped his chin, smiled, then returned to watching over the edge of the great wall. A plateau sat below him and, on it, the practice field. The faint rumble of horses' hooves and the sound of steel hitting steel told her the men were in full swing, training in the lower bailey.

Her attention drifted to the west gatehouse, one of only two entrances into Drachaven. A stone bridge lay on the other side of the high archway, sloping down to join the training area. She hesitated, her feet missing a beat as she wondered if Xavian was out on the field. So far she hadn't found him there, but…

No, she must stick to the plan. He was too good at evading her. The moment she stepped foot outside the porticos he would disappear, leaving her with nothing but disappointment and a boatload of frustration.

Dratted man. He was driving her daft.

Passing through the stable's double-wide doors, Afina paused to scan the gloomy interior. The scent of fresh hay and horses kicked up along with twinkling dust motes as she searched the shadows, looking for the stable master. She didn't want to run into Ritz. A battleaxe of a man, he always stuck his nose where it didn't belong. And really, the last thing she wanted was to explain herself—or the reason she needed a rope.

On her tiptoes, Afina crept down the wide center aisle, seeing Ritz in every shadow, around each corner, and behind piles of crates. The sound of her pulse throbbed in her ears—the relentless thump-thump-thump sounding more like horses' hooves than her heartbeat. Pausing next to an empty stall, Afina pushed the half door open, ready for the stable master to jump out at her.

She wouldn't put it past him. Ritz was a wily old coot.

Like everyone in Drachaven, he'd been stolen from somewhere. Xavian, for some reason, didn't understand the word no. He took whatever he needed, including people. Mitza, the cook, had been kidnapped in Ismal; Ritz from some fancy lord's stables; Carmen, the bee keeper and resident ale brewer, from a tavern near Constantinople; and Jersey, the smithy, from his bed inside the armory at Corvinesti Castle.

She could go on forever. The list was endless. Everyone had been taken by stealth, but more incredibly, no one seemed to mind. They all accepted Xavian and loved living at Drachaven.

Which was insanity to the next power.

But then, she understood it to some degree. Foolishly felt it herself. In the two weeks since her arrival, Drachaven had become home. Now if only Xavian would cooperate…

Afina frowned, irritated all over again, and stopped in front of the back wall. Rope, coiled and tied into loose bundles, hung from metal hooks hammered into the mortar joints. She bit her bottom lip, trying to decide. The selection was mind-boggling. Leather, twine, and braided cloth ropes, thick and thin, long and short, marched like soldiers along stone: orderly, neat, ready to be used.

Oh, goddess, what was she doing?

Up in her bedchamber, it had seemed like a marvelous idea. Now she wasn't so sure. Could she go through with it? Afina rubbed her fingertips with the pad of a thumb, her gaze hopping from one rope to the next. Xavian would no doubt kill her if she… But Goddess help her! She couldn't take the distance anymore.

She missed him so much. Missed the scent of forest musk and man and the sound of his voice. Missed his sharp intelligence and quick wit and gentle hands. But more than anything, she missed how he made her feel: strong and able and maybe even a little bit brave.

Feeling that way felt good. So right, in fact, she refused to let it go. She'd learned something from Xavian: how to fight and take what she wanted. It was simply unfortunate—at least for him—that she was about to use the same tactics he'd taught her against him.

Poetic justice.

Yes, that was it. Xavian had started the battle between them. She would end it, using any means available to her…rope included. Now all she had to do was corner him.

Chewing on the inside of her cheek, Afina examined her choices again. The braided cord made of cloth was probably the best option. The last thing she wanted to do was hurt him, and the other ropes would no doubt cut into his—

"Priestess."

With a squeak, Afina swung around, her heart a tangled mess inside her chest. She put her hand over it, telling it to calm down. It paused a moment then sped up again as she spotted the intruder. Planted in the middle of the center aisle, Garren stood, arms crossed and expression intent.

His gaze narrowed on her. "Up to no good, I see."

Afina swallowed. A prickle of fear shivered through her and her fingertips throbbed, her magic responding to the unspoken threat. Her body always reacted the same way whenever Garren was around. Something inside her knew he didn't like her—would hurt her if given half a chance. Shifting a little, she widened her stance to match his, preparing for whatever he threw at her.

"Relax, Priestess. No one needs to get hurt here."

His tone was lazy, unconcerned, but most of all unthreatening. Afina resented it. She hated the fact he scared her so badly. A close second on the annoying scale? He never called her by name. It was always "Priestess," as though using anything else might cause him to forget the past and her family's crimes.

"I have a name, dragon," she said, giving tit for tat. If he wanted to play rough, she would meet him and raise the stakes. She wasn't a fragile flower. Not anymore. "And what I do is none of your concern."

"Itching for a fight, are you?" One corner of his mouth hitched up, he tilted his head, studying her. "Not that I blame you. Frustration will do that to a female."

"Go away, Garren."

"And what...leave you bereft? Without the benefit of my advice?"

"I do not need your advice."

"Truly," he said, raising a dark brow. Afina curled her hands into fists, fighting the urge to yank the offending eyebrow back down. "You are not doing very well on your own and...I am good at tying knots."

Afina blinked, surprise momentarily lowering her guard. "How—"

"It is written all over your face," he said, a spark of amusement in his eyes. "Of course, it doesn't hurt that I am privy to your thoughts as well."

She clenched her hands so hard her fingernails bit into her palms. Wonderful. A runaway dragon with mind reading capabilities. Just what she needed. By the goddess, she wanted to hit him...just once.

"Striking me will not solve your problem, Priestess...or bring Xavian closer."

"Stop it," she said, warning in her tone. "Get out of my head, Garren."

"As you wish," he murmured, dipping his chin in a mock bow.

The pompous ass. He was a nightmare come to life. "Do you always intrude where you are unwelcome?"

Garren shrugged. "It is a hobby...of sorts."

"I'm sure," she said, her tone without bite. Closing her eyes, Afina rubbed the spot between her brows and huffed, the sound half-laugh, half-sob. She was so tired; tired of fighting with Garren, tired of chasing Xavian, tired of always being on the losing end. "All right, Garren. You've had your fun. Now could you please just...leave me alone."

His boots scraped against the limestone floor as he stepped toward her. Afina's head snapped up. What was she doing? She knew better than to take her eyes off him. He was dangerous—a predator on the hunt—and she was nothing but an intriguing bit of prey.

She raised her hands. Magic pulsed in her fingertips.

Instead of charging, he stopped six feet away and held both hands, palms up and to the sides. The universal sign for "I mean no harm." Afina studied the hard planes of his face, waiting for the trick, the ambush that would tear her apart.

"You are in pain, Priestess," he said, tone soft, expression without a hint of the anger he always showed her.

"Come to gloat?"

"No...to help."

"Why would you bother?" She crossed then uncrossed her arms, feeling uncomfortable in her own skin. "You hate me."

"Hate is too strong a word, Afina," he said, causing her to flinch. Coming from him, her name sounded strange, like it belonged to another person. "Besides, he suffers too."

Afina swallowed past the lump in her throat. "Then he wouldn't stay away."

Giving voice to the thought made her head ache and her heart hurt. The truth of it was terrible, like being sideswiped by a runaway horse and dragged through gravel. She was raw, completely bare, and didn't know how to reset her defenses. Garren didn't need to touch her to cause her pain. Like any warrior, he'd found the chinks in her armor and thrust the blade home.

Fighting tears, she told herself to walk away before he did more damage. Her feet refused to listen, which in turn encouraged her runaway mouth, and she said, "If Xavian truly wanted me, he wouldn't—"

"Hristos, woman." Garren scowled, his expression so black Afina took a step back. She bumped into the crate behind her, wobbled then reset her balance as he ran a hand through his dark hair. "That bitch really didn't teach you a thing, did she?"

"Not much besides pain," she whispered, viselike pressure banding around her rib cage.

Garren stared at her, puzzlement and uncertainty in his eyes. After a moment, the hard planes of his face relaxed, softening until she got a glimpse of the man behind the dragon. "I am going to clue you in. But if you tell him I told you..."

A peace offering...from Garren? There must be a catch. Was he sending her into a trap; one designed for his own amusement? Afina rubbed a hand over her heart, mistrust warring with the need to know. She needed information—wanted to understand— and Garren was the closest thing she had to a mentor. He'd been there from the beginning, had known her mother, understood magic and what Afina was capable of. She would never find a better teacher.

Swallowing her fear, she took a chance. "I won't tell him, I swear."

Garren frowned and, rolling his shoulders, gave her another stern look.

"Promise."

He sighed. "You and Xavian have bonded, Afina. The connection is one of mind, body, heart, and soul. Once forged, it is unbreakable. You need each other. He drains the excess magic in your blood and keeps you healthy. You bring him power, increase his natural abilities, help him heal quickly, among other things. If one of you dies, the other will not survive long."

"But my father died when I was—"

"He and your mother were never truly mated. The connection between them was not a strong one." A crease between his brows, Garren scanned the assortment of rope hanging on the wall behind her. The blue streaks at his temple winked in the low light as he moved to stand alongside her, closer than he'd ever been before. Afina tensed, ready to flee when he turned and planted his shoulder against a timber post. "Xavian cannot help but want you. It is in every breath he takes...in all that he is. Whether he admits it or not, he is a bonded male now. A dangerous thing without his female. The longer he is away from you, the more aggressive and territorial he will become. Not a good thing for a male who is built that way to begin with."

"But he is avoiding me and I..." She paused, feeling inadequate. Talking to Garren about her lover was like airing dirty laundry: unpleasant and embarrassing. But what choice did she have? He was willing to help. She wasn't getting anywhere on her own, and Xavian was suffering too. The thought was unbearable. "What can I do? No matter how hard I try, I cannot get close to him. Please, tell me what to do."

"First thing?"

She nodded, chin bobbing, ears and heart wide open.

"Stop thinking about tying him up. A male such as Xavian is too proud for that."

"But—"

"Touch him, Afina." Garren pushed away from the post. His massive form cast a shadow, falling over her head and shoulders as he pivoted toward the exit. "All you need do is touch him."

Afina huffed. "How am I supposed to do that when I cannot find him?"

"He is in his workshop. South side of the courtyard, behind the smithy. 'Tis where he sleeps, too, so you will be comfortable enough."

"Thank you," she whispered, her throat so tight she could barely force the words out. Brushing an errant tear from the corner of her eye, she reached out without thinking. As her hand touched his forearm, he went stiff. "Thank you, Garren."

His chin tilted down, he stared at her hand then brought his violet gaze up to meet her own. A silent understanding passed between them, a truce of sorts. Giving him a squeeze, she let him go before she overstepped her bounds. His eyes narrowed, he studied her a moment then moved off, long legs striding toward the double doors. Just before he crossed the threshold, he pivoted and tipped his chin in her direction.

"One more thing." One corner of his mouth curved, Garren put his large hand between his legs and cupped himself. "Touch him here, lass…with your mouth."

Afina's eyes went wide as the naughty image tumbled through her mind. It hit the rocks somewhere between unlacing his trews and—

She shook her head. Not a chance. No way she could… would…be able to—

"Trust me," he said, the devil in his eyes. "No male worth his salt can resist such a thing."

Irresistible was good. Very good, she decided as the dragon-shifter stepped into the sunshine and disappeared from view.

❦✠❦

The rasp of metal joined the clang of the smithy's hammer as Xavian drew the whetstone along the blade of his carving knife. His rhythm was sure but his mind was elsewhere. Normally 'twas what he liked most about carving. It took him to another place, away from the past, out of the future, leaving him grounded in the now.

The *now*, however, was presenting a problem. One with dark hair and hazel eyes and a body that—

He needed to stop thinking about her.

Xavian dropped his tools on the table and shucked his tunic, tossing the balled-up linen onto the chair behind him. No matter how well made, he couldn't stand the fabric against his skin. 'Twas too soft. Reminded him too much of Afina and the silk between her thighs.

"Hell…'tis where I am," he muttered, testing the edge of the blade with his thumb. After a few more swipes, he set the whetstone back in its wooden box and turned to his newest sculpture.

Three feet high by almost six feet long, the piece sat on the center table of his workshop. It was the largest he'd ever attempted, its size an exact match to the enormity of the distraction he was feeding. The room he was nursing it in should have helped. Instead it felt like a pine box; one that was already six feet under.

Sandwiched between the curtain wall and the blacksmith's, the large, timber-beamed structure he worked and slept in blended so seamlessly into the smithy it was difficult to find. And thank Christ for that. The stone walls and sloped roof gave him what he needed most—privacy. A scarce commodity on a good day. But essential now that Afina was flitting around the keep.

Hell, Drachaven was his home, normally a bastion of calm in the sea of his life. Not anymore. Trying to do the right thing was tearing him apart…and he was hurting Afina in the process. He felt her pain. Could distinguish her moods better than his own—all without getting anywhere near her.

He knew when she spent time with Sabine and his lads, her happiness a living thing that enlivened his heart and steadied his soul. The vibration changed when frustration took hold, like now, radiating until his skin prickled and his muscles tightened. Xavian shifted, discomfort a slow draw that chipped at his calm, making him want to stab something.

He ran his free hand over the nape of his neck, pulling at tension. Christ, what a mess. Mayhap Cristobal was right. Mayhap he should be selfish and take what he wanted. The problem? Afina would suffer more with him than without him. So he ignored his friend's prodding and stayed away, following at a distance like a lovesick lad.

But worse than that? He was driving his staff mad: pestering Cook to make sure Afina ate enough, quizzing the maids to ensure she had enough blankets at night, prodding Mistress Kent about the new gowns he'd ordered for her, beating the snot out of his men on the practice field to ease his frustration. All this to combat the one thing he wanted most...to hold her while they talked, lazing the day away in bed.

Xavian smoothed his hand over the half-formed carving. Made of basswood, the fine grain gleamed in the low light, its golden hue a soft stroke against his palm. When he'd placed it on the table, he'd been tempted to stand it upright and carve a person. But the only one he saw was Afina, and the last thing he needed was to see her lovely face at the start of each day.

'Twould send him over the edge...one he was perilously close to already.

Raising his blade, he leaned in and made a precise cut along the block's flank. A wood curl, about the width of his thumb, gleamed against the knife tip. It fell away and landed on the surface of the table as he twisted his wrist, ending the line. He continued on, cutting a series of grooves until a hind leg took shape and form. Next he moved onto the foot, working on the claws.

He was doing the carving from memory, and though he'd only seen the dragons in the dark, the likeness was good. Garren would no doubt try and burn it. The man-dragon hated having his beast carved—had threatened to skin him alive when Xavian had told him why he wanted the large block. Xavian grinned. He needed to finish fast. Couldn't wait to defend the carving. Even if he lost and the piece got roasted, the fight would give him what he craved...release.

Blade working in quick strokes, he lost himself in the rhythm, sinking beyond his shop into another world. Moving around the table, he sculpted, defined and redefined, care in each curve and deep-set line. Just as he started on the scaled torso, a tingle swept the back of his neck. Xavian's head came up so fast it nearly snapped off his shoulders.

Eyes narrowed, he glanced toward the doorway. Jesu. It couldn't be. He'd made certain she didn't know where—

"Xavian?" Afina's voice drifted through the open doorway.

The husky timbre washed over him like summer rain: warm and gentle and tempting. His body responded, the traitor behind his laces hardening so fast he grabbed the edge of the tabletop to keep from doubling over. A death grip on the knife hilt, Xavian closed his eyes.

He was in trouble. Serious—the-kind-a-man-didn't-get-out-of—trouble.

Panic picked up his heart and slammed it against his rib cage. He dropped the knife. As it clattered on the table, he pivoted toward the back of his shop. He needed to reach his bedchamber and the sliding panel behind his wardrobe before she touched him. Or he got a look at her.

Escape was the only option.

And the secret passageway concealed by the large cabinet was his best bet. It would take him into the labyrinth beneath Drachaven. Carved out of solid rock, the maze was a useful tool, one he often used to move from place to place around the castle, but never more than in the last sennight. Without it, he would never have been able to watch Afina without her knowing he was there.

Halfway to the chamber door, Xavian heard a mad scramble behind him. He picked up his pace.

"Xavian!" Her voice was sharp with warning. He kept going, teeth clenched, hands fisted with determination. Something crashed behind him, sounded like a wooden chair hitting the floor. "Oh, no. Don't you dare!"

He did and, lengthening his stride, came even with the door-jamb. The air crackled, became hot and thick, but Xavian didn't look back. She was too close, and he was too needy. If he laid eyes on her at this range, he'd have her beneath—

His head snapped back as he hit some sort of barrier. With a "Christ," he stumbled back a step, searching for whatever he'd smashed into. Warped, the air in front of him waved, a shimmering undulation in midair.

Rahat, magic. What the hell did Afina think she was doing?

With a snarl, he swung around to face her. A sensible person would have run in the other direction when they saw his expression. Afina kept coming, hazel eyes aglow with green. He shifted left, preparing to counter her. But she was already on him, slapping her hand in the center of his bare chest, pushing him backward until his arse hit the edge of the sideboard.

Wooden figures rattled as his shoulder blades bumped the shelves and the cupboard rocked against the wall behind it. He grabbed her wrist, desperate to get her hands off him. She resisted and, shoving him off balance, bumped his knee out to step between the spread of his thighs. Jesu, she was stronger than she looked. And now her hips were precisely where he didn't need them—and exactly where he wanted them.

"Afina, back away." His voice was more plea than command. God, he didn't want to hurt her. Was trying to be gentle. But with her scent and softness all around him, he couldn't take much more. "You don't want—"

"Be quiet." She applied pressure, keeping her palm pressed to his skin and him perched on the lip of the sideboard. "I know exactly what I want."

Balanced against his chest with her fingers spread wide, she aligned their bodies and scrambled his wits. The warmth of her breath touched him first, fanning over his collarbone an instant before she flicked him with the tip of her tongue. He shuddered as she drew away then came back to flick him again. Once, twice...Christ, he lost count as she licked her way to the base of his throat. She hummed against his skin and kissed his pulse point. With a groan, Xavian tipped his chin up to give her more access. He should stop her...should use his strength against her and fight his way free.

"Hmm...you taste so good, Xavian."

The muscle roping his stomach tightened as she leaned in hard, pressing her breasts to his chest. He sucked in a breath and cupped the nape of her neck, intending to pull her away—to set himself to rights and find the will to deny her.

Afina beat him to it, drawing away a little at a time. His gaze glued to her face, Xavian frowned, wondering at her game. She'd cornered him, had the upper hand, why was she retreating?

A wicked gleam in her eyes, she sank down between the splay of his knees. There was a quick tug. He stiffened as understanding lit him up like a lightning strike. Jesu, she'd tricked him; distracted him with her mouth while she unlaced his trews. And now...

"*Rahat*," he gasped as she pulled hard on his waistband. The sideboard biting into his arse, he grabbed for her hand. She was too quick. Unwrapping him like a birthday gift, she palmed his shaft, sliding her small hand deep inside his trews.

Air left his lungs in a rush. All thought disappeared. His body ceased to cooperate as, slack-jawed, he watched her lean in. Like liquid fire, her mouth closed around the head of his shaft. He shouted—half curse, half plea—and arched as her hot, wet tongue swirled, sending him past right and straight into wrong.

CHAPTER TWENTY-NINE

He tasted glorious. Pure sin with a hint of sweetness.

On her knees, Afina stroked Xavian with her tongue, listening to him groan and curse. His scent all around her, she watched him through the veil of her lashes. The ecstasy on his face said it all. He loved this. Loved having her mouth on him. Each swirling lick and gentle suck dragged him deeper, unraveling the threads of his control.

He whispered her name, so close to release now. The truth was in the flex of his muscles, in the rapture riding the planes of his face. His will was cracking...and she was winning. Another lick, a swirling suck, and she would have everything she craved. Total surrender. Him inside her.

Afina wanted to shout her victory. She stroked harder instead, relishing the reversal of power.

She rarely got to lead. Xavian was too strong to play the subordinate for long. He liked command too much, especially when it came to her. It was the reason he loved hearing her beg. Lord knew she enjoyed it too. But now she held the upper hand. He was enthralled, a prisoner to her pleasure.

Part of her wanted to keep him there.

The insight surprised her. Holding another captive had never held much appeal. But with Xavian? Afina couldn't get enough. She wanted to dominate, just for a while. The risks were enormous. He could push her away, deny her a home…break her heart. None of that was enough to stop her. The reward was too great to ignore: a happy home and long future together.

Afina yearned for both. Wanted to share her secrets and worries, her small successes and bigger victories. Wanted to be in his arms every night and wake up that way each morning. But first, Xavian needed to bend. Not a lot, just enough for her to slip through his defenses.

Afina tongued him again, wielding desire like a weapon. She wanted him tangled up, tied down, a slave to her and his need. He gripped the lip of the sideboard, his knuckles white as he arched, begging for more. She gave it to him, exploring him from root to tip. He grew longer, harder, so thick she couldn't contain him. Bringing her hands into play, she stroked him while her tongue circled.

Hmm, he was glorious…glorious with a dash of incredible.

"Jesu…" Xavian rolled his hips against her. She opened wide, taking him so deep he touched the back of her throat. Lips parted, spine arched, he groaned. Afina took him deeper. *"Rahat!"*

He pulsed against her tongue. With a hum, she eased the rhythm, soothing him with gentle licks, pressing her thumb to the base of his shaft to settle him. She didn't want him to finish yet. Some other time she'd have the taste of him in her mouth, but not now. When he came, she wanted him buried to the hilt inside her. Nothing less would do. She'd waited so long to have him this way. Had fought to find and subdue him. No chance in Hades she would allow her opportunity to slip away.

Xavian twisted against her, so close to coming he throbbed inside her mouth.

"Easy, my love." Kissing along his length, she caressed the outside of his thigh. "Not yet."

"*Draga*...please." He buried a hand in her hair.

"More?"

His grip moved to the nape of her neck, but he didn't answer. He was too busy waging an internal war...stay or go. Afina could see the indecision as regret collided with want. The battle played in his expression, and Afina's heart ached. She understood that kind of agony, the fear he would never be good enough. But Xavian was wrong. He was more than enough—all she needed and better than she deserved.

She flicked him again, swallowed the white pearl sitting like a crown on the tip of his shaft. Goddess, he was delicious...and so sensitive. Each lick sent him closer to the edge—beyond reason...precisely where she wanted him.

"God!" With rough hands, he jerked her to her feet. Hauling her against him, he lowered his head and invaded her mouth.

Afina hummed, opened wide, and wrapped her tongue around his. She had him now. No holds barred. No chance of retreat. His intensity told her that and something more. He was past civilized—beyond gentle and headed into greedy.

Hands buried in his hair, breasts pressed to his chest, she held on as he pushed away from the sideboard. His tongue still deep in her mouth, he grabbed fistfuls of her skirt and, raising the wool, walked her backward. Cool air washed over her calves and up the backs of her thighs. The chill lasted mere moments before his hands found her. Calloused and warm, his palms slid against her skin, arousing her, making her want more.

She bumped into something solid. The sharp edge pressed in. Afina barely noticed. The table behind her didn't matter. Xavian's hands were busy beneath her skirt. Holding her steady, his fingers stoked across her belly. Afina held her breath, waiting for him to move lower. He brushed her curls and she spread her thighs, anticipation bubbling inside her.

Nipping her bottom lip, his fingers slid home. "Jesu, you are so slick, love."

"O-oh...please," Afina gasped as he caressed her, circling the hard nub at the top of her sex. But it wasn't enough. She longed to take him deep; to feel him thick and hard, rhythm wild as he loved her.

As though he'd read her mind, he growled, "Hard and fast, *draga*."

The violence in his tone shivered through her, and she couldn't wait. She wanted him...right now. Her nipples hard pearls against her chemise, Afina pressed her breasts to his chest, desperate for relief.

Fingers still circling, he wound her tighter, pushing her higher with each mind-numbing caress. She needed more: more pressure, more heat...more everything. How could he tease when—

His teeth grazed her cheekbone. The rasp of his whiskers followed as he worked one finger inside her. She moaned, swirled her hips, begging without words. He held her still and thrust a second finger deep, stretching her, preparing her for deeper penetration. "I won't be gentle. Can you handle me that way?"

"Yes...anything. Please."

"Anything?" His growl reverberated, sliding between her ribs to surround her heart. "Foolish, love, to give me such leeway. But I'll take it."

His hand slid from between her legs and he stepped back. Afina keened as she lost her grip on him. She reached out, afraid he meant to leave her. But she needn't have worried. The heat in his eyes as they met hers told her all she needed to know. He wasn't leaving and she was in for the ride of her life.

Shoving his trews over his hips, he grabbed her wrist and spun her until her back was to his front. Cupping the nape of her neck, Xavian bent her over the table. The wooden edge bumped her hipbones and cold air touched her bottom as he shoved her skirt up and out of his way.

"*Rahat*, you're beautiful." His touch was light, almost reverent as it ghosted over her, tracing her curves. His hand slid up, anchored her hips before he pressed his thigh between her own. "Spread your legs."

With a moan, she walked her feet out to the side.

"Wider."

Goddess, he was demanding. Exquisitely so, making her surrender all. The realization made her pause. Bent over the table, she didn't have a scrap of leverage. She was helpless to his powerful, weak to his strong. He wouldn't hurt her, she knew that, but—

"Do it," he said, his tone steely yet somehow soft. "Now."

The command was one Afina couldn't deny. Palms planted against wood, she widened her stance, giving him all the space he needed to move between her thighs. His hips touched her bottom, and the tip of his shaft brushed her core. Afina sucked in a breath and grabbed for the edge of the tabletop. Her hand curled around the wooden lip an instant before he pressed in. He took her hard, stretched her wide, burying himself to the hilt in one thrust.

Pleasure, wild and wonderful, hit her full force. It spiraled out, eclipsed inhibitions, made her toes curl and her fingertips tingle. She pushed back against him, demanding he move.

"Christ, aye." Big hands bracketing her hips, he withdrew and came back.

True to his word, he set a fast pace, one designed to drive her mad. Each swirl of his hips and hard thrust brought her so close to climax she pulsed around him. She wanted to go over—to leap from the ledge and fly with him—but he pulled her back, left her teetering on the brink, suspended a breath away from bliss.

"Xavian!" Reaching behind her, she wrapped her hand around his wrist. Had she been able to she would have begged. But he'd stolen her air, filled her so full her brain went blank as she cried, "Let me…oh, yes…oh, please…please, please, please…"

The rush picked her up and threw her into a cataclysm of color so bright Afina sank beneath the wave, resplendent in the glory Xavian gave her.

Pressed deep, Xavian throbbed inside her. She could feel him struggling to hold on, to keep his climax at bay. With a shudder, he planted his hand next to her cheek and leaned over her. As his chest settled against her shoulder blades, he kissed her temple and swirled his hips.

"Again, *draga*." He rocked against her, pressing her into the table, employing a rhythm meant to revive.

Afina shook her head, weak from the pleasure, a limp mess in his arms.

"One more time, love."

Pulling back, he plunged forward, his hips driving hers. He wasn't gentle. He was ruthless, bringing her body back to life one merciless stroke at a time. Then again, he'd warned her. This coupling was about need and lust, about his drive to dominate, not coddle her. But even as he ruled her body he murmured, telling her she was beautiful—how much he needed her, wanted her, couldn't live without her.

His words and heat and heart awakened her own, and she rose, mind, body, and soul to meet him. She took him all. She took him deep, rocking into each thrust, taking him on a trip of unmitigated delight as she showed how much she loved him.

❀✟❀

Xavian's bed was the nicest she'd ever slept in. Not that it was bigger than the one in the master chamber. The mattress wasn't thicker. The bedding wasn't softer. There were no tassels, fluffy pillows, or fur throws. In fact, the bed was just that—a bed with an ordinary patchwork quilt thrown over the whole. Although the posts rising from each corner were undeniably spectacular. Hand carved, the wood gleamed with high polish, each pillar the image of a woman, the uneven stone walls the only frame for her beauty.

Afina's gaze roamed from one post to the next. Each paid homage to a different season. Winter dressed warmly. Spring held a sprig of new growth. Summer wore little more than a thin robe. And fall's arms overflowed with the bounty of harvest. But the woman's face was the same in each, the grace of her features sculpted into every hollow and curve.

Afina frowned. She knew that face, had—

A big hand curled around her breast. Hmm, here was the reason she liked this bed best. Xavian was in it with her. Afina turned toward him, arching into the warmth of his touch. Pushing up onto one elbow, he hummed and lowered his head. His thumb caressed the thrust of her nipple as his mouth paid homage to its mate. He suckled gently and she twisted, more than ready for another bout of lovemaking.

Beautiful man.

He'd loved her so well the second time, slow and sweet, without the urgency. She'd enjoyed him both ways. Dominant and demanding, reverent and gentle...it didn't matter. She wanted him however he came to her.

Afina slid her hands into his hair. The curling ends played between her fingers, painting her palms with softness. He flicked her with his tongue. She moaned, shifted beneath him, asking for more. He raised his head. His gaze met hers and searched, wandering deep as if to solve some great mystery.

A slight crease between his brows, he broke eye contact to focus on one of the bedposts. "Mother Nature."

Afina sighed. Drat. He wanted to talk instead of make love. She squashed her sudden burst of frustration. There were worse things than lying abed naked with Xavian...and not many better.

"Goddess of all things," she murmured, her gaze drifting to spring. "You carved each one?"

Xavian nodded. "I dream of her often...have since my youth."

The breath stalled in Afina's chest. "Who...the goddess?"

"Aye."

Mother Mary. The goddess had visited him. Afina didn't know whether to be offended or not. Jealousy was a petty reaction, she knew that, but Afina couldn't help herself. The goddess had made the trip for Xavian while never once bothering with her. She'd spent her youth floundering, vulnerable to her mother's many attacks. And where had the goddess been when she needed her? Drifting around in Xavian's dreams.

It was a bitter draught to swallow. Afina swallowed it anyway. None of what had happened to her was Xavian's fault. He'd been under attack too—fighting to survive—and if the goddess had helped him through those awful years? Good on her.

Afina had always had Bianca, a warm place to sleep, and good food to eat. Xavian had possessed none of that.

Her throat tightened. He'd endured so much with Al Pacii. Henrik hadn't wanted to tell her at first, but with every conversation she'd pulled more out of her brother...until a river of information had flowed. She knew what Xavian had been—and in some ways still was.

She stroked her hands over the tops of his shoulders. None of that mattered to her. She accepted him for what he was...for what he'd been trained and tortured to become.

With gentle fingers, she traced the arch of his eyebrow. "Does she speak to you?"

He shook his head.

"What, then?"

"Naught." He shifted, as though uncomfortable with the question. "They were just dreams, Afina. A lad's imaginings, naught more."

Afina's fingertips slowed then stilled, coming to rest on his biceps. He was hiding something...and lying to her. Oh, no. Xavian—the one who insisted on honesty—was skirting the truth.

A prickle of unease ghosted beneath her skin. "Xavian...look at me."

His brows contracted so hard a ridge pushed up between them.

"Please."

Muscle rippled, responding to his tension as his shoulders bunched up hard.

Afina chewed on the inside of her cheek. What tack should she take with him? He was shutting down, resetting his shields, and Lord knew, that was the last thing she needed from him. The bond she sensed growing between them wasn't strong enough yet to survive his retreat. If he left now, before they'd settled the rest, he would go and never come back.

His hand slid from her breast, leaving her cold. Her heart responded, kicked into a gallop, urging her to wrap her arms around him and hold on tight. She stilled the need. That wouldn't work. Not with Xavian. The harder she held on, the faster he'd slip away. The trick was to move slowly, to draw him in with soft words until his vulnerability gave way to trust.

She raised her hand and cupped his cheek. He flinched but remained with her, allowing the caress. With a murmur, she smoothed her hand along his jaw, taking in the sharp prickle of whiskers and the deep furrow between his brows. Gentle but sure, she turned his face toward her own. His throat worked and he refused to meet her gaze.

"Xavian?" Her tone was soft, undemanding, more entreaty than question.

" 'Tis insane."

"No," she whispered, understanding a loud echo in her mind. He was embarrassed over some imagined weakness. And like all warriors, weakness of any kind was never welcome. "She visits me too."

His gaze shot to hers. Surprise shimmered in the light blue depths.

"I heard her voice after...ah, when we made love in the stable," she said in a rush. He was so close to leaving her. Afina sensed it, saw it in his face. "Then she came to me at the burn...when you gave me the trews...and...I spoke with her. She warned me of the dragons and promised to visit me."

"Here?" Both his brows rose. "At Drachaven?"

Afina nodded.

"Have you spoken to her before?"

"No, but I've always known she exists…my mother told me so." Even though she told herself not to, her hands tightened on his arms. She couldn't let him go, not now, not ever. "She is real, Xavian. You did not imagine her."

He glanced away. His chest rose and fell. Afina breathed with him. In. Out. Mimicking his movements. The sound of the smithy's hammer echoed, clanging as the fire crackled, interrupting the silence. Uncertainty burned in the center of her chest. She felt like the ash beneath the flame, grey and useless, without the strength to influence the blaze above.

The logs shifted on the grate and a cracking pop burst into the chamber. Xavian stared at the embers, expression set, eyes serious.

"As a lad I needed her."

His voice was low and full of gravel, but his hand returned, sliding along her thigh. His palm in the hollow, he curled his fingers around her hip, anchoring himself, pleasing her. Thank the Gods. His shields were coming back down. He was going to talk to her. Afina murmured, encouraging him to continue.

Xavian cleared his throat. "I'd close my eyes, go to sleep, and she would…"

"What?"

His gaze flicked to hers then away. "Hold me. Keep me safe in my dreams, away from Halál and the horrors of the day."

She brushed the hair away from his forehead. "I am glad."

"She never comes anymore."

"You are a grown man now. Strong enough to protect yourself and others. And mayhap…"

"Mayhap?"

"She no longer visits because you no longer need her…" Afina took a deep breath, setting her courage. "Because you have left Al Pacii."

Xavian went rigid. His hand flexed then bit into her hip.

She stayed perfectly still. Mentioning the group of assassins was a risk, but she needed him to know that she knew. Henrik had told her everything. She understood where Xavian had grown up; what Halál had done to him and her brother. The bastard had hurt them so badly. Xavian needed to know she would never judge him for his past. He didn't need to hide it from her… there was no shame in what he'd been made to do. The fact he'd survived—been able to walk away with his soul intact—was a miracle.

"Henrik," he growled, murder in his voice.

"Yes. I have spent a lot of time—"

"Rahat!"

A muscle jumped in his jaw as he rolled away from her. Afina clung to him, following the explosion. Wrapping her arms around his shoulders, she threw her leg over his thighs and straddled his hips. He sat up on the edge of the bed and, spanning her waist, prepared to toss her aside.

She hung on, her grip desperate, her heart galloping like a runaway horse. "Don't!"

"Jesu, you do not know me—"

"Yes, I do."

"—or what I am capable of. You shouldn't—"

Afina slapped her fingers over his mouth. "Be quiet…be quiet and listen."

His jaw tightened beneath her hand, but merciful goddess, he stayed silent.

"I do know you…better than I know myself." He tried to protest. She pressed against his lips. If she was going to win, she must have her say…without him interrupting. "I know you think it's important…your past, all of the things you've done. But I don't care about any of that. I want you regardless and need you more."

"Afina…" His hands flexed on her waist. Afina dug in, arms firm around his shoulders, knees pressed to the mattress. "I am not the man you think I am."

"True. You are much more."

"Christ, you have no idea wh—"

"Why do you think the goddess visited you all these years?" Looking him square in the eye, she pushed him past his doubts and into the truth. "Why, Xavian?"

He shook his head, shifting a little beneath her.

"She was keeping you safe until you held the skills you needed…to protect me. The goddess doesn't do random, my love. She chose you for me."

Xavian stared at her, open-mouthed.

"I am sorry for what you endured with that mad man. If I could, I would take it all away, but I need you as you are. Strong, skilled, smart…sometimes brutal like you were with the slavers. Who else can protect me but you?" She kept her tone soft, but without a hint of remorse. The instant he detected pity, he'd throw her off and disappear. "I am not ordinary. Much as I wish otherwise, I have accepted it. I cannot have an ordinary mate…I need *you*."

"*Draga*," he whispered, the pain in his eyes almost more than she could bear. "I am damaged goods. You do not know what you are asking."

"Yes, I do." Holding his face in her palms, she leaned in to kiss him softly. He allowed the caress, but didn't kiss her back.

"You are mine as much as I am yours. We are bonded and I...I love you. I cannot survive without you now."

"You love me?" He whispered the words slowly, as though he spoke a foreign language, one he didn't understand.

She nodded. "And you love me too."

As she pulled away, Afina saw the truth. The love he'd tried to hide was there for her to see, but so too were regret and guilt. She murmured, the sound pleading. Xavian closed his eyes. On a rough exhale he bowed his head. Afina tilted her chin, making space as he nestled his face against the curve of her throat. She cupped his nape with one hand and stroked his spine with the other, willing him to relax, wanting him to accept.

"Be with me, just...*be* with me. We will face the future together."

His arms slid around her, brought her closer as a shudder racked him. "I am no good for you."

"Not true."

"Jesu, I had it all planned, but I never expected..."

Holding him tight, Afina waited.

Finally he said, "You. I never expected you."

"Too bad," she said, rocking him in her arms. "I am here to stay."

He huffed, the laugh half-amusement, half-despair, and Afina knew she had won. Whatever the future—however soon her enemies attacked, uncertain or not—he would stay and fight by her side.

CHAPTER THIRTY

Shay crouched behind a large rock, close enough to see, far enough to stay out of view. Damnation, Vladimir Barbu was smart. The bastard wasn't approaching Drachaven from the usual paths. He was making his own, cutting through heavy brush to reach the great fortress undetected. Most of his men remained five leagues away, tucked away in the forest. With only a handful of men he approached on silent feet, looking for weaknesses, weighing his options, calculating the odds.

From his position thirty feet away, Shay watched Barbu motion to his men. He spread them out, keeping ten paces between each man. Canny. The distance kept the sound of their boots in the underbrush to a minimum. Not as quiet as his, but effective nonetheless. Christ, the bastard was dangerous. Not good for Ram. Even worse for the woman Barbu was after.

A healer by all accounts: dark-haired, hazel-eyed.

He'd gotten the details last night while the moon hung high and the wolves called. The great oak above Barbu's head had provided concealment enough to get close and listen in. Belly down, flat against a thick tree limb, the rough bark had bitten through his tunic while the campfire blew smoke in his face and Barbu laid out his plans.

The bastard had grand ambitions—the lordship of all Transylvania.

Shay shook his head. One side of his mouth worked its way into a snarl, dragging amusement with it as he left the rock and sifted like a phantom in Barbu's wake. Deep shadows and crooked bracken touched his tunic, rasping against leather and the steel he had sheathed inside it. The scent of fall—damp earth, decaying leaves, and wet wood—followed, greeting the morning chill. He quickened his pace, predatory awareness in every step.

He could take Barbu now...if he wanted—gut him and be away before his men knew what hit them. Selfishness stilled his hand. He needed a way inside Drachaven. A feat great enough to prove his loyalty to Ram. Declaring it would never be enough. Ram wasn't stupid—canny, brutal, unforgiving? Aye, all of those, and Shay hoped trust might be counted among the qualities... for a price.

The price was Barbu—his movements and plan given on a silver platter.

Something had changed on Shay's journey through the mountains. He no longer wanted to die. Surprising, really. But as he'd made his way, the stories he'd heard in the villages and marketplaces had given him hope. Drachaven had become a refuge— a safe place amid the wilds—and Ram accepted strays. He gave them a home and a second chance.

A *home.*

Shay clenched his teeth and kept his feet moving. Silent as death, thick longing welled inside him. A place to belong, to be trusted and accepted and needed in the normal way. His ribs drew in tight, restricting his lungs for a moment. Pausing in the gloom, he crouched behind a fallen tree, pressed his hand to the slick moss that covered dead bark. Black birds with red-tipped wings flew in Barbu's wake. They called to one another, their song sharp as they flitted from branch to branch, leaving a dark trail of blurry wings overtop Barbu's men.

Christ, what he wouldn't give…a *home* among his own kind.

He pushed away from the log. The woman was the key. From what little he knew, Ram valued her. Gossip was scarce—mayhap even wrong—but little was better than naught. Barbu wanted her. Ram protected her. And Shay would bide his time, prepared to give aid however his former comrade needed it. 'Twas the only way to win Ram's trust. The only way through the gates to Drachaven and into the fold.

She felt so damn good in his arms. But then, that was no surprise. From the moment he spied Afina in the market of Severin, Xavian had wanted her this way—warm and sweet, tangled up with him amid quilts and soft sheets.

Propped on his elbow, one thigh between her own, he adjusted the covers around them. She hummed, the sound soft with contentment as she sank deep into slumber. He studied her face, watched her chest rise and fall, the rhythm even, her trust absolute.

Xavian stewed about that for a moment.

He didn't deserve her trust. Didn't deserve to be sated from her loving much less hold her while she slept. But in the middle of his bed, with the afternoon waning and Afina in his arms, he couldn't help but be thankful. Before her, he hadn't known life could be so sweet.

"*Draga.*" Xavian murmured the endearment, heard the reverence in his tone as his hand ghosted over her: tracing, worshiping, committing her to memory. He needed to remember her like this...always. "I love you."

The words came out low, a thick tangle on his tongue. Afina's eyelashes flickered, and he froze, one hand on the curve of her hip, breath gone still in his throat. *Please, not yet.* He needed her to sleep awhile longer. Wasn't ready to face her yet. Uncertainty was still using him for target practice, leaving holes the size of arrowheads in his confidence.

He exhaled as she settled and said the words again, tasting fear in each syllable. Were they true? Did he love her? Afina believed he did. Had told him what he felt was more than passion. On some level, he knew she spoke true. Aye, there was lust aplenty and yet...

Was that *something more* love?

Having never loved someone, Xavian couldn't be sure. All he knew was that what he felt grew deeper with each passing moment. Christ, he could hardly contain it.

Dipping his head, he kissed the curve of her shoulder, brushing his mouth over her birthmark. The moon-star glowed faintly, a soft shimmer against her pale skin.

The touch of the goddess...the one who'd visited in his dreams.

Xavian frowned. He'd been so young, only seven, barely a month in Halál's camp when the dreams started. He suppressed a shudder, recalling that brutal time, those first days, how frightened he'd been. Closing his eyes, he pushed that memory away and reached for another. Red-haired, green-eyed, she rose in his mind's eye. The irony wasn't lost on him. He couldn't remember his mother's face but he remembered *hers*.

He should feel guilty about that...or sad. All he could manage was regret. And a keen sense of foreboding. The warning stirred inside him, an echo he'd not felt before. 'Twas telling him to get all in order, to stock Drachaven, arm his men, and prepare for war. The reaction smacked of paranoia, but he couldn't deny the urgency.

He'd ignored it at first, dismissing the itching claw as naught more than his response to Afina. But the sensation plaguing him now was different; completely unlike the gentle current he drew from the lass in his arms. More aggressive, it streamed from another source, something outside Drachaven. Something dark and unnatural.

"Warrior." The whispered greeting drifted across the chamber.

Xavian went stone still. Logs shifted in the hearth. The cracking pop echoed, almost in warning as a potent wave bubbled into the chamber. Magic. He recognized the smell. 'Twas a thousand times stronger than Afina's, but the resonance was the same.

The goddess had arrived.

Long-standing habit made him reach beneath his pillow. He never met anyone new without a weapon in his hand.

As his fingers closed around the hilt of his favorite dagger, he glanced over his shoulder toward the hearth. Bare feet planted on the cowhide rug in front of the fire, she regarded him with cool, green eyes. White gown knotted over one shoulder, she wore majesty like a cloak, her power on display, magic the jewel in her crown. An intimidating picture. Xavian wasn't impressed, although his heart reacted, slamming against the wall of his chest.

"Goddess," he murmured, his tone polite, his posture aggressive. 'Twas the best he could manage. Until he knew her purpose, he refused to give way. She was in his home—one he'd fought hard to secure—and goddess or nay, he held sway here. "Welcome to Drachaven."

"Best you can do?" She raised a brow.

He shrugged. "Depends."

"On what?"

"Your purpose."

Her lips curved as she glanced away to take in his chamber. Xavian kept his focus on her. He didn't need to follow her gaze to know she saw a sparse chamber: stone walls, simple hearth, timber-beamed ceiling, a few stools, one chair, and a scallop-edged wardrobe. The only extravagance in the room was his bed. Her amused expression transformed into a true smile when she swept the bedposts, examining each one in turn. Xavian clenched his teeth, tamping down a sudden surge of embarrassment. He never should have carved the posts in her image. He'd done it on a whim, as tribute to his boyhood savior.

"Don't let it go to your head." He nodded toward the bedposts and shifted onto his other hip, careful to shield Afina. He didn't want his back to the goddess or Afina out in the open.

"As compliments go, it is a beautiful one." Stepping off the rug and onto flagstone, she approached the bed. Xavian tightened his grip on the knife, prepared to defend the only way he knew how...with brute force. The goddess stopped at the end of the bed, even with the footboard and the first post. Her mouth curved as she raised her hand and traced the sheaf of barley the carving of fall held with a fingertip. "You have astonishing skill with a blade, assassin."

The double meaning wasn't lost on Xavian. Aye, his skill was legendary, but the one she spoke of had naught to do with wood and everything to do with human flesh. A lump, heavy as a lodestone, settled in his belly as the goddess moved on to examine winter. He shifted again, the balls of his feet sinking into the mattress as he rolled into a crouch.

What the hell did the goddess want? Why approach him now…when Afina was asleep?

The answer to his question came with dizzying speed. This visit was for him. Whatever the goddess hoped to accomplish she didn't want Afina to overhear. Or mayhap she'd come to take her away…for the training the goddess had promised Afina at the burn. Aye, he knew of it. Had listened to Afina as she told him of their conversation.

But that wasn't going to happen.

Afina belonged with him. She needed him to ease her, to drain the excess magic in her blood. Without him, she would suffer and so would he. Not physically, but in every other way. No matter how much his independent nature wanted to deny it, he knew he couldn't live without her now.

"Why are you here, Goddess?" His voice sounded harsh, even to his own ears, but he couldn't help it. Suspicion made him tense, ready to use the knife in his hand.

Still at the foot of his bed, she ignored his question and said, "No need for a weapon, Xavian."

"There is always need."

"Not this time," she said, bare toes visible from beneath the hem of her gown.

Leaving off her examination of winter, she pivoted and, as though out for an afternoon stroll, returned to the fire. The rug rippled under her feet, and she raised her hand. Xavian tensed as the armchair next to the hearth shot out from the wall. Wooden legs bumping across the flagstone floor, it came to a stop a hair's breadth from the goddess's outstretched hand. Grasping the wide chair back, she turned the seat to face him and sat, lowering herself onto the cushion with a grace that complemented her beauty.

"Though I am glad you have taken to your duty."

His gaze swung from the chair's usual spot to the woman now sitting in it. Jesu, why was he so surprised? Afina could blast a full-grown dragon, for Christ's sake. One puny chair was hardly a match for the goddess. "Duty?"

"You protect her well." Bending her knees, the goddess settled into the chair, curled like a cat in its favorite spot. "I am grateful...though you will have to learn to share her."

His eyes narrowed. "Share how?"

"Territorial males." Waving a hand in the air, she rolled her eyes. "Bane of my existence."

Xavian stayed silent. The insult he could handle. What he couldn't take was the idea of losing Afina. What was the goddess playing at?

Careful to protect his position, he moved to the edge of the bed. Afina grumbled as he withdrew, protesting the loss of warmth. His gaze pinned to the goddess, he murmured to soothe her and pulled at the quilt, drawing it over her sleeping form. She sighed and, turning, curled onto her side, nestling into the spot still warm from his body.

"Even in sleep she craves you," the goddess said, an odd pang in her voice, her expression wistful as she watched Afina settle.

"In that we are well matched." He swung his legs around and settled on the bed's edge, bare feet flat on the floor. The chill of flagstone crept from heel to toe, but Xavian didn't move. The goddess sat, and so would he, to better shield Afina. "What do you want?"

The goddess's focus dropped to the blade he held by his thigh. The steel tip gleamed silver in the low light. Her eyes crinkled at the corners. "A moment alone with you, nothing more."

"Why?"

The goddess arched a brow. "You are her mate now...her forever male. We must come to an understanding."

An understanding, his arse. She wanted to lay the ground rules, to put him in his place. The problem? Xavian knew exactly where he stood, now and in the future. Afina might be the magic wielder, but she needed his strength and touch to survive. Naught would get in the way of that...not even the goddess.

"I enjoy your intelligence, Xavian. For a male, you are astute. You know your purpose and what Afina needs. For this alone, I accept you." A slow smile spread over her face, taking her from beautiful to breathtaking. "But you must give if you wish to take, warrior. Balance in all things...it is the way of this world. Afina is as much mine as she is yours."

"Xavian?"

Full of sleepy confusion, the whisper came from behind. The husky timbre stroked him like a lover. His muscles flickered. His mind took flight, reminding him Afina lay without a stitch on behind him. The image brought a groan to his throat. He bit it back, ignoring the shift below his navel and the need that caused it. Now was no time to become distracted.

The covers rustled and Afina murmured his name again.

Exhaling long and smooth, he adjusted the quilt across his hips, hiding his body's reaction to her closeness. "Go back to sleep, love. 'Tis all right."

More rustling, as though she had shifted in his direction. He steeled himself, afraid she might...*rahat*, she did. Xavian swallowed, suppressing a shiver as her hand drifted down his spine. She drew warm circles on his back, a motion meant to soothe, and said, "Then why do you have a knife in your hand?"

Christ, his plan was shot to hell. So much for keeping her away from the goddess. "We have a visitor."

His tone was harsh, rife with warning. Afina took the hint. A tug on the sheet, more rustling before she rolled to her knees behind him, using his back as a shield. Smart lass. Her small hand flat against him, she peeked over his shoulder.

"Oh, it's you," Afina said, warm welcome in her tone. Shuffling on her knees, she looped her arm around his neck, snuggling against his back.

"Greetings, daughter," the goddess said, voice soft, gaze bouncing from him to Afina. "You have come to terms with your male, I see."

Her hair brushed him as she hugged him closer. "Yes."

One syllable. Such a simple response, but it hit Xavian like a lodestone. She'd claimed him...in front of the goddess. She meant to keep him. Had accepted him with word and deed.

Why that surprised him, he wasn't sure. She'd told him earlier, but hearing her say it out loud to another made it real. He wasn't just her bedmate, a plaything she would tire of and throw away. She was his mate, and he was hers and...*Rahat*. That made him want to lay her down and love her all over again.

"Good." Satisfaction gleamed in the goddess's eyes. "It will make what comes next easier for him to bear."

Xavian's eyes narrowed. "Easier for you, mayhap."

Afina went tense against him. Xavian felt her fear an instant before she asked, "What do you want from him?"

"Easy, *draga*." He kept his voice soft, wanting her calm. He needed to keep his wits about him and her upset would only serve to distract him. Reaching behind, he settled his hand on her thigh and squeezed, transferring his need—and reassurance—through touch. "Let me handle this."

"I'll try," she murmured, just loud enough for him to hear. Kissing the back of his shoulder, she leaned away to wrap the sheet over her breasts. He felt her secure it then shuffle sideways. She ended up sitting beside instead of behind him.

Tousled and rosy-cheeked, she rose like a queen from the wrinkled sheets, straight-backed and regal. But her posture lied. He saw her clenched hands, the ones she hid in the sheet folds, along with the worry in her eyes. Flipping the dagger to his left hand, he reached for her with his right. She latched onto him, entwining their fingers, squeezing them hard.

A crease between her brows, the goddess said, "I had hoped it would not come to this, but…"

Xavian brushed his thumb over Afina's palm. "But?"

"There is little choice now." Brushing a stray lock of hair from her forehead, the goddess tossed an apologetic look at Afina. "Forgive me, child, but I must take your male—"

"No!" Shaking free of his hold, Afina scrambled to her feet. She planted herself in front of him so fast Xavian barely saw her move. "He stays with me."

With a curse, Xavian surged behind her, ready to take the hit if the goddess struck in anger.

"Afina," the goddess said, voice sharp, eyes narrowed, magic throbbing in the air around her. "You will listen first and ask second. Otherwise I will do as I wish…without your consent."

Aggression rolled beneath Xavian's skin. He didn't like the goddess's tone or the fear it evoked in Afina. Reaching for his trews, he shrugged them on, pulling the laces tight before settling his hand on Afina's shoulder. "I'm not going anywhere, love."

A tremor flickered through her as she turned and slid into his embrace. Curling his arm around her, Xavian tipped his chin toward the goddess. "Explain."

With a nod, the goddess raised her hand. Milky white, perfectly round, a sphere rose from her palm. Grower larger, it levitated, floated in midair for a moment before splitting down the middle to form a flat panel. Afina sucked in a quick breath, her rib cage expanding against him as a picture formed on the pale background. Snow capped the top and bottom of the globe, but most of the mass was covered by blue. Blotches of brown and green interrupted the indigo flow, some connecting, others leagues apart.

"A bird's-eye view of the world you live in." The goddess flicked her fingers and the image wavered, became blurry, then spun into another. Xavian's brows collided as a forest came into view followed by a mountain range and, last, a ribbon of blue… the Jiu River. Christ, they were flying above the ground, looking down upon the land. "This is your home…sun and moon, land and sea, earth and sky."

Another flick of the fingers. The image whirled once more.

Xavian tensed as the lush green of the forest turned black. Like skeletons, trees stood at odd angles, charred limbs above barren ground. The Jiu no longer sparkled in the sun. Naught more than a sunken pit, the riverbed lay cracked beneath fish bones and dead weeds. The mountains loomed above it all, the peaks devoid of snow cover, pointing to a scorched sky. Yellow clouds swirled, and Xavian swallowed, feeling bile rise in his throat.

"And that is what your world will become if balance is not restored."

"Mother Mary," Afina whispered, her gaze fastened to the horrific images flying across the panel. "What must we do?"

"You already do your part, Afina. The instant you came into your magic, you began your journey." The goddess stared at the burned-out landscape, expression full of regret. With a sigh, she dragged her gaze away to look at Afina. "You are my conduit, child…the means by which magic passes from my world into yours. Through you my power is transformed into the life-giving essence the earth needs to thrive. In this way all things grow and balance is achieved."

Afina frowned. "Why can't you do this yourself?"

"My magic is too potent to be spread upon the earth without first being filtered. Too much is as damaging as too little," the goddess said. "Without you, my essence will not flow onto earth and balance will never be maintained. I chose the women of your family millennia ago. In this way, they have always served."

"Until my mother." Sorrow in her eyes, Afina pressed deeper into Xavian's side. He tightened his arm around her, encouraging her to lean on him as he searched for the words to soothe her. He didn't know what to say. Family had never been his strong suit.

"Ylenia was a fool, Afina. Her betrayal was her failing, not yours."

The goddess fisted her hand and the white panel shattered, images falling away in a cloud of dust. Caught up by firelight, the faint sprinkle lingered for a moment then disappeared as the goddess paced the length of the chamber. She passed the end of the bed. Xavian shifted his stance, keeping Afina out of the line of fire.

Nose to wardrobe door, she spun back toward them, the fury in her gaze so fierce it painted the stone walls the color of moss. "When your mother chose the dark path, nature lost its keeper. The forests ceased growing, the flowers failed to bloom, the soil grew stale, and man's crops became less plentiful every year."

"The beech trees that surrounded my cottage were dying," Afina said, sadness in her tone. "I could feel their thirst."

The goddess murmured, echoing the same distress as she glanced at Xavian. "Have you not noticed these things?"

"I am a warrior, Goddess, not a farmer," he murmured, his gaze on the goddess, his attention on Afina. Pushing Afina's hair aside, he cupped the nape of her neck. Fingers searching, he massaged, attacking her tension.

The goddess gave him a pointed look.

He conceded, answering her question. "I have heard grumbles, the worry of those who work the land. Each year produces less, the markets lack the variety they once boasted, and livestock becomes thinner with the change of each season. Many talk of famine."

"One without end...which would come but for Afina."

"But you have her now," he said, not grasping the reason for her continued concern. She'd reached her goal. Afina stood ready to do her duty, and still the goddess wasn't happy. "Afina's magic will reverse the decay. Your problem is solved."

"If only it was that simple."

"Naught ever is."

"True enough, warrior," she said, her attention now focused on him. "I cannot fight this battle alone. In truth, I cannot fight it at all."

"An enemy plagues you?"

"A powerful one. He was contained until...Ylenia turned dark." Pain made an appearance on her face before she smoothed her expression. "Using the black arts, she opened the gates into the underworld. Gates that can never be closed. And now dark forces stir in the underbelly. *Things* that were never meant to see the light of day."

Afina shivered against his side. He tightened his hold on her, the sense of foreboding he'd felt since returning to Drachaven reaching a fevered pitch. "You need a fighter to put them back in their box."

The goddess shook her head. "I need a leader of men…one touched by the conduit, one with her magic in his blood. One with the skills to wage war."

Exploding from his side, Afina threw off his hold to plant herself in front of him once more. "No. He has endured enough… has finally found a home and the peace he has dreamed of. Do not drag him into a war. I can do what is needed, Goddess. Let me—"

"No, you cannot, child." The goddess took a step toward them, holding her hands palms up, arms out to the sides. "I am the Mother of all things and you are an extension of me. I made a vow long ago never to harm another soul. We are nurturers at heart, Afina…healers. It would pain you to kill another and lessen your effectiveness as a conduit. I need warriors who will not shy away from what must be done. No matter the circumstances."

"Trained killers," he murmured.

The stir of excitement hit Xavian gut-level. Finally. His purpose revealed; one beyond caring for Afina. The kind Henrik had always possessed and Xavian never had. Jesu. This was his chance. The opportunity he needed to put his mind and skills to work for the greater good, to atone for the sins of his past.

"If you like," the goddess said, inclining her head toward him. "Armand, king to the underworld, rises. Like me, he cannot wield his power here on earth, but seeks out those willing to serve his purpose. Even now, he builds his army. I must do the same."

Xavian flexed his shoulders, turning the possibilities over in his mind.

No doubt seeing his interest, the goddess pressed, enticing him. "You and your men will be my first line. The *Defenders*. The sharp end of my sword and teachers to those who follow you.

Drachaven will be my stronghold against those now awakening in the bowels of the earth."

"Afina stays with me?"

"You are her male, warrior. I would never take you from her."

"Then—"

"Xavian, no." Laying her palms flat on his chest, Afina met his gaze. His heart clenched at the despair he saw in her eyes. "I am what I am…that cannot be changed. But you have a chance at what you have always wanted. Freedom. Do not give it away."

"I am an assassin, love," he said, stating it plainly for the first time.

She went stiff an instant before her obstinate chin thrust forward. "You are more than that."

"Mayhap," he said, softening his tone to help her accept. "But ignoring my past will not make it go away."

On the verge of crying, she pushed against his chest.

Xavian curled his arm around her, refusing to allow her retreat. As much as he craved her good opinion, he wanted honesty between them more. "What good am I if I do not use my skill to serve the greater good? The years with Al Pacii, all the training and punishment…if not for this then what? I want to believe there is a reason for what I endured. The goddess's purpose gives meaning to the suffering." He dropped his blade to the mattress. It bounced once as he secured his hold on Afina. "*Draga*, I will protect you always, but this is something I must do."

"Then we are agreed?" Soft and true, the goddess's tone spun a thin web around him. Once he committed, the threads that tied them would be absolute. As strong as the bond she shared with Afina.

A tear rolled over Afina's lashes. Xavian wiped it away, waiting for her to accept his decision. When she lowered her eyes and tucked her face against his chest, he said, "You have my sword, but..."

The goddess raised a brow, waiting for him to continue.

"My men choose for themselves. I will not force them into your service."

"Your men will follow where you lead, warrior. You know this as well as I."

"True enough," he said, glad for their loyalty even as he prayed he didn't lead them astray.

CHAPTER THIRTY-ONE

"War?" Tossing the knife into the air, Henrik's eyes gleamed with interest. He caught the blade mid-flip, twirled the hilt in the center of his palm, and threw it again. "With who?"

Xavian crossed his arms over his bare chest and leaned back against his worktable, wondering where to start. From the beginning? Or should he just hammer them with the bottom line? He vacillated a moment then tossed it into the open. "King of the Underworld."

Cristobal choked. A piece of the apple he was eating hit Xavian square in the chest. "That sounds challenging."

"And promising," Henrik murmured, dagger hilt now planted against his palm.

Turning his half-eaten apple over in his hand, Cristobal said, "Positively engaging."

"No trouble believing me, Cristobal?" Flicking the apple chunk off his skin, Xavian raised a brow. He wasn't worried about Henrik. Afina's brother knew of the goddess, had already accepted that magic existed in the world. His other men weren't so well versed. "'Tis a lot to swallow."

"Shit, I saw Garren shift in the glen last week," Cristobal said, dark eyes flashing. "After talking to a dragon, I'm apt to believe anything."

Xavian bit back a smile. Trust Garren to bring his men into the fold. The shifter knew how much he valued each one. That he'd made it his mission to reveal himself to those closest to him said a lot about his loyalty...and his cunning. Another reason to be glad. He needed the dragons in the battles to come. Whatever form the fighting took, their skill and strength would give him the advantage.

Too bad he didn't have a few more specifics.

As it was, he was flying blind. The goddess hadn't provided any details. Which led Xavian to believe there weren't any. A problem. But one that was easily solved. People talked. Word of such things always traveled. If King Bastard was building an army, there would be signs: supply wagons, workers, whispers to point him in the right direction.

Whittled down to naught more than its core, Cristobal tossed the apple at the wooden refuse box beside the door. It bounced on the rim, teetered a moment, then fell with a thud. "When do we start?"

"Soon?" Henrik asked as he sheathed the knife in his chest holster and took out another. Testing the midpoint, he balanced the blade on the tip of his finger and shot Xavian a hopeful look.

Xavian snorted. Only his best friends would look forward to fighting what amounted to the devil—or at least his minions. But he couldn't fault them. He was having trouble curbing his own excitement. Christ, a challenge—one in which he would get to hunt again. 'Twas ironic, really. All his life he'd yearned for a home, a place to call his own. But now that he held Drachaven he realized the day-to-day running of it bored him. He was a hunter at heart, built to attack in order to defend, not sit on a wall and wait for conflict. That his men saw themselves in the same light was no real surprise.

Catching movement in his periphery, Xavian lowered his voice. "We start when everyone is on side and in the fold."

"We keep it close?" Henrik's eyes narrowed, catching a flash of color from inside Xavian's bedchamber.

"Very. Only the core of us...the ones we trust...will know the truth." Xavian pushed away from the table, flexed his hands, rolled his shoulders, running through a list in his mind. He wanted Drachaven and all who lived inside his walls prepared to defend, no matter the circumstance. His home was now Afina's, his walls her safeguard. By the time he finished with the castle, a groundhog wouldn't be able to burrow anywhere near them without his knowing about it. "I do not want Afina exposed any more than that. Her purpose and ours must remain a well-guarded secret."

"Hmm, secrets," Afina said, coming through the open door-way to his chamber. "Sounds intriguing."

Gowned in the green silk he'd taken from Ismal, she tipped her head to one side and drew a fine bone comb through her hair, smoothing the knots. Xavian followed each sweep through her raven locks, trying not to notice the color of the gown matched the flecks in her eyes. The strategy didn't work, and shifting focus to cool his ardor, his gaze jumped to her hands. A mistake. Watching her brush out the tangles made him realize he'd put them there—had made her thrash against the pillows in his bed. And that made him remember other things...like the way she tasted and how good she felt around him.

He tightened in reaction, the traitor behind his laces keen for another round. Xavian wanted to give in to the urging. He had two choices: slam the door in his friends' faces and carry her to bed or stay and finish the conversation. It was a close call. He teetered on the edge for a moment before he found control and reined himself in.

Holding out his hand, palm up, he invited her to come to him. She crossed the workshop, hips swaying, comb forgotten, skirting the table and his half-carved dragon to reach him. As her hand slid into his, the connection they shared flared. Afina smiled and his heart flip-flopped, thumping hard in his chest. With a gentle tug, he reeled her in until she rested against his side.

Cristobal grinned. "About time."

"Goddamn it." Henrik scowled at Cristobal then turned his fury on Xavian.

He dug in, tossing Afina's brother a warning look of his own. His friend was obsessed. What did Henrik expect him to do? Pull a priest out of his arse, for Christ's sake? Besides, there'd been no time to discuss marriage. He'd been too busy—first claiming Afina and second, meeting the goddess. Prepared for all-out war, he opened his mouth to tell his friend to shove off and mind his own affairs.

Afina beat him to it. "Stay out of it, Henrik."

"Christ, Afina." Henrik's knuckles went white around his dagger hilt. "I warned—"

"I mean it," she said, her voice so sharp Xavian flinched, feeling the razor edge of her tongue.

In a move contrary to his nature, Henrik snapped his mouth shut.

Cristobal chuckled.

Xavian gave Afina a gentle squeeze. "Where are you off to?"

"The keep." She hurled another dark look at Henrik, no doubt to ensure her brother stayed mum, then turned her gaze up to meet his. "The boys will be done with their lessons soon. I want to take them and Sabine out for a while…run their little legs off."

Xavian nodded. Jesu, she was a marvel…made him so damn proud. She'd taken to his lads without hesitation, and in less than a fortnight had won them over, becoming the mothering influence he wanted for them. Even Dax, the oldest and most damaged of his wards, accepted her with open arms. Forgetting was impossible—Xavian knew that better than most—but mayhap now they would begin to heal, to move past the pain and embrace a new future.

Dipping his head, he pressed a kiss to Afina's temple. As far as "thank-yous" went, it wasn't much. But with his throat gone tight, it was all he could manage.

"Ram?" A folded piece of parchment in his hand, Qabil hesitated between the shafts of the doors of his workshop. "A missive just arrived for you."

"From?"

"Ivan of Ismal."

"Shit," Henrik muttered, of a sudden very interested in the tip of his blade.

Afina grimaced, a flush spreading over her cheeks. "Sherene's husband?"

"Aye." Xavian raised a brow, curiosity piqued by the siblings' reactions. What the hell had they done to his seamstress? Hmm…a mystery, one worth investigating. But not now. Qabil had that look about him. The one that said whatever he carried held great importance. Giving Afina an encouraging nudge, he pointed her toward the door. "Go, love. See to the children. I will meet you for the evening meal."

Color still high, Afina headed for the exit. She smiled at Qabil, murmuring a greeting as she passed him. The lad turned an interesting shade of scarlet but remembered his manners and nodded before she rounded the doorframe and was out of sight.

"What does it say, lad?" Cristobal flicked his fingers, inviting Qabil into their meeting.

"News from Grey Keep." Worry in his eyes, Qabil raised his hand. The vellum crackled between his fingertips. "More boys are to be delivered to Al Pacii."

With a snarl, Henrik pivoted and hurled his dagger. Steel whistled before it struck wood, the twang audible as the blade bit into the doorframe. "Fucking Halál."

Xavian ignored the damage to his chamber door. Henrik's outburst was one he could get behind. He understood that kind of hatred. Felt it himself for the man responsible for their pain. "How many?"

"Ivan doesn't say, but word is they are transporting them via the North Trail."

Cristobal cracked his knuckles. "When do we leave?"

"An hour before dawn," Xavian said, their route already mapped in his head. The North Trail snaked through the mountains, the terrain rough at best, deadly at worst. They would reach it by traveling through Gully Pass, come out of a hidey-hole positioned above the path. 'Twas the perfect place for an ambush.

"I will see to the supplies and tell the men to prepare." With a nod, Cristobal headed for the exit. "Come, lad. You may help."

"How long will we be gone, Ram?"

Asked without heat, and still the query held the power to shift his foundation. He understood Henrik's worry—couldn't help but feel it himself. "Afina will be all right, H. Until today, I hadn't touched her in a fortnight. A sennight without me will do her no damage."

"You'll check with Garren to be sure?"

"Aye," he murmured, needing reassurance as much as his friend.

Short absences from her couldn't be helped. Especially now that he served the goddess. But he needed to know how long she could go without him. Xavian prayed the shifter held the answer. Leaving her would be hard enough. Leaving her to suffer would be unbearable.

Safe behind Drachaven's walls, Afina stood on the ramparts, looking out over the forest. A thin mist hovered, playing between the sway and creak of treetops. Thick evergreens, tall maples, stout beech trees pushed skyward eager for the sun's first rays. In the stillness of the closing night, she sensed them lean toward the east, impatient for the coming day to banish the gloom.

Afina placed her hand flat against stone, between two blocks jutting up like sharp teeth from the outer wall. The granite pressed into her palm, scraping her skin. The chill leached into her hand as she leaned out, trying to see past the tree line.

It was no use. She couldn't see them anymore.

Mother Mary, what was she doing? They'd been gone over an hour—Xavian with them. No amount of looking or wishing or praying would bring them back.

Rubbing a circle over her heart, Afina searched the lip of the forest one last time. She was being foolish. Xavian was a warrior with a warrior's purpose. He couldn't spend all his time with her. Knowing that, however, didn't make his leaving any easier to bear. The good-bye had been so hard. On him too, she knew. He hadn't wanted to leave her any more than she'd wanted him to go. Although she couldn't deny his farewell had been spectacular.

Not the hard kiss. Not the pat on her behind. Nor the part where he'd told her to "behave" before he mounted Mayhem. But beforehand…in his chamber, up against the wall. Well now, a good-bye didn't get much better than that.

Afina sighed. She needed a distraction.

The more she thought of Xavian—skilled bed-play or otherwise—the more she missed him. And as much as she ached to have him home, she refused to carry on this way the entire time he was away. For one thing, it was unproductive. For another, she wasn't a lily-livered ninny without a brain in her head. Drachaven and its people needed her care. And she would make certain they got it. No matter how woebegone she became over Xavian's absence.

Turning away from her perch, Afina snugged her cloak up to cover the nape of her neck and headed toward the east tower. Footfalls as heavy as her heart, she listened to her boot heels click against stone on the battlements.

A thick shadow shifted in the guardhouse and stepped down to her level. Afina nodded to the huge man now blocking her path. Wide of shoulder with long legs and muscled arms, the captain of the guard was a fierce specimen whom those with any wisdom gave a wide berth. Taken from a country far to the north, Hamund's ferocious expression hid a gentle soul, though with his sword unsheathed one would never know it.

"Good morrow, Hamund."

"'Tis barely that yet, my lady." The captain's mantle parted to reveal his throwing knives as he cupped his hands and blew on his fingers. His eyes narrowed on her thick cloak and boots. "You'll not be wandering off today, will you, my lady? Ram wants you inside the walls while he's gone."

The news made Afina grit her teeth. Of a sudden, Xavian's short command to *behave* took on a whole new meaning. What did he expect her to do? Stay cooped up inside the whole time he was away?

"I thought to walk the woodlands," she told the guard. "Midmorning, mayhap."

Hamund grunted, the sound as ominous as his expression. "Not wise, that."

Probably not, but she itched to get outside Drachaven for a while. The sensation had taken hold the moment she lost sight of Xavian from the wall. His leaving left an empty space inside her, one the forest would soothe. The evergreens called to her. The maples murmured and the beeches lured with quiet insistence. Each whispered in its own way, voices distinct, craving the life-giving essence she carried with her. Not that they needed her among them to receive it. She felt the flow now, gave the goddess's power without effort. Connected in a web, each tree reached out to touch the next, spreading the energy between them, passing it along until everything—to a single blade of grass—received what it needed to flourish.

Afina breathed deep, filling her lungs with autumn's chill and the smell of morning dew. The freshness—the vibration she felt as nature hummed—lightened her heart. Finally she was part of a solution, not in the middle of a problem. She was helping reverse her mother's mistake. Making right a terrible wrong.

"An hour, no more, Hamund," she said, a pleading note in her tone. She needed out, if only for a while. To hear the birds call. To touch the leaves and see squirrels play. To walk among the roots, lay her palm to tree trunks and listen to the hum beneath the rough bark. "And I'll take a guard."

He gave her a dubious look.

She folded her hands in the prayer position. "Please...I'll go mad cooped up inside. I miss Xavian already and the woodlands will keep me happy until he comes home."

"More than one, then."

"A dozen burly guards with mean swords and even worse scowls."

Hamund's lips twitched. "All right. But only when the sun's high. And you stay within sight of the walls."

"Deal." Releasing a breath, she gave him a big smile.

He shook his head. "Off with you then. I'll fetch you mid-morning...after I've found guards with fierce enough scowls."

With a laugh, Afina skirted the captain and hurried along the outer wall to the rounded archway at its end. Thrown into shadow by the stone vault above, the planked door face looked more black than brown, and Afina fumbled a moment, searching for the iron pull. The smoothly hooked handle chilled her palm as she thumbed the latch, swept passed the barrier, and into the chamber it protected. Stone dust and the scent of disuse swirled as the door thumped closed, sending the sound of wood on stone echoing in the quiet.

Carved into the rock face, the turret was neither round nor square, but some shape in between. The odd curves in the main chamber were charming, really, and as Afina crossed the empty space she imagined it as her healing room. East facing with a sheer drop from the windows to the river below, it was close to the battlements, accessible to the men from the wall. Treating wounds quickly and cleanly saved lives. The chamber was well situated to do both should they ever be attacked.

Afina paused to look up at the domed ceiling. Ancient symbols stood in relief against the pale stone. She studied them a moment then pushed the door opposite the one she'd just entered open and stepped into the corridor beyond. Ten feet apart, limestone walls marched alongside her as she hurried through the gloom. The boys along with Sabine would still be asleep, but she needed to see them, if only to count heads.

They hadn't taken the news of Xavian's departure well. But then, she couldn't blame them. Her own reaction had been less than superb.

Reaching the entrance to the nursery, Afina cracked the door open. Coals glowed in the hearth, throwing enough light into the chamber for her to see. Beds marched like soldiers along the far wall, matching quilts mounded in the centers over little bodies. Her gaze lingered on Sabine a moment, taking pleasure in the wealth of blond curls visible above the blankets.

Another victory. She'd kept her promise to Bianca. Her little girl was safe.

Afina sent a quick thank-you heavenward and continued to count. She pursed her lips as she got to the last bed. Just as she suspected. Dax was gone.

Her heart went still in her chest then sent up a dull throb. The ache swirled out, rushed through her veins along with her worry. Her poor lad. He'd had another bad dream. It was the only explanation. Although he was the wanderer of the group, Dax never left his adopted brothers or the nursery at night. He was scared of the dark, though at ten years old he would sooner die than admit it. But Afina couldn't blame him. The lad had seen more in four years with Al Pacii than most men saw in a lifetime. Xavian assured her the nightmares would go, but each time Afina heard Dax scream in his sleep and ran to soothe him, a part of her screamed along with him.

The bastards. Those filthy, rotten bastards.

Anger curled her fists tight as magic pulsed in her fingertips. What kind of monster preyed on children? One that needed to be wiped from the face of the earth. By the goddess, she hoped Halál accompanied his men this time...and got within range of Xavian's swords. She wanted the piece of filth in a shallow grave where he belonged.

Taking a calming breath, Afina pulled the door closed, shutting her babies safely away in the nursery. They wouldn't be up for another hour, and she needed to find Dax. He could be anywhere, inside Drachaven or outside the walls. Afina bit her bottom lip, hoping it wasn't the latter. Somehow, though, she knew he wasn't in the keep. The lad loved the forest as much as she did and would choose the upper limb of a tree over a dark corner in the castle any day of the week.

The ache in the center of her chest grew stronger as she pictured him curled up, knees to chest, trying to be brave, unwilling to let anyone hear his whimpers and see his fear. One day mayhap he would come to her instead of running away, but today was not that day.

Pivoting on her heel, Afina headed back toward the battlements and Hamund. She needed to tell him Dax was missing. If the lad stayed true to form, she would be venturing outside the walls sooner than the captain expected.

From his hiding spot amid large ferns and dense foliage, Vladimir surveyed the beast. He'd come at the great fortress from behind, hoping to find a weakness on the cliff side or, at the very least, the postern door. So far he hadn't found it—or anything else for that matter: no weak points, no deficiencies, an Armageddonlike arsenal manning the walls.

Drachaven was a veritable monster.

Not unlike the man who called it home. The assassin was unbeaten hand-to-hand, but his home...Damnation. 'Twas a thing of beauty. Stone walls and cliffs colliding to form an impenetrable stronghold. And shit, he hadn't even begun to examine the gatehouse. At first glance, he guessed three portcullises. That meant navigating three sections separated by metal gates before reaching the outer bailey. No doubt with murder holes, countless places through which to launch arrows or pour boiling oil on the soldiers below. If anyone made it through alive, the inner gatehouse awaited. Vladimir could only imagine...and salivate. What he wouldn't give to hold Drachaven for himself.

But first things first. He must get his hands on Afina.

Stepping over a fallen log, Vladimir leaned around a fern head to get a better view. He scanned the battlements again. Spaced at even intervals, men-at-arms lined the walls, looking far too alert. Hell, the sun wasn't even up, yet there they were, armed to the teeth and ready to fight. Ramir must be cracking the whip and busting heads open while he was at it. 'Twas the only explanation for the kind of diligence he saw on Drachaven's walls.

But then, the assassin wasn't a fool. Ramir protected a prize. A woman with more power than the bastard had the wit to recognize. He needed to get in there...or find a way to force Afina out. Reaching into the pouch at his waist, Vladimir stroked the choker he'd had made especially for her. The gemstones caressed his skin and heated his blood. He couldn't wait to force it on her, to claim what belonged to him by right and the will of God.

Careful to leave the foliage undisturbed, Vladimir moved left, his eyes on the base of the great wall. He must locate the postern door. Even if it was well defended from above, a midnight raid might prove successful. He dodged around a massive oak, heard his men move with soundless precision behind him, and caught movement. A shadow skirted the angled foundation stones, moving on quick feet away from him and his men. Vladimir crouched on his haunches and waited. A heartbeat passed then two before the slight form slipped from the shadows and made for the lip of the forest.

Grey cloak swirling behind him, the dark-haired lad paused at the tree line to glance over his shoulder. Vladimir's eyes narrowed. It didn't take a genius to know the boy was important. His garments were well made, his leather boots too expensive to be anyone other than one of Ramir's brats. Aye, he'd heard the rumors—knew the assassin raised a tribe of boys no one else wanted. Now, it seemed, he would get to put that knowledge to work…along with the screams of one very unlucky lad.

Lips curved, Vladimir veered away from Drachaven's wall and went after the boy…the bait to set his trap.

CHAPTER THIRTY-TWO

They stood in the center of the inner bailey, shifting from ordinary men into organized killers. The sight sent a shiver down Afina's spine. Her gaze moved from the guards' faces to Hamund's broad back. A piece of parchment in one hand, a fletched arrow in the other, the captain curled his fingers into a fist. Vellum crinkled, giving way beneath the force of white-knuckled fury.

Message delivered by arrow. Never a good thing. But today its delivery might mean terrible rather than just plain bad.

Dax was still missing. She couldn't find him anywhere. A chill sank deep, making her bones ache. Her gaze drifted around the semicircle again, taking in each man's war-honed expression. Whatever the message in that note, it wasn't friendly. An enemy with an ultimatum. A threat to give fair warning. Either was a possibility, but the first made more sense.

The morning sun spilled over the walls. The other children were breaking their fast, and Dax never missed a meal. He'd gone hungry too often before finding a home at Drachaven to take Cook's fare for granted…no matter how fearsome his dreams. Afina rubbed her damp palms on her skirt. The soft wool absorbed the sweat, soothing her skin but not her mind. She went over the list again in her head. Drachaven held a number of good hiding spots. She'd checked them all, starting with Dax's hidey-holes. He wasn't in the keep, which left one possibility. He was outside the walls, no doubt headed for his favorite place.

The swings. The ones she'd insisted be hung a fortnight ago.

Afina squeezed her eyes closed and cursed herself. Goddess be merciful, what had she done? Had she not demanded a play area—a place away from the constant clash of swords and threat of violence—Dax would never have ventured out to the great oak. Swinging soothed him, the rocking rhythm draining the angst that so often gripped him. Afina couldn't blame him for needing it. Xavian's departure had hit him harder than the rest. Something about her mate calmed Dax, made him less restless, more confident, better able to cope with all he had suffered.

But Xavian wasn't here to bring him home...to keep him from danger. That duty now fell to her.

Her eyes on the crumpled parchment in Hamund's hand, Afina forced her feet to move. Dread made the short trip across the inner courtyard seem like a trek into the mountains. Everything felt heavy, as though the earth bore down, yoking her shoulders, pulling on her legs, dragging her heart into her stomach. Even the air smelled thick, damp with the scent of wood smoke and evergreens, clogging her lungs until she found it difficult to breathe.

Keeping to Hamund's back, she approached the men, footfalls silent on frosted cobblestones, ears attuned to the low masculine rumble. Armed to the teeth, focus trained on their captain, each man leaned in, listening intently as Hamund laid out the ground rules. Afina caught the tail end of Hamund's instructions as he said, "Quill, Monk...circle round behind the bastards and report back. I want to know what we're into before we go after the lad."

Dark eyes set in identical faces, the twins nodded. Quill checked his throwing knives. Monk scowled so fiercely Afina's knees knocked together. Merciful goddess. Dax was in trouble.

"Bear...find Afina." The captain tipped his chin to the man on his immediate right. "Make sure she stays in the nursery."

"At what cost?"

"Lock her in if you have to, but keep her contained."

Afina curled her hands into fists, fingertips prickling as magic begged for release. She kept it contained, allowing the power to swirl in the center of her palms. The big dolt. What did he think he was doing? Lock her in, indeed. There wasn't a prison—never mind a chamber—in all of Transylvania strong enough to hold her. Not when Dax needed her.

Bear grumbled, a look of distaste on his face.

Afina pursed her lips. Well, at least one of them possessed a modicum of wit. Bear might have found himself smacked upside the head had he looked pleased about following his captain's orders. Hamund, however, was fair game. The captain was perilously close to being bashed from behind.

"Too late." Afina heard the snap in her voice but didn't care. If the captain thought for one instant she would stand by—sit sewing or something—while someone threatened her family, he was in for a nasty surprise. "I am already out."

Hamund tensed and pivoted to face her, eyes grave, expression wiped clean. "My lady, go back to the keep."

"Do not even try it, Hamund." She leveled him with a lethal look then dropped her gaze to the note. "What's happened? Where is Dax?"

His lips set in a grim line, he crossed his arms, hiding the missive under an elbow. Afina scowled. The captain's eyes narrowed, and silent as a stone, he stared at her, no doubt expecting her to scamper back to her chamber like a good girl. Well, she wasn't scampering anywhere and good didn't begin to describe her. Not now...not when worry outweighed caution.

"Tell me, Hamund. If Dax is in trouble, I need to know."

A muscle twitched in his jaw. "What you need to do is go back to the keep."

No chance of that. Afina held out her hand. "Let me see the missive."

His brows collided and his eyes went dark. Afina bit the inside of her cheek, withdrew her hand, and shuffled back a half step. Mayhap demanding wasn't the soundest approach. Hamund, for all his gentleness, was a warrior with a warrior's way. Strong-arming him wouldn't work. He was too controlled, too stubborn, too set on shielding her from the truth. She could see it in his expression, his desire to protect her from something awful.

"Please, Hamund," she whispered, rubbing her palms together.

"Do not worry, my lady," he said, his tone full of understanding even as he established boundaries. "I will handle this."

"I know you will. Xavian trusts you and so do I, but..." she trailed off, hating to follow the statement of faith with a "but." It wasn't about trust, it was about sanity. Hers. She would go stark raving mad if the men rode out without telling her who held Dax and why. The thought made her throat go tight. Goddess help her, he was just a little boy. Only ten years old, no matter how much he wanted to believe otherwise.

"Whatever it is, please tell me. He is my child, Hamund...my son, no matter who birthed him. I need to know what is happening...if he is all right. It is my right as a mother and the Lady of Drachaven." Hamund's face went tight as she pulled rank. Afina hated to do it, but reminding him of her station was necessary to make him see reason. She held out her hand for the second time. "May I see it...please."

His knuckles went white around the parchment. "I will have a promise from you first."

Afina squirmed, knowing she would never give her word. She knew what he wanted—her safety above all else. Even over a little boy's life. "What?"

"You will stay inside Drachaven...tend the other children, mix your healing potions, pace the halls...whatever. But you will not involve yourself in this." He brought his hand forward, missive clutched in his fist, leaving no doubt what "this" meant. "You will allow me to do my duty without worrying you'll do something foolish."

"Hamund—"

"Otherwise I will lock you away...in the dungeon, if necessary." He gave her a savage look, one meant to frighten her enough to listen. "Xavian will kill me, Afina. One bruise on you and he'll kill me. If you have any liking for me at all, you will do as I say."

"You fight dirty."

"Only when I have to."

Afina sucked a breath in through her nose, blew it out her mouth. Hamund held a special place in her heart. He was her friend, and she hated cornering him. She didn't want him hurt anymore than she did Dax. If she believed for one moment Xavian would touch him, she would have listened. But she didn't. Her mate would no sooner kill the captain than he would put a bruise on her. Meeting his gaze head-on, she tucked the promise he wanted inside her cheek and held out her hand.

"Christ."

Palm up, her hand bounced in midair, asking without demanding. With a growl, Hamund placed the ball of parchment in her hand. Her fingers trembled as she pulled at the vellum, unrolling the corners before smoothing her thumbs down the center of the small sheet.

Her knees nearly gave out. "Goddess help us."

She read the note again, all the fear she'd carried for two years culminating in a giant ball in the center of her chest.

Assassin,

I have your brat. The Dower cliffs before noonday. Send Afina. Alone. Or I deliver Dax to Drachaven's gates, one piece at a time. I'll be kind and start with his fingers.

Vladimir, Voivode of Transylvania

The captain grabbed her elbow to keep her on her feet as she swayed, listing backward. "My lady?"

Hamund's voice came from far away, through a tunnel with fuzzy edges. Afina closed her eyes, a picture of Dax in her mind's eye. Dear goddess, his hands...his small, little-boy hands. The swine would take pleasure in putting a razor-sharp blade to Dax's fingers and...

Afina gagged, fighting to keep her breakfast down. Her nails bit into her palms and she took a shaky breath to settle her stomach. "I am going with you."

"No chance in hell. Goddamn it, Afina—"

"He'll do it, Hamund. If I don't go...if he doesn't see me, he will slice Dax to ribbons."

The captain's eyes narrowed. "You know the bastard?"

"I ran from him two years ago." The memories stirred, stripping the scab from the festering wound deep inside her. Guilt and sorrow flowed like the finest poison, leaching into her mind. If only she had stayed and faced him then, Dax and the people of Drachaven would be safe now. "I am so sorry. I brought him to your gates."

"Your gates now too." Hamund gave her a meaningful look, one that said—don't be foolish, find your courage. "Do not forget who you belong to, my lady."

Xavian. I belong to Xavian.

The thought gave Afina strength, allowing her to see past her fear. She smiled a little, grateful for Hamund and the reminder. "We need a plan."

"No shit." Eyes steady on her, Quill scraped a whetstone along one of his dagger blades.

The motion should have scared her, but somehow Afina drew comfort from the sound of steel on stone. It gave her hope, reminded her of Drachaven's strength and each man's skill. If Xavian's warriors couldn't pry her lad from Vladimir's grip, no one could.

The quiet threatened to swallow him whole. Xavian reveled in the soundlessness, the absolute certainty he would find a fight here, amid narrow dirt paths and jagged stone teeth. 'Twas his kind of terrain, the sharp edges and violent cliff angles companions to the predator inside him. Caged most of the time, the killer stirred, looked out through prison bars waiting for the moment Xavian swung the door wide and allowed his counterpart out into the light of day.

The hunt. His beast loved it…yearned for it the way a child did sweet cakes and honey.

Xavian understood the restlessness, the need. Had lived with it most of his life. Today, though, it felt different...tempered by another craving of equal value. He wanted to go home...missed Afina so much he ached inside. Christ, he'd only been gone a day—one day!—yet the compulsion to see her face, hear her voice, wrap himself up in her threatened his control. Xavian clenched his teeth. When had he become so weak? He frowned. Nay, 'twasn't weakness, but love.

He loved her.

Even now, after a full day of knowing the truth, it still held the power to send him back a step. Xavian swallowed. He'd never imagined someone might love him. Dreamed of it, aye, but hope was a nasty beast. It made great promises that rarely, if ever, came true. But Afina was real...what she felt for him was real.

She wanted him. Needed him. Loved him for who he was, despite the ugliness and all his flaws.

He took a deep breath, combating the sudden tightness in his chest. Hell. No wonder he didn't want to stay away from her. Why would he? He'd been spared, saved from a lonely life and empty future. Only an idiot wouldn't cherish a gift such as that.

But he couldn't return to Drachaven. Not today. His heart could play tug-of-war with his mind all it wanted. He refused to forsake his mission. The lads he sought to rescue deserved his full attention and Afina, no matter how lovely a distraction, was one he couldn't afford. Later, only when the assassins he hunted lay dead, would he allow his thoughts to wander home, toward his mate and her needs.

Balanced on the balls of his feet, perched in a crevice between two rock faces, Xavian scanned the trail below. Pebbles, worn by time and effort, kept their secrets, hiding tracks, both human and animal alike. Such a good place for an ambush. Al Pacii knew it, and so did he.

His lips curved. Soon. Very soon, he would have some small measure of revenge. Not much of one by any stretch, but enough to hammer his intentions home yet again. He would take all comers...wouldn't stop until Halál was destroyed and the boys the bastards preyed upon were safe. Grim determination settled him as he backed out of his hidey-hole and made for the edge of the ridge. His men were in position, but a new plan needed to be made. The silence told him more than the hoofprints Cristobal had tracked through the forest and into the foothills.

The bastards wanted to be found...were leaving just enough for him to follow. Their intention? To draw him out into the open, into a well-laid trap.

Xavian shook his head, finding humor in the game, and skirted a boulder. Footfalls silent, he dodged the limb of a lone tree on the narrow lane. Roots spread like tentacles, the evergreen clung to a crevice in the rock, twisting at odd angles to reach the awakening sun. A small hawk sat in its arms, half asleep, enjoying the soft breeze ruffling its feathers.

Placing his hand flat on the hump of stone beside the tree, Xavian leapt, soaring until his feet landed on the flat plane below. Poised above the North Trail, Cristobal glanced at him from his periphery, acknowledged him with a nod before returning his attention to the pathway below.

Xavian rotated into a crouch beside his friend. "Anything?"

"Not yet. But the bastards are around." Cristobal stroked the hilt of one of his daggers still safely sheathed. "'Tis too quiet."

"A good sign."

Cristobal rolled one shoulder then the other, alleviating the stiffness that always came with staying still so long. "If Valmont leads them, they'll come looking for us soon. The bastard was never patient enough to play hide-and-seek."

"Pray it's Valmont." Xavian's gaze swept the tumble of rocks on the other side of the North Trail and forced his muscles to relax. One by one, they unlocked, keeping him calm on the outside while he seethed inside. Valmont, that sick bastard. Just the sound of his name made him want to stab something. "'Twould be a gift."

"Michaelmas comes early." Cristobal's dark eyes gleamed as he grinned. "Have you been a good lad this year?"

Xavian's mind skipped from now to then—landing one short day ago when he'd held Afina in his arms. He heard her moan his name, gasp with pleasure, telling him without words how *good* she found him. His body picked up the thread, and he went hard behind his laces. "I have been *very* good."

His friend chuckled, the sound quiet and low. "I'm going to tell her you said—"

The womp-womp of heavy wings sounded overhead.

Cristobal looked to the sky. So did Xavian, searching for the beast that had become his friend. A large shadow slithered over rock, spreading over the cliff face like a stain. A rush of air followed, stirring the hair at his nape before dark scales flashed blue in the sunlight. Light as an angel dove, the dragon's clawed feet touched down on the ridge above them.

"What have you found?"

"Twenty-eight Al Pacii. Heavily armed. Hunkered down beyond the foothills." Garren settled, shifting his weight from one claw to the other before folding his wings. "No boys."

Henrik appeared on the ridge. Laying his hand against Garren's scaled shoulder, he said, "An ambush…twenty-plus assassins strong. Hell, Ram, you must be doing something right. Halál's pissed off enough to put a big price on your head."

Xavian performed a mock bow. "I live to please."

Garren snorted. Twin tendrils curled from his nostrils, sending a cloud of smoke and the smell of sulfur tumbling over the rock face.

With a grin, Henrik left his perch, jumping to join them on the narrow ledge. Vestiges of dragon smoke swirled around his boots as he sank to his haunches beside them. "Just as well. Wipe out many with one blow. Better than chasing one or two around the countryside."

"Glad you approve, H," Cristobal murmured, his mouth tipped up at the corners. Shaking his head, he returned his attention to the landscape spread out in front of them. "Don't know about you two, but I don't feel much like hiding anymore."

"Seek and destroy." Henrik settled his elbows on his knees, solidifying the crouch. "A much more enjoyable game."

Xavian raised a brow. "Want to even the odds a little, H?"

"Got a method in mind?"

"How many can you get with your bow before we go in... three?"

Henrik fingered the tip of an arrowhead. "Four minimum... before they take cover."

"Good." Xavian glanced over his shoulder at Garren. "The others?"

"Tareek keeps watch in human form from the trees." The dragon dipped his head, bringing his gaze level with theirs. "Cruz watches from on high, hidden in a mountain crevice."

"Can you reach them?"

"Aye," Garren said, the growl in his voice unmistakable. "I will inform them of the plan through mind-bond. When you engage, they will shift and come."

Xavian nodded then met his men's gazes, each in turn. "They expect us from the north. We will come from the south. H, find high ground…on my signal, unleash hell."

With a murmur of agreement, they pushed to their feet, moving as one. Xavian saw the shift in each, felt it himself as he unlocked the cage that imprisoned the beast inside him. Free rein. He allowed the monster free rein, moving with quiet precision down the mountainside. The sooner he finished with his former comrades, the better. He needed to go home to Afina.

CHAPTER THIRTY-THREE

Back in borrowed trews, a hauberk strapped to her chest and a knife to her thigh, Afina shuffled to the edge of the boulder, hoping for a different view. No such luck. Her imagination hadn't exaggerated. She chewed on the inside of her lip, stared at the trailhead and the narrow pathway beyond. Twisted and bent, tree limbs hung like ghouls, sawtooth leaves dripping from thick canopies. Rain-soaked trunks tunneled into the forest, deepening the gloom, creating a passageway that shoved her courage in the wrong direction.

She pivoted on the balls of her feet, anchoring her boots in soft earth. The scent of wild mint and morning mist rose around her, not letting her forget—neither the circumstance that kept her huddled in the midst of the forest nor the reasons she must go on. She wished she could block them out, if only for a moment. Mayhap then her hands would stop shaking.

Afina swallowed the bitter taste in her mouth. She didn't want to go in there. Her hand slid to the small of her back, to the second blade Hamund insisted she carry. The first was a decoy, easily removed. The second was Xavian's, concealed by the flap of her leather hauberk and one the swine wouldn't expect. Vladimir would take the one strapped to her thigh, never suspecting she had the courage or smarts to come packing another. Arrogant bastard.

Skin-warmed steel settled against her palm, the hilt heavy in her hand. She gripped it tight, thought of Xavian…pictured his face and wrapped herself in his strength.

"Are you certain about this?"

The whisper made the back of her neck tingle. She tossed Hamund the fiercest look she owned. What kind of question was that? Of course she wasn't certain. No one in their right mind would be…but what other choice did she have? "Stop asking me that or I will find a branch and bash you with it."

Hamund cleared his throat, cutting off a snort.

"Don't laugh at me."

"Wouldn't dream of it." He sounded strained; the tremor in his voice said it all. The dolt found the idea of her hammering him amusing.

"Goddess help me," she muttered, smothering the urge to turn and smack the smirk she just knew he wore right off his face. "I need a club, not a knife."

"I will get you one…after." Hamund bumped the outside of her thigh with his knee. Afina teetered on the balls of her feet. She grabbed a rambling weed to keep from falling on her behind, reestablished her crouch, and tossed him another dirty look. His lips twitched. "You may hit me all you like when Barbu is dead and you are safely home."

A shiver slithered up her spine. "Promise."

"No word of a lie."

She huffed—half laugh, half despair. It was the best she could do under the circumstances. Her chest was too tight, rib cage pressing in, lungs getting smaller by the moment. A full breath would have been nice—good even—but she settled for Hamund's distraction instead. Goddess bless him. She needed the diversion, something to keep her focused on what she must do and not what might happen.

Afina glanced skyward. Heavy branches flowed into delicate ones, the jagged leaves changing from green to orange and gold. A gentle breeze caressed their veined underbellies, tousling the tips, mocking the gathering storm in her mind. How could everything look so normal on the outside when inside she was less than an echo, barely enough? No answer came; no rush of comprehension or relief from the pain…from the picture of her mother lying on the stone floor, a red pool spreading beneath her white gown while Vladimir stood over her, bloody blade in his hand.

She pressed her palms flat against the rock face. Damp moss pushed back, tickling her fingertips as the chill sank into her skin. The cold settled her, gathered her in its embrace until her focus narrowed. Opening her senses wide, she listened then reached out and connected to the hum of the woodlands: heard the trees murmur, an eagle call, and the water miles beneath her feet gurgle and rush. Each sound, unique and alive, reminded her of the magic and her purpose.

No. She wouldn't run. If she did, the monster who haunted her sleep and hurt her people would win. She'd come too far—learned too much—to make the same mistake twice. Dax needed her. The men trusted her. All of Transylvania was relying on her. For once she would do as she promised, be the high priestess fate had made her.

Shifting to the right, she opened her eyes. The narrow trail didn't look so scary now. A bird called, the tone pitch-perfect, but man-made. Hamund answered, whistling with the soft song of a lark.

Afina tilted her head, ear to shoulder, first to one side then the other. Tight muscles protested before uncoiling one strand at a time. "It's time?"

"Aye. The men are in place. They will not be able to see you, Afina. They will stay back until I give the signal."

"You don't wish to give away our advantage," she murmured, finishing Hamund's thought before he could. He must think she had brain damage. He'd made her recite the plan at least a dozen times since leaving Drachaven.

"Exactly." The captain bumped her again. Afina understood the silent entreaty. She glanced over the curve of her shoulder. Dark eyes bore into hers. "Tell me again."

She wanted to sigh—to tell him she understood, could recite the plan backward and forward, probably in her sleep. Instead she nodded. "Distract. Divide. Retrieve. Retreat."

"Simple. Straightforward. Keep your eye on Dax, Afina. The moment you have him...run like the devil. We will do the rest."

Which meant kill Vladimir.

Afina liked the plan...especially the last part. "Got it."

"Go, then." Hamund gave her a pat on the shoulder. "I will keep you in sight...be no more than ten paces behind you the entire time."

His words should have brought her some small measure of comfort. They didn't, and as she slid from her hidey-hole and crept onto the path her mind laid out images. Each one flashed, vivid, colorful, like the past was only moments away instead of two years ago. She slammed the lid on the memories shut. Too late. They were already out in the open, asking questions she didn't want to acknowledge, much less answer. Why had her mother not fought back, used her magic to save her life? What kind of monster was Vladimir Barbu? Did he have power of his own...a way to deflect the goddess's essence? Afina flexed her hands as she tiptoed closer to the trail entrance. And if he did, what chance did she have against him?

Her magic wasn't exactly mature. She hadn't practiced what little she knew, and that knowledge was sketchy at best. Afina swallowed. She should have cornered Garren, insisted he teach her...well, at least the basics. Like how to protect herself.

Halfway down, the tunnel rolled into a blind curve. Afina paused, gripping the hilt of the knife strapped to her thigh. She took the outside track, moving to her left to see around the wild shrubs tangled with a clump of saplings. Shadows pressed in, entombing her like a funeral shroud. It was an apt description. She felt like she was being buried alive. The smell of wet dirt and pungent pine did nothing to dissuade her morbid imagination. All she needed now was a hole: two feet wide, six feet deep, and just as long.

The wind picked up and tree limbs moaned, creaking as they clattered against their neighbors. Another gust. Another push from behind. Afina took the hint and, goose-bumped, dry-mouthed, rounded the bend.

Sunlight greeted her. The yellow rays spread like fingers, penetrating the gloom, illuminating the almost perfect circle of the tunnel mouth. Afina blinked. From spine-bending scary to cheery in a few short steps. Ridiculous. Thank the goddess. She needed the reprieve, if only for a moment, to catch her breath, to settle her spirit, to ready her mind for the violence to come.

She thought herself ready for it. Now she knew better. No matter how certain she'd been—standing in the inner bailey at Drachaven, discussing strategy, making plans—following through was something else entirely. The goddess was right.

She was a nurturer at heart, not made for violence or able to inflict it without hurting herself.

Oh, how she missed Xavian. Not for his skill with a sword, but his ability to soothe her. Afina closed her eyes. She wanted his arms around her, to hear his voice and feel the magic flow between them. Cowardly, she knew, but she couldn't stop the yearning...the need to touch and be touched in return. Reaching deep, she searched for their connection, the essence of him. More than the physical, she needed his spirit, that intangible something...the what and who that made him hers.

She shivered as it bubbled up, surrounded her heart, loosened her lungs, gifting her with her first full breath since leaving the safety of Drachaven. The rumble followed, rolling through her like an earth tremor. Afina froze, surprise morphing into dismay as a stream of magic surged down her legs. A lightning bolt sensation followed, zigzagging out of the soles of her boots and into the ground. Her feet followed the quake, shuffling toward the edge of the pathway. Grabbing a nearby shrub, she stopped her forward progress, heart slamming in her chest, breath coming in shallow bursts.

What was that?

A *pssst* came from behind her. Afina glanced over her shoulder and found Hamund crouched in the foliage, the agreed-upon ten paces away. He tipped his chin, waved his hand, encouraging her to move. Forgetting the odd surge of magic, she took one step then another. The last few feet were throat-gripping, muscle-twisting awful.

Was Vladimir waiting for her beyond, haloed in sunlight?

Afina almost snorted. *Haloed.* Right. The only halo the swine would wear was one of fire when he fell from this world into the one below and met the devil. She set her teeth, praying the plan worked and the bastard met his maker, preferably sooner rather than later.

Her hand flexed around the knife hilt. Staying low, she crept forward, past tree roots and thornbushes. She paused beneath the boughed archway to get the lay of the land. Almost a perfect oval, the clearing boasted a knoll at its center, rolling out to large trees on three sides. Giant, sharp-toothed stone slabs rose at odd angles on the fourth, guarding the path down the mountainside. Dower Pass…it was exactly as Hamund had described it, but for one thing: It was empty. Not a soldier in sight. Not a branch out of place. No swine to be found.

Vladimir was playing his usual game. The bastard had never met a lie he didn't favor.

So what now? How could she get to Dax if she couldn't find him? A sharp pang hit her chest level. The sensation clawed at her throat and desperation pushed her feet forward, looking for a clue, no matter how small.

A dark blob shifted in her periphery. Heat surged along her spine, burned in her fingertips as Afina spun and, hands up, unleashed magic. With a soft shriek, air rushed, blasting a hole near the base of a huge oak. The dirt exploded, mushrooming before it came down in a pitter-patter of wet earth. Fingers curled, she stood stone still, waiting. A squat shrub bobbed, bouncing beneath a swath of grey fabric.

Each exhale choppy and chilled, Afina glanced right then left. She was still alone. No one was coming through the trees or attacking…yet. Wiping her damp palms on her trews, she tiptoed toward her only clue. Hollowness threatened to swallow her whole when she reached the lip of the clearing. Oh, no. A piece of Dax's cloak—perfect stitches torn, wool ripped down the seam—lay over the clustering shrub. She fingered the soft lining. Rabbit fur caressed her palm as she brought it to her face. It smelled like her little boy...sweet with a hint of the soap she made Dax use at bath time. Under duress...always under duress. It was one of the things she'd learned about lads his age—they didn't see the need for cleanliness. Bathing, after all, cut into their playtime.

Afina's throat went tight. She clamped down on the swell of grief. Finding his mantle didn't mean Dax was dead. *Stay calm. Stay even.* 'Twas the only way she'd see Vladimir's trap.

The calculating swine never played by the rules. He was setting an ambush...but where? The mountain passes kept their secrets. The bastard could be anywhere.

Like an apparition, Hamund appeared at the tree line. She lifted her hand and showed him the piece of mantle. The captain mouthed a curse and—

A scream vibrated through the forest.

High pitched, the terrified shriek thundered up her spine, collided with the back of her skull. The fine hairs on the nape of her neck spiked, and without stopping to think, Afina sprinted toward the path that descended the mountainside. Hamund shouted her name. She ignored him. Vladimir was cutting her lad. Oh, no, his beautiful little fingers.

Fear whipped through her, lending her strength as she sliced between two giant slabs of stone. Small pebbles unbalanced her, rolling beneath her feet. She caught herself and kept going, following the narrow trail, dodging boulders and sheared rock. To hell with caution and consequence. Vladimir was a dead man. She would rip him apart, blast him off the mountainside...smile as she listened to him shriek on the way down.

Another spine-chilling scream. Then another. And another.

Afina's heart slammed and her legs pumped, hurtling her through a jagged maze. Dax's name echoed inside her head. *Please, Goddess…shield him, save him, keep him alive.*

She gripped the edge of a flat-faced stone. Her skin gave way, leaving her palm raw as she pushed off, looping and bobbing around obstacles. The sun beat down and sweat rolled, drenching the small of her back. With a final push, she lunged across a series of low-lying rocks and vaulted into the expanse beyond.

Flat to the point of perfection, the area was huge, mayhap fifty feet wide and twice as long. Rimmed by small shrubs, sheared sheets of rock formed haphazard piles before giving way to a plateau that rolled out to the edge of a cliff. A whimper, a choked sound of protest, sounded to her right. Her boots sliding on stone dust, Afina pivoted, afraid to look yet unable to turn away.

Her heart hiccupped behind her breastbone.

Her enemy stood behind Dax, a blade pressed to his slender throat. Bloody hand cradled against his chest, Dax's eyes were huge in his small face. Afina's hands curled into fists. One false move and Vladimir would use the knife…slit her lad from ear to ear. Suppressing a surge of panic, she met her enemy's gaze, looking him in the eye for the first time in her life. And wished she hadn't. Madness lived there, a dark gleam that said he enjoyed the power he held.

"Afina." He hummed her name as though tasting it. "Welcome."

The sick satisfaction in his tone made her stomach roll. "Let him go."

"M-mama." Dax reached for her with his uninjured hand. The bastard twisted her lad's hair, yanked him backward.

"I'm right here, love," she said, keeping her voice soft to smooth out the hitch. He'd never called her Mama before, not once…not even when she tucked him in at night. Afina breathed in through her nose, out through her mouth, struggling to stay calm.

Flexing her hand around the dagger, her gaze swept the plateau, looking for a weakness. Vladimir had to have one. The swine was too arrogant—too sure of himself—to believe another capable of besting him. But she'd done it once already, and so she searched, examining the rocks and twisted sycamores behind him. The trees hid something…a narrow trail, mayhap?

"Toss the knife away, Priestess," Vladimir said, tone pleasant as though he stood in a great hall conversing about the weather. "Or I gut your lad."

Dax whimpered.

Afina swallowed one of her own and unsheathed the blade strapped to her thigh. Steel clinked against stone as she threw it away. "It's all right, darling. Everything is going to be all right."

"Liar." The bastard's whisper drifted, echoing like a shout off the rock face. "I'm going to slit your throat and take your mother."

"S-sorry, Mama." Twin tears rolled, leaving streaks on his dirty face. "S-sorry."

"It isn't your fault, Dax." Afina took a step closer, wanting to blast Vladimir so badly her palms throbbed. But what if she missed? The swine would do as he said and Dax would die. "I am here, Vladimir. I kept up my end. Now keep yours. Let him go."

The bastard grinned over the top of her lad's head. "Come and get him."

"Bastard," she said, tone soft, more snarl than curse. Gravel crunched beneath her boot heels as she shifted left to find a better angle. She needed to see what lay beyond him. He'd chosen his position for a reason. Were his men hunkered down in the trees, behind the boulders, waiting for his signal? Afina swallowed. She hoped Hamund wasn't far behind her.

"Tsk, Priestess. Such language." His eyes traveled over her trews. Speculation mingled with lust, washing his cheeks with color. "You've grown...in all the right places."

"You have no idea." Afina itched to show how very much she had changed. Show him she was no longer a frightened rabbit, ready to flee at the first scent of danger. She was mated now and the magic flowed, moving through her veins with vicious intent. Rubbing her fingertips with her thumb, she held onto the urge as well as the power. It was too soon. The possibility of hitting Dax instead of her target was too real. "Forever the coward, aren't you, Vladimir...using a lad as a shield?"

A muscle twitched in his jaw. "'Tis intelligence, *chère*...not cowardice."

Chère. He called her his sweetheart. Afina wanted to vomit. She swallowed the burn, mind racing to form a new plan. Where were Hamund and his men? No doubt regrouping, trying to find a way onto the plateau. It wouldn't be easy. A sheer rock face on one side, a cliff on the other, the trail she'd used seemed the only way in. Her saving grace? She knew they would never leave her.

"Not too smart. I managed to evade you for over two years," she said, wanting to keep him talking. Whatever his plan, it wouldn't unfold here. It was too isolated a place, without any true means of defense. The longer they lingered the better her advantage and the more time Hamund had to reach them. "Me...a woman without skill or experience."

He sneered. "Bianca helped you. Little whore."

Anger bubbled up. Afina pushed it back down. The idea was to taunt him, keep him distracted. Not rise to the bait herself. "My sister was—"

A battle cry ripped through the canyon. A clang of swords followed, rising up from the trail behind her. Tension cranked her muscles one notch tighter. The swine's men-at-arms had been there all along, hiding in the rocks, waiting for her guards. Goddess, she was an idiot. She'd done what Vladimir expected. Now Xavian's men would suffer for her mistake.

"Ah, your men...and not a moment too soon. You walked them right into my trap. Not too smart, Priestess." Vladimir smiled, throwing her words back in her face. "Did you think they would save you?"

The sound of battle grew closer. Men shouted and blades clashed, brittling her insides. "I don't need them to save me."

The words jolted her, leaving her disoriented for a moment. She said them again, this time with more conviction. They circled, coming together, giving birth to something new...something shiny and good and *right*. Afina embraced the truth of it, let it grow until years of self-doubt sank beneath a rising wave of confidence. The power inside her shifted, seething for release. With a growl, she let the magic enfold and take her, mold her into aggression.

"Nay?" Vladimir scoffed, laughing at her.

"No." Chin tipped down, Afina glared at him from beneath her brows. "I can save myself."

"Right, and I am the King of—"

She raised her hand, giving body to the magic in her blood. A blue current snapped between her fingertips, forming a perfect sphere. The orb settled in the palm of her hand, white lightning striking inside the orb.

Vladimir's eyes went wide. "You are—"

"Mated to Xavian." She smiled, a mere curve of the lips, but it conveyed the message. *Take that, you filthy swine.* "You will never control me."

"You are mine!" Fury set the lines of his face as he bared his teeth.

"No." One word, a simple denial that set the final piece in place. She belonged to Xavian by choice. Her destiny was her own to control. "I am not."

The bastard pressed his blade harder to Dax's throat. Blood ran, trickling from under his chin, soaking the collar of his cloak. Afina clenched her teeth to mute her cry of outrage. Another round of lightning cracked inside the sphere. She tightened her grip on it. She couldn't throw it…not yet. Not until he shifted into the open.

Forcing a calm she didn't feel, she flipped the orb into the air and caught it on the down arc. "Careful, Vladimir. The lad is the only leverage you've got…kill him and I blast you."

"Come then…retrieve your wee bastard." Dark eyes narrowed, Vladimir lifted the knife, planted his foot on Dax's back, and kicked. Her lad stumbled forward, a red rivulet rolling down his throat.

The moment Dax was clear, Afina hurled the lightning ball at Vladimir's head. The air crackled. Fire hissed as blue flame streaked across the clearing. The swine ducked and leapt right. Rock exploded, raining a downpour of shards. Afina launched another. Vladimir rolled. Dirt flew skyward and wood cracked. Brown debris clouding the air, the acrid scent of scorched sycamore drifting, she vaulted toward Dax. She knew it was a mistake the moment her feet moved.

Vladimir was down, not dead.

But the need to reach her son overpowered self-preservation. *Retrieve. Retreat.* That was her mission.

A foot away from Dax, Vladimir shouted, "Now!"

A flurry of movement erupted above her. Something brown and weighted slammed into her back. The air left her lungs as she hit the ground chest first. Wheezing, she planted her palms in the dirt and pressed up, flipped over, fighting confinement. Rough rope scraped her cheek. She tore at the netting. Heat seared her skin and pain met the smell of burning flesh. Afina jerked away from the web and stared at her hands. Blisters were already forming. Blood crystals...everywhere, sewn into each junction.

She tried to scream, to let Hamund know she was in trouble. No sound emerged. She reached for Dax. Crumpled on an exposed piece of granite, he lay just feet away. Her hand inched out. The gemstones contracted, becoming a prison around her. Mother Mary, she needed to get to him. If she didn't, he would bleed to death.

Uncaring of the agony, Afina yanked on the rope again. More burns. More bubbling blisters as magical bars stronger than steel closed around her. She felt the sucking draw—the same awful pull as when Tareek had held the medallion to her throat—and she knew she was lost. The blood crystals had gone to work, siphoning her strength one gulp at a time. Helplessness arrived, dragging desperation with it as the magic left her, moving in the wrong direction.

Afina slumped, cheek pressed to wet stone, her gaze on Dax. As her heartbeat slowed to an inaudible thump, she fought the darkness as it came to her...fought to stay with her lad. *Live.* The whisper echoed inside her mind. She pushed the command toward Dax, across the scant few feet separating them. *Live.* She willed it, thrust her determination into his heart and soul, giving him all she had.

The tips of Vladimir's boots came into her line of vision. "Foolish Afina...but predictable, at least."

Smeared with pain, her vision blurred. Her fingers curled, filling her hands with stone dust. She murmured Dax's name, more sob than whisper. Goddess forgive her, she'd failed him, just as she had failed them all.

Grey clouds of smoke billowed toward a clear blue sky. Sap bubbled on tree trunks and flames roared, devouring shrub and evergreen alike. The inferno raced along the lip of the dell, rimming the large, flat expanse, colliding with the adjacent rock face. Fire licked at Xavian's boot heels, hemming Al Pacii in along with his men.

Xavian wiped the sweat from his eyes. Good Christ. What the hell had Cruz been thinking? Not that he minded roasting the enemy, but there was a time and place...preferably one without a forest full of kindling to feed the blaze.

He glared at the dragon behind him. Oblivious, happy in the hellfire, Cruz growled and, raising his clawed forepaw, stomped on one of the assassins. He bared his fangs, grinning as bone crunched, and pivoted to face another. The scaled bastards were having a ball destroying the enemy. Tareek had even eaten one, for Christ's sake.

He shook his head and unsheathed his swords. Afina was going to kill him. The damage to her precious woodlands would take years to reverse. He and Cruz needed a sit-down, face-to-face—or rather fang—conversation. Nature and Afina's purpose must be respected by all who served him...regardless of their penchant for using their mouths as flamethrowers.

The price of having dragons for comrades. Jesu. Fire-eating idiots.

Twin blades reflected the flames as Xavian joined the fray. Pivoting, he ducked beneath an enemy sword and his steel met flesh. He drew his slice through, cutting muscle from bone. The man screamed, crumbling to one knee before Xavian reversed course. One powerful stroke and the bastard's head left his shoulders. Brown hair streaked scarlet flipped end over end to land with a thump on scorched grass.

Xavian stepped around the headless corpse, engaged another Al Pacii, took him down. Fire nipping him from behind, he checked his position. Cristobal fought ten feet away, blades whirling as he engaged two assassins at once. Seasoned and well-built, they were after his friend's head. Xavian sheathed one of his swords and replaced it with a dagger. A third closed in behind Cristobal.

The bastards didn't know how to fight fair. But then, neither did he.

He waited a moment, wanting the optimal angle, then yelled, "Down!"

Cristobal dropped, rolling left. An enemy blade missed his friend by an inch, and Xavian loosed the dagger. His steel sank deep, catching the third man's throat dead center, just beneath his chin. Thrown back by the impact, the bastard dropped his sword. He clutched at the hilt pressed against his flesh and stumbled back a step. The fire took over, completing the kill.

Back to back now, he and Cristobal made quick work of the assassins around them. He needed to reach the rise, the one beyond Garren. Valmont was fighting there. Per usual, the bastard was holding his own. He wanted a piece of him before Al Pacii lost and Valmont tucked his tail between his legs and fled.

Xavian had no doubt he would run...leave the remaining assassins to die while he made a clean escape.

'Twas the bastard's way. Halál's way.

Xavian's swords cut through the air faster. Cristobal kept pace. Working as one, they slashed their way to the blue dragon. Garren flicked an assassin away with a tip of his claw. The man went flying, hit the ground and rolled...winded but still alive. The dragon swung his massive head in their direction. Teeth bared, violet eyes lethal, he inhaled. With a curse, Xavian jumped right, out of the incendiary path. Upon recognizing them, Garren swallowed the fireball and grinned.

Cristobal scowled back. "Would you just kill them, for shit's sake?"

Garren shifted to shield them, using his body to deflect a flurry of arrows. The steel points bounced off his scales as he raised a brow. "'Twould be over too quickly if I did that. Need some small challenge, you know?"

"Well then, eat them."

"I'll leave that to Tareek." The dragon grimaced as though tasting something foul and muttered, "Never developed a liking for human flesh."

"Good to know." Xavian leaned around the dragon's shoulder, scanning the terrain. The battled stilled raged, but little by little his men evened the odds. Al Pacii had come prepared with a full contingent of seasoned assassins. Much as he wished it, Valmont wasn't stupid. He watched the bastard fight a moment... watched Andrei's swords flash, matching Valmont's stroke for stroke. "Garren, cover me. I need to get to that rise."

The dragon tossed another man with his snout, sending him ten feet in the air. He glanced at him from his periphery. "You want a piece of the dark one?"

"Aye." Xavian planted his boot on the dragon's foreleg. "I'm going up and over you."

"I'll clear a path," Garren said then eyed his friend. "Cristobal, what the hell are you doing?"

"Staying here to kill the ones you toss." Cristobal sheathed one of his swords in favor of a throwing knife.

"Hristos, you'll ruin my fun."

"Get over it, dragon."

Garren snorted, the sound one of disappointment. "On my count, Xavian."

On three, Xavian pushed off, vaulting over the dragon's spiked spine. He sighted the ground an instant before his feet hit. Rolling, he grabbed the hilts of his swords, unsheathing them in one pull, and attacked. Set in a semicircle around their leader, the assassins closed ranks, keeping him out and Andrei in. He took on two at time, pushed them back, made Valmont adapt as the circle around him became smaller. Henrik came from the other side, collapsing the loop from the right. Almost there. One more slice, another thrust and—

A tremor rumbled beneath his feet.

With a violent shiver, it vibrated up through the soles of his boots and along his spine to collide with the base of his skull. Xavian faltered, dropping his guard. An enemy blade slipped through, gouging his bicep. Pain ripped through him as blood ran to his forearm. Pushing the discomfort aside, he reset his balance, but it was too late. He'd lost ground and his focus. A dull thump started, squeezed his lungs, whispered inside his head. Not words exactly, but he understood the urgency all the same.

"Jesu, Afina." His mate was in trouble.

"Garren!" His sword clashed with the assassin's. Steel rang against steel as Xavian backtracked. Retreat wasn't something he liked, but he did it anyway. Afina needed him. He didn't know how he knew—why the earth pulsed beneath his feet—only that he must return to Drachaven. Without delay. Splitting Valmont in two would keep for another time.

The blue dragon swung his spiked tail. It hit the ground inches from his boot heels then whipped around, sending the bastards following his retreat into the rock face. Garren watched them thud against stone and growled, "What is it?"

"Afina." Xavian breathed in smoke and spit out dread. He could feel her. She was hurting and so afraid her fear gripped his heart. "I need to go home...now."

"Get on." Garren lowered one shoulder. "Cristobal...you too."

Xavian hesitated less than an instant. Riding a dragon was naught compared to the urgency thumping in his veins. Garren's wings would get them home faster. And fast was very, very good.

Grabbing the twin spikes behind Garren's shoulders, he leapt into position. Cristobal settled in behind him. The blue dragon roared once, calling the others, and unfurled his wings. His men followed; Andrei and Kazim on Cruz, Henrik and Razvan on Tareek. Clawed paws spread and muscle rippling, Garren pushed off, launching them into the sky. A death grip on the beast's spikes, Xavian sent a desperate prayer heavenward.

Please, let her be all right.

But even as he released it into the ether, he knew that she wasn't.

CHAPTER THIRTY-FOUR

Sunlight filtered through the trees, making the leaves look like birds of prey. Caught fast by the net, Afina stared up at them, watched the flicker and wane as Vladimir's men dragged her behind them on the narrow dirt trail. Numb inside, apathy spread, infecting her like disease. She sighed. 'Twas lovely, really. Total oblivion wrapped up with a touch of unreal.

The blood crystals hummed, drawing her in until her body didn't belong to her anymore. Instead she watched them drag her, floated above the sheared cliff faces and knotty pines, unable to feel anything.

"*Afina.*" The goddess's voice whispered through her mind. "*Fight, child.*"

She blinked, her eyelids so heavy she struggled to reopen them. A patch of fog floated between her temples, obliterating thought, unhinging reason. Afina frowned. What had the voice said? What—

"*Remember, Dax, daughter. Fight.*"

Oh, right. Dax. Such a wonderful lad. So smart and—

The amulet thumped against her chest. Afina glanced down at the white crystal. Bright light swirled at its center, pulsed once, pulled her in until her mind caught hold of a thought. Another followed, linking together until the mess in her mind cleared. A jolt roared through, made her muscles tense, thrusting her into awareness.

Good Goddess, what was she doing? Her son needed her and she was giving in, succumbing to black magic.

The blood crystals hissed. Afina fisted her hand around the amulet, absorbing its power through her palm, and twisted in her prison. The rope held, pushing down as she thrust up, looking for a weakness in the threads. Sticks and jagged stone gouged her as she turned onto her side and reached for Xavian's dagger. Numb fingers defied her and she missed, overshooting the flap of her leather hauberk. Afina gritted her teeth, demanding her body cooperate. But every movement felt weighted—difficult— like slogging through a bog of quicksand.

She tried again, caught the lacing that ran like a road up her spine. Hanging on to the ties, she rolled right to avoid a rock. It missed her shoulder by a scant inch. The men dragging her cursed, yanking her back around.

One of the beasts chuckled. "Do you see any more, Oscar?"

"There's a sharper one around the bend," the second brute said, anticipation in his voice.

"Good. Let's see how well the witch avoids that one."

Pressing her boots into the ground, she used her heels to steer. The boulder rose on the trail in front of them. The animals dug in, ramping into a run. She kicked right. The guards swung her back and she hit dead center. Pain struck, clawing at her arm and shoulder as the collision flipped her up and over, vaulting her into air. She landed hard, the guards' laughter ringing in her ears as her rib cage contracted around her lungs and the trail gave way to grass.

The sliding stopped in the middle of a clearing. Horses nickered nearby. The brutes dropped the net, leaving her in a pool of sunshine. Hiccupping gasps of air, Afina lay on her side, her hand still clutched around the white crystal, fear sitting like a stone at the bottom of her stomach.

Where was Hamund?

She closed her eyes, hope a barely formed thought in her heart. The fighting sounded far away now, a distant clang that spoke of disaster. The captain and his men were tangled in Vladimir's web and she'd walked right into the trap. Afina swallowed her dread. She was on her own now, alone with a monster intent on murder and, worse, domination.

Damn her mother to hell and back. Had Ylenia loved her like a mother should, the swine wouldn't be here and neither would she.

Something landed with a thud beside her.

She didn't want to look, but couldn't help it. The sweet smell of soap and blood mingled, telling her what they'd dropped next to her. Dax. One arm trapped beneath him, he lay on his back, neck marred by dry blood. Afina's eyes stung and, desperate for a sign, watched his chest. It rose then fell, the movement barely there, but just enough. He was still alive. She had half a chance to get him home.

Afina blew out a slow breath. *Home. Yes…think of Drachaven.*

Envisioning the strong walls, she pictured the guards atop them, armor set, weapons at the ready. Their courage helped rouse her own, helped her hold on to Xavian. Clear as day, his face took shape and form in her mind's eye. She saw his blue eyes, his beautiful face…his unfailing spirit. Reaching deep, she embraced his strength and made it her own. The amulet pulsed against her palm and her magic stirred, rising to fight the blood crystals' cage around her.

One of the guards kicked at her feet. "Not so tough now, are ye, witch?"

Vladimir shoved his man aside, sending him sprawling arse-first in the dirt. "She is mine. Remember that, Oscar, and you will live to see another day."

"Aye, my lord." Oscar gained his feet and brushed off his backside. As he turned, he glared at her, lips curled in a snarl.

"Apologies, *chère*," Vladimir said, his voice smooth as silk, his attention on his man-at-arm's retreating back. "No need for such unpleasantness...especially since you will soon be wedded and bedded." He turned his gaze away from Oscar and met hers. "Though not in that order."

The thought of him touching her made her skin crawl. "Xavian will kill you."

"He will have to find me first. By then 'twill be too late."

The certainty in his tone rubbed her raw. The terrible glint in his eyes catapulted her fear to new levels. He knew something she didn't...but what? The mystery—all those nasty unanswered questions—hinged on his knowledge. "What did you do to my mother?"

"Besides kill her? Not much. The question you should be asking, little witch, is what she did to you." Vladimir reached into the pouch at his waist. His movements slowed, prolonging the moment as he pulled a piece of jewelry from the leather opening. The golden links slid across his palm, dangling from his finger-tips. A choker. One with oval blood crystals set in a diagonal pattern. Afina sucked in a quick breath. The half-smile he wore turned into a full grin. "'Tis a lovely dog collar, don't you think? Fit for a high priestess."

Dread sank like a stone in the pit of her stomach. Her mother had made the necklace. Afina recognized her work, smelled the black magic in each link. The stench carried a vile imprint, the same one used to imprison the dragon shifters.

And if Garren—with all his strength and cunning—had not been able to resist the spell, what chance did she have to defeat it?

"You'll never get it on me."

"'Tis why I have them to hold you down," he said, waving his free hand. Afina glanced over her shoulder, trying to avoid the blood crystals sewn into the net. Four men stood behind her, looking keen and battle-ready.

Vladimir swung the choker on the tip of his finger, the sway hypnotic...terrifying. "Now let's get you muzzled, shall we?"

"No!"

"Come now, *cherie*. 'Twill not hurt...much." Crouching at her feet, he unsheathed his dagger and set the sharp point to the net. The four pigs shifted, boxing her in, one to hold each limb when her prison gave way. Vladimir cut the first junction, met her gaze, and whispered, "Soon you will spread your lovely thighs for me, Priestess."

"Never."

Vladimir smirked and cut the first link in the net.

Afina dropped the amulet and curled her hands into fists, muscles coiled, waiting for the moment the rope fell away and the black magic retreated. She was weak, yes, but not entirely defenseless. The buffer—the wall surrounding the core of her magic—was still intact. It wasn't much...hardly enough...but a little was better than nothing. She needed to keep that *thing* away from her neck. "I will never forget Xavian. He is and will always be my mate."

"So much spirit." Vladimir chuckled, cutting another joint. "I will enjoy breaking you, Afina."

Five more to go...now four. Afina counted, held her breath, felt her magic flicker as the netting loosened around her.

The swine cut through the last tie. He glanced at each of his men, a warning in his gaze. "Get ready."

With a quick flick, Vladimir threw the blood crystals aside. Afina exploded through the opening, feet and fists flying. Her heels slammed into shins. Her knuckles connected with bone. Her fingernails gouged, raking their cheeks. The men cursed. She scrambled sideways. Cruel hands grabbed her, pulled her back, pinned one wrist then the other. Kicking out with her feet, she swung right, shoulders arched, boot heels tearing at the ground. She couldn't let them get her feet. She couldn't—

One calf hit the ground under a brutal hold. The other followed, pinned by the fourth bastard's shin. Her curse turned into a sob. She called on her magic, prayed for the answering rush—the heat and power—but knew it would never come. The blood crystals had taken too much...left her vulnerable to the vermin holding her down. Still she fought their grip, howled her fury, refusing to surrender. If she lost the battle, Dax would die. Xavian would suffer. And she would turn into a monster...just like her mother.

Vladimir stood watching, calm in the face of her storm. "Now, now, Priestess. Give up...you are defeated."

"I am going to rip your head off and feed your body to the wolves!"

"And I am going to fuck you here...in the dirt," he murmured, still twirling the choker around his fingertip. Skirting the guard holding her right wrist, the swine stopped even with her head. She tensed when he nudged her with his boot, pressing the sole to her cheekbone. Wet dirt smeared her skin, mixing with the smell of leather before he lifted his foot away and sank to his haunches beside her. "Do you think my men will enjoy watching us? Enjoy the sight of your bare flesh in the sunlight, mud on your knees, my cock in your mouth?"

Afina's bottom lip quivered, betraying her fear.

Vladimir raised his hand, brushing away the mud he'd left on her face. "Now chin up, *chère*. 'Tis time."

She pinned her chin to her chest. "Get away from me!"

His fingers dipped, trailing down her face to curl beneath her jawbone. Vladimir pressed up. She resisted, protecting her neck. Applying more pressure, he used his thumb, digging into her pulse point. Pain shot into her ear, down the back of her throat, gagging her. With a growl, she bared her teeth and sank them into the muscle below his thumb.

"Damnation!" He jerked and shook free of her hold.

Afina tasted blood and, gathering her salvia, spit in his face. "Swine."

Disgust turned the corners of his mouth down as Vladimir wiped the mess from his cheek. Cold fury in his eyes, he tipped his chin in Oscar's direction.

"With pleasure," Oscar said, fisting his hand in her hair. Lifting, he slammed the back of her head into the ground. Agony hit her like a flail, driving its spikes into her skull. The bastard raised her head again.

Vladimir grabbed his arm. "Flip her over."

The band of fresh fear tightened its grip around her chest, squeezing a sob from her throat. Five against one. The bastards. She would never be able to fight with him sitting on her back.

"Good idea, my lord." The pig holding her arm down laughed. "Want to take her that way too?"

"Mayhap," Vladimir murmured, excitement sifting beneath the word.

Her stomach rebelled. Afina tasted bile and desperation, fighting to keep them from flipping her over. Their collective grip was brutal, squeezing in her muscles, compressing the bone beneath. Her chest touched down first then her belly and hips. Vladimir's knee settled between her shoulder blades.

No. Goddess help her, no. "Xavian!"

She screamed his name like a battle cry, over and over… until her voice gave out and shadows gathered in her mind. Like demons winged with blood, they settled deep as the swine wound her braid around his hand. His fist pressed to her nape, he pulled until her chin came off the ground.

His mouth brushed the shell of her ear. "Now you become mine."

Afina bucked beneath his weight. "Go to hell."

Vladimir retreated to loop the choker beneath her chin. She cringed, arched her spine more to avoid the inevitable. The crystals hummed, a breath away, reaching for her skin. An instant before gemstones touched her, a whoosh sounded above her. The bastard holding her wrist jerked and toppled backward. A long blur streaked past. Blood arched, splashing across her cheek as the second guard collapsed, an arrow shaft through his eye socket. Both hands now free, Afina reared. Vladimir hung on, tightening his grip in her hair. She made a sound, more animal than human, and twisted, unbalancing the swine on her back. The choker flew, flipping end over end as Afina brought her arm up. Bone cracked against bone as she planted her elbow in Vladimir's face.

With a howl he flailed, falling backward, one hand over his bloody nose, the other reaching for her. As his arse met the ground, Vladimir bellowed, telling his men to keep hold of her legs. The man holding her right ankle pressed down. Another whistle sounded. Chest heaving, heart thumping, Afina ducked. The bastard behind her gagged, the tip of a dagger protruding from his throat. Scrambling madly, she kicked out, slamming her foot into Oscar's chin. His head snapped back and he lost his grip, liberating her other foot.

Wet earth pushing beneath her fingernails, Afina lunged toward Dax. She needed to get them both to the lip of the forest. The arrows had come from her left. Her salvation lay in that direction. If she could just—

A man she didn't recognize leapt over a huge boulder at the edge of the dell. His feet hit the ground, and he rolled, loosing a dagger as he came out of his crouch. The blade struck home, sinking into an enemy chest. Vladimir shouted, rousing his guard. At least twenty strong, they unsheathed their swords.

The stranger skidded to a halt beside her. Drawing two arrows from his quiver, he set his bow with both and took down more of Vladimir's guard. "Get behind me, healer."

Afina didn't stop to think, much less argue. The warrior dressed like Xavian and his men, black from head to toe. The only real difference was his hair. Trimmed to his skull, the cut emphasized the planes of his face. Set in lethal lines, his green eyes flashed as his arrows flew, using the swine's men as pincushions. But they were growing wise, taking cover to release their own. An arrowhead cut through the ground beside her, leaving a trench an inch deep.

The warrior in front of her snarled, unsheathing his twin swords. "Get moving, woman."

"Where?"

"Take cover in the trees. I will follow."

A death grip on Dax, Afina heaved his weight. Oscar outflanked her, blood running from the corner of his mouth. Sword in hand, he cut off her escape from the left. Another guard came around from the right, blocking the last path to freedom. Setting her son down gently, she palmed Xavian's dagger. "Ah, warrior?"

"What?"

"We've got problems."

"No shit." Steel slid beneath an enemy chin. The warrior drew his blade through, slitting the man's throat.

Oscar took a step toward her, a hideous grin on his face. "I'm gonna get your brat, witch."

"Come any closer..." Afina trailed off, watching two more pigs arrive. They were setting a perimeter, encircling them from all sides. She adjusted her grip on the knife hilt and held it out in front of her. "And you're a dead man."

Shielded behind Oscar's back, Vladimir snorted. "Away you go, Oscar. Kill the bastard...bring me Afina."

The warrior took a step back. He reset his stance, keeping them back-to-back with Dax lying between them. "You know how to use that, healer?"

"Afina."

"Shay," he said, deep voice rumbling as he returned the favor and told her his name. Mayhap it was stupid, but she needed to know it. If she was going to die with the man, she wanted to know what to call him. He threw her a sideways glance, blades raised, a brow arched. "Do you?"

She flexed her free hand, felt a prickle in her fingertips. Her breath hitched on hope as heat gathered at the base of her spine. With the blood crystals gone, her magic was returning. It wasn't much, but enough mayhap for a diversion...for one of the invisible domes she'd used on the dragons.

"I'll manage." Afina shifted to the balls of her feet, picturing a warrior's shield. She held the image in her mind's eye, watched, waited for Oscar to make his move. "You fight...I will watch your back."

Oscar shook his head. "Put it down, witch. You are no match for—"

A dark shadow rolled over the clearing, blotting out the sun. Awareness shivered through her. Afina glanced up an instant before the war cry rippled, rising on the wind. Time slowed, every man froze, swords poised in midair, eyes on the sky. Trees trunks bent sideways, making way for a dark wing. The sharp tip angled in, sliced down, creating a path for its cargo. Xavian leapt from his perch, vaulting through tree limbs, an avenging angel dressed in black leather. As his feet hit the ground, he unsheathed his swords, a roar on his breath, murder on his blades.

"Christ." Shay glanced at her over his shoulder. "You'll remember I helped you when this is over?"

"I've got your back," she said to Shay, reassuring him as she set her stance, feet planted, dagger up, magic swirling in her palms. She smiled—more snarl than grin—at Oscar. "Now you're in for it."

The bastard's eyes narrowed. "He has to reach you first, witch."

A black blur landed behind him, blades at the ready. Afina tipped her chin, greeting the warrior now standing at Oscar's back. "Andrei."

"Afina."

"About time you got here."

Andrei grinned. "Better late than never."

The pig roared and, ignoring Andrei, lunged toward her. Sunlight rippled along his sword, the razor-sharp tip leading the charge. Heart in her throat, Dax still at her heels, Afina shifted and raised her hand. A moment before she threw up her shield, Shay pivoted. Steel met steel, the clashing blades inches away from the top of her head. A low ring started in her ears as she got low, hunching over Dax to protect him from the backlash. It didn't come. Skilled and brutal, Shay controlled the thrust and, with a quick twist, planted his foot in the middle of the bastard's chest. Oscar stumbled back toward Xavian's man.

"My thanks." His gaze on Oscar, Andrei took a step back, allowing his enemy to regain his balance. The urge to bash him over the head almost overcame her. Good goddess, he was fighting fair, adhering to some strange *man code*.

"Not a problem."

Afina threw them both a dirty look.

Andrei shrugged, a dangerous twinkle in his eye.

With a grin, Shay returned to the fray, guarding her from the other side.

Aware now was no time to lecture them on the merits of a quick kill, Afina sheathed her knife and grabbed hold of Dax. She needed to get him out of the clearing, away from the fighting… somewhere she could tend his injuries in relative safety.

Retrieve and retreat. Retrieve and retreat.

She looked one way then the other. A lane opened, giving her a clear path into the forest. Her feet moved before her brain told her to go, heading north toward the cliffs. Dax's head bobbed against her arm. Afina tightened her grip, willing strength into her legs. Her muscles shook, giving in to exhaustion. She needed Xavian's touch and the ease he always gave her, but that would have to wait. The chaos was too thick. Men were screaming. The horses were shrieking. Steel rang against steel, sound clashing with the scent of freshly churned earth and sweet pine. Afina clung to the mixture like comfort, blocking out the other smells: the blood and sweat and urine.

Almost there…almost there.

The chant sounded inside her head, pushing her forward. The air cooled as she half-dragged, half-carried Dax beneath the canopy of a huge oak tree. Exposed roots made her stumble. She found her footing and kept going, all her focus on the forest and the safety it provided. A dark shadow rose in her periphery. Fuzzy at first, it gathered speed then sound, snarling from three feet away. Shielding Dax, Afina ducked and rolled, breaking their fall with her shoulder. A bloody hand, curled like a claw, swiped at her, passing overhead.

Palming her blade, she spun into a crouch. Vladimir whirled to face her. The choker clutched in his hand, he bared his teeth. Afina snarled back, daring him to come closer. Not the best move, but she didn't have another. She needed him at dagger point. Her magic would only reach so far. The flickering heat was almost gone, warming little more than her fingertips.

"Come on then...you coward," she said, taunting him.

"Little bitch." He spat the words, but took the bait and charged.

Knife at the ready, she raised her free hand. The bastard lunged, reaching for her neck. Almost at her throat, Afina threw up her shield. His wrist buckled as he collided with the invisible barrier. The blood crystals shattered, exploding in a spray of uneven light. Black magic surged, filling her mouth, closing her throat, attacking her lungs. Her rib cage contracted and, choking on poison, Afina used the last of her strength to thrust the dagger forward. Steel found flesh and bone. She rammed it through to Vladimir's heart.

Blood bubbled over the hilt to coat her hand. Too weak to stand, she hung on, watched the life drain from her enemy's eyes and felt the emptiness in her heart. The bastard was dead. He couldn't hurt her anymore.

"Afina!"

Her name sounded warped, coming through thick layers, as though her head was under water. Her body felt it too, becoming weightless as Vladimir fell, taking her with him. The ground rose up then grabbed hold, slamming into her shoulder first. Sunlight flickered before the darkness won, stealing her focus. A shadow appeared at her side, the fuzzy outline somehow unthreatening.

"Jesu...*Draga*." Gentle hands brushed her face then altered course. With quick efficiency, they ran over her, checking her limbs, the back of her head. Afina flinched, protesting when he touched the cut on her arm. "Easy now...be easy."

Hmm, she recognized that voice: the strength and rhythm and warmth. "X-Xavian..."

"Shh, now. 'Tis all right."

Her eyes slid closed. She forced them open. "I g-got him."

"Aye, you did." Strong arms slid beneath her shoulder blades. The pain made her cough. "Breathe, love."

Footfalls sounded then ceased beside her. A second shadow joined Xavian's. "Goddamn it."

"Not now, H." Xavian rolled her to one side and pulled, unlacing the ties at her back. "Where are the others?"

"Hamund and his crew are running the bastards down."

Afina tried to raise her hand. She wanted to touch Xavian, stroke his face, tell him how much she loved him...how happy she was to see him. Her arm didn't move. "Xavian."

"Here, *draga*." He cupped her cheek then shifted her again. Her hauberk went flying.

Cool air washed over damp skin. A violent shiver shuddered through her. "H-home."

Setting his mouth to the corner of hers, he tugged her tunic from her leather trews. She sighed as his skin touched hers. Magic flowing between them, he murmured, "Home it is."

CHAPTER THIRTY-FIVE

Steam drifted off the surface of the water, rising toward the painted dome. Torches, seven strong, stood in their brackets, lending light to mosaic tiles and round half-pillars. Styled in the way of the Greeks, each column boasted detailed leafing, more decorative than useful. Xavian liked them anyway. The bathing chamber was one of his favorite places. A private oasis nestled deep in the earth, hundreds of feet beneath Drachaven's great hall, surrounded by stone, protected by a fortress full of warriors.

Xavian's lips curved. An *oasis*. Christ, he was turning into a poet. One of those sappy, lovelorn fools, and he didn't mind a bit.

The reason lay curled in his lap, warm and rosy, all soft skin and ready curves. So enticing…so beautiful. Full-blown temptation come to life.

Shoulder-deep in the water, Xavian shifted against the rounded tub back, struggling to put a lid on his need. Afina wasn't ready for his loving…not yet. Despite the hypnotic pull of the hot spring, she was still too tense, more in her mind than her body.

Xavian cuddled her a little closer. He could feel her pain, wanted to take it away—banish the hurt she held in her heart—but knew he couldn't. He'd experienced the ache enough times to know there wasn't a quick fix. All he could do was hold her and wait…be ready when she decided 'twas time to talk.

Holding her, though, was almost as good. She made him lighter somehow. Touched the soft side beneath his armored exterior until he felt, well…happy, for the first time in his life. Satisfaction had always been the safe emotion, one based on action and his accomplishments. What he felt now was different: softer, gentler, more meaningful. 'Twas hard to fathom, but he'd never been truly content, not once…until Afina.

He rubbed his chin against the top of her head. She drew a shuddered breath, tensing as a violent shiver shook her. His arms tightened around her. Jesu, he hated that she was hurting; it made him want to slay her demons and banish the shadows in her eyes. But she didn't need another battle. She needed patience and a gentle hand.

Murmuring a simple cadence, more hum than words, he drew soft circles along her spine. Sweeping warm water over the curve of her shoulder, he chased away her goose bumps and slid a little deeper into the sunken pool. The hot spring gurgled, followed the movement, and lapped at them, disturbing the quiet.

The stillness was one of the things he liked best about the chamber. He often descended into the tunnels and came here to think, to study the mosaics spread like tapestries between the columns, watch firelight dance and listen to torches hiss. Most everything made sense to him shoulder-deep in the hot spring while the quiet hummed and the world above faded to naught. He'd come to the bath almost a half hour ago, hoping it would do the same for Afina.

He swept his hand along her thigh, worry getting the better of him. She was so quiet, so still…not like her at all. Xavian couldn't stand it anymore.

Twirling her dark hair around his hand, he brushed the heavy mass over her shoulder, exposing the nape of her neck.

She whimpered, turning her face into his shoulder. He answered the call and stroked her gently. Little by little, she surrendered, letting him unravel her tension, one corded muscle at a time. The strange current they shared helped, moving like a whisper between them. Xavian breathed a silent sigh of relief as the magic gained speed, soothing her, empowering him, lending strength where he normally held none.

Like butterfly kisses, Afina's eyelashes brushed his chest. Good, she'd opened her eyes, but was she ready to talk…to share her pain?

Xavian waited, searching for the right words.

"It's almost healed," she said, tracing his injury with her fingertip, voice so soft he barely heard her.

"Aye," he murmured, glancing at his arm. The gash delivered by an Al Pacii sword was almost gone. Healed by her magic, naught but a faint line remained. Soon even that would go, leaving him without a scar to show for the pain. "You are good for me."

She huffed, half-sob, half-laugh. "Hardly. I almost got you killed…again."

"*Draga*," he said, tone gentle yet full of warning. She wasn't to blame; not for Dax or the fact Vladimir Barbu had tracked her to Drachaven. "'Tis over, love. Let it go."

She drew her knees in closer, bumping his rib cage. "I can't."

"Aye, you can…'tis best and right that you do." He nudged her chin, encouraging her to raise her head. With a shiver, she denied him, tucking her face into his chest, not wanting to meet his gaze. Xavian wanted to sigh. Instead he hugged her tighter, using his body to comfort her. "All is well, Afina. Dax is safe. His wounds will heal and the men returned home safely."

"Even Hamund?"

Xavian hung onto his temper. Hearing the captain's name made him want to hit something. Damn fool. What the hell had he been thinking? He'd let Afina walk in there all alone, for Christ's sake.

"You didn't hurt him, did you?" she asked, her voice small, her index finger drawing loops on his collarbone. "It wasn't his fault. I didn't give him a choice."

He knew that too. 'Twas the reason Hamund was still alive. Not that the captain wouldn't be sporting a few spectacular bruises from Xavian's well-placed fists come the morrow. But Afina didn't need to know about that. "Don't worry about Hamund."

"What about Shay?"

Rahat. Why must she worry over everyone but herself? 'Twas her nature to nurture, he knew, but...Christ. She deserved equal attention. "Look at me, and I'll tell you."

She shook her head. He cupped her nape, massaged as he coaxed her chin up. Her lashes lay in wet, spiked layers on her cheeks. Lowering his head, he kissed the corner of her mouth, nipped her with his teeth, wanting inside. Waiting for her wasn't working. She needed a push, a distraction to take her mind off her troubles and put it squarely on him. Eyes still closed, she parted her lips and, with a sigh, accepted his tongue. Hmm, she tasted good, a delight that never failed to please him. He went a little deeper, worked her a little harder until she rose in his lap, curled her hands in his hair, demanding more.

With a flick, he withdrew, and when she followed, he kissed her again. 'Twas short, sweet, not half of what he wanted, but all she needed. "Shay is playing chess with your brother."

Afina blinked. "What?"

"In the great hall."

She met his gaze for the first time, relief shadowing the pain. "You're letting him stay?"

"For now." Palming her waist, he lifted her from his lap and nudged her legs open. She settled astride him without complaint, knees pressed against his hips, bottom cradled by his thighs. One hand on her hip, he cupped her face with the other, holding her still as he searched her gaze. Her pupils were still too large, but the eye color had shifted, becoming less green. "I know he saved your life, but until I know more he bears watching."

"Do you think he's a spy?" With a sigh, she turned her cheek into his palm, accepting his caress.

"Could be." Xavian shrugged, not convinced one way or the other. He hoped it was the *other*. The young assassin fought well and seemed sincere. Whether he joined their ranks and made Drachaven his home, however, remained to be seen. Though the thought was seductive. With Shay in the fold, their number came to seven. The old Al Pacii prophecy circled...

And out of the ashes seven warriors shall rise. Bringers of death, they shall wreak vengeance upon the earth, until shadow is driven into darkness and only the light remains.

Jesu, how often had he heard that? Too many times to count. Was the goddess's purpose for him tangled up with the fate of his friends...the assassins who had followed him from Grey Keep? Was it wishful thinking come to life or the fallacy he'd always believed? Whatever the case, it deserved his consideration, but not now. Now was for Afina.

"Halál is clever. Sending Shay to win my trust is not far-fetched. What better way to disturb my plans than to plant a mole at the heart of Drachaven?"

"It makes sense," she said, nodding once before her brows drew tight. "I wish Halál had been there...I wish you'd killed him."

"The way you did Vladimir," he said, pushing the door she'd just opened wide. She shook her head, tried to slam it shut, deny herself peace and him a chance to help her. Xavian wedged himself in tight, refusing to allow her retreat. "Nay...don't. I am here to listen. Talk to me, Afina...get it out."

A hitch in her breath, she glanced away. He watched her closely, tried to be patient, wondering if he needed to lay her down—love her outright—to help her let go. The traitor between his legs loved the suggestion. His mind rebelled, not wanting to use the tactic. Aye, he yearned to make love to her, but not like this...when she was hurting so badly. He needed her to confide in him, not because he ruled her body, but because she wanted to. Foolish, mayhap, but it all came down to trust. She loved him, aye, but did she trust him enough to tell him her secrets?

Just as the silence got to be too much, she said, "It hurts inside...right here."

An ache throbbed behind his breastbone, squeezing his rib cage so tight he tasted the burn. Raising his hand, he placed it atop hers, right over her heart. "Heavy? Like a huge weight is pressing down and you cannot breathe?"

She nodded and choked out, "Goddess, how do you stand it?"

Sometimes he didn't. Sometimes he just held on, clung to the hope peace would come, along with forgiveness. "Taking another's life is never easy. But 'tis less difficult for me. I was trained to fight...to take...from an early age. You were not." He paused, brushed the hair from her temple, choosing his words with care. "Sweet love, 'twas a necessary thing, taking Vladimir's life. 'Twas kill or be killed."

"Don't you think I know that?" she asked, her voice pained, fraught with frustration and shame. "In my mind, I know there was no other way...but in my heart..." She tapped her chest, struggling to find the right words. "In my heart...Xavian, I looked into his eyes...saw the light drain away. It was different the first time...You remember...the slaver and the axe?"

"I remember."

"But I...was so close. Felt the dagger go in, all the blood on my hands and...his eyes, they..." she trailed off, bottom lip trembling. He kissed the quiver away, murmured against her mouth, encouraging her to continue. He understood the pain, the guilt...the need to justify. But more than that, he knew she needed to give the hurt a voice. 'Twas the only way the healing would begin. "I just...I mean, I know there was no choice. He would have enslaved me, killed you, but inside...the tightness won't go away."

"'Twill ease with time."

She dipped her head, nestling in against him. Voice muffled, she whispered against his throat, "Promise?"

"Promise," he murmured, holding her tight. They stayed that way for a while, chests rising and falling in time. Warm water lapped at them, a slight echo against limestone. The quiet sound should have calmed him, but it didn't, and as Afina relaxed his tension built. 'Twas time...time to tell her everything. But now that he stood on the precipice, he didn't know where to start. Did he leap first and look later? Or take the safe route and ease in? Xavian swallowed. Easing in sounded good.

"Afina..."

"Hmmm."

"Do me a favor?"

The seriousness of his tone brought her head up. "What?"

"Don't go off alone again," he said, his chest so tight the words came hard. He cleared his throat. "I need to tell you something. 'Tisn't easy for me…I'm not…"

Patient and gentle, she raised her hand, stroked his hair, giving him time.

A moment passed, stretched, turning into many. The silence wasn't welcome this time. It wound him tight, cranking until the pressure became too much and he leapt in, feet first. "If anything were to happen to you, I don't know what…I couldn't…Afina, I love you." Her gasp encouraged him and he plunged deeper, emptying his heart, confessing all. "You give me purpose, beyond what the goddess wants. I am your shield. You are my reason. I cannot live without you now."

"Xavian," she whispered his name like a benediction, love in each note. "You are so much more than just mine. You are goodness and strength…kindness and honor. My mate. My love. My life."

He touched his mouth to hers, overwhelmed by her and all she gave him. "I am yours for all time."

Her breath hitched. He tasted her tears as she whispered, "I love you too."

"How did I get so lucky?" The question was rhetorical, one not meant to be answered, but served its purpose. He felt Afina's mood rise, lighten as she huffed. After giving her a gentle squeeze, he drew away to see her face and gauge her reaction. "And now we need a priest."

Her lips parted before coming together to form a beautiful little "O." "You want to…to…truly?"

"Aye," he said, warming to Henrik's demand. In truth, it seemed more his idea now and not much like his friend's at all. "Will you wed with me, love?"

The smile reached her eyes before he saw it on her mouth. "When?"

"As soon as one can be found and brought to Drachaven."

Something in his tone tipped her off and her eyes narrowed. "You won't steal the priest, will you? You'll ask him to come, right?"

His lips curved. He couldn't help himself. She knew him so well. Stealing people was part of what he did and exactly what he had planned.

"Xavian," she said, a warning in her tone. She backed it up with a stern look. "You cannot go about taking people from their homes."

"Why not? It's how I got a hold of you…and look how well that turned out."

She scowled at him.

Xavian grinned. Jesu, he loved her temper. Though how she thought to lecture him while sitting naked in his lap was anyone's guess. She managed well for a moment or two before he turned the tables and started to tease. A flick of the tongue here, a heated touch there had her gasping, arching, demanding more. Settling in for a long loving, he gave her what she wanted and he craved, setting a pace designed for her pleasure. But he knew the truth, he pleased himself too…hadn't lied. He *was* the lucky one. Afina was the light in his darkness; her acceptance more than a gift. 'Twas his salvation, and no matter the challenges that lay ahead, the future looked bright.

ACKNOWLEDGMENTS

At thirteen years old, I never imagined a chance meeting with a history book would lead me here. Surprising really, but falling in love with the medieval era set me on a path...the one I was most meant to walk. This book is proof enough of that.

Many thanks to Christine Witthohn, literary agent extraordinaire. You believed in me first and worked hard to make it happen. You are the absolute best!

To Eleni Caminis, my amazingly talented editor. Thank you for all your hard work, dedication, and support. But most of all, for believing in this book and being as excited about the Circle of Seven series as I am. And the entire Amazon Publishing team whose talents, energy, and enthusiasm never cease to amaze me. I so enjoy working with all of you!

With love to my family. None of this would be possible without you. Thank you a thousand times over.

Last but not least, to Kallie Lane, critique partner, fellow writer, and friend. Thanks for all the BS sessions, insights, and laughter. It's always a blast! And to the MTL gang and ORWA. I always learn a ton when you're around.

I raise a glass to all of you!

ABOUT THE AUTHOR

Image © Julie Daniluk

As the only girl on all-guys hockey teams from age six through her college years, Coreene Callahan knows a thing or two about tough guys and loves to write about them. Call it kismet. Call it payback after years of locker room talk and ice rink antics. But whatever you call it, the action better be heart stopping, the magic electric, and the story wicked good fun.

After graduating with honors in psychology and working as an interior designer, Callahan finally succumbed to her over-active imagination and returned to her first love: writing. And when she's not writing, she is dreaming of magical worlds full of dragon-shifters, elite assassins, and romance that's too hot to handle. Callahan currently lives in Canada with her family and her writing buddy, a fun-loving golden retriever.